MW01274183

THE LAST FALL OF BABYLON
... and the coming Kingdom

Daniel J. Erasmus

English translation by K. Arpin

Edited and revised by D.J. Erasmus

PRESS

The Last Fall of Babylon
by Daniel J. Erasmus

Printed in the United States of America

Library of Congress Control Number: 2002116424
ISBN 1-591604-09-5

Unless otherwise indicated, Bible quotations are taken from
the *King James Version* of the Bible.

Xulon Press
10640 Main Street
Suite 204
Fairfax, VA 22030
(703) 934-4411
XulonPress.com

To order additional copies, call 1-866-909-BOOK (2665).

"For the testimony of Jesus is the spirit of prophecy"
Revelation 19:10

CONTENTS

Introduction xi

1. Shining Light of the Prophetic Word! 17

2. Startling Signs...41

3. The Unique Role of Israel 81

4. The Middle East – Flashpoint of the World 141

5. The Last Fall of Babylon 165

6. All Roads Lead to Rome 189

7. A Week Has Seven Days 207

8. The Time of Jacob's Trouble 239

9. When is Christ Coming? 257

10. The Seventh Day – The Coming Kingdom 299

11. The Glory of Heaven 321

Endnotes 333

"In the latter days ye shall consider it perfectly"
Jeremiah 23:20

"And none of the wicked shall understand;
but the wise shall understand"
Daniel 12:10

INTRODUCTION

At the beginning of the 21st century, or of far more importance - the beginning of the third millennium after Christ, there is a fierce onslaught on the life of the Christian who sets his faith solely on the Bible. There are many varying points of view today concerning various Bible truths and often the ordinary church member is left in the dark over the real truth, and if it is in any way attainable. It also seems that not everybody is searching for the truth with the same earnestness and persistency.

If one compares available literature concerning the subject of 'the last days' or specifically the second coming of Christ, one finds, in certain cases, that some have done only superficial research and Bible study on the subject. Some find it totally impossible to concede to certain truths about the time shortly before Christ's return, while others diminish the Bible's teachings of the last days as if all prophetic passages in the Bible should be regarded as merely spiritual or symbolic.

Nearly every time a person shares this view however, it becomes more than apparent that these theologians or authors spiritualize most of the Bible - especially the book of Revelation.

It results in the problem that the time of 'great tribulation' (Mt. 24:21), is not being regarded as nearly as significant and serious as the Bible portrays it.

If one contemplates the book of Revelation using this perspective, that all those things already happened in the past or that it should be understood (in whole) merely in a symbolic way, it is understandable that the study of the last days or eschatology will not be regarded as of any imminent importance.

We are living in an age, more than ever, where the Bible is being read and studied very shallowly by a great number of Christians. This implies that the Bible's absolute authority, particularly for our generation, is being disregarded in many ways. The Bible is being regarded as very broad and vague and merely as a 'general manual' by which we may choose to live. It seems that certain truths in the Bible are being ignored, as if it doesn't really have any meaning for our generation. The numerous distinct Bible prophecies which have come to fulfilment in our time, are pushed aside by many, seemingly because it could not be interpreted 'as literally' or because it have 'nothing in common with our generation.'

This modus operandi can be very dangerous. It poses the threat of stripping our generation of true knowledge of the Bible as well as of insight into the age that we live in. In this day and age we have far more literature from a Christian perspective than, for example, a century ago. It seems though, if we consider the prevailing situation in our society, that this still has little impact. Is the current interpretation of the Bible not possibly too vague and unclear? Is it not far too broad and way too general? Does the Bible not speak to us much more distinctly than what appears to be the case today?

This matter requires attention. Our generation will also come to an end and may God help us, that we will not stand accused and be regretful to the fact that we diminished His Word into merely something of academic importance.

For this reason, amongst others, this book is addressed to you at the start of the third millennium. It is your own prerogative to study the content thereof prayerfully and with the Bible at hand. Jesus Christ said that we shall *"know the truth"* and that the truth shall *"make you free"* (John 8:32). He also said that the Holy Spirit will *"guide you in all truth"* and that He (the Spirit of truth) will even *"show you things to come"* (John 16:13)!

September 2002

"behold, I have foretold you all things"
Mark 13:23

1

SHINING LIGHT OF THE PROPHETIC WORD!

"We have also a more sure word of prophecy; whereunto ye do well that ye take heed, as unto a light that shineth in a dark place" (2 Pet.1:19)

"Despise not prophesyings." (1 Thes.5:20)

Which book written on earth could be compared to the Word of God? Which book was written to announce not only the beginning but also the end of time?

The God of all creation did not keep mankind, that He also created, in the dark over future events. No, He left a letter to all mankind - the Bible - His infallible Word, so that man may know the plan of his Creator. This God Himself had declared: *"I am God, and there is none else; I am God, and there is none like me, declaring the end from the beginning, and from ancient times the things that are not yet done, saying, My counsel shall stand, and I will do all my pleasure"* (Is. 46:9,10).

It makes one think, but does concrete evidence exist to support this?

Recently I read an article by an author warning very sternly that we shouldn't try to make the Bible 'God.' He persists that the Bible is merely a directive for man to lead an admirable and exemplary life by.

The author maintains that he is a Christian, but repeats that one shouldn't make more of the Bible than one is supposed to. How much are we then supposed to make of the Bible? Is it true that people erroneously try to make too much of God's Word? Did the almighty God not proclaim: *"In the beginning was the Word, and the Word was with God, and the Word was God."* (John 1:1)?

The Apostle John continues in John 1:14: *"And the Word was made flesh, and dwelt among us, (and we beheld his glory ...)"* John writes in Revelation 19:13 pertaining to Jesus' second coming and regarding Him which he had seen: *"And he was clothed with a vesture dipped in blood: and his name is called the Word of God."*

Interestingly God Himself proclaims that He is the Word.

The question now remains, can we put absolute faith in the Word and can we always trust the authority of the Word. Numbers 23:19 tells us: *"God is not a man, that he should lie ... .hath He said, and shall he not do it? Or hath he spoken, and shall he not make it good?"*

It highlights the fact that we need faith. What is true faith? Dare we advance in blind faith and put our trust in God unconditionally or is there another side to be considered? Is faith really all we need? Many believe that we merely have to believe. Thus faith in faith and not necessarily believing in the one true God. For many, merely believing already became an idol. The living God affirms in the Bible what type of faith we should acquire and how to attain it. Rom.10:17 reads: *"So then faith cometh by hearing, and hearing by the Word of God.*" There is no true faith if not based on the Bible - the Word of God. The rest are mere assumptions. Exclusively and only the Bible preaches the end of things from the very beginning - through the prophetic Word. The facts in this Book were tested repeatedly and verified many times.

Rom. 10:14 emphasises just how important the preaching of the gospel is. It is the method chosen by God to convert people to faith in Him and His Word. Have you ever attended a sermon delivered on the prophetic word - a sermon pertaining to the numerous biblical prophecies which came to pass and are currently going into fulfilment faster then ever before? It is this aspect that has repeatedly proven the Bible to be the infallible and inspired Word of God.

The truth remains that the Word is the complete revealed will of God to the human race. If Christ is the incarnated Word, it is true that the entire Scripture refers to Him. All the prophecies in the Bible refer in one way or another to Jesus Christ. This is not unfamiliar to Scripture as Rev. 19:10 tells us: *"For the testimony of Jesus is the spirit of prophecy."* No prophecy in the Bible remains separate from Him who is God Himself. This seems very logical, but is not readily accepted as such in our day and age. Many attest of new revelations and apparitions that are out of line with the Bible. It is however presented as if coming from God. Any prophecy can be put to the proof by asking: Does it carry the evidence of Jesus Christ? For this reason we refer to the words of Jesus in John 15:26: *"But when the Comforter is come, whom I will send unto you from the Father, even the Spirit of truth, which proceedeth from the Father, He shall testify of Me."*

The Holy Spirit always testifies of Jesus Christ and not of Himself or anybody else.

It is not difficult to discover that all the Old Testament

prophecies point to the first coming of Jesus to the earth or to His return - the second coming, in one way or another. It incorporates the preparations for His coming, the coming itself, His actions and much more.

Why do we then have to have faith in God and His Word? Is the Bible truly infallible?

May or do we have to take it just as it is written or may we spiritualize the Scriptures without much ado?

The Bible itself will answer the question.

PROPHECIES ABOUT THE MESSIAH'S FIRST COMING

We are going to look at the phenomenal prophecies, written hundreds and even thousands of years prior, which prophesied that a Messiah would come, that He would die in an unfamiliar way and about numerous other events surrounding His coming. This is the test of the Scriptures and will prove if God really is whom He says He is. In Amos 3:7 we read the remarkable words: *"Surely the Lord God will do nothing, but he revealeth his secret unto his servants the prophets."*

God always informs man that He created about what He is going to do, before He goes into action and does it to the letter - and so brings His Word into fulfilment.

Near the beginning of the book of Genesis (the well-known chapter 3:15) we encounter the first prophecy of the Bible and it is followed by numerous other prophecies relating to the coming Messiah.

The bewildering fact is that each and everyone - note each and everyone - went into fulfilment literally!

Here follows a list of more or less 60 Old Testament prophecies, in chronological order, relating to Jesus Christ's first coming to earth - with its New Testament fulfilment in cursive (emphasis added):

The first promise and prophecy

Gen. 3:15 and I will put enmity between thee and <u>the woman</u>, and between thy seed and <u>her seed</u>; it shall bruise thy head, and thou shalt bruise his heel

Gal. 4:4 But when the fulness of the time was come, God send forth his Son, <u>made of a woman</u>
Gal. 3:16 Now to Abraham and his seed were the promise made. He said not, And to seeds, as of many; but as of one, <u>and to thy seed, which is Christ.</u>

Covenant with Abraham

Gen. 12:3 ... And in thee shall all families on earth be blessed

Gal. 3:8 And the scripture forseeing that God would justify the heathen through faith, preached before the gospel unto Abraham, saying , In thee shall all nations be blessed

Passover lamb refers to Christ

Ex. 12:46 In one house shall it be eaten; thou shalt not carry forth ought of the flesh abroad out of the house; <u>neither shall ye break a bone thereof</u>

Jn. 19:33 But when they came to Jesus, and saw that he was dead already, <u>they brake not his legs</u>

Manna refers to Christ

Ex. 16:4 Then the Lord said unto Moses, Behold, I will rain <u>bread from heaven for</u> you; and the people shall go out and gather a certain rate every day, that I may prove them, whether they will walk in my law, or no

Jn. 6:51 <u>I am the living bread</u> which came down from heaven: if any man eat of this bread, he shall live for ever

The purple robe of Christ

Ex. 28:31,32 And thou shalt make the robe of the <u>ephod all of blue</u>. And there shall be a hole in the top of it, in the midst thereof, it shall have a binding of woven work round about the hole of it, as it were the hole of an habergeon, <u>that it be not rent</u>

Mk. 15:17 And they clothed him with <u>purple</u>
Jn. 19:23,24 ... the coat was without seam, woven from the top throughout. They said therefore among themselves, <u>Let us not rend it</u>

The star of Bethlehem

Num. 24:17 I shall see him, but not now: I shall behold him, but not nigh: there shall come a <u>Star out of Jacob</u>, and a Sceptre shall rise out of Israel

Mt. 2:2 Where is he that is born King of the Jews? For we have seen <u>his star</u> in the east, and are come to worship him

Jesus - the Prophet that would come

Deut. 18:15,18,19 The LORD thy God will raise up unto thee a <u>Prophet</u> from the midst of thee, of thy brethren, like unto me; <u>unto him ye shall hearken</u>; ... I will raise them up a Prophet from among their brethren, like unto thee, and will put my words in his mouth; and <u>he shall speak unto them all that I shall command him</u>. And it shall come to pass, that whosoever will not hearken unto my words which he shall speak in my name, I will require it of him

Acts 3:22 For Moses truly said unto the fathers, A <u>prophet</u> shall the Lord your God raise up unto you of your brethren, like unto me; h<u>im shall ye hear</u> in all things what-soever he shall say unto you

The curse of the cross

Deut. 21:23 ... for he that is <u>hanged</u> is <u>accursed</u> of God

Gal. 3:13 Christ redeemed us from the curse of the law, being made a curse for us: for it is written, <u>Cursed is every-one that hangeth from a tree</u>

Conspiracy against Christ

Ps 2:2 The kings of the earth set themselves, and <u>the rulers take counsel together, against the LORD, and against his anointed</u>

Acts 4: 27,28 For a <u>truth against thy holy child Jesus,</u> whom thou has anointed, both <u>Herod and Pontius Pilate,</u> <u>with the Gentiles and the people of Israel, were gathered</u> <u>together,</u> for to do whatsoever thy hand and thy council determined before to be done

God, the Holy Spirit conceived Jesus Christ

Ps. 2:7 I will declare the decree: The LORD hath said unto me, <u>Thou art my Son</u>; <u>this day have I begotten thee</u>

Mt. 1:20,21 For that which is conceived in her is <u>of the Holy Ghost</u>. And she shall bring forth a son, and thou shalt call his name Jesus

Jesus would rise from the dead

Ps. 16:10 For thou <u>wilt not leave my soul in hell</u>; neither wilt thou suffer thine Holy One to see corruption

Acts 2:24 Whom God hath raised up, having loosed the pains of death; <u>because it was not possible that he should be holden of it</u>

Jesus' words on the cross

Ps. 22:1 <u>My God, my God, why hast thou forsaken me</u>? Why art thou so far from helping me, and from the words of my roaring?

Mark 15:34 And at the ninth hour Jesus cried with a loud voice, saying, Eloi, Eloi, lama sabachthani? which is, being interpreted, <u>My God, my God why hast thou forsaken me</u>?

Scorners encircling the cross

Ps 22:7,8 All they that see me <u>laugh me to scorn</u>; they shoot out the lip, they <u>shake the head saying</u>, He trusted on the Lord, that he would deliver him: <u>let him deliver him</u>, seeing he delighted in him

*Mt. 27: 39,40 And <u>they that passed by reviled him, wag-</u>
<u>ging their heads,</u> And saying, Thou that destroyest the tem-
ple, and buildest it in three days, <u>save thyself.</u> It thou be the
Son of God, come down from the cross*

Jesus' agony in Gethsemane

Ps. 22:11 Be not far from me; for <u>trouble is near;</u> for
there is none to help

*Lk. 22:41,42 And he ... prayed, Saying Father <u>if thou be</u>
<u>willing, remove this cup from me</u>: nevertheless, not my will
but thine, be done*

Thirst on the cross

Ps. 22:15 My strength is dried up like a potsherd; and
my <u>tongue cleaveth to my jaws</u>

*Jn. 19:28 After this, Jesus knowing the all things were
now accomplished, that the Scripture might be fulfilled,
saith, <u>I thirst</u>*

Crucifixion depicted long before its manifestation

Ps. 22:16 For dogs have compassed me: the assembly of
the wicked have inclosed me: they pierced my hands and my
feet

*Lk. 23:33 And when they were come to the place, which
is called Calvary, there <u>they crucified him,</u> and the <u>malefac-</u>
<u>tors</u> one on the right hand, and the other on the left*

Jesus, broken for us

Ps. 22:17 <u>I may tell all my bones</u>: they look and stare upon me

Mk. 15:15 Pilate ... delivered Jesus, when he had <u>scourged</u> him, to be crucified

Jesus' robes divided amongst the guards

Ps. 22:18 They <u>part my garments</u> among them, and <u>cast lots</u> upon my vesture

Lk. 23:34 And they <u>parted his raiment,</u> and <u>cast lots</u>

False witnesses accused Jesus

Ps. 27:12 Deliver me not over unto the will of mine enemies: for <u>false witnesses</u> are risen up against me

Mt. 26:60 though <u>many false witnesses</u> came, yet found they none

Jesus commits His Spirit to the Father

Ps 31:5 <u>Into thine hand I commit my spirit</u>: thou hast redeemed me, O LORD God of truth

Lk. 23:46 And when Jesus had cried with a loud voice, he said, Father <u>into thy hands I commend my spirit</u>: and having said thus, he gave up the ghost

His bones would not be broken

Ps. 34:20 He keepeth all his bones: <u>not one of them is</u>

broken

Jn. 19:36 For these things were done, that the scripture should be fulfilled. <u>A bone of him shall not be broken</u>

Jesus' immense suffering

Ps.38:6-8 I am troubled; I am bowed down greatly; I go mourning all the day long. For my <u>loins are filled with a loathsome disease</u>: and <u>there is no soundness in my flesh</u>. I am feeble and sore broken: I have roared by reason of the disquietness of my heart

Heb. 2:9 But we see Jesus, who was made a little lower than the angels for the <u>suffering of death,</u> crowned with glory and honour; that he by the grace of God <u>should taste death for every man</u>

His disciples deserted Him

Ps. 38:11 My lovers and my friends stand aloof from my sore; and <u>my kinsmen stand afar off</u>

Lk. 23:49 And that all his acquaintance ... <u>stood afar off,</u> beholding these things

His crucifixion planned slyly and deceitfully

Ps. 38:12 <u>They also that seek after my life lay snares</u> for me; And they that seek my hurt speak mischievous things, and imagine deceits all the day long

Acts 4:26 The kings of the earth stood up, and the rulers were <u>gathered together against the Lord, and against his Christ</u> (also Ps. 2:2)

Jesus is silent before his false witnesses

Ps. 38:13 But I, as a deaf man, heard not; and I was a dumb that <u>openeth not his mouth</u>

Lk. 23:9 Then he questioned him in many words; <u>but he answered him nothing</u>

A confidant would betray Jesus

Ps. 41:9 Yea, mine own familiar friend, in whom I trusted, <u>which did eat of my bread, hath lifted up his heel against me</u>

Jn. 13:18,26 ... that the Scripture may be fulfilled: <u>He that eateth bread with me hath lifted up his heel against me</u> ... and when he had dipped the sop, he gave it to Judas Iscariot

Hated without cause or reason

Ps. 69:4 They that <u>hate me without a cause</u> are more than the hairs of mine head: they that would destroy me, being mine enemies wrongfully, are mighty

Jn. 15:25 that the word might be fulfilled that is written in their law, <u>They hated me without a cause</u>

His own brothers despised Him

Ps. 69:8 I am become a stranger unto my brethren, and <u>an alien unto my mother's children</u>

Jn. 1: 11; 7;5 He came unto his own, and his own received him not ... For neither did <u>his brethren believe in him</u>

He would keep the temple holy

Ps. 69:9 For <u>the zeal of thine house hath eaten me up</u>; and the reproaches of them that reproached thee are fallen upon me

Lk. 19:45 And <u>he went into the temple</u>, and began to cast out them that sold therein, and them that bought

Gall and vinegar to eat and drink

Ps. 69:21 They gave me also <u>gall for my meat</u>; and in my thirst they gave me <u>vinegar to drink</u>

Mt. 27:34 They gave him <u>vinegar to drink mingled with gall</u>

He would speak in parables

Ps. 78:2 <u>I will open my mouth in a parable</u>: I will utter dark sayings of old

Mt. 13:34,35 All these things spake Jesus unto the multitude in parables; and <u>without a parable spake he not unto them</u>: that it might be fulfilled which was spoken by the prophet saying, <u>I will open my mouth in parables</u>; I will utter things which have been kept secret <u>from the foundation of the world</u>

He is the firstborn, among many

Ps. 89:27 Also I will make him my <u>firstborn</u>, higher than the kings of the earth

Rom. 8:29 For whom he did foreknow, he also did pre-

destinate to be conformed to the image of his Son, that he might be the <u>firstborn</u> among many brethren

Judas replaced by Mathias

Ps. 109:8 Let his days be few; and <u>let another take his office</u>

Acts 1:26 And they gave forth their lots, and the lot fell upon Mathias; and <u>he was numbered with the eleven apostles</u>

Jesus is the corner stone

Ps. 118:22 The stone which the builders <u>refused</u> is become the <u>head stone of the corner</u>

1 Pet. 2:6 Behold, I lay in Zion a chief <u>corner stone, elect, precious</u>: and he that believeth on him shall not be confounded

Jesus, born of a virgin

Is. 7:14 Therefor the Lord himself shall give you a sign; Behold <u>a virgin shall conceive</u>, and bear a <u>son</u> and shall call his name <u>Immanuel</u>

Mt. 1:18 When his mother Mary was espoused to Joseph, <u>before they came together</u>, she was found with child of the Holy Ghost
Mt. 1:22,23 Now all this was done, that it might be fulfilled which was spoken of the Lord by the prophet, saying, Behold <u>a virgin shall be with child and shall bring forth a son, and they shall call his name Immanuel</u> which being interpreted is, God with us

The birth of Jesus

Is. 9:6 For unto us <u>a child is born, unto us a son</u> is given: and the government shall be upon his shoulder: and his name shall be called Wonderful, Counsellor, The mighty God, The everlasting Father, The Prince of Peace

Lk. 2:11,12 For unto you is <u>born</u> this day in the city of David <u>a Saviour, which is Christ the Lord</u>. And this shall be a sign unto you; Ye shall find the babe wrapped in swaddling clothes, lying in a manger

Jesus - descendant from David.

Is. 11:1,2 And there shall come forth a rod out of the stem of Jesse, and a branch shall grow out of his roots: and <u>the Spirit of the Lord shall rest upon him</u>

Mt. 1:1,2,6 <u>The book of the generation of Jesus Christ, the son of David</u>, the son of Abraham. Abraham begat Isaac; ... <u>and Jesse begat David the king</u>

He judged the poor with righteousness

Is. 11:4 but <u>with righteousness shall he judge the poor</u>, and reprove the equity for the meek of the earth

Lk. 21:3 And he said, Of a truth I say unto you, that <u>this poor widow hath cast in more than they all</u>

Jesus, light of the world

Is. 49:6 I will also give <u>thee</u> for a <u>light to the Gentiles,</u> that thou mayest be my salvation unto the end of the earth

Jn. 8:12 Then spake Jesus again unto them, saying, <u>I am the light of the world</u>

He was abused

Is. 50:6 <u>I gave my back to the smiters,</u> and my cheeks to them that plucked off the hair: I hid not my face from <u>shame and spitting</u>

Mt. 27:26 He had <u>scourged</u> Jesus
Mt. 26:67 Then they did <u>spit in his face,</u> and buffeted him; and others <u>smote him with the palms of their hands</u>

He became unrecognisable and marred

Is. 52:14 As many were astonished as thee; <u>his visage was so marred more than any man, and his form more than the sons of men</u>

Mt. 26:68; 27:29 Who is he that <u>smote</u> thee ... they had platted a <u>crown of thorns, they put it upon his head</u>

He came to be despised, a man of sorrows

Is. 53:2,3 He hath no form nor comeliness; and when we shall see him, there is no beauty that we should desire him. <u>He is despised</u> and rejected of men;<u> a man of sorrows,</u> and acquainted with grief; and we hid as it were our faces from him; <u>he was despised and we esteemed him not</u>

Mk. 9:12 and how it is written of the Son of man, that <u>he must suffer many things and be set at nought</u>

Crucified for our sins

Is. 53:4,5 Surely <u>he hath borne our griefs</u>, and carried our sorrows: yet we did esteem him stricken, smitten of God, and afflicted. But <u>he was wounded for our transgressions, he was bruised for our iniquities</u>: the chastisement of our peace was upon him; and <u>with his stripes we are healed</u>

Rom. 4:25 who was <u>delivered for our offences</u>, and was raised again for our justification
1 Pet. 2:24 Who his own self bare <u>our sins in his own body</u> on the tree
Mt. 8:17 <u>Himself took our infirmities</u>, and bare our sicknesses

Jesus did not defend Himself

Is. 53:6,7 All we like sheep have gone astray; we have turned every one to his own way; and the Lord hath laid on him the iniquity of us all. He was oppressed, and he was afflicted, yet <u>he opened not his mouth</u>: he is brought as a lamb to the slaughter, and as a sheep before her shearers is dumb, so <u>he openeth not his mouth</u>

1 Pet. 2:23 who, when he was reviled, <u>reviled not again</u>; when he suffered, he threatened not
Mt. 26:63 but Jesus <u>held his piece</u>

He was made to be sin for us

Is. 53:8 for the transgression of my people <u>was he stricken</u>

2 Cor. 5:21 For <u>he hath made him to be sin for us</u>, <u>who knew no sin</u>; that we might be made the righteousness of

God in him

A wealthy man laid him to rest

Is. 53:9 And he made his <u>grave</u> with the wicked, and <u>with the rich in his death</u>, because he had done no violence, neither was any deceit in his mouth

Mt. 27: 57, 59, 60 A <u>rich man</u> from Arimathea ... named Joseph ... had taken the body ... laid it in his own <u>new tomb</u>

His blood justify and sanctify us

Is. 53:10,11 Yet it pleased the Lord to bruise him; he hath put him to grief ... by his knowledge shall my righteous servant <u>justify many</u>; for he shall bear their iniquities

Heb. 13:12 Wherefore Jesus also, that he might sanctify the people <u>with his own blood, suffered</u> without the gate

He prayed for his malefactors

Is. 53:12 because he hath poured out his soul unto death: and he was <u>numbered with the transgressors</u>, and he bare the sin of many, and <u>made intercession for the transgressors</u>

Mk. 15:28 he was <u>numbered with the transgressors</u>
Lk. 23:34 Then Jesus said, Father <u>forgive them; for they know not what they do</u>

Israel would cry for her children

Jer. 31:15 Thus said the Lord; A voice was heard in Ramah, lamentation, and bitter weeping; Rachel <u>weeping for her children</u> refused to be comforted for her children, because they were not

Mt. 2:16 Then Herod, when he saw that he was mocked ... was exceedingly wroth, and sent forth, and slew all the children that were in Bethlehem, and in all the coasts thereof, from <u>two years old and under</u>

Jesus, forsaken by His own

Dan. 9:26 And after threescore and two weeks <u>shall Messiah be cut off, but not for himself</u>

Jn. 1:10 He was in the world, and the world was made by him, and <u>the world knew him not</u>

Jesus would visit Egypt as a child

Hos. 11:1 When Israel was a child, then I loved him, and <u>called my son out of Egypt</u>

Mt. 2:14,15 When he arose, he took the young child and his mother by night, and <u>departed into</u> Egypt: ... that it might be fulfilled which was spoken of the Lord by the prophet, saying, <u>Out of Egypt have I called my son</u>

Jesus to be born in Bethlehem

Mic. 5:2 But thou, <u>Bethlehem</u> Ephratah, though thou be little among the thousands of Judah, yet <u>out of thee shall he come forth unto me that is to be ruler in Israel</u>, whose goings forth have been from of old, from everlasting

Mt. 2:1 <u>Jesus was born in Bethlehem of Judea</u>

Jesus would enter Jerusalem upon a donkey

Zech. 9:9 Rejoice greatly, O daughter of Zion; shout, O daughter of Jerusalem: behold, <u>thy King cometh unto thee</u>: he is just, and having salvation; lowly, and <u>riding upon an ass</u>, and upon a colt the foal of an ass

Lk. 19:30,31,35 at your entering ye shall find a <u>colt</u> tied, whereon yet never man sat ... the Lord hath need of him ... they brought him to Jesus: and they cast their garments upon the colt, and <u>they sat Jesus thereon</u>

Jesus sold for thirty pieces of silver

Zech. 11:12 And I said unto them, if ye think good, give me my price; and if not, forbear. So they weighed for my price <u>thirty pieces of silver</u>

Mt. 26:15 What will ye give me, and I will deliver him unto you? And they covenanted with him for <u>thirty pieces of silver</u>

Judas bought the potter's field

Zech. 11:13 And the LORD said unto me, Cast it unto the potter: a goodly price that I was prized at of them. And <u>I took thirty pieces of silver, and cast them to the potter in the house of the LORD</u>

Mt. 27:7 And they took counsel, and <u>bought with them the potter's field</u>, to <u>bury</u> strangers in

Jesus pierced by a spear

Zack. 12:10 ... and they shall look upon <u>me whom they have pierced</u>

*Jn. 19:34 but one of the soldiers <u>with a spear pierced his</u>
<u>side,</u> and forthwith came there out blood and water*

John the Baptist would come

Mal. 3:1 Behold, <u>I will send my messenger, and he shall</u>
<u>prepare the way before me</u>: and the Lord, whom ye seek,
shall suddenly come to his temple, even the messenger of
the covenant, whom ye delight in: behold he shall come,
saith the LORD of hosts

*Mk. 1:2-4 As it was written in the prophets, Behold <u>I</u>
<u>send my messenger before thy face, which shall prepare thy</u>
<u>way before thee. The voice of one crying in the wilderness,</u>
<u>Prepare ye the way of the Lord, make his paths straight</u> ...
.John did baptize in the wilderness*

THE FAULT FACTOR IS ZERO!

We are dealing with the almighty, everlasting, truthful God!

This is but a few of the more than 330 prophecies that
have gone into fulfilment with Jesus' first coming to earth.
Not one of these prophecies were fulfilled merely symboli-
cally or figuratively, but as can be seen very clearly, it went
into fulfilment literally.

In the same manner there are about 318 prophetic references to the second coming of Christ in the New Testament
alone - a great number more than about baptism and the holy
communion together.

If it was not for the literal fulfilment of the prophetic
word of the Old Testament, we would not have had a
Saviour today. God proved however, whom He was and that
He was truthful according to His Word - when He sent His

Son Jesus Christ (Himself God - 1 Jn. 5:20) to leave heaven and venture to earth as a mere mortal. By doing so, God proved that He is the God of love - the only God of love!

This is what fundamentally distinguish the Bible from any other earthly scripture. The holy Bible is history that was previously recorded. Yes, the Bible is more up to date than tomorrow's newspaper. The prophetic Word is the means which God utilises to prove to humanity that He is truly God. He had done so previously, with the Israelites in the times of the Old Testament. He had often sent them prophets to foretell great details about their future. God Himself then brought the prophesies into fulfilment - that Israel may comprehend that He is God. No other God could achieve this. This is why we have to take urgent heed to the prophetic word - every day, every moment.

God relates in His Word: *"Surely as I have thought, so shall it come to pass"* (Is. 14:24). Nobody can alter any of this in any way. We have to fit in precisely with God's perfect plan. He is not going to fit in with our man-made contrivances. Everything that had to have happened previously, happened. That which have not gone into fulfilment yet, will surely do so in future - and in the near future. We may be certain of this fact. All prophecies point in one way or another to Jesus and He is God, therefore all will be fulfilled.

Jesus Christ Himself is the incarnated Word and our only salvation. We have the Word in our midst and every born-again Christian possess in him or her the Holy Spirit. It was of the Holy Spirit that Jesus proclaimed: *"Howbeit when he, the Spirit of truth, is come, he will guide you into all truth: For he shall not speak of himself; but howsoever he shall hear, that shall he speak: and he will show you things to come."* (Jn. 16:13). We as children of God are therefore never left in the dark pertaining to the future. All prophecies referring to the second coming of Christ, will go into fulfilment just as literally as all the previous prophecies went into fulfilment. If He affirms that He will return, He shall bring it about in all truthfulness. He notes that we may well know the season of His return (Mt. 24:32,33), and have to acknowledge it with our whole heart. The question remains if we are going to acknowledge the Word of God with an earnest and sincere heart. What are we doing with the prophetic Word of the living God today? Take heed to not be caught off guard! May He, when He returns, find us waiting, vigilant and absorbed in His majestic, reliable Word.

2

STARTLING SIGNS

In these days many are of the impression that man was left in the dark over quite a number of Bible issues. Is this true? Is this what God had in mind when the Bible was being chronicled for us? On the other hand, is the complete opposite true?

In many places in the Bible, it is quite clear that God wants to reveal future prophetic events to us.

Note the following (emphasis added):

Deut. 29:29 – *"The <u>secret things</u> belong unto the Lord our God: but <u>those things which are revealed</u> belong unto us and to our children for ever, that we may do all the words of this law."*

Ps. 25:14 – *"The <u>secret</u> of the LORD is with them that fear him: and he <u>will show</u> them his covenant."*

Prov. 25:2 – *"It is the glory of God to <u>conceal</u> a thing:*

but the honor of kings is to <u>search out a matter</u>."

Is. 45:11 – "Ask me of <u>things to come</u>…"

Is. 46:10 – "declaring the end from the beginning and from ancient time the <u>things that are not yet done</u>"

Is. 48: 5-6 – "I have even from the beginning declared it to thee; before it came to pass I showed it thee … <u>I have shewed thee new things from this time, even hidden things, and thou didst not know them.</u>"

Dan. 2:28 – "But there is a God in heaven that <u>revealeth secrets</u>,"

Mt. 13:11 – "He answered and said unto them, Because it is given unto you to know the <u>mysteries</u> of the kingdom of heaven, but to them it is not given."

Mk. 13:23 – "But take ye heed; behold , <u>I have foretold you all things</u>."

Rom. 11:25 – <u>"For I would not, brethren, that ye should be ignorant of this mystery,</u> lest ye should be wise in your own conceits, that blindness in part is what happened to Israel, until the fullness of the Gentiles be come in."

Rom. 16:25,26 – "Now to him that is of power to stablish you according to my gospel, and the preaching of Jesus Christ, according to <u>the revelation of the mystery, which was kept secret since the world began, but is now made manifest, and by the scriptures of the prophets,</u> according to the commandment of the everlasting God, made known to all nations for the obedience of faith:"

1 Cor. 15:51 – " *Behold, I <u>show you a mystery</u>; We shall not all sleep, but we shall all be changed, in a moment, in the twinkling of an eye, at the last trump.*"

Eph. 1: 9-10 – *"having made known unto us the <u>mystery of his will</u>, according to his good pleasure which he hath purposed himself: that in the dispensation of the <u>fullness of times</u> he might gather together..."*

Eph. 5:27,32 – *"that he might present it to himself a glorious church, not having spot, or wrinkle, or any such thing: but that it should be holy and without blemish ... This is a great <u>mystery</u>: but I speak concerning Christ and the church."*

How many Christians will one day regret that they have never searched the mysteries in Scripture, or just plainly for the reason that they have studied the Bible so seldom? In eternity, we are going to deal a great many times with the Word (Christ) – as the Word will endure unto all eternity.

Is. 40:8 reads: *"The grass withereth, the flower fadeth; but the Word of our God <u>shall stand forever</u>."*

THE ABSOLUTE UNIQUENESS OF THE 20TH CENTURY

If we understand that God did not leave us in the dark concerning future events, many things become much more clear to us – especially regarding this current age that we find ourselves in now. The world change dramatically over short periods of time and thus many sudden reforms are typical of our time, but was this always the case?

It is good to slow down once in a while and to have a bit of retrospect over the just expired 20th century. To tell the truth, it is of critical importance that we shall look at the past hundred years or more - what happened in the world and what changes took place. The demands that the time we live in have upon us, sometimes results in us not being able to keep a sober perspective on where we came from and where we are going. We live in a time where everything is happening fast – very fast. Faster than ever before in the history of the human race. It may seem this way, but is the age in which we find ourselves really so different from the previous centuries and millennia? Is this the case, or is it all a mere illusion?

A bit of retrospect here for a minute: Five thousand years ago, the main means of transport used by man were a horse or a donkey. A thousand years ago, this was still the case. Five hundred years ago, it remained very common practice. Even two hundred years ago, this was true. A hundred years ago, it definitely was still the case. Yes, even as little as fifty years ago horses, mules and donkeys were still the most common mode of transportation worldwide. Can we say the same today? Definitely not. The automobile is by far the most commonly used mode of transportation right across the world. There are places where poverty restricts the use of motorcars, but seen from a worldwide perspective, petrol driven automobiles have taken over the world. This in a period of just fifty years! Yes it is true that the first motor was fabricated by Ford in 1896, but initially very few were lucky enough to own one. We have to admit that the world changed dramatically in the last hundred years. Especially in the last fifty years – even more dramatically! For more than five thousand nine hundred years, man found his way by his trusty steed, but in the last five decades, there came a turn around unknown in the history of man. We move in luxury vehicles, busses, trains, airplanes and even space shuttles! The world did indeed take a drastic turn.

Let us look in short at a few of the greatest discoveries

and developments of the past slightly more than one hundred years, which have had such a huge impact on the world – and still does, even more so now:

1876 – the invention of the telephone.
1880's – the light bulb
1890's – electricity
1895 – the radio
1896 – the automobile
1903 – the airplane
1930 – the first computer
1930's – the audio cassette
1940 's – the television
1940's – the atom bomb
1956 – atomic energy
1957 – the space shuttle
1960 – the communication satellite
1971 – the microchip
1970's – the video
1979 – the compact disc (CD)
1993 – the Internet breakthrough
This breakthrough is almost shocking. Now anybody with a computer and a telephone can visit anybody else's computer on earth (through e-mail) and literally see and research millions of pages of information on any subject that exists.
1997 – cloning of a sheep
2000 – unraveling of the human genetic code (DNA)

A few years ago, it was estimated that the information in the world multiply at such a tempo, that it was doubled every two years. It may well have accelerated way beyond this by now.

'Where this is going to end, nobody knows,' people always say. If one studies the Word of God in a serious way, one will be quick to realize that everything in this world will come to an abrupt end some day when Jesus Christ will return. No, we are not going to live on other planets and fly around each with our own space ship one day. There will be however, a much more wonderful end for every person that knows Jesus Christ personally and serves Him above all else.

The Bible, the infallible Word of God, warned us long ago that everything would change drastically towards the end of time. In the book of Daniel we read the following prophetic words:

"But thou, O Daniel, shut up the words, and seal the book, even to the time of the end: many shall run to and fro, and <u>knowledge shall be increased</u>." (Dan. 12:4)

Knowledge regarding the Word has increased, as has knowledge in general. The 20th century has indeed been totally unique. Never has there been a time or a period that could even compare with it. The dramatic changes in the world over the last hundred years, is a clear indicator of the nearness of the second coming of Christ. Many unfortunately, in our day and age, make the fatal error in concluding that amidst all these changes, God Himself has also changed. The Word of God though presents the right perspective in Heb. 13:8: *"Jesus Christ [is] the same yesterday, and today, and for ever."* His unchangeable Word also still remains the same for us today. Yet, many in our generation are very ignorant of this fact and as they changed with everything around them, they are of the impression that God also changed in a similar way.

There does however, through God's mercy, come a time when one can actively meditate on all that have happened around you and rethink your position regarding the present and the near future.

A CONTROVERSIAL SUBJECT

Eschatology or the biblical teaching on the *last things*, has always been regarded as a controversial subject throughout the church dispensation. There may be particular reasons for this, but the fact that most people just cannot foresee that there will really come a moment when Christ will literally return to this earth and make an end to this current dispensation, is most certainly not the least of them.

The history of the church has shown that there are basically four interpretations regarding the book of Revelation and therefore also regarding the return of Christ and the role of the Antichrist in the end times.
Following are in short the four interpretations:

1. The Spiritual interpretation

Augustine and others advocated this way of interpretation. This states that the book of Revelation is merely a symbolic or spiritual book and that the Antichrist is merely an evil system that the church has to guard against. By doing so the biblical prophecies regarding the end times, the second coming of Christ and the Antichrist are merely spiritualized - it thus points in no way to a specific time and also not to a specific fulfillment. As a result, everything is vague and unclear and no one can with any certainty say which of the biblical prophecies already came into fulfillment and which did not. Further, as a result, the numerous specific prophesies that went into fulfillment so literally with Christ's first coming (for example Is. 53) are not used as a guideline for the prophecies regarding His second coming. The belief that God's previous judgments was to an extent literal, is upheld, but when it comes to the judgments of the future - that are clearly predicted in the Bible - it is merely spiritualized. This doctrine also firmly believes that the Lord rejected

Israel as a nation in a finale way and that all God's promises, which were previously directed to Israel, are now transmitted to the church. The church, in other words, replaced the literal nation of Israel. To this day this is the viewpoint of the Roman Catholic Church, the Anglican Church and even most of the Protestant churches. This is in spite of God's admonition in numerous places in Scripture that He is not rejecting Israel for all eternity, but that they were to suffer hardship in many places for the sake of the other (gentile) nations in the world (Rom. 11:25-28). God also said that He would change their destiny in the last days. (More regarding this at a later stage).

2. *The Preteristic interpretation*

In the 17th century, a Jesuit from the Roman Catholic Church, Alcazar, played a fundamental role in the establishment of this interpretation. It entails that everything John had written in his letters and in the book of Revelation, as well as concerning the Antichrist, already went into fulfilment during his time – the end of the first century. According to this interpretation, the Antichrist was the Roman Caesar, Nero. The fact that the Antichrist and his armies will be defeated during the last war (Armageddon – Rev. 16:14, 16; 19:19) thus clearly in the future, is left out of the picture. It is true that Nero reigned in 64 AD. The apostle John wrote the book of Revelation only in 96 AD. Note the following: He referred in Rev. 17:12 to the ten kings *"which have received no kingdom as yet"* (thus not yet in the year 96), but they will receive their kingdoms with the appearance of the beast – the coming and final Antichrist. It could not have been Nero or his immediate successors. He was at most a strong type of the Antichrist.

3. *The Historic interpretation*

This view entails that everything that had been written in

the book of Revelation (also regarding the Antichrist), have transpired already - spaced through the course of the church period (of 2000 years). It is mere history today. They however use bizarre methods to interpret the Scriptures. As a result, the earthquake in Rev. 11:19 may be interpreted as the French revolution of 1789. The Bible is merely interpreted as portraying the meaning that best suit their needs. It also entails that the Bible means many different things to many different people. If an earthquake is a war, what is a war then? Perhaps an earthquake? This is a strange way of interpretation. If everything has happened already, when were the Antichrist and the false prophet cast into the lake of fire? (Rev. 19:20). When were the inhabitants of the earth forced to take the mark of the beast? (Rev. 13:16,17).

(If it is merely a spiritual mark, when did they take this mark then)? The most important question remains, when did Jesus Christ come to end the big war of Rev. 19:11-21? To this the advocates of this historic interpretation have no satisfying answers. If some of these events are still to happen, the historicists are then presently more futuristic as they would have one believe.

4. The Futuristic interpretation

This term is probably not a very good description of what this group believes. This interpretation takes into account that the first three chapters of the book of Revelation is history – there really were seven such churches in Asia Minor. The letters to the seven churches however also have a clear prophetic meaning. Every church points to a prophetic time, from the beginning of the church age (Pentecost) up to the second coming of Christ. Presently, we are prophetically spoken in the time of Laodicea, which 'by chance' means *human rights* or *people's rights*. The rest of the book of Revelation - and as a result all the prophecies regarding the final Antichrist - are still in the future. Further, this also does not mean that there have not been any antichrists in the past. We read more on this in the latter part of 1 John 2:18. This interpretation entails that the prophecies in the book of Revelation, together with the other prophecies pertaining to the end of time still have to go into fulfillment. Therefore, the prophecies in which the final Antichrist plays an important role could not have gone into fulfillment yet. The fact that the Antichrist will be a specific person - a man - is not doubted in any way.

Further, the distinct symbolic parts of the book of Revelation are held in tact. To interpret it however in whole as a 'symbolic book', is seen as a total exaggeration. There are in truth quite a few images and symbolic passages that are used in this final book of the Bible, for example the following:

- Christ is represented as a Lamb (Rev. 13:8). He is not really a lamb, but because the Bible name Him as such, it surely does not mean that He has to be seen as merely symbolic.
- The Antichrist is being represented as a beast with seven heads (Rev. 13:1). There is no beast with seven heads in existence and it is easily identifiable as symbolic language, but it does not at all mean that the Antichrist has to be seen as merely symbolic. *A symbolic image always refers in one way or another to a literal entity.*
- Satan is being depicted as a dragon and a serpent, distinctly symbolic (Rev. 12:9). In other parts he is however called by his known name. This does not mean that he is a dragon or a serpent, but he carries some of their characteristics. That he does exist literally however, is an absolute fact – just recall for a moment all the murders and violence in the world and especially the growing interest in witchcraft and hardcore Satanism.

• The woman of Rev. 17 sits on a scarlet-colored beast, but also on *"many waters"* (verse 1). It is a symbolic reference, because in Rev. 17:15 the Word itself explains: *"The waters which thou sawest, where the whore sitteth, are peoples, and multitudes, and nations and tongues."*. The 'waters' is only an image of another literal truth. It is not something vague, which has no true meaning. Our wonderful God is a God of order and a Master in His description of the most important and eternal concepts. Images and symbolism never replace literal truth, but merely describe and illuminate them further.

If and when current world events are taken into account, it will become clear that we have already entered the time surrounding the second coming of Christ. It is indeed true that nobody will know the specific day or hour of His return, but that we are in the season of His return is more than clear. To study the prophetical word is a command from God (1 Thes. 5:20; 2 Pet. 1:19) and contains a very special blessing for every Christian (Rev. 1:3) – especially in the time that we live in!

The futuristic interpretation of Bible prophecy will consequently, for the greater part, be our point of departure in this study of the amazing end time scenario. It has to be mentioned though, that all the other interpretations have, to a greater or lesser extent, made a contribution to explain the Bible's prophetic passages. This will become quite clear in this study. To tell the truth, every interpretation contains some truths, but according to the Jewish way of prophetical interpretation, a prophecy can have multiple fulfillments – thus deeper and clearer each time. We then arrive at a type of cyclical fulfillment of the prophecies of the Bible. If we for example examine a subject like the Antichrist, this pattern of prophetic fulfillment becomes quite evident. There have been numerous antichrists, and there most certainly are some present in the world today, but eventually they all point to the last or final Antichrist (see 1 Jn. 2:18). Prophetic fulfillments always progress towards the climactic and final fulfillment!

The question now remains, where are we today on the prophetic calendar of God. Should there be any uncertainty about this?

THE BIG APOSTASY

A British weekly reported early in the year 2000 on the way of thought in Britain's Christian churches. In a *Gallup* survey, tragic and shocking statistics were being recorded. One of the sections of the survey included persons who viewed themselves as Christians, who had to relate if they still believed in the following issues or not. The results among these self-proclaimed Christians were as follows:

64% did not believe there is a devil
62% did not believe there would be a second coming
60% did not believe in hell
39% did not believe in life after death
33% did not believe that Christ was born of a virgin
33% did not believe that Christ was resurrected
23% did not believe in heaven
15% did not believe in God [1]

If this is what Christians believe, we do not even have to wonder what other people believe in this regard. The words of Christ in Lk. 18:8 – that when He returns, will He still *"find faith on the earth"*? – now becomes very clear to us.

What would be the reason for this great apostasy away from the truth of the infallible Word? That this situation at the time of the end, was foretold in the Bible, cannot be doubted.

Just consider for example Mt. 24:11; 2 Thes. 2:3; 1 Tim. 4:1; 2 Tim. 3:1-5 etc.

There are however quite a few present day factors that can be brought into consideration regarding this. A newspaper heading read as follows (translated):

"TV-WATCHERS 'BRAIN-DEAD' IN COMPARISON TO READERS" and continued:

"Research have shown that people who are addicted to watching television are 'brain-dead' compared to people who read ... people who constantly watch television, do not really utilise their brain. Science has already proven that a person's brain is more active when he sleeps than when he is watching TV." [2]

People today are becoming dull and numb toward God and His Word, and the role of the television in all of this can not be underestimated. In 1995 a study was conducted by the *Nielson Media Research* group in the USA and they found that the average child watches 15 000 to 30 000 hours of television before he or she finishes school. At the same time the child will only spend 11 000 to 16 000 hours in school, and on average only 2 000 hours (of quality time) with his or her parents. [3]

It was also found that an average child views between 800 000 and 1,5 million acts of violence on TV, which includes 192 000 – 360 000 depictions of murder – before he or she finishes with school. [4] Can this truly have nothing to do with the culture of violence that is sweeping the world at present? Alternatively, would it not add tremendously towards the growing apathy towards God and the Bible?

To misjudge this would be very unwise and to deny it altogether, certainly foolish.

THE BEGINNING OF SORROWS

In Mt. 24 the Lord Jesus Christ announced unmistakable signs that would mark the season of His return. After He described a whole list of signs that His disciples should be on the lookout for, He urgently warned in verse 8 that *"All these things are the beginning of sorrows"*.

This is a reference to the beginning of the greatest time of tribulation that the human race will ever face (verse 21). Today however, there are many who hold to the belief that Mt. 24 has no reference to our current generation, but that it had already and completely gone into fulfillment around the year 70 AD and shortly thereafter. The reason given for this, is found in Mt. 24:1,2 where Jesus told the disciples that no stone of the temple would be left on another. Directly after this, they asked Him when all these events would take place and when His second coming and the end of the world (or final age) would be. In the year 70 AD the temple was destroyed by the Roman armies under General Titus, but surely Jesus did not return at that time and clearly it was not the end of the world. It was merely thirty eight years after his ascension that the temple and Jerusalem were destroyed. It seems very short sighted to declare that the remainder of Mt. 24 also went into fulfillment during that time. There were false christs in that time like Nero and others and surely there were earthquakes, pestilences, famines and wars during that time, but the end did not yet arrive. The Jews were scattered throughout the whole world at that time, as the Word prophesied, but surely the end did not come. The Word of God declares in numerous places in the Old and New Testament (Ezek. 36:24-29; Rom. 11:28) that the end will only come after the Jews return to their land. God Himself would eventually bring this into a miraculous fulfillment and He is currently still engaged in that process. In 1948, Israel miraculously became a nation again and from that time, Jews from all over the world are returning to their country. The great majority of them, however, are blinded to the fact that God still wants them to repent of their sins (like everybody else) and accept the Lord Jesus Christ as there risen Messiah and Saviour. Those that will not adhere to God's call, will enter the biblically prophesied time of great tribulation that cannot be a far-off event now. The 'end' and the second coming of Christ could thus technically not have come before the fulfilment of the great and amazing event that came in the year of 1948.

Only now do we live in the generation of which Jesus Christ Himself had said: *"Verily I say unto you, This generation shall not pass, till all these things be fulfilled. Heaven and earth shall pass away, but my words shall not pass away."* (Mt. 24:34,35).

Not all of Mt. 24 went into fulfilment around the time of 70 AD. Presently, however, few seem to realize what is currently happening on the world stage, although it is coming to pass right in front of our eyes.

It also needs to be mentioned that Mt. 24 is reflected in a remarkable way in Rev. 6. This proves even more distinctly that Mt. 24 refers to the future time of great tribulation. Only in Rev. 19 will this time period come to an end. These sorrows may be compared to a woman who is in travail. The Greek text of Mt. 24:8 confirms this, as the Greek word translated as 'sorrows' may also be translated with 'birth pains' or 'birth pangs'. All these signs and events that are mentioned in Mt. 24 and Rev. 6, are intensifying and moving to a climax, comparable to birth pangs. As time speeds on, the intensity and frequency of the pains get greater. Everyone that takes note will realise that something or someone will be born shortly and that it surely will not be of an enjoyable nature. (In connection with birth pains, also compare Is. 13:8, Is. 26:17,18 and 1 Thes. 5:3).

In Mt. 24:16 God warned the Jews (*"them which be in Judaea"*) that they should flee to the mountains when this happens (especially with the coming of the Antichrist). Surely, the Lord would not warn them to flee from the wonderful 'new time' that would supposedly be just around the corner.

THE DECEPTION WAS FORETOLD

- *"And many false prophets shall rise, and shall deceive many."* Mt. 24:11
- *"For there shall arise false Christs, and false prophets, and shall shew great signs and wonders; insomuch that, if it were possible, they shall deceive the very elect. Behold, I have told you before."* Mt. 24:24,25

Nearly two thousand years ago the disciples asked Jesus: *"what shall be the sign of thy coming, and of the end of the world?"* His first, immediate and distinct answer was:

"Take heed that no man deceive you." (Mt. 24:3,4)

In our day and age, we are forced to look closely at this prophecy. Beside the above-mentioned warning of the Lord Jesus, there are numerous similar warnings recorded for us in the New Testament. Mt. 7:14-16 illustrates why this is such a serious matter. It reads:

"because strait is the gate, and narrow is the way, which

leadeth unto life, and few there be that find it. Beware of false prophets, which come to you in sheep's clothing, but inwardly they are ravening wolves. Ye shall know them by their fruits."

The Lord Jesus makes it clear that few will be saved and that false prophets will be a major obstacle in the way of those He would have liked to reconcile with Himself. If these preachers stand in the way of people reaching the cross and Christ, we have to take it into account in the most serious manner. Eph. 5:11 states very distinctly: *"And have no fellowship with the unfruitful works of darkness, but rather reprove them."* The Lord did in fact say: *"and ye shall know the truth, and the truth shall make you free."* (Jn. 8:32).

Nobody on earth is set free by lies. Why then would you want to be misled, if you can know the truth and it has the ability to set you free? You can then also lead others to the truth.

Jesus Christ Himself said: *"I am the way, the truth and the life:"* (Jn. 14:6). There is no truth if not within Jesus. A false prophet will only be declared false if he is measured againt the Word of God and thus found to be a liar. Christ is the incarnate Word (Jn. 1:14). The Word is the absolute truth. This has been verified on numerous occasions. Any person who is under the impression that he or she is filled with the Holy Spirit, but at the same time despises the truth of the Word openly, needs to be declared as false – by the authority of the Word of God. Paul, Peter, John, Jude (filled and led by the Holy Spirit) warned the church of their time on numerous occasions and in all earnestness that they are to be on the lookout for false prophets. The exact same apply to us today. Here are a few examples:

"For I know this, that after my departing shall grievous wolves enter in among you, not sparing the flock, Also of

your own selves shall men arise, speaking perverse things, to draw away disciples after them. Therefore watch, and remember, that by the space of three years I ceased not to warn every one night and day with tears." (Acts 20:29-31).

The most disturbing fact seems to be that men from inside the church will rise with false teachings and that some (if not many) will follow them. Why do people get so upset when they are cautioned about these things? Paul himself cautioned in tears!

"But there were false prophets also among the people, even as there shall be false teachers among you, who privily shall bring in damnable heresies, even denying the Lord that bought them, and bring upon themselves swift destruction. And many shall follow their pernicious ways; by reason of whom the way of truth shall be evil spoken of. And through covetousness shall they with feigned words make merchandise of you;" (2 Pet. 2:1-3).

"Beloved, believe not every spirit, but try the spirits whether they are of God: because many false prophets are gone into the world. Hereby know ye the Spirit of God: Every spirit that confesseth that Jesus Christ is come in the flesh is of God: and every spirit that confesseth not that Jesus is come in the flesh is not of God: and this is that spirit of antichrist, whereof ye have heard that it should come; and even now already is it in the world." (1 Jn. 4:1-3).

Many tend to believe nearly anything and everything that is offered to them from a 'Christian' perspective. How small a number of people remain who examine and test everything – on the basis of Scripture?

All Christian groups acknowledge in one way or another that Jesus Christ existed. Watch out for those however who do not center their evangelism around the crucifixion, death and resurrection of Jesus Christ. A church should be preaching and presenting the message of the cross (the gospel – 1 Cor.15:1-4) to the human race which is going astray. Every person who receives salvation from God through Christ's atonement will be transformed to live a holy life and will serve God in all sincerity. Such a life will be in line with that of Jesus when he walked on the earth. Remember that Jesus Himself said that the Holy Spirit will remind us of everything He had said (Jn. 14:26; 15:26). This is what it really means to profess that Jesus came in the flesh. Paul wrote in 1 Cor. 2:2 to the church of the Corinthians: *"For I determined not to know any thing among you, save Jesus Christ, and him crucified."* God spoke these words. Any other imitated message points to the Antichrist.

The word faith, is very cheap these days, but what does God's Word say about the true faith:
"Beloved when I gave all diligence to write unto you of the common salvation, it was needful for me to write unto you, and exhort you that ye should earnestly contend for the faith which was once delivered unto the saints. For there are certain men crept in unawares, who were before of old ordained to this condemnation, ungodly men, turning the grace of our God into lasciviousness, and denying the only Lord God, and our Lord Jesus Christ." (Jude 3,4).

What became of the faith that was once delivered to the saints? Today there are numerous examples of 'permissiveness' in churches and in the lives of many who call themselves Christians. Yes, false prophets did creep in and the damage is already unimaginable.

The now already infamous 'Jesus Seminar', a group of theologians and 'intellectuals' that enjoy tearing the Bible to shreds, recently re-convened to decide which part of the

Bible is true and which should be rejected.

The following excerpt from an article shows there line of thinking:

> "After declaring that Jesus was not born of a virgin and that many biblical reports of his life were conjured by early Christians, the Jesus Seminar is taking on God. ... 'We are opening up a new phase of the seminar', said the group's founder, Robert Funk, ... <u>'We are discussing the future of God, so to speak'</u> ... " [5] (emphasis added).

This is clearly blasphemous, but as of yet, they do not realize that God foretold their future a long time ago.

"The wise men are ashamed, they are dismayed and taken: lo, they have rejected the word of the Lord; and what wisdom is in them?" (Jer. 8:9).

"in the latter days ye shall consider it perfectly. I have not sent these prophets ... ye have perverted the words of the living God, of the LORD of hosts our God." (Jer. 23:20,21,36).

ADD TO AND OR DIMINISH FROM THE WORD OF GOD

"Ye shall not add unto the word which I command you, neither shall ye diminish ought from it." (Deut. 4:2).

"Add thou not unto his words, lest he reprove thee, and thou be found a liar." (Prov. 30:6).

"For I testify unto every man that heareth the words of the prophecy of this book, If any man shall add unto these things, God shall add unto him the plagues that are written in this book: and if any man shall take away from the words

of the book of this prophecy, God shall take away his part out of the book of life, and out of the holy city, and from the things which are written in this book." (Rev. 22:18,19).

This warning was not heeded by most in the days of Israel and most certainly it is not heeded today.

Just think of the Jesus Seminar's so-called 5th gospel!

"A wonderful and horrible thing is committed in the land; the prophets prophesy falsely, and the priests bear rule by their means; and my people love to have it so: and what will ye do in the end thereof?" (Jer. 5:30,31).

The Scriptures teach us distinctly to not believe everything and everybody, but that we have to differentiate and discern between good and evil (1 Jn. 4:1; Phil. 1:9-10). Moreover, we are able to discern as a result of our knowledge of the Word. Without it we would not be able to see the difference.

Is. 5:20 reads: *"Woe unto them that call evil good, and good evil; that put darkness for light and light for darkness"* The Word goes on in declaring: *"A good tree cannot bring forth evil fruit, neither can a corrupt tree bring forth good fruit,"* (Mt. 7:18 – especially in context of false prophets). Rom. 16:17,18 holds the answer: *"Now I beseech you, brethren, mark them which cause divisions and offenses contrary to the doctrine which ye have learned; and avoid them. For that are such serve not our lord Jesus Christ, but their own belly; and by good words and fair speeches deceive the hearts of the simple."*

To summarize one may use the words of Paul to Timothy: *"Now the spirit speaketh expressly, that in the latter times some shall depart form the faith, giving heed to seducing spirits, and doctrines of* devils;" (1 Tim. 4:1) and continues:

"For the time will come when they will not endure sound doctrine; but after their own lusts shall they heap to themselves teachers, having itching ears; and they shall turn away their ears from the truth, and shall be turned into fables." (2 Tim. 4:3,4).

FALSE CHRISTS

Through the centuries, there have been numerous false Christs, but today it seems to be the case more than ever.

Note the following:

'Jesus' in the clouds

"Numerous TV-watchers were quite convinced that they saw 'Jesus' face' on a TV image. Shortly after the TV broadcast CNN in America was overwhelmed by telephone calls. Many viewers were convinced that 'Jesus' face' was clearly to be seen on a photo that was taken by the Hubble-space telescope." (translated) [6]

'Jesus' in Iran

"Large crowds have been gathering in front of a house in the Iranian capital … after rumors spread about the apparition of Jesus Christ there."

The article continued and reported that an image of Jesus with a beard, dressed in white with a cane in his hand, appeared on a wall of a house in Teheran. It is interesting that the image only appeared at night. [7]

The Word however says: *"Then if any man shall say unto you, Lo, here is Christ, or there; believe it not."* and *"Wherefore if they shall say unto you, Behold, he is in the desert; go not forth: behold, he is in the secret chambers;*

believe it not." (Mt. 24:23 and 6).

Christ will not return in this manner. He is coming in the clouds to take His bride with Him to heaven! (1 Thes. 4:16,17).

Another report tells of the large number of messiahs that make their appearance in Israel. It is reported that some declare themselves to be Christ, some Moses, others Elijah and others again see themselves as Mary, David or even Samson. People take linen from their hotel rooms, drape it around them and walk through the streets of Jerusalem. Doctors there named it the 'Jerusalem Syndrome.' A Doctor is reported as explaining how he himself treated several 'Christs.' The article asks the question that if the real Messiah appears (for whom many Jews are presently waiting) how will they recognize him as the true Messiah? How will they know which one is the right one? [8]

This is not all. Even Muslims await a 'Messiah Jesus' that must still appear. At the end of 1999 some Muslims in Lebanon adhered to the call of a religious leader who asked them to move to the mountains "... to witness the arrival of the messiah Jesus and the establishment of the kingdom of justice," [9]

We are living in strange days and many people believe that they are the long awaited one. Note the following amazing statistic:

"There's been a boom in false 'messiahs.' The number of self-appointed religious saviours has never been greater than today, when more than 1 500 people claim to be an incarnation of Jesus Christ," [10]

WARS

"In Mt. 24:6 the Lord says: *"And ye shall hear of wars and rumors of wars."*

Until 1948, most of the wars on earth were fought between the big nations. Think about France against Germany, England against France. During the two world wars of the 20th century it was also nation against nation. It was Japan against America and the other way around. Germany against other countries and so on. In the day and age we live in, a change is taking place. The wars or conflicts of the last decade or so were very specifically ethnic in nature. Think about Bosnia Herzegovina and Croatia as well as the Serbs and Bosnians against each other over the same territory – ethnic. Serbs and Albanese in Kosovo – ethnic. North and South Korea – ethnic. North-Ireland (Catholic against Protestant) – ethnic. Rwanda – ethnic. Burundi – ethnic. The Congo – ethnic. Zaire – ethnic. Angola – ethnic. Mozambique – ethnic. South Africa (especially Kwazulu-Natal) – ethnic. Why is this so important, one may well ask. Did you know that the Greek word used in Mt. 24:7 translated with nation, is the word *ethnos*? There we read: *"For nation shall rise against nation, and kingdom against kingdom."* It refers specifically to ethnic violence and wars. How much blood was not already shed through this type of violence and conflicts. The Lord Jesus Christ who knew the future in His omniscience, knew that these wars would be occuring shortly before His second coming.

Look at the following facts:
- The ethnic war that still rages in Rwanda and Burundi already claimed more than a million lives in the last decade. In 1998, there were conflicts and wars in more than a quarter of the states on the continent of Africa. [11]

- International weapon trade in 1999 amounted to $809 billion. [12]
- In the year 1998 alone, there raged 27 wars on earth – mostly ethnical. [13]
- The year 1999 boasted a record number of wars: "the number of wars fought world-wide increased significantly in 1999, when there were no fewer than 40 armed conflicts being fought on the territories of 36 countries..." [14]

Wipe out all life?

Another verse in Mt. 24 that relates distinctly to wars reads: *"And except those days should be shortened, there should no flesh be saved,"* (Mt.24:22).

The British Premier, Tony Blair delivered a speech at the end of 1998 that confirms these prophetic words without a doubt. He declared that Iraq was in possession of enough weapons for chemical and biological warfare to destroy the world's population three times. This came after a United Nations inspection group visited that country. [15]

This is a far reaching issue. The current generation on earth is the first in history to posess weapons which could destroy the whole world's population so that 'no flesh' will be saved. A thousand years or even a hundred years ago this would have been unimaginable, but not any more. Atomic and nuclear weapons merely exist from 1945. It is one of the clearest indications that our generation is nearing the end and that God will intervene shortly.

FAMINES

"There shall be famines..."

Presently, famines poses unimaginable threats to the world's population if something drastic is not done. The question remains, do some world leaders really want to do something about it. This may sound strange, but it is a matter that needs urgent attention. We regularly hear about great, well-known nations that deliver thousands and thousands of tons of food to starving nations to assist them in their need. Numerous reports however, also reach the media that the people on the ground do not always receive this food. Sometimes armed gangs and even government officials of these countries (often terrorists groups) take posession of the food to resell it.

The following statistics from the last 5 years or so, give us a glimpse on the crises at hand:

- The crises in Ethiopia, Somalia and other African countries are already very infamous. In Sudan, in October 1997, there were 2,5 million people already totally dependent on international provisions just to survive. [16]
- From Lusaka it was reported in 1998 that 800 000 Zambians were staring acute starvation in the eye. [17]
- In North Korea the situation have been very critical for a long time now. Programs on telvision were even aired to inform inhabitants what types of grass they could consume.
- Up to 3,5 million people in North-Korea already died as a result of that immense famine – and only since 1995. This occurred without most people having even known about it. [18]

In Rev. 6:5,6,8 we read of the 'black horse' that will arise early in the time of tribulation and that starvations will be part of that dark time.

The world today is very conscious of the rapidly changing weather patterns. If this is as a result of El Nino, La Nina or because there are someone tampering with the weather, does not matter - it has a direct effect on the planting of crops. There is no doubt that the earth has the necessary natural resources to provide enough food for the earth's billions, but there are other factors that comes to mind. This include the weather, as mentioned, a great variety of pests that destroy crops, and the question of knowledge in agriculture and food production. The other question is whether all governments want there people to produce food or not. That many in the world however, are looking starvation right in the face, is not to be doubted.

- The United Nations published a report stating that nearly 20 million people in East-Africa alone are experiencing a severe famine. [19]
- It is now calculated that up to 60 000 people per day die as a result of starvation [20]
- According to a report of *Earthwatch*, 1 out of every 6 people are now constantly hungry. It means that 1 billion people are now always hungry. [21]
- According to a UN report there are 1,2 billion (one thousand two hundred million) people on earth that have to live on less than $1 per day. According to them one third of the whole world's population lives in extreme poverty and as a result already on the edge of starvation. [22]
- More recently the "World Food Programme has warned that 12.8 million people are on the brink of starvation in southern Africa [alone] and urgently need food aid. ... Hundreds have already died in Malawi ... " [23]

The Word predicted this for the last days. It wasn't like this before. The worst is yet to follow. (Rev. 6:8).

PESTILENCES

"....and pestilences..."

Medical scientists will be quick to assure anybody who wants to doubt it, that the field of medical science is presently on the farthest point of development in the history of man. This is a clear fact. What is however accurate as well, is the fact that there have never before been such a big war against such a wide variety of viruses and infections at the same time in history. The medical scientist cannot deny this and admit to it candidly. Consider the following in this regard:

"Antibiotics can no longer save the world. ... Illnesses like influenza and pneumonia, measles and cholera ... tuberculosis, meningitis, malaria, bubonic plague, and Hepatitis B that have returned vigorously to kill off the human population. A third of all deaths in 1995 was as a result of these illnesses, says the World Health Organization." (translated). [24]

Prof Lafras Steyn of the Department of Microbiology at the University of Cape Town in South Africa states quite frankly: "No new class of antibiotic could be developed in the past twenty years." (translated). He also said that new types of antibiotics are merely permutations of existing ones. [25]

- The magazine, *Insig,* again reported on this and mentioned that medical researchers speak about the year 2007 as D-day, as they are not able to develop new antibiotics fast enough. [26]
- There are also diseases or pestilences that hit livestock. (food for the human race). In the wellknown case of the 'mad cow' disease, 2,3 million herd of cattle were slaughtered in England at the end of 1996 alone, to stop the spread of this disease. [27]

- In the USA, similar action was necessary to keep this dangerous situation in tact. If this continues, it may pose far-reaching results for the human race. Recently, there are also huge numbers of fish that are found dead from various viruses, around the world.
- In Russia, in 1997 alone, 392 000 Russians were infected with syphilis. The number of children younger than 14 years that were infected with this sexually transmitted disease, increased by 31%. This is how Russia look after all that is filthy from the West were welcomed there. [28]

The deadly disease aids has to be put under the spotlight here more than any other though. If this is not God's judgment for the drastic increase in immorality of this day, only the Day of Judgment will prove otherwise. In Rom. 1:27 we see clearly that sinners will bear: "...*in themselves that recompense of their error*"

Study the following statistical information regarding this disease and decide for yourself if it is merely an ordinary, normal or natural phenomenon:

- More than 1 600 South-Africans are infected daily with the HIV virus that causes aids. [29]
- In Zimbabwe in 1999, already 240 people per day died as a result of aids related illnesses. It represents 1 680 people per week. At hospitals, bodies are being removed 24 hours per day. [30]
- In South Africa alone, the persentage of HIV positive people increased from 0,22% in 1988 to a staggering 32,8% of the population in 1999. These numbers were made available by the Department of Health. [31]
- The aids virus took the lives of about 12 million inhabitants on the continent of Africa since the start of it. [32]
- The situation in Africa is worsening dramatically:

"over 30% of the adult population [is] infected in some countries" according to the United Nations. Overall "more than 28 million Africans were HIV-positive" [33]
- In China it looks even worse that that:
  "China is facing an aids epidemic that has led to the infection of 80 percent of the population in some areas. ... the *China Daily* ... made the first official mention of the towns where infection rates are higher than any in Africa." [34]
- At least 15 000 people worldwide are infected daily with the HIV virus that causes aids [35]

Malaria is another disease that takes yet a bigger toll. 3 000 children under the age of five are currently dying each day as a result of malaria worldwide. "Every thirty seconds, a child dies of malaria." Nearly 500 million cases of acute malaria were reported in 1999 world wide – it is five times more than aids, tuberculosis, measles and leprosy together! [36]

Approximately 13 million people worldwide die annually as a result of diseases.

Since 1945, 150 million people have died from illnesses like aids, malaria and tuberculosis - according to the Red Cross' *World Disaster Report.* [37]

➜ In Deut. 28:58-61 the people of Israel were seriously warned by God that this scenario would become reality among them as it also becomes a shocking reality in our day among all the nations of the world.

EARTHQUAKES

"...and earthquakes..."

It is true that there have always been earthquakes. This is also not the point of departure here. We need to remember however that sensitive seismographic equipment (for the measurement of earthquakes) was only manufactured in the 20th century for the first time. The Chinese philosopher Chang Heng though probably invented the first basic seismograph in 132 AD. Earthquakes have thus been measured for quite a lengthy period of time.

What is however true, is that the number of stations where earthquakes can be registered, increased drastically during the 20th century. In 1931 there were about 350 such stations around the world and today there are about 4000 stations where data on earthquakes is received via telex, computer and satellite. God declared that this will be a sign of His return and He made sure that nobody will have an excuse. Through the ages, earthquakes were always an incident that reminded men of His return and today this is ever so much more the case. We have to comprehend that we are dealing with a perfectly righteous God. He gives everybody an equal good change to understand that He fulfills His Word and that He will let come to pass exactly that which He had said He would. It is this that reminds us that we are dealing with the living God. There have never been so many reports on earthquakes in the media and never before could such great a number of people be sure of the second coming of Christ. Here follows a list of the current average annual incidence of earthquakes in the world (Information from the *United States Geological Survey* and *Earthquake Information Center*):

Giant earthquakes 8 and higher on the Richterschale – 1
Major 7-7.9 – 18
Large 6-6.9 – 120
Medium 5-5.9 – 800
Light 4-4.9 – 6 200 (estimated)

Small 3-3.9 – 49 000 (estimated)

Very small < 3.0 2-3 on average 1 000 <u>per day</u>
1-2 on average 8 000 <u>per day</u>

A summary of 1999's reported earthquakes showed that there were also more major earthquakes than the expected annual average – 20 major earthquakes (7.0 – 7.9) were registered in 1999. Coinciding, the number of deaths were doubled that of the expected annual average – 22 000 people died in earthquakes in 1999. It is interesting to notice that the Bible, in Lk. 21:11, declare specifically that:

"<u>great</u> earthquakes shall be in divers places"

The largest group of earthquakes - that increased the most in our time - are the earthquakes between 6.0 – 6.9 on the Richter scale. There are many more of these quakes than those between 7.0-7.9 and many more people die annually in these quakes.

- Another illuminating fact regarding the incidence of earthquakes is the following: From a list of the most destructive earthquakes of all times (quakes which killed at least 50 000 people at a time) it appears that 10 of these 21 quakes <u>occurred in the 20th century</u>. The first of these 21 earthquakes occurred as early as 856 AD. There has been, as can be seen, a distinct increase (at least in knowledge) in the occurrence of these quakes in the last millennium.
- The other shocking fact surrounding this type of destructive earthquakes is that not one of these 21 earthquakes which killed 50 000 or more people occurred in a predominantly Christian (Protestant) Western country. Most of these quakes occurred in China (the land of the dragon, where the biggest quake

in 1556 killed 830 000 people) and Arabic nations like Iran, as well as in Russia and surroundings. One was in Japan and five in predominantly Roman Catholic countries such as Italy, Portugal and Peru. [38]

The enormous and extremely tragic earthquake that occurred in India in January of 2001 brought about the death of more than 20 000 people (some estimated more than 30 000). This earthquake that measured 7.7 on the Richterscale also collapsed Islamic mosques and palaces and severely damaged Hindu temples and shrines. An old 11th century sun temple was also cracked at the time. [39] Is this a foretaste of the last fall of Babylon?

Recently, in El Salvador, "2 massive earthquakes that killed more than 1,200 people have been accompanied by thousands of smaller jolts ... sending people fleeing in panic to the streets day after day. ..."
During that time it was reported that "Many believe the end of the world is coming." [40]

RECORD NUMBER OF NATURAL DISASTERS

In 1999 there were a record number of 755 natural disasters in the world. In 1998 there were 701 and in 1995 around 600. In 1999 there were, amongst others, 225 windstorms, 190 floods, 111 geological catastrophes like big earthquakes and volcanic eruptions. At least 70 000 people died in 1999 in natural disasters and the economic loss was about R700 billion (about $80 billion at the time). The economic effect of natural disasters increased eightfold from 1987 to 1997. [41]
This is exactly like the birth pangs Scripture predicted!
Lk. 21:25 reads: *"And there shall be signs in the sun, and in the moon, and in the stars; and upon the earth <u>dis-</u>*

tress of nations, with perplexity: the sea and the waves roaring; men's hearts failing them for fear, and for looking after those things which are coming on the earth."
(Emphasis added).

ECOLOGICAL DECAY AND THE GROWING WORLD POPULATION

There are many cases of ecological decay in the world around us. We all know that, but do we really know to what extent the decay is progressing at the moment. Here are just some examples:

According to news sources, *Worldwatch* recently made a shocking announcement. One out of every four (a quarter) of the world's vertebrate species (birds, mammals, reptiles, amphibians and fish) are nearing extinction or had already become extinct. [42]

The following unbelievable information about the earth's coral reefs also necessitates our attention:

> "More than a quarter [25%] of the world's coral reefs have been destroyed ... most of the remaining reefs could be dead in just twenty years. In ... the Maldives and Seychelles islands in the Indian Ocean, up to 90 percent of coral reefs have been killed during the past two years [1998-2000]... "
>
> This means that many species of fish – food for the human population – will now be at risk of extinction. [43]

In 1998 the *World Nature Fund* announced that half (50%) of the world's fresh water ecological systems died out from 1970 to 1995. Could this be – in just 25 years?

This was not all they had to say. According to their *Living Planet Report*, the earth is annually losing natural forests the size of England and Whales combined. [44]

Are we living in the last days or can this problem really be solved? No chance without intervention from the living creator God.

The world population is another startling sign that this world will never exist for another thousand years – as some still believe the case might be.

- The world population doubled since 1970! This in only 30 years! There are now more than 6 billion people on planet earth. Interesting that we reach the number 6 billion after approximately 6000 years of human history. To think that the first billion was reached only in 1850 and that in the next 150 years alone another 5 billion people was added to the world population. The world population now grows at 76 million annually or 145 people per minute! This is the official growth rate, thus after the death rate was already taken into account. It is quite clear that things cannot carry on like this for very much longer. The more people on earth, the bigger the crises – think here in terms of diseases, famines etc. [45]

Will God let it go on like this for much longer?

HARDSHIPS OF THE LAST DAYS

The escalation in violence across the world, is no surprise to the Lord. This tragic situation in the world that depresses so many people did not surprise the God of heaven and earth. No, it is also not true that He lost control or gave up on the human race. All these things now happening - in front of our eyes - were prophesied thousands of years ago.

If there is one sign of the nearing return of Jesus, that nobody can deny, it is the fact that crime and violence increased dramatically during the last few years. This is a phenomenon that is noticed worldwide. South Africa surely never knew such a plague of violence as is experienced currently. It is extra-ordinary. We can all admit easily that today's world is rife with violence.

In Gen. 6:11 and 13 we learn about a long passed but corresponding era that occurred on this earth. We read there: *"The earth <u>was also corrupt</u> before God; and the earth was filled with violence...And God said unto Noah, The end of all flesh is come before me; for the earth is <u>filled with violence</u> through them"* (emphasis added).

God repented at that moment that He made man and had to exterminate all flesh, except Noah and his family. He promised however to never do it again through water, but the next time by fire.

We read in 2 Pet. 3:7 the following words: *"but the heavens and the earth, which are now, by the same word are kept in store, reserved unto fire against the day of judgment and perdition of ungodly men."*

As in the days of Noah, God will not let this senseless culture of violence continue under His presence. It is going to be brought to a swift and abrupt end. We read in Mt. 24:37-39 that the days of Noah will be a lesson in judgment for those living at the end of time and that similar conditions will prevail on earth then. This will be the situation on earth shortly before Jesus returns and clearly it is. He Himself will end the violence.

We know quite well that the current state of affairs is not normal. Unusual circumstances are at the order of the day. People in South Africa and all over the world are being murdered without reason.

Since 1994, (in South Africa) more than 1 000 police officers were murdered. [46]

The number went up even higher thereafter.

Tens of thousands of people were also murdered in the cruelest of ways, during this time in our beloved country.

In 1998 alone, 18 000 people were murdered in South Africa. This means an average of 1500 people per month and an average of fifty per day! [47]

We hear of new cases everyday on the news. It keeps getting worse, with no end in sight.

Take note of this, "For every three crimes committed in South Africa, one is an act of violence." And "From every 1 000 acts of crime only 450 are reported." Not even half are being reported. [48]

From America the following is reported: "A recent study found that 61 percent of TV shows depicted violent acts in 1997. Viewers see an average of six acts of violence per hour." [49]

Television programs of the 'modern time' fuel the culture of violence of our day and age. Violence is not just an illusion on TV, but an absolute reality in our society.

Presently there are numerous violent computer games for children. In the Netherlands, the government intervened to keep the computer game, Carmageddon (referring to Armageddon), from being sold to children younger than 16. In the game, points are awarded for killing pedestrians by running over elderly people, children and animals. [50]

These things are horrible and make the life very unpleasant for many. There are few people left that can truly live a peaceful life. This is however still the good news, things are going to get even worse.

God foretold these tendencies in His omniscience and wrote it in His Word as a sign of the future. In Mt. 24:10 we read about the signs of the time and specifically these words: *"And then shall many be offended, and shall betray one another, and shall hate one another."* Moreover, verse 12 continues: *"And because inquity shall abound, the love of many shall wax cold."* These things have to happen and will escalate.

We also read in 2 Tim. 3:1-4 : *"in the last days perilous times shall come. For men shall be lovers of their own selves, covetous, boasters, proud, blasphemers, disobedient to parents, unthankful, unholy, without natural affection, trucebreakers, false accusers, incontinent, fierce, despisers of those that are good, traitors, heady, high-minded, lovers of pleasures more than lovers of God;..."*

There is much suffering on earth, but man himself is responsible for this. Abortions are another immense atrocity of our times. Only in the first two years since the legalization of abortion in South Africa, 70 000 abortions were committed in the country. [51]

Our generation is more than ever one 'without natural affection.' God's judgment is without any doubt hanging over this sin filled world. We cannot change it, but this time will be short in span and eventually will not return ever again. Times of peace and solace under the presence of the Lord are on the way. We have to fix our eyes on Jesus – He is the coming Prince of peace. In Ps. 34:7-10 we read these words of comfort: *"The angel of the Lord encampeth round about them that fear him, and delivereth them. O taste and see that the Lord is good: blessed is the man that trusteth in him. O fear the Lord, ye his saints: for there is no want to them that fear him. ... they that seek the Lord shall not want any good thing."*

PAGANISM ON THE INCREASE

In the day we are living in, there is a greater interest than ever in witchcraft, the occult and similar activities.

The following gives an example to what an extent paganism (heathen religion) and the practice of magic are growing among the youth worldwide:

"More than 100 young people, mostly girls, approach the Pagan Federation in the UK each month for advice on witchcraft, ... "

It appears that television programs like Sabrina the Teenage Witch and books like the Harry Potter series "encourage an interest in magic ... "

Can this really be harmless fun for teenage chldren?

A Pagan Federation spokesman reacted to this, saying: "We don't get asked how to become a witch, but rather we get asked <u>what a young witch should do</u>," [52]

(Emphasis added).

Defenders and supporters of the Harry Potter series of books initially maintained that the books help young children to develop a general interest in reading. This was later found to be not the case when a study was conducted amongst youth readers in Britain:

- In the year 2001 less youth books were sold than in the previous year despite the great sales of the Harry Potter books
- No new youth readers were added to the existing group
- Most readers of the Potter books were adults [53]

These type of books, of course, do introduce young people and older ones, for that matter, to occultic ways. This will not get you closer to God at all. The opposite is true and this is something that is very serious indeed.

In Gal. 5:19-21 we read that "witchcraft" is one of the abominations that (if not forgiven and cleansed by Jesus' blood) will keep a person from entering the kingdom of God. In the time of tribulation that is to come, we read that witchcraft will be an everyday occurrence in the world – Rev. 9:21. Rev. 22:15 also declares that the "sorcerers" will remain outside with the dogs and other like sinners.

The logical question comes to mind, why then does God allow these things to happen on earth. Why does he not stop it – He is God. Alternatively, is He really God, some may ask? The answer is that God according to His Word wants the measure of sin to come to a fulfillment. Only hereby will man see that without the creator God there is no way out. He is in fact very patient with the human race and His grace is amazing and indescribable. To solve this problem forever, Christ died for us on the cross. It is the time factor that is difficult for us to come to grips with, but for that we have the Bible. The fact remains that this world (as we know it today) has to come to an end, so that a wonderful new dispensation may follow – free from all these mentioned problems.

3

THE UNIQUE ROLE OF ISRAEL

Many are familiar with the history of Israel as it is portrayed in the Old Testament. Most Christians are well acquainted with God's miraculous acts with this people as well as with their extraordinary experiences over long periods of time. Where does Israel stand in today's world though? Is the church Israel? Who are the 144 000 sealed described in Rev. 7 and 14? These questions leave many unanswered questions amongst various Christian groups. Is the current church of Jesus Christ (God's true and born again children) the new Israel of today? Numerous church denominations believe that they have replaced the ancient people of Israel and that all the blessings that were meant for the people of the Covenant, now transfers to them. However, is this what the Word says?

DID GOD REJECT ISRAEL OF OLD COMPLETELY?

Is there an easy answer to this question? The only

answer is to be found in the Word of God. It may well be the case that many theologians reject the idea of God still having a plan with the literal people of Israel, but it still does not alter the Scripture's message. The Bible directs us in all matters, and even today, there is no greater authority than the Holy Scripture. From His Word, we may understand the miraculous way in which God deals with this people group that was formerly chosen by Him for a very special reason.

In Jer. 31:36,37 He says: *"If those ordinances depart from before me, saith the Lord, then the seed of Israel also shall cease from being a nation before me for ever. Thus saith the Lord: If heaven above can be measured, and the foundations of the earth searched out beneath, I will also cast off all the seed of Israel for all that they have done, saith the Lord."*

This is but one of the passages that proves that God shall never reject the ancient people of Israel. The reason for them being eventually forgiven though, will only be as a result of them sincerely repenting and surrendering to His will at the time when He returns (Zech. 12:10-14). On that day they will call on Him with sincere hearts and He will forgive them all that they have sinned. The same applies to every sinner today (from whatever people or nation) that has gone astray and wants to come to God with a sincere heart, deep regret and a full admission of his sin. 1 Jn. 1:9 is applicable to all sinners, the Jewish nation included.

In Titus 1:2 we read about *"God, that cannot lie."* He gave us the prophecies in the Bible and we have to understand that it will go into fulfillment to the last letter.

Read the following Scripture passages and decide if God will ever reject his formerly chosen people forever:

- *"And yet for all that, when they be in the land of their enemies, I will not cast them away, neither will I abhor them, to destroy them utterly, and break my covenant with them: for I am the Lord their God."* (Lev. 26:44)

- *"Now therefore hearken, O <u>Israel</u>....And the Lord shall scatter you among the nations, and ye shall be left <u>few in number among the heathen</u>, whither the Lord shall lead you...When thou art in tribulation, and all these things are come upon thee, even <u>in the latter days</u>, if thou <u>turn to the Lord thy God, and shalt be obedient unto his voice</u>; for the Lord thy God is a merciful God; <u>He will not forsake thee</u>, neither destroy thee, nor forget the covenant of thy fathers, which he sware unto them."* (Deut. 4:1,27,30,31).

Theologians of our day surely do not believe that only a small number of Christians of the current church will be left to endure the end of time, do they? The church has never been scattered amongst the nations – she stems from all nations, however!

- *"But thou, Israel, art my servant, Jacob whom I have chosen, the seed of Abraham my friend. Thou whom I have taken from the ends of the earth, and called thee from the chief men thereof, and said unto them, Thou art my servant; I have chosen thee, and not cast thee away....Fear not, thou worm Jacob, and ye men of Israel..."*(Is. 41:8,9,14).

- *"I say then, Hath God cast away his people? God forbid. For I also am an Israelite, of the seed of Abraham, of the tribe of Benjamin. God hath not cast away his people which he foreknew...I say then, Have they stumbled that they should fall? God forbid....blindness in part is happened to Israel....until the fullness of the Gentiles be come in. And so all Israel shall be saved..."*(the believing remnant at the end of the days) (Rom. 11:1,2,11,25,26).

Will God not be unique in his approach to this nation – because Jesus, the Saviour of the world, was born from their midst. May He not act as He pleases?

Another big misconception people in our day and age have, is that God will not cast his blessings on the unsaved Jews. That is why the current return of the Jews to Israel bears no real importance to them. The fact remains that God will surely not bless an unsaved Jewish people. As mentioned earlier, they will suffer tremendous tribulation in Israel and only after that will the remainder – which was previously mentioned – receive true salvation in Christ Jesus. Only after they will become converted, will God bless them again!

JACOB BECOMES ISRAEL

In Gen. 32:24-30 we read about Jacob wrestling with a *"man"* at the river Jabbok. It was God with whom he had wrestled, because Jacob says in verse 30 that he saw *"God face to face"*, yet his life was preserved. We know, however, that no one can see God in His full glory and still live (Jn. 1;18 and 6:46). This *"man"* was none other than Jesus Christ Himself. The Word teaches us that He existed from the very beginning of the world and that all was created through Him (Jn. 1:1-3). Jesus appeared to Jacob as an angel, for we know that He would only be born as a man thousands of years later in Bethlehem. The Old Testament refers to Jesus Christ as an angel in many places (Gen. 18:10,13; Judg. 13:20-22). After the *"man"* saw that he could not subdue Jacob, he struck him on the thigh and asked him to let him go *"for the day breaketh"* (verse 26). The fact that the day broke could refer to the bright morning star and to the light of the world – Jesus Christ, who would return many years later as a human to pay the price for the sins of the world on the cross. God's indescribable love is manifested through this. The fact that God wrestled with

Jacob, points to His need to have community with the human race whom He has created. To this day, this is God's desire – to be in relationship with everyone He had created.

If man does not aspire to make contact with God out of his own (and no one does by the way), God will do everything in His power to fix the broken relationship that came to be after the fall of man. God is indeed the One who seeks man first, as Rom. 3:11 says: *"there is none that seeketh after God."* No man will receive eternal life without wrestling with God or without *"much tribulation"* (Acts 14:22). The fact remains that the *"man"* could have 'overpowered' Jacob on the physical level, but God chose to 'overpower' him on the spiritual level. Today, God wants us to also rather live in the spirit than in the flesh. Jacob did not want to let God go before he was blessed by Him. By doing this, Jacob proved that He was serious with God. His faith was what God was searching for and God blessed him on that day – hereafter he could not continue to be the same old Jacob (the liar). Jacob then became part of God's plan and this gave rise to an indescribable blessing for the whole of human kind. Jacob may have limped away, but it became the sign to forever remind him of God and of the day when the Creator of heaven and earth had blessed him. In body – and flesh – God's children will bear suffering in life, but within their souls they will realize that they are saved and experience peace that exceeds all understanding. Only after Christ's second coming will we receive transfigured and glorified bodies and will we never know pain again (1 Cor. 15:53). Jacob, now carried on his body the mark that he had wrestled with God. Years later Paul also wrestled with the thorn in his flesh and God did not want to take it away from him. These soft spots in the flesh refer to man's total dependence on God as well as Jesus' crucifixion when his body was pierced and broken for our sins (Is. 53:5). Jesus Christ will, on the day of His return, present the marks on his hands and feet to the Jewish nation and then they will realize that He is the true Messiah (Zech. 12:10; 13:6). This is still applicable today. The perishable body of man still carries the marks of the Fall and it will remind every child of God of the day Jesus endured the pain in his body for our salvation.

The *"man"* also changed Jacob's name and said to him: *"Thy name shall be called no more Jacob, but Israel"* (verse 28). Israel means to *wrestle with God* or to *persevere*. It can also be translated with *prince*. If you wrestle with God and give yourself over unconditionally - and you persevere, you will be victorious in Christ and will live like a prince or the child of a king (spiritually spoken) in this dispensation. It is of utmost importance that the person who wants to be a true servant of God, has to die to himself and has to humble himself before God (Rom. 6:8; Mt. 18:4). The Lord will exalt such a person Himself in the right time (1 Pet. 5:6).

All true believers in Christ Jesus are also children of Abraham (Israel's grandfather), in a spiritual way (Gal. 3:7-9). That is why Abraham is called the father of the faithful. Rom. 4:17 also proclaims this when God relates in His Word regarding Abraham: *"I have made thee a father of many nations"*. We know that Abraham is the literal father of many nations only in a certain sense (Israel and nations descending from Ishmael). This verse is therefore rather speaking of spiritual descendents – the born again children of God. A Christian from Japan or Sweden is one with Abraham in God through faith, but in the literal sense they did not become Jews or Arabians. That is why we know that the true church or the bride of Christ is not the new literal Israel (a replacement thereof), but rather the spiritual children of Abraham. Jesus Christ was also born from his line.

Although the church is not Israel, the Old Testament is still a spiritual guideline for the church as Rom. 15:4 and 1

Cor. 10:11 clearly explain. Many great spiritual lessons are to be found in the pages of the Old Testament and besides that it points us to Christ through the hundreds of shadows and prophetic passages concerning His coming to earth.

The misconception of the British-Israelism groups, that certain western nations are the ten lost tribes of Israel, stems specifically from the notion that they are the literal Israel. Nobody can replace the literal nation of Israel or undo God's promises to them. The Jewish people were chosen by God to bring His perfect plan, of reconciliation with man, to a fulfillment. Not only for Israel, but also that *"the blessing of Abraham might come on the Gentiles through Jesus Christ; that we might receive the promise of the Spirit through faith."* (Gal. 3:14).

As a result, the nation of Israel stands on the one side and the gentile nations on the other. The Jews however, most definitely need to convert to Jesus Christ, exactly like individuals from the gentile nations. A converted Jew then becomes part of the bride of Christ and is not under the law anymore, from that moment on. Gal, 3:28 reads: *"There is neither Jew nor Greek...for ye are all one in Christ Jesus."* This verse speaks only of those in Christ – they are all one, spiritually spoken.

This of course does not mean that all unregenerate gentiles from all nations are also one, as if in one big brotherhood. This is typical Babylonian and New Age line of thought that is taught almost everywhere today.

Greeks (and individuals from all other nations for that matter) and Jews who received salvation through Jesus Christ is spiritually spoken not Greek or Jewish anymore, but are now children of God in the first place. The dispensation of the law and circumcision now expires for the Jew, but it is now all fulfilled in Christ. These Christian Jews are then also excluded from God's other dealings with the literal people of Israel, who will endure terrible persecution during the time of the coming great tribulation. Only those Jews who have accepted Jesus Christ as their Messiah, will escape it. The Word is very clear in this regard: *"For they are not all Israel, which are of Israel."* (Rom. 9:6). All Jews are as a result not necessarily part of the church or body of Christ – they did not all become a 'prince' with God. All the literal descendants of Abraham - in the flesh - are surely not children of God. No, only the Christian Jews can claim this together with all God's other children from all nations on earth – people who have been converted through the Holy Spirit and therefore now lives in Christ. God is righteous and the Jewish people will not receive eternal life simply because of their nationality as some believe today. There is another great truth though, that *"the salvation is of the Jews"* (Jn. 4:22), meaning that Jesus Christ was born from them (Rom. 9:5) and unto all eternity nobody is able to alter this. God's eternal promise to the fathers Abraham, Isaac and Jacob and His covenant with them is the second reason why the Jewish people still are a special people.

The words in Gal. 6:16 concerning the *"Israel of God"* could in a way be a spiritual reference to the church – made up from Jews and gentiles in Christ. The previous verse speaks about a *"new creature"* and that not the circumcision or the non-circumcision are of importance anymore. This verse also distinctly refers to all true Christian Jews. If they receive Christ as their Saviour and Messiah, they now become, as a result of the New Covenant of the New Testament, the real 'Israel of God'. The Bible is not one-dimensional. There are different levels of interpretation and the one does not exclude the other, but reaches deeper, more so when it relates to prophetic matters. The epistle to the church of the Galatians was written specifically to those who pursued the idea that all, Jew or non-Jew, should still adhere to the Jewish law to earn salvation. Paul brings this into perspective, that true faith in the gospel of Christ is the only way towards salvation. The Scripture does not profess that God has ceased all his literal plans with the nation of Israel. The God from the Old Testament is the same as the God of the New Testament. He always prevails. His earlier promises to the nation of Israel did not come to an end with the new dispensation. No, only the converted Christian Jew has now received salvation from the previous dispensation. The remainder of the Jews that are not saved, will find themselves in an anxious situation as a result of their denial of Christ. They remain slaves of the previous dispensation. It is tragic, but true. In Is. 40:2 we read that they will be judged by God and that Israel receives from the Lord *"double for all her sins."* In this regard, God acts differently with this nation than with any other nation on earth. It is as a result of them being so privileged initially, because He chose them and because He Himself revealed His power through them. Specifically because Christ was born of from amongst them.

THE LITERAL PEOPLE OF ISRAEL

"Take heed, and hearken, O Israel; this day thou art become the people of the Lord thy God." (Deut. 26:18,19)

"And the Lord hath avouched thee this day to be his peculiar people, as he hath promised thee, and that thou shouldest keep all his commandments; and to make thee high above all the nations which he hath made, in praise, and in name, and in honor, and that thou mayest be a holy people unto the Lord thy God, as he hath spoken." (Deut. 26:18,19)

In Gen. 11:31 we read that Terah took Abram, Sarai and Lot and *"went forth with them from Ur of the Chaldees, to go into the land of Canaan."* After they had lived in Haran for some time, Terah, the father of Abram died there. Abram descended from the line of Noah, a righteous man in the eyes of the Lord. In Gen. 12:1-3 we read this remarkable words of God to Abram: *"Get thee out of thy country, and from thy kindren, and from thy father's house, unto a land that I will show thee: and I will make of thee a great nation, and I will bless thee, and make thy name great; and thou shalt be a blessing: and I will bless them that bless thee, and curse them that curseth thee: and in thee shall all families on earth be blessed."*

God had chosen Abram with a very distinct reason in mind. The Word teaches us clearly that God does not judge by appearance, but by what lies hidden in the heart. (1 Sam. 16:7) Further in Gen. 12 the Bible tells how Abram reacted to God's request and this tells us about his heart: *"So Abram departed, as the Lord had spoken unto him."* A man with faith like few before and after him (Heb. 11:8,9). The Lord still seeks people like this, for without faith, no man can please God (Heb 11:6).

We know that God later changed Abram's name to Abraham because he would become *"father of many nations"* - spiritually spoken (Gen. 17:5). From the line of Abraham was born, Isaac and later Jacob (or Israel as God renamed him). It is of utmost importance to understand the role of the nation of Israel in the history of mankind. Without it, one can hardly comprehend the prophecies of the Bible. The literal nation of Israel is the key to numerous Holy Spirit inspired prophecies regarding the end of time and the nearing second coming of Jesus Christ.

THE CHOOSING OF ISRAEL

"For thou art a holy people unto the Lord thy God: the Lord thy God hath chosen thee to be a special people unto

himself. Above all people that are upon the face of the earth. The Lord did not set his love upon you, nor choose you, because ye were more in number than any people, for ye were the fewest of all people: But because the Lord loved you, and because he would keep the oath which he had sworn unto your fathers.....” (Deut. 7:6,7,8a)

God had chosen Israel above all the other nations on earth. There were many other and more powerful nations to choose from, but the Lord chose the smallest of all nations. Jesus also often sought the most simple ones of society during his earthly ministry, to speak to and to console. God is not reluctant to be with the outcasts or to associate with them. With His first coming to earth, He made it wellknown that He came to seek and to save, those whom are lost – meaning those who admit that they are lost, because the Word teaches that we are all lost as we were conceived and born in sin. Man's pride however stands in God's way and therefore most refuse to admit that they are indeed lost. God hates pride and arrogance in people (Prov. 8:13).

Back to Israel's amazing role as the chosen people. We read in Ps. 135:4 : *“For the Lord hath chosen Jacob unto himself, and Israel for his peculiar treasure.”* The Psalmist uses a distinct definition to disclose God's divine love for His chosen people. In Ex. 4:22 the Lord says: *“Israel is my son, even my firstborn.”* We can only thank God that He did not leave it at that and that all nations received an opportunity, through Israel, to be reunited with God. God's absolute righteousness is but one of his many perfect attributes. That Israel remains close to God's heart is accentuated with these words: *“Thou shalt be blessed above all people:”* (Deut. 7:14a).

Few people accept these words though. Israel is without any doubt the most unique nation on earth, not because they are without sin, to the contrary, but because God chose them for a specific purpose.

THE GOD OF ISRAEL

"I am the Lord, your Holy One, the Creator of Israel, your King." (Is. 43:15)

"For thy Maker is thine husband; The Lord of hosts is his name; and thy redeemer the Holy One of Israel; The God of the whole earth shall he be called." (Is. 54:5)

The God of Israel is also the God of all that serve Him and that align themselves to His will. The God of Israel, is however, in a literal and specific way the God of the literal nation of Israel. This God has numerous attributes, too many to understand or mention. Through His Word, directed to His people of Israel, one may however learn a great deal about what lives in His heart. Lev. 20:24b, 26 reads: *"I am the Lord your God, which have separated you from other people. And ye shall be holy unto me: for I the Lord am holy, and have severed you from other people, that ye should be mine."* Today, God still wants His children (His true bride) to separate themselves from the world to serve and surrender to Him in all things. We live in the world, but are not of this world (1 Jn. 3:1). This does not mean a withdrawal from society or the community, but rather to a distinct separation or denouncement from the things of this world. Everything that brings separation between you and God is of this world and a complete break with it is the only way to lead a holy life before God. We have to be grateful that the Lord always stays loyal, even when we do not. In 2 Tim. 2:13 we read: *"he cannot deny himself"*. In the same way, He will be true to His promises to be the Lord of Israel unto all eternity. Nobody has the ability to alter this because we know *"God is not a man, that he should lie: neither the son of man, that he should repent: hath he said, and shall he not do it? Or* hath he spoken, and shall he not make it good?" (Num. 23:19).

Often times, the greatness and power of God are too much for us humans to comprehend and this is why we underestimate Him many times. In Is. 55:8,9 the Lord warns us to never underestimate Him: *"For my thoughts are not your thoughts, neither are your ways my ways, saith the Lord. For as the heavens are higher than the earth, so are my ways higher than your ways, and my thoughts than your thoughts."*

THE COVENANT WITH ISRAEL

The Lord made a covenant with Abram in Gen. 15:18. *"In the same day the Lord made a covenant with Abram, saying, Unto thy seed have I given this land, from the river of Egypt unto the great river, the river Euphrates:"*

God reaffirmed this covenant with Isaac. We read in Gen. 26:3 *"for unto thee, and unto thy seed, I will give all these countries, and I will perform the oath which I sware unto Abraham thy father."*

The same covenant the Lord also confirmed with Jacob. Gen. 35:12 reads: *"and the land which I gave Abraham and Isaac, to thee I will give it, and to thy seed after thee I will give the land."* God will never go back on His Word and His covenant, but honours it unto this day and forever. The Word continues in Jer. 32:40 concerning the people of Israel: *"and I will make an everlasting covenant with them, to do them good; but I will put my fear in their hearts, that they shall not depart from me."*

Note that we are dealing with an eternal covenant! Israel did turn away from God initially, but they will turn to Him again. It is an everlasting promise of God that He gave (written down) in His eternal Word. The above-mentioned verse is to a certain extent a confirmation of the covenant with Abraham, Isaac and Jacob. Not only is God's covenant with the nation of Israel confirmed in the Old Testament, but also in the New Testament a covenant is mentioned. Heb. 8:8-12 quotes Jer. 31:31-34, when it relates about a new covenant (referring to salvation in Christ). The Lord says: *"I will make a new covenant with the <u>house of Israel</u> and with the <u>house of Judah</u>.... I will put my laws into their mind, and write them in their hearts: and I will be to them a God, and they shall be to me a people....For I will be merciful to their unrighteousness, and their sins and their iniquities will I remember no more."*

This covenant will apply to those Jews that will become born again – to those that will be in Christ and thus will become part of the Church. This new covenant though, will in no way end the old covenant for *the unsaved Jews* – those outside of the Church.

We know that the house of Israel and the house of Judah, as mentioned in the verses above, do not refer to the Church and they never will.

Here, the Lord refers specifically to His literal people of Israel, whose remnant will convert to Him at the end of the great tribulation (Zech. 12:10-13:9). Here the Scripture explains: *"And it shall come to pass, that in all the land, saith the Lord, <u>two parts therein shall be cut off and die</u>; but <u>the third shall be left therein</u>....they shall call on my name, and I will hear them: I will say, It is my people: and they shall say, the Lord is my God!"* (Zech. 13:8,9). Like the doubting Thomas, they will first need to see the scars of the wounds inflicted upon Christ, and then they will convert to true faith in Him. This is all because they have been temporary blinded by God (Rom. 11:25) for the sake of the gentile nations. This period is fast coming to an end though. In Zech. 13:1 we read: *"In that day there shall be a fountain* *opened to the <u>house of David</u> and to the <u>inhabitants of</u> <u>Jerusalem</u> for sin and uncleanness."* Many will be converted, though a small persentage overall. The Church is not the house of David and does not reside in Jerusalem. The Scripture in Zech. 12:11-14 depicts distinctly how these Jews will become converted in their separate generations. This will happen in and around Jerusalem. There is no reference to the Church here. Zech. 14:1-5 clearly speaks of the last war and how Jesus Christ will stand with His feet on the Mount of Olives with His return to earth. It is during this time that the amazing events will occur in Israel. What a time of refreshing and quickening in the presence of the Lord this will be.

THE LAND AND BORDERS OF ISRAEL

"And the Lord said unto Abram...Lift up now thine eyes, and look from the place where thou art northward, and southward, and eastward, and westward: for all the land which thou seest, to thee will I give it, and to thy seed for ever." (Gen. 13:14,15)

The Lord is quite clear in His description of the land He had promised to the nation of Israel. It will be their eternal heritage. There are theologians who have researched and found that God has promised the land of Israel to the Jews, in more than 1 400 places in the Scripture. This is not a 'spiritual promise' for the Church at all. The Church has received many wonderful promises of her own in the New Testament. The history of the people of Israel in the Old Testament does however serve as a source of deep spiritual instruction for the Church and the individual Christian. Many, however are not able to comprehend these mysteries. They contemplate: 'Why would God still have a plan with the Jews, or Israel, after they have rejected and crucified

Him nearly 2 000 years ago? Why would the covenants of the Old Testament still be in effect after all that Israel has done to God?' The fact remains that God is a God of grace and that the final fulfillment of the covenant concerning the borders and land of Israel will become a reality right at the end of this dispensation. This however will only come to a fulfillment when the remnant of the Jews convert to Him at His second coming.

Every true child of God from the other nations, will through His grace, share in this promise in different ways during the millennium of real peace that will prevail on earth after the second coming. After the thousand years of the reign of Christ is completed, the Holy City, the New Jerusalem of God, will descend from heaven and will come to rest on the new earth. (Rev. 21:1,2). This Kingdom period will end, but the New Jerusalem will exist unto all eternity. This will prevail on the new earth, because we know that the first earth will perish. The area where the current Jerusalem is situated could very well be the center point of the New Jerusalem. We know that this city will be 1 500 miles wide, long and high (Rev. 21:16) because there will be no more oceans (Rev. 21:1) and the New Jerusalem will be in the midst of the new earth.

The Lord amazingly enough planned it that the current Israel and Jerusalem are situated on the center point of the earth. (Ezek. 38:12b). Also regarding this we read in Is. 19:24 that: *"In that day shall Israel be...a blessing in the midst of the land"*. The day that is referred to here is certainly not the New Jerusalem and certainly not the present time. This is the 7th day, the Sabbath or day of rest of 1 000 years that will become a reality shortly after this current dispensation. (Rev. 20:1-6). If one reads Is. 19 (God's warning to Egypt), verse 16-25, the words *"in the day"* occurs regularly, as well as a clear description of life during the coming millennium of peace. The nations will live in peace amongst each other during this time, as the devil will be bound for a thousand years so that he can no longer mislead the nations (Rev. 20:2,3). The fact that God gave the land to Israel unto all eternity reflects from the following: *"And I will give unto thee, and to thy seed after thee, the land wherein thou art a stranger, all the land of Canaan, for an everlasting posses-sion; and I will be their God."* (Gen. 17:8).

The boundaries that God specified for the twelve tribes of Israel, are mentioned in Num. 32:32-42 (Reuben, Gad and half of the tribe of Manasseh) as well as in Num. 34:1-13 (the other 9 and a half tribes).

In Gen. 15:18 the Lord said to Abram: *"Unto thy seed have I given this land, from the river of Egypt unto the great river, the river Euphrates."* Never in the history of Israel, did they occupy this entire area. In the days of kings David and Solomon, Israel did however succeed in conquering nearly the whole area. (Also, compare Deut. 11: 24 and Josh. 1:4).

Read this quote of a recent Turkish leader, Necmettin Erbakan, previous Islamic premier:

"(The Israeli flag) represents a state which strives to conquer all territory between the Nile and the Euphrates." [54]

This is almost prophetic words coming from a Turkish premier.

It will however, most certainly, become their heritage with the return of Christ, when He will reign as King on earth. God promised it with an oath and therefore it will cer-tainly come to pass. These boundaries will include a land area much larger than the territory occupied by Israel today and will most probably be from the Wadi el Arish or 'Stream of Egypt' to the River of Euphrates in the current Iraq. The Lord will never forget the *"covenant which he made with*

Abraham, and of his oath unto Isaac; and hath confirmed the same to Jacob for a law, and to Israel for an everlasting covenant, saying, Unto thee will I give the land of Canaan, the lot of your inheritance." (1 Chr. 16:16-18). We have to remember whom God really is and that He will never disregard His Word.

The fact that the current Israel will be way to small for the generation to come in the Kingdom of peace, is explained in the Word. In Is. 49:18-20 the Lord says to Israel: *"Lift up thine eyes round about, and behold: all these gather themselves together, and come to thee...shall even now be to narrow by reason of inhabitants ... The children which thou shalt have, after thou hast lost the other, shall say again in thine ears, This place is too strait for me: Give place to me that I may dwell!"* The same Lord says in Is. 54:2,3 *"Enlarge the place of thy tent, and let them stretch forth the curtains of thine habitations: spare not, lengthen thy cords, and strengthen thy stakes; for they shalt break forth on the right hand and on the left; and thy seed shall inherit the Gentiles, and make the desolate cities to be inhabited."* Presently we are seeing Jews returning from all over to Israel and before long the small, humble country will be too small for all the inhabitants.

THE PUNISHMENT OF ISRAEL

"And the Lord shall scatter thee among all people, from the one end of the earth even unto the other; and there thou shalt serve other gods, which neither thou nor thy fathers have known, even wood and stone. And among these nations shalt thou find no ease, neither shall the sole of thy foot have rest: but the Lord shall give thee there a trembling heart, and failing of eye, and sorrow of mind: and thy life shall hang in doubt before thee; and thou shalt fear day and night, and shalt have none assurance of thy life: and in the morn-

*ing thou shalt say, Would God it were even! And at even thou
shalt say, Would God it were morning! For the fear of thine
heart wherewith thou shalt fear, and for the sight of thine
eyes which thou shalt see."* (Deut. 28:64-67)

God had proclaimed it, and so it is. The Jewish nation is
scattered right across the world and one finds them in almost
every country on earth. No other nation in the whole history
of the world was ever scattered like the Jews. One may also
note that no other nation on earth was ever stricken with
such hardship and persecution as the Jewish people. In Deut.
28. the Lord presented a list of blessings and curses to the
nation of Israel. If they would submit to His laws and institutions, He would bless them greatly. If they however would
not obey God, they would have to face many difficult days
and severe punishment. We know that the latter came true
and what sorrowful days the Jews did not endure because of
their sins against God. The Lord, however, is always righteous and warned them that it would be this way if they did
not leave their wrongful ways. The Lord says in Ezek. 36:19
*"I scattered them among the heathen, and they were dis-
persed through the countries; according to their ways and
according to their doings I judged them."*

In Deut. 4:27 we read that the Lord says to the people of
Israel: *"...and ye shall be left a few in number among the
heathen, whither the Lord shall lead you."* Presently, this is
the case, not for long anymore though. There are numerous
prophecies regarding God's punishment of Israel that went
into fulfillment literally through the course of history. In
Deut. 28:53 we read about the almost unimaginable, that the
nation of Israel, during a siege and in dire distress, would eat
their own children. Ps. 79:1-3 speaks about a large number
of bodies that could not even be buried and of the blood that
was shed around Jerusalem. Both of these cases refer to the

Roman siege of Jerusalem in 70 AD. Nearly a million Jews died during that siege. That which was foretold in Scripture, happened to the letter, many years later. The historian Josephus described these events in detail. In recent history, in WO II, Hitler ensured that nearly 6 million Jews were exterminated. Satan hates the nation of Israel and incites world leaders against them. The aim being to destroy them completely because Jesus Christ of Nazareth was a descendant of them. The devil leads the Jewish people astray and then God has to punish them, because His Word, through which He had warned them, stands fast. Anti-Semitism or hate towards Jews that is so rife worldwide today, is further proof of the accuracy of the Bible. God said that this nation would be hunted and it is still no different today. The immense persecution of the Jewish people will however reach an unparalleled climax in the seven years of tribulation (Mt. 24:21; Dan. 12:1). Especially during the last three and a half years, the time of 'Jacob's trouble' (Jer. 30:7) the Antichrist and his accomplices will explode in all severity against Israel. This time will be unprecedented.

Even if we realize that the Church is not Israel, every human being and nation can learn a great deal from the wrongdoings of Israel. Throughout the Old Testament we read of the sins and transgressions of the nation of Israel and how God punished them. The Scripture teaches us in 1 Cor. 10:11 regarding Israel *"Now all these things happened unto them for ensamples: and they are written for our admonition, upon whom the ends of the world are come."* Rom. 15:4 also helps us focus: *"For whatsoever things were written aforetime were written for our learning, that we through patience and comfort of the Scriptures might have hope."* For this reason it is so tragic that so few individuals and so few nations give heed to what had happened previously and how God acts upon sin. That is why so few are ready for the second coming of the Lord today.

THE RESTORATION OF ISRAEL

"And say unto them, Thus saith the Lord God; Behold, I will take the children of Israel from among the heathen, whither they be gone, and will gather them on every side, and bring them into their own land: and I will make them one nation in the land upon the mountains of Israel; and one king shall be king to them all" (Ezek. 37:21,22))

"For I am the Lord thy God, the Holy One of Israel, thy Saviour: I gave Egypt for thy ransom.....Fear not; for I am with thee: I will bring thy seed from the east, and gather thee from the west: I will say north, Give up; and to the south, Keep not back: bring my sons from far, and my daughters from the ends of the earth" (Is. 43:3,5,6)

These quotations do not refer to Israel's return after the Babylonian captivity. Babylon (today's Iraq), lies to the east of Israel and during that exile, the Lord did not scatter the Israelites to the ends of the earth. The Lord said that He would collect His people from all the nations (from all four wind directions) and that He would bring them in their land – and this is what is happening today. Jews from all over the world are returning in vast numbers to their country. This is not mere chance, but a fulfillment of a covenant the almighty God made.

In Deut. 30:4,5 the Lord says: *"If any of thine be driven out unto the outmost parts of heaven, from thence will the Lord thy God gather thee, and from thence will he fetch thee: and the Lord will bring thee into the land which thy forefathers possessed, and thou shalt possess it"* Is anything in heaven or on earth to wonderful for our Lord. Will He say something and will it not prevail? The nation of Israel will regain their country, the country of which there is left so little today. There is however a day in the near future when they will take into possession the whole of the territory promised by the covenant. The Lord will never reject Israel like many skeptics and unfaithful believe. The Word is very clear about it in Jer. 30:11: *"I make full end of all nations whither I scatter thee, but I will not make a full end of thee"* Lev. 26:44 explains it even more distinctly: *"when they be in the land of their enemies, I will not cast them away, neither will I abhor them, to destroy them utterly, and break my covenant with them"* We have to understand that God speaks here and that we should be silent and listen closely.

In 1948 Israel was reaffirmed as a nation and received their land back after nearly 1900 years. It was one of the greatest wonders of all times. God said in His Word that Israel will return to Him in the last days and that He will restore them in the land of their heritage. All the tribulation and suffering of the Jews will eventually come to an end. The Lord said: *"When thou art in tribulation, and all these things are come upon thee, even in the latter days, if thou turn to the Lord thy God, and shalt be obedient unto his voice; ... he will not forsake thee"* (Deut. 4:30,31). We are to a certain extent already living in that time. Never before in all history have so many Jews converted themselves to Christ, as is the case currently. All glory to God.

In Ezek. 36 and 37 the full restoration of Israel on political and spiritual level is explained dramatically. The same way God is collecting Israel literally from all the different nations, He is also busy collecting a holy 'nation' for Him from every tongue, tribe and nation on earth. They are the true Church or Bride of Christ that are being prepared for the big meeting with their heavenly Bridegroom. Are you part of this bride – holy and without blemish – cleansed by the blood of the Lamb?

There are numerous quotations from Scripture that explain Israel's return to their country and their final restoration. A few examples:

- The Lord will change the destiny of this nation – Jer. 30:3, Zeph. 3:20 and Amos 9:14
- God will sift the house of Israel among all nations – Amos 9:9
- He will not destroy the house of Jacob – Amos 9:8
- He will plant them in their land – Amos 9:15 and Jer. 32:41
- He stretches His hands out for a second time to recover the remnant of His people – Is. 11:11,12
- God will return them to Israel – Jer. 16:15, Jer. 30:3, 10,11; Zech. 8:7,8 and Ezek. 36:24

THE CITY IN ISRAEL

"...Jerusalem, the city which I have chosen me to put my name there." (1 Kgs. 11:36b)
"...for thy city and thy people are called by thy name." (Dan. 9:19).

Jerusalem – the city of David, the city of God. An unique city, stipulated in the decree of an unique God.

In 1996 it was precisely 3 000 years since king David had conquered Jerusalem. After all this time there is still no other city in the world which captures the imagination like the city on the mountains of Zion. This city plays a cardinal role in the last moments of the current dispensation and the time surrounding the Lord's blessed return to earth. In Zech. 8:3 we read: *"Thus saith the Lord; I am returned unto Zion, and will dwell in the midsts of Jerusalem: and Jerusalem shall be called A city of truth; and the mountains of the Lord of hosts, the holy mountains."* This is not the New Jerusalem or the heavenly Jerusalem as described in Rev. 21:2 and Heb. 12:22,23. When Jesus Christ returns to earth, He will rule from Jerusalem for a thousand years and the saints will rule with Him on earth. (Rev. 20:1-6; Is. 21:1-4). In Zech.

12:6b the Lord clarifies that He speaks of the earthly Jerusalem when He says: *"and Jerusalem shall be inhabited again in her own place, even in Jerusalem."*

The fact that the Lord will also preside there, proves that the city will be prepared for that day. God Himself will prepare the city for the time to come. In Ps. 147:2 we read *"The Lord doeth build up Jerusalem: he gathered together the outcasts of Israel"* In the same Psalm, in verse 12, the author of the Psalm praises the Lord on behalf of the inhabitants of the city: *"Praise the Lord, O Jerusalem; praise thy God, O Zion."*

In Is. 62:6,7 the Word speaks of the watchmen on the walls of Jerusalem and that they should always *"make mention of the Lord ... And give him no rest, till he establish, and till he make Jerusalem a praise in the earth."* Jerusalem shall also be called *"The city of the Lord, The Zion of the Holy One of Israel."* (Is. 60:14b). Currently this city of Jerusalem is, however, a *"cup of trembling"* and a *"burdensome stone"* to many nations (Zech. 12:2,3). These nations are going to hurt themselves with it quite seriously however. The nations of the world do not argue over and fight over any other city in the world, the way they do over Jerusalem. Why is there no such strife over London, Paris, New York or Tokyo? What do the nations of the world want from the dusty roads of this ancient city? One answer may be that they intend to rule the entire world from this location. Jerusalem lies in the center of the inhabited world and is strategically very well situated to launch a one world government. The second answer may be the tremendous riches the Dead Sea offers, but the most important reason seems to be that God chose this city for Himself and that the devil will try all he can to bring that fact to nothing. That is why even many of God's children will be ignorant regarding the biblical truths concerning the city of Jerusalem. Therefore many just go about and spiritualize almost all the prophecies regarding this city. If Christians from all nations would rather study Ps. 122:6 earnestly and *"Pray for the peace of Jerusalem,"* for then the Psalm writer says: *"they shall prosper that love thee."*

THE GENTILE NATIONS AND ISRAEL

"For thus saith the Lord of hosts; After the glory hath he sent me unto the nations which spoiled you: for he that toucheth you, toucheth the apple of his eye." (Zech. 2:8)
"let people serve thee, and nations bow down to thee: be lord over thy brethren, and let thy mother's sons bow down to thee: cursed be every one that curseth thee, and blessed be he that blesseth thee." (Gen. 27:29)

This latter verse were Isaac's words to Jacob (Israel) when he received the blessing that was supposed to go to Esau. It was God's will that Jacob had to be blessed by his father, because He wanted the nation of Israel to be born this way. The Lord chose Israel and they are the apple of his eye. Throughout the ages, He saved them wondrously from many 'hopeless' situations and will do so again. The fact that so many nations hate the Jewish nation only brings God's judgment on them. In Is. 41:11,12 the Lord says to his people: *"Behold, all they that were incensed against thee shall be ashamed and confounded: they shall be as nothing: and they that strive with thee shall perish....they that was against thee shall be as nothing, and as a thing of nought."* If a nation wants to harm the apple of God's eye, they have to do it at own risk. God says to Israel: *"When thou passest through waters, I will be with thee; and through the rivers, they shall not overflow thee: when thou walkest through the fire, thou shalt not be burned; neither shall the flame kindle upon thee. For I am the Lord thy God, the Holy One of*

Israel, thy Saviour" (Is. 43:2,3) and *"whosoever shall gather together against thee shall fall for thy sake. No weapon that is formed against thee shall prosper; and every tongue that shall rise against thee in judgment thou shalt condemn."* (Is. 54:15,17). These mentioned Scripture quotations could of course also be applied to individuals (spiritually) - but in the first place they apply to the literal people of Israel.

There are many prophecies in the Bible regarding other nations and how they interact with and against Israel. The Word prophesies that a time will come when a nation from the North, together with many other nations will come against Israel. The Lord Himself will bring it to pass that these nations will invade Israel. We know that this will be happening in the future, as Scripture says: *"it shall be in the latter days"* (Ezek. 38:15,16). During those dark times, God will however rescue Israel again, as He did so many times before. These nations will be conquered on the mountains of Israel through the hand of God (Ezek. 39:3,4). The nations who want to engage in war with Israel, will necessarily have to face the God of heaven and earth. Even in recent years, there were numerous examples of how God saved His people in the most extraordinary of ways during the most dangerous of situations. In the last 40 years, He came to Israel's salvation at least five times when dark clouds arose around them. It happened in 1948, 1956, 1967, 1973 and also in 1982. Study the history of these wars and how Israel was victorious every time. The purpose of the war of Ezek. 38,39 will be, like the previous ones, to manifest God to all nations so that they realize that He is the Lord God (Ezek. 38:23).

In the final war of this dispensation, the war of Armageddon, the Lord will convene people form all the nations against Israel (Zech. 12:9; Zech. 14:2,3). He will also bring a quick end to them (Rev. 19:15, 19-21; Zeph. 3:8).

Although many Jews or Israelis have lost their lives in wars over the centuries, Israel as a nation, will never be totally destroyed. In the end the nations that remain after the last war " ... *shall see and be confounded at all their might: they shall lay their hand upon their mouth*" and they will approach the Lord in fear (Mic. 7:16,17). There will come a day when the Lord will make Israel *"a witness"* to all the nations and *"a leader and commander to the people,"* because the Lord says:... *"thou shalt call a nation that thou knowest not, and nations that knew not thee shall run unto thee, because of the Lord thy God, and for the Holy One of Israel; for he hath glorified thee."* (Is. 55:4,5). In Deut. 28:10 God already told Israel: *"And all people of earth shall see that thou art called by the name of the Lord; and they shall be afraid of thee."* This prophecy will be fulfilled in the time of the millennial reign of Christ in a literal, final and complete way.

THE PLAN WITH ISRAEL

"for salvation is of the Jews" (Jn. 4:22)

God chose Israel so that His only son Jesus Christ could be born of them - on earth. Jesus Christ Himself was a Jew and so were all the authors of the books of the Bible (except Luke). It was the way which God chose to conclude His plan of redemption – to reconcile man with Him. God wanted to reveal Himself to man and chose the Jewish nation to fulfill His plan. In. Gal. 3:16 this truth is confirmed when the Word speaks about the covenant with Abraham and his seed: *"He saith not, And to seeds, as of many; but as of one, And to thy seed, which is Christ."* As early as Gen. 3:15 the Lord gave this promise of the seed and therefore He fulfilled it as He is God and His Word infallible. God became human and lived on earth for around 33 years, His own creations crucified

Him, but His eternal plan of salvation was completed for all eternity when Jesus Christ was resurrected from the dead. Never again would anybody need to pay the price of sin. This gift of grace became attainable from that day on to everyone who was willing to accept it. Nobody is forced into accepting it, it is free and will remain that way until the end of time. If somebody repeatedly rejects it, there remains no more sacrifice for sins (Heb. 10:26) and we know that everybody sinned and *"come short of the glory of God"* (Rom. 3:23). The difference between the indescribable splendour of heaven and the unthinkable horror of hell is so huge, but in spite of it most will receive the latter part as their inheritance for all eternity, because they reject this incredible gift of salvation – because they reject Christ (God) Himself (Mt. 7:13,14; Lk. 13:22-30).

We have to remember that in our daily lives we live either to the glory of God, or to the glory of the opponent of God – Satan. These are the only two choices we have. Israel also merely had these two choices and failed most of the time because they relied on their own strength. God's standard is very high, but He supplies the strength to everyone who kneels to Him in prayer. The Lord never exalts a person or a people merely for the sake of themselves, but what He does, He does to make His greatness and glory known to all. This is distinctly illustrated by the following: *"Thus saith the Lord God; I do not this for your sakes, O house of Israel, but for mine holy name's sake, which ye have profaned among the heathen, whither ye went."* (Ezek. 36:22). The Lord makes it clear that He did not return the people of Israel to their country because they were such special people, but for His glorification. Israel profaned His Name among the nations, instead of glorifying it and sharing the everlasting gospel with them. The Lord will hold them accountable for this during the time of great tribulation especially. God did scatter Israel among the heathen nations as a result of their sins, but at the same time, He used this opportunity to spread the gospel to these people in one way or another in spite of Israel's disobedience. There also was a remnant of the Jews that converted themselves to God, even though they had to serve Him amongst foreign nations (Rom. 11:4,5). There, the remnant confessed Jesus Christ and the true gospel of salvation was heard for the first time in many countries. The apostle Paul and those who worked with him are clear examples of converted Jews who spread the message of Christ in the gentile nations. In Acts 15:24 we read that *"God at the first did visit the Gentiles, to take out to them a people for his name"* From the very beginning it was God's plan to gather for Himself a bride from amongst every tongue, tribe and nation. The Lord blinded Israel for a period of time so that they are not able to see, and He made them deaf so as not to hear (Rom. 11:8,10). In doing this, He fulfilled His perfect plan to convert a people for Him from among the gentiles as well. In Rom. 11:11 we read this remarkable words regarding Israel: *"Have they stumbled that they should fall? God Forbid: but rather through their fall salvation is come unto the Gentiles, for to provoke them to jealousy."* In verse 13 Paul notes that he is an apostle who labours among the gentiles and in verse 14 he says: *"if by any means I may provoke to emulation them which are my flesh, and might save some of them."* God put Israel and the gentile nations against each other so that His people from both groups may be saved and His name glorified across the whole earth. This plan of God is an eternal plan. Paul refers to this in Rom. 11:25 and 28 when he says that he does not want *"that ye should be ignorant of this mystery, lest ye should be wise in your own conceits, that blindness in part is happened to Israel, until the fullness of the Gentiles be come in"* and also *"As concerning the gospel, they are enemies for your [the gentiles] sakes: but as touching the election, they are beloved for the fathers' [Abraham, Isaac and*

Jacob] sakes."

God will never put aside or forget His covenant. That most of today's Jews still do not believe that their Messiah had already come and that they cannot comprehend that He died for their sins on the cross as well, is very tragic. They are suffering for our sake so that we may realize and understand the plan of salvation that God foresaw for the human race. There will be a day however, that the fullness of the gentiles will come and from that day God will turn to Israel, the literal people of His covenant. At the end of Rom. 11 in verse 33, we read the words: *"O the depth of the riches both of the wisdom and knowledge of God! How unsearchable are his judgments, and his ways past finding out!"*

THE RECENT HISTORY OF ISRAEL

"For the children of Israel shall abide many days without a king, and without a prince, and without a sacrifice, and without an image, and without an ephod, and without teraphim: afterward shall the children of Israel return, and seek the Lord their God, and David their king; and shall fear the Lord and his goodness in the latter days." (Hos. 3:4,5)

Indeed, Israel was left for a long time without king or prince. Since 70 AD, when the temple and city of Jerusalem was destroyed, until 1948, they did not have a country of their own. Thereafter it changed dramatically however. Since Israel became a state again, a few million Jews have already returned to their land. This is happening before our eyes and what makes it so special is that the Lord foretold it all in His Word. More than that, He prophesied that it will occur during the latter days. The return of the Jews to Israel remains the most distinct piece of evidence that we are living in the end of times, very close to the second coming of the Lord Jesus Christ. God brought Israel back to their land after nearly 2 000 years or 2 days (2 Pet. 3:8), just as He had promised. It is therefore not strange to find a clear pronouncement regarding this in Hos. 6:2 *"After two days will he revive us: in the third day he will raise us up and we shall live in his sight."* Israel was scattered for two days (2 000 years) among the nations and was 'dead' as a nation. The third day refers to the thousand years of peace that will follow after the two days are completed. During this time, the remnant of Israel will live literally in the presence of the Lord in their allotted land. In Luk. 13:32 Jesus Christ makes a similar pronouncement when He says that He will be busy for two days and that He will be finished on the third day. Both these statements are also typical of Christ's crucifixion and resurrection on the third day. Since Jesus' ascension to heaven to the present time, thus a period of 2 000 years or 2 days, He is busy in heaven interceding for all who will come to God through Him (Rom. 8:34; Heb. 7:25). At the beginning of the third day, He will be finished – and He will return to earth.

Recent years have seen the tremedous build up of tension in the Middle East. The Arabic nations surrounding Israel and the Arabs that support the Palestinian Authority in Israel, want the country for themselves and refuse to agree that the land belongs to Israel. The media often does not report events there in a realistic way. Large pieces of Israeli territory were segmented and handed over to the Palestinians in recent years. This includes the Gaza strip and the West Bank. The Palestinian flag now even flies in Bethlehem of all places. The Golan Hights and parts of Jerusalem are also in jeopardy. The separation of the borders of Israel is high on the list of priorities between the PA and the Israeli government. God, however, made very clear what area He gave to the people of Israel. In Joel 3:1 He says that

He will change the fate of His people, and continues in verse 2: *"I will also gather all nations, and will bring them down into the valley of Jehoshaphat, and will plead with them there for my people and for my heritage Israel, whom they have scattered among the nations, and <u>parted my land</u>."* The nations have indeed parted the land of Israel and therefore God will judge them at the last war.

In the last 100 years numerous Bible prophecies regarding Israel went into literal fulfillment.

To mention but a few:

In 1897, a group of Jews from around the world convened in Basel, Switzerland, to consider the re-acquisition of their country Israel. A few years later, it became a reality and some land was bought back, letters were signed and the first Jews began to return to their land, although at this time it was not officially recognized by the other nations and only some Jews started returning. In Jer. 32:42-44 we read about this extra-ordinary prophecy of the Lord, recorded by the prophet Jeremiah. In 1917 (during the first world war), while Jerusalem was under Turkish rule, the Lord used England and when their simple airplanes circled Jerusalem, the Turkish people fled. The city was liberated after numerous centuries and the Word went into fulfillment again, this time it was Jes 31:5. This happened on 9 December 1917. On the Jewish calendar, that day was the 24th day of the 9th month, Kislev. Hag. 2:18,19 prophesied that the Lord would bless His nation from that day on. Everything that God says in His Word goes into fulfillment literally. He is no mere human, no fortuneteller, but the living and almighty God. An interesting scenario to be considered here is Josh. 19:48, where we read that the last of the twelve tribes of Israel regained their territory after they invaded the Promised Land under the guidance of Joshua. It reminds one of 1948 when the Jews regained their land. Is the hand of God not in this as well? Nothing in Scripture is by mere chance, but surely according to the will of a God of order for a specific reason. A lack of faith could deprive you of many blessings. In 1948 large numbers of Jews returned to Israel by air and by sea. In Is. 60:8,9 the Lord had it prophesied that such days would come.

THE FUTURE OF ISRAEL

"And I will pour upon the house of David, and upon the inhabitants of Jerusalem, the spirit of grace and of supplications: and they shall look upon me whom they have pierced, and they shall mourn for him, as one mourneth for his only son, and shall be in bitterness for him, as one that is in bitterness for his firstborn. In that day shall there be a great mourning of Hadadrimmon in the valley of Megiddon." (Zech. 12:10,12)

"In that day there shall be a fountain opened to the house of David and to the inhabitants of Jerusalem for sin and for uncleanness. And it shall come to pass, that in all the land, saith the Lord, two parts therein shall be cut off and die; but the third shall be left therein. And I will bring the third part through the fire, and will refine them as silver is refined, and will try them as gold is tried: they shall call on my name and I will hear them. I will say, It is my people: and they shall say, the LORD is my God." (Zech. 13:1,8,9)

Almost exactly the same happened to the doubting Thomas in Jn. 20:28,29. He is a typical example to the people of Israel.

This is not a description of the church of Jesus Christ. The true church (al those who are saved) is not the house of David nor the inhabitants of Jerusalem. This is a reference to the literal Israel, they who crucified Jesus and pierced Him with a spear. Two thirds of the church will not be wiped out so that only a third remains. It has to be noted that it will only be the remaining third of Israel, after they have been tested and tried, that will convert to the Lord. All this will happen with the return of Jesus Christ at His second coming – at the end of the great tribulation, when He will stand with His feet on the Mount of Olives (Zech. 14:4). We also read in this regard in Deut. 4:30 (as previously cited) that Israel will at the end of the days, when they are in dire need, return to God and listen to His voice. In 2 Kgs. 19:31 Scripture states regarding the third of Israel that will remain: *"For out of Jerusalem shall go forth a remnant, and they that escape out of mount Zion."* There are numerous other places in Scripture where these events in Jerusalem, at the end of time, are also prophesied, for example in Mic. 2:12. Israel's future stands firm and is established by God. Nobody can undo this.

There will be such a day in the near future of Israel that the remnant will turn their eyes to the almighty God of their forefathers – and they will be a great blessing to all the nations. The Lord says in Zech. 8:13: " *... as ye were a curse among the heathen, O house of Judah, and house of Israel; so will I save you, and ye shall be a blessing..."* and also *"Yea, many people and strong nations shall come to seek the Lord of hosts in Jerusalem, and to pray before the Lord. Thus saith the Lord of hosts; In those days it shall come to pass, that ten men shall take hold out of all languages of the nations, even shall take hold of the skirt of him that is a Jew, saying, We will go with you: for we have heard that God is with you."* (Zech. 8:22,23). These quotations refer to that specific time in the existence of the nation of Israel after they are spiritually healed. Christ's millennial reign of peace on earth will indeed be a special time of refreshment for all who will be there. If we look at what Scripture says regarding Israel during that time, we will find clear guidelines about the land's borders and the division of their territory. The Lord gives in His Word, in Ezek. 48, a clear description of how the territory will be divided among the different tribes. That is if we merely study the Bible and take the Lord upon His word. The Jewish people will live to the praise and glory of God during that untroubled time and will fulfill their purpose, to exalt God, at long last. I believe that this time period will have its commencement in the near future. In Rev. 7 we read about the 144 000 sealed persons and what a big influence they will have during the time of tribulation. From verses 1-8 we see very clearly that this group of people will be literal Jews from the twelve tribes. In Rev. 14:1-5 we also read about these Jewish Christians. They are definitely not the church of God as the Jehovah's Witnesses proclaim. Also, they clearly are not Christians from other (gentile) nations. To this day, there remain Jews from all twelve original tribes. God preserved them as such. In Rev. 7:9 and 14 we read that the 144 000 will be like missionaries, because a great multitude of saved people appear in heaven shortly thereafter. This number of Jews surely is not a symbolic reference to all those who were saved from all times, from all nations. If we will only accept God's Word as it is written, we will understand it so much better and the blessing will be so much greater. We need to be faithful to believe in the Word, but it is also only faith that will please God – faith like that of a child (Mt. 18:3-6).

ISRAEL AND ETERNITY

"For the Lord hath chosen Zion; he hath desired it for his habitation. This is my rest forever: here I will dwell; for I have desired it." (Ps. 132:13,14)

In the previous verses the Lord makes it clear that He is speaking of the land of Israel, because He mentions the *"throne of David"* and the *"mighty God of Jacob"*. This habitation is the mount Zion in Israel, where the eternal reign of the Lord will commence. God desired to have Jerusalem as His residence for all eternity. First, Christ will reign in the earthly Jerusalem for a thousand years and after that the heavenly one, the New Jerusalem will appear. After Jesus Christ brings to an end the other kingdoms at His second coming, He will hand over all to His Father whom will reign eternally (Dan. 2:34,25,44). They will reign together as one for Jesus and His Father are one according to Jn. 10:30. Never again will there be another earthly kingdom. His earthly kingdom will convert to His heavenly kingdom. The first will still be imperfect, but will convert to the perfect. It will be the advancement to the unequalled climax in God's council. We know that Jesus Christ Himself is God (1 Jn. 5:20) and that is why His reign will last forever.

In Mt. 19:28 the Lord said to His Jewish disciples that they who followed Him, will themselves sit on 12 thrones and judge the 12 tribes of Israel. It will commence when the Son of Man Himself will sit on His glorified throne. This proves that God will never destroy the memory of the nation of Israel, but that all will be reminded of them unto all eternity. In the New Jerusalem, the holy city from heaven, there is another reference to Israel. The Word says in Rev. 21:12 that the city has *"Twelve gates...and names written thereon, which are the names of the twelve tribes of the children of Israel."* The apostles, all Jews, also get a place of honour in the New Jerusalem. In verse 14 of Rev. 21 we see that *"the wall of the city had twelve foundations, and in them the names of the twelve apostles of the Lamb."* They were fundamental in the establishment of the church of Christ here on earth – first from the Jews and also from the Greeks (gentiles). God never stops thinking about the people of His covenant. In conclusion, I will mention Ps. 105:8 where the Word declares clearly: *"He hath remembered his covenant for ever, the word which he commanded to a thousand generations."*

ISRAEL TODAY

It was mentioned that presently the Jews are returning to their country. Most return from the economic unstable Russia and surrounding regions. The Jews are the only people on earth that return to their land of origin on such a large scale. They are also the only nation on earth, that in spite of having lived in other countries for numerous generations, have kept their own unique identity. They remain Jews. To be called a Jew means far more than just a person from Jewish descent, it has to do with their religion too – unlike all other nations under the sun. The Jews are presently returning and many are currently also learning to speak Hebrew. Numerous training schools for this purpose now exist in Israel.

Israel is much talked about today. Peace treaty upon peace treaty are signed in connection with this small strip of land, but in most cases the signatures are not even worth the paper it was written on.

Many people today and also many Christians have much against the Jewish people. Reasons vary, but some have it against them because some Jews are very rich people and because they control many banks in the world etc. Some of them are also actively involved in the pursuit of a new international world order. Yes, some want to control the world and are in a way successful at that. The same though, could be said of many individuals from the gentile nations, but people forget that. The majority of the Jewish people are merely blinded (temporarily, as was explained earlier) and therefore many are involved in different anti-Christian actions. Presently many Jews are 'new agers' and live far separated from the true God. They do not realize what they are doing, but will be judged for this in the near future. These people need the gospel of Jesus Christ very urgently. God is only allowing this to happen for a certain time frame, but do not forget that He is still totally in control of Israel's and the world's destiny. All these things do not however undo the promises of God regarding the future of Israel. Never will God go back on His Word. Everything will eventually change, as the Bible predicts. Today that time is at hand.

Sadly, quite a few British and American people as well as some others, believe that they are Jews and try to keep certain Old Testament Jewish rituals. The Old Testament is of great importance to us, but not for this reason. There are today for example some British people that believe that Prince Charles will shortly ascend to the throne of 'his father David'. Some of these people believe that they are from the so-called 'ten lost tribes of Israel.' The truth however is that no Jewish tribe got lost at all. In Jas. 1:1 we read that this epistle was written specifically and in the first place to: "*the twelve tribes which are scattered abroad.*" Many Jews presently, have knowledge to what tribe they belong.

The Bible warns us in Rev. 2:9 and Rev. 3:9 against "*them who say they are Jews, and are not.*" This warning is also applicable to every church today that teaches that they have replaced the nation of Israel and therefore became God's new Israel themselves. Many of these churches are under the impression that God is finished with the literal people of Israel and that they have no further role to fulfill. How wrong can they be?

We did indeed reach a very late hour in the history of the human race on earth. In this whole process, the nation of Israel became a clear beacon to us of just how late it is. The Jewish nation has always been the clock that indicated to other nations where they found themselves on the prophetic calendar of God. In the days that will follow it will be the case even more. Interesting times remain and the nation of Israel's part in it will only become greater and greater.

To follow are a number of extra-ordinary signs that went into fulfillment or are currently going into fulfillment in the land of Israel and which points without doubt to the fact that we are nearing very exciting and also unique times in man's existence on earth:

ISRAEL BORN IN ONE DAY

On 14 May 1948, the state of Israel was re-born – a total miracle from the almighty God. Previously, Israel was a nation, but ceased to be one for nearly 1900 years and then suddenly the unexpected happening (to most) that astonished the world. The Bible though, new all about this day.

Is. 66:8 declares: *"Who had heard such a thing? Who hath seen such things? Shall the earth be made to bring forth in one day? Or shall a nation be born at once? For as soon as Zion travailed, she brought forth her children."*

ISRAEL THE FIG TREE

Mt. 24:32,33 reads: *"Now learn the parable of the fig tree; When his branch is tender yet, and putteth forth leaves, ye know that summer is nigh: so likewise ye, when ye shall see all these things, know that it is near, even at the doors."*

How do we know that this is referring to the ancient nation of Israel?

Jer. 24:5,6 declares: *"Thus saith the Lord, the God of Israel; like these good figs, so will I acknowledge them that are carried away captive of Judah...For I will set mine eyes upon them for good, and I will bring them again to this land: and I will build them, and not pull them down; and I will plant them, and not pluck them up."*

Hosea 9:10 declares: *"I found Israel like grapes in the wilderness; I saw your fathers as the first ripe fig tree at her first time."*

God sees Israel as a fig tree. Israel, the fig tree, was planted dearly in their country - in 1948! What a remarkable prophecy this is that we find in the infallible Word of God.

PROPERTY IS STILL BEING BOUGHT IN ISRAEL

Jer 32:43,44 reads: *"And fields shall be bought in this land, whereof ye say, It is desolate without man or beast: it is given into the hand of the Chaldeans. Men shall buy fields for money, and subscribe evidences, and seal them, and take witnesses in the land of Benjamin, and in the places about Jerusalem, and in the cities of Judah and in the cities of the mountains, and in the cities of the valley, and in the cities of the south: for I will cause their captivity to return, saith the Lord."*

Since 1897 the Jews are buying property in Palestine, and specifically so since 1948. It is true that many Jews bought property there through the centuries, but even very recently (the late nineties) wealthy Jews of America bought property in Israel again. Note the following newspaper article:

'OVERSEAS JEWS SECRETLY BUY PALESTINIAN HOMES'

"Wealthy overseas Jews have put up $40 million ... to quietly purchase Palestinian properties in Hebron and else-where in the occupied territories, ... The purchasers are primarily ultra-Orthodox Jews from the United States committed to what is being called 'redemption of the land' before it is lost to Palestinian self-rule." [55]

FOREIGNERS ARE WORKING ON KIBBUTZIM IN ISRAEL

Is. 61:5 read: *"And strangers shall stand and feed your flocks, and the sons of the alien shall be your plowmen and your vinedressers."*

What country on earth is better known for their communal farming activities than Israel? Even South African's venture there in search of employment.

NATURE PROSPERS IN ISRAEL

Is. 27:6 reads: *"He shall cause them that come of Jacob to take root: Israel shall blossom and bud, and fill the face of the world with fruit."* It has happened. The fig tree has already sprouted and Israel export fruit to numerous Eastern countries and Europe. In the coming millennium of peace, it will be fulfilled in a more complete way.

MOUNT OF OLIVES READY TO SPLIT IN TWO

Zech. 14:4 reads: *"And his feet shall stand in that day upon the mount of Olives, which is before Jerusalem on the east, and the mount of Olives shall cleave in the midsts thereof toward the east and toward the west, and there shall be a great valley; and half of the mountains shall remove to the north and half of it towards the south."* According to a publication in Israel there is already an earthquake fault line from west to east through the area of the Mount of Olives. [56] Verse 15 of Zech. 14 speaks of such an earthquake as well as the book of Revelation, chapter 16:18.

JUDAH CAN NOW DO BATTLE IN JERUSALEM

Zech. 14 :14 says: *"And Judah also shall fight at*

Jerusalem;"

The mentioned verse refers to the last war, because the whole of Zech. 14 describes the events surrounding it. This prophecy could never have been fulfilled before Israel became a state in 1948. Further, in 1967, with the infamous six-day war, Judah fought in Jerusalem for the first time in centuries and regained control over the city of God. They will surely battle there again – perhaps very soon!

EAST GATE OF JERUSALEM CURRENTLY CLOSED

Ezek. 44:1,2 reads: *"Then he brought me back the way of the gate of the outward sanctuary which looketh towards the east; and it was shut. Then said the Lord unto me; <u>this gate shall be shut</u>, it shall not be opened, and no man shall enter in by it; because the Lord, the God of Israel, hath entered in by it, therefore it shall be shut."*

In chapter 43:1,2 of Ezekiel we read that the Lord will enter into the city of Jerusalem, early during His millennial reign, through the east gate. Presently the east gate is still shut. Years ago, Muslims blocked up the gate because the Bible proclaimed that the Messiah would enter Jerusalem through it. They loose sight that Jesus has a glorified body and since His resurrection, no shut gate can keep Him out. Shortly after His resurrection, He appeared a few times to His disciples where they convened behind closed doors (Jn. 20:19).

TERRITORY NOW AGAIN DIVIDED IN ISRAEL

Joel 3:1,2 reads: *"For, behold, in those days, and in that time, when I shall bring again the captivity of Judah and Jerusalem, I will also gather all nations, and will bring them down into the valley of Jehoshaphat, and will plead with* *them there for my people and for my <u>heritage Israel</u>, whom they have scattered among the nations, and <u>parted my land</u>."*

Large pieces of Israel's rightful territory had already been segmented and given to the Palestinians. Currently the 'peace makers' are again urging Israel to denounce the whole Golan Hights for example so that it may be handed over to Syria. The Palestinians also want the whole of Jerusalem for themselves. This is according to the infamous 'land for peace' scheme. Arafat is long being known for saying that he would conquer Israel, 'piece by piece by peace'. It is for this reason that God will gather the nations against Israel for this last enormous war that is approaching fast now.

HIGHWAY IN AND TO ISRAEL NOW A REALITY

Is. 19:23 reads: *"In that day shall there be a highway out of Egypt to Assyria,"*

Today a highway stretches from Egypt through Israel to Iraq and even further to the East. Rev. 16:12 speaks about the road on which the kings of the East will advance towards Israel. In Israel, another big highway is being build with the name: 'Trans-Israel Highway'. The news announced it: "....construction is ready to start for the Trans-Israel Highway." [57]

TWO RED MOONS OBSERVED IN ISRAEL IN 1996

Joel 2:31 reads: *"The sun shall be turned into darkness, and the moon into blood, before the great and the terrible day of the LORD come."*

In 1996, exactly on two Jewish feastdays – in April and again in September, the moon appeared red - from Jerusalem.

Early in the year 2000 another report about a red moon

came from Britain: "The Moon went a deep shade of red as it turned out of the light of the Sun and into Earth's shadow." 58

Lk. 21:25 also mentions this as a sign of the times.

OIL DISCOVERED IN ISRAEL

Deut 33:19,24 reads: "*...they shall suck of abundance of the seas, and of <u>treasures hid in the sand</u>...Let Asher be blessed with children; let him be acceptable to his brethren, and let him dip his <u>foot in oil</u>.*"

Is. 45:3 reads: "*and I will give thee the treasures of darkness, and hidden riches of secret places, that thou mayest know that I, the Lord, which call thee by thy name, am the God of Israel.*"

In the Middle East, oil is probably the biggest source of wealth that a nation can be endowed with. Israel discovered oil on the southwest side of the Dead Sea. Note the following article:

"A new flow of oil south of ARAD has been discovered, ... The find, between Arad and the Dead Sea, flowed at a rate of 600 barrels a day ... In July [1996], the government awarded the first five licenses to drill for oil in Israel's deep waters in the Mediterranean." 59

Very recently Israel discovered gas on the west side of the country – in the Mediterranean Sea – this could also mean that oil will be discovered there soon:

"The Israel Electric Company has signed an 11-year contract with Israeli companies that have <u>discovered gas off the Israeli coast outside Ashkelon.</u> The gas for the $150-million-a-year contract will be piped to an installation on the Ashdod shore, and from there to the Electric Company's power stations. The arrangement is scheduled to begin at the beginning of 2004. ... the deposits discovered outside

Ashkelon could supply all of Israel's needs" [60]

Soon Israel could also find oil close by to where the territory of the tribe of Asher was on their northwest coast (see quote from Deuteronomy 33). On an ancient map the area of Asher looks like a foot that touches the sea. It is in that area that they are also drilling for oil now.

What an immense effect such oil discoveries could have on the whole Arabic and Muslim world?

THE TEMPLE WILL BE REBUILD

Rev. 11:1,2 reads: *"Rise and measure the temple of God, and the altar, and them that worship therein. But the court which is without the temple leave out, and measure it not; for it is given unto the Gentiles"*

Yasser Arafat of the Palestinians declared a few years ago that he got his hands on a drawing of the new Jewish Temple – something that understandably disturbed him greatly. The *Temple Mount Faithful* group in Israel already did much to prepare the instruments of the temple and to train Levitical priests for the big day. The corner stone is also in readiness. The *Arutz 7* radio station reported on 26 July 1999 that even secular Jews are now supporting the rebuilding of the temple.

There are consistent news reports concerning the templemount area. Note this incredible piece of information from an Israeli newspaper:

"A proposal to divide the Temple Mount area into four sections, each containing a different mix of powers for the two sides, has been discussed in the talks between Israel and the Palestinian Authority ... The four sections would be: Al-Aqsa Mosque and the Dome of the Rock shrine; the Temple Mount plaza; the external wall; and the subterranean spaces." [61]

This could have serious prophetic implications. With such a division Rev. 11:1,2 can go into fulfillment easily. The Muslims (gentiles) already have the area that could have been used for the temple's outer court. According to the prophecy though, the rebuild temple would not need that area. Because this is the case, the fulfillment of this prophecy could now come any day. This is not all. Jewish rabbis have plans to build a synagogue on the Temple Mount and the Muslims warned that they will wage war if this happens:

"Palestinian leaders warned Israel … that a plan to build a synagogue on the Temple Mount in Jerusalem could provoke a war in the Middle East. [62]

WATER IS FLOWING FROM THE TEMPLE MOUNT

Ezek. 47:1,2 reads: *"Afterwards he brought me again unto the door of the house; and, behold, waters issued out from under the threshold of the house eastward … the waters came down from under, from the right side of the house, at the south side of the altar."* Also, read Joel 3:18 and Zech. 14:8 in this regard.

This prophecy refers quite clearly to the Kingdom or millennial period that is to come, but something is happening already. The *'Temple Mount and Land of Israel Faithful Movement'* reported as follows:

"Important news about the water flowing from the Temple Mount comes from the Israeli newspaper, *Ha Tsofer*. In the 15th May [1999] edition of the Journal, (pg 5) … the Arabs … have done everything possible to stop the flow of water, … the Arabs, … are busy with very intensive excavations on the Temple Mount, … during these diggings they broke into one of the water sources and … the water started to flow out of the rock" [63]

The *Temple Mount Faithful* group in Israel also confirmed this in their newsletter with the name *The Voice of the Temple Mount Faithful*, (Spring 2000). In the newsletter a long article appeared with the title: '*Water Flowing from the Rock: A Sign of Redemption.*' They are of the impression that this occurrence points to the speedy coming of the Messiah. It is true however that many deny the 'water story' completely, especially the Muslims.

Recently, news about the flowing of water near the temple mount again made headlines:

"Water began dripping among the stones of the Western Wall ... The water was discovered on the upper right side of the Western Wall, on the men's side of the plaza, ... The water has so far dampened a 40 centimeter section of the wall." [64]

JERUSALEM IS A CUP OF TREMBLING

Zech. 12:2,3 reads: "*Behold, I will make Jerusalem a cup of trembling unto all the people round about, when they shall be in the siege both against Judah and against Jerusalem. And in that day I will make Jerusalem a burden stone for all people*"

Jerusalem is in the news nearly every day and the ongoing 'peace process' concerning this city is one of continual failure. All the nations on earth's eyes are on Jerusalem – more than on any other city on earth.

In 1998 the United Nations accepted 3 resolutions that declare that Israel has illegal control over Jerusalem. Also in 1998, the United Nations said that "Israel [is] illegally in Jerusalem" [65]

Can you believe this? If ever there is a country that could claim Jerusalem, then it is Israel. The whole Bible and numerous historic writings confirm this repeatedly. This is however, how it will be, because the Bible have to go into fulfillment. God does exactly what He said he would.

The peace negotiations in September 2000 in America did not succeed, but note the main reason given for the failure: "Jerusalem was said to have been the stumbling block at US sponsored talks at Camp David..." [66]

It is almost the exact words of the above-mentioned passage from the book of Zechariah.

Also look at the following amazing declaration from a Palestinian of high authority:

"In a speech to the European Parliament in Strasbourg, Ahmen Qureia [speaker of the Palestinian parliament] said the Palestinians would support internationalizing all of Jerusalem ... both parts of Jerusalem east and west should be a unified international Jerusalem....not just the capital of Israel or Palestine, but a capital of the world, ... The proposal ... still remains part of the European foreign policy...." [67]

(Emphasis added. Note the role of Europe and Rome later on).

There will come a day when Jerusalem will be the capital of the world, but only in the millennial Kingdom of Christ. That which is currently happening is an imitation of what is to come and the coming Antichrist will govern there for a short period of time.

ISRAEL IS A COUNTRY WITHOUT WALLS

Ezek. 38:11 reads: "*and thou shalt say, I will go up to the land of unwalled villages; I will go to them that are at rest, that dwell safely, all of them dwelling without walls, and having neither bars nor gates.*"

Even though Jerusalem still have a few old walls and gates, the modern Israel is not known for their walls and gates. It was completely different during their ancient history. The war of Ezek. 38 will take place during the time when they are in *"unwalled villages."* This is today!

ITS NEIGHBORS WANT TO DESTROY ISRAEL COMPLETELY

Ps. 83:3,4 reads: *"they have taken crafty counsel against thy people...They have said, Come, and let us cut them off from being a nation; that the name of Israel may be no more in remembrance."*

Compare Ezek. 38. In Ps. 83 follows all the nations surrounding Israel by name. To this day it remained the same. Note the following recent statements of Israel's current enemies:

"Iranian supreme leader Ayatollah Ali Khamenei called ... for the destruction of Israel, saying it was the only way to solve the problems of the Middle East." [68]

"Libyan leader Colonel Maummar Gaddafi has warned that Israel has no future in an Arab environment, and advised Israeli's 'to go and found a state in Alaska.' Palestine will be the graveyard for the Jews, he said" [69]

(Emphasis added).

Rethink this clearly for a moment. This sign regarding the nation of Israel could only have gone into fulfillment after the Jewish nation returned to their own country. Remember, they were without a land and state for nearly 1900 years. Not one of the mentioned passages of Scripture that has to do with the second coming could have gone into fulfillment before 1948. Think about this clearly. The most striking is that these signs are now going into fulfillment at the same time. It speaks volumes. The second coming is thus nearer than any of us could have imagined.

Note the words of Ps. 102:13-16, it confirms what we have just said: *"Thou shalt arise, have mercy upon Zion [Israel and Judah]: for the time to favor her, yea, the set time is come. For thy servants take pleasure in her stones, and favor the dust thereof.*" (Many Christian archaeologists are currently working in Israel and their work confirms that the Word of God is absolutely true.)

"*So the heathen shall fear the name of the Lord and all the kings of the earth thy glory. <u>When the LORD shall build up Zion, he shall appear in his glory</u>.*" The rebuilding of Israel as a state and the second coming of Christ – the Messiah, is almost synonymous!

ISRAEL A THOROUGHFARE FOR MILLIONS OF BIRDS EACH YEAR

"*Thou shalt fall on the mountains of Israel ... and the people that is with thee: I will give thee unto the ravenous birds of every sort ... to be devoured.*" Ezek. 39:4

"*thus saith the Lord God; Speak unto every feathered fowl, ... Assemble yourselves, and come; ... upon the mountains of Israel, that ye may eat flesh, and drink blood.*" Ezek. 39:17

"*And I saw an angel standing in the sun; and he cried with a loud voice, saying to all the fowls that fly in the midst of heaven, Come and gather yourselves together unto the supper of the great God; That ye may eat the flesh of kings ... and the flesh of mighty men, and the flesh of horses, ...* " Rev. 19:17,18

Roughly 500 million birds pass through the land of Israel every year and not only that – they pass through twice every year, in spring and autumn:

"Israel's unique location at the junction of three continents, Europe, Asia and Africa, makes it a site for an extraordinary phenomena: some 500 million migrating birds cross its skies twice a year." [70]

These are birds of all kinds, but of very specific interest

is the fact that quite a number of them are birds of prey, also called raptors. These raptors come through Israel every year: "Between one and two million raptors migrate through Eilat, Israel each spring. They arrive via south Sinai, Egypt, largely on a south-west to north-east course indicating that they have left Africa by crossing the Gulf of Suez, Egypt, at its southern end."

This information comes from a scientific study and was reported by the *OSME,* the *Ornithological Society of the Middle East, Caucasus and Central Asia* in their journal. [71]

The *Raptors 2000* conference that was held in Eilat, Israel, from 2 – 8 April 2000, further serves as an example that this small biblical country has lots of birds of prey within its boundaries. It was a joint meeting of *The Raptor Research Foundation* and *The World Working Group for Birds of Prey.* [72]

The following is also very interesting and significant:

"According to Dan Alon, Director of the Israel Ornithological Center, this area is one of the best bird-watching regions in the world. There are 390 bird species in the area and the season lasts from October until the end of March. In the Hula Valley ... 30 types of bird of prey, pelicans, ducks and geese" can be seen amongst others.

A bird-watching festival was also held in Israel in the year 2000:

"The festival include[d] guided tours to the best bird-watching sites (Hula Valley, Mt. Hermon, Beit Shean Valley, Jezreel Valley, Sea of Galilee)" [73]

The most astonishing of all is that the valley of Jezreel is also mentioned as one of the great gathering places of birds in Israel. Of course you know where that is – it is right next to the infamous valley of Megiddo! Revelation 16:16 also speaks of this place and that final awesome day.

The Bible is literally true to the last word.

EXPLOSION OF KNOWLEDGE SINCE 1948

We have already mentioned that the 20th century is absolutely unique in comparison to the previous centuries. The most interesting here is the role of the Jewish nation in the whole knowledge explosion:

Since around 1948, the world has seen and experienced all kinds of inventions that made life easier and also a lot faster.

Even before 1948, Jews were prominent in this regard. Alexander Graham Bell 'invented' the telephone but he got his knowhow from a Jew in Europe. Albert Einstein, whom was also a Jew, was instrumental in the developement of the atomic bomb and also the color television. Madam Curie who discovered radium had a Jewish mentor. Henry Ford built the first car, but Jews from Europe invented the combustion engine at first.

In the 1950's the transistor was developed and after that it never stopped. It surely appears that 1948 was a defining year in terms of the technology explosion that we now experience daily. Computer chips revolutionized the way we are living and more is to come soon. Knowledge is now doubling every two years – at least.

Apart from the knowledge explosion, since roundabout 1948 many great world institutions also came into existence for the first time:

1945 – United Nations
1945 – World Bank
1945 – International Monetary Fund
1945 – World Court
1948 – World Council of Churches
1949 – North Atlantic Treaty Organization
1949 – Council of Europe (forerunner of the current European Union)

Is this all merely a coincidence?

ISRAEL – A HIGHLY DEVELOPED COUNTRY

Most people lose sight of the fact, but the recent history of the country of Israel is an amazing one, in all sectors:

"From a nation whose economy was based on agriculture – 30 years ago, it captured 70% of all exports – Israel has turned into a high-tech country. Agricultural products have fallen to 3% of total exports. Few countries have carried out a revolution such as this, and in a very short period. During the ... six years [1990-1996], Israel's technology industries have themselves doubled. The pace of growth is now 25% annually in the telecommunications and 20% in the others." [74]

It is and remains one of the most amazing manifestations in the history of the world – how the nation of Israel developed from almost nothing to a strong economic infrastructure. We have to remember however that there is a God in heaven that planned everything to the tiniest detail and who will fulfill it to the last letter. The Jews' view of their future and how they want to shape it, may however take a huge turn shortly.

THE RETURN OF THE JEWS

Since 1948, when the nation of Israel was reborn, probably more than 3 million Jews returned to their land. (Numerous Jews also returned between 1917 and 1948 in the hope of regaining their status as a state and nation).

The *Jerusalem Post* newspaper of April 8, 1989 had the following front-page heading:

'MASSIVE EXODUS OF SOVIET JEWS PREDICTED' and they were quite right.

It coincided with the so called 'End of the Cold War', after Russia finally opened their doors for the Jews to return to their country. It is tragic that so few Christians and church leaders are really aware of the extent of this truth, because this is a major intervention by the living God into affairs on earth.

Merely in the 10 year period from 1989 to 1999, nearly 800 000 Jews streamed into Israel from Russia and surroundimg countries alone. An increase of 129% in Jews returning from Russia was noted from 1998 to 1999. [75]

Yes, in 1999, Jewish emigration from Russia was more than double the figure of 1998. Nearly 30 000 Russian Jews returned to their country in that year in comparison to only 13 000 in 1998. [76]

If one studies a map of the world and you look at the location of Russia in comparison to Israel, then it becomes apparent that Russia is situated exactly north of Israel. Moscow lies exactly north from Jerusalem. That is how we can understand the outflow of Jews from the North very clearly – The Lord had it prophesied that He would bring this forth in the last days. The book of Jeremiah, chapter 31:8 reads: *"Behold, I will bring them from the north country, and gather them from the coasts of the earth, and with them the blind and the lame, the woman with child and her that travaileth with child together: a great company shall return thither. ...* [and verses 10,11] *Hear the word of the Lord, O ye nations, and declare it in the isles afar off, and say, He that scattered Israel will gather him, and keep him, as a shepherd doth his flock. For the Lord hath redeemed Jacob, and ransomed him from the hand of him that was stronger then he. ...* [also verse 16] *Thus saith the Lord; Refrain thy voice from weeping, and thine eyes from tears: for thy work shall be rewarded, saith the Lord; and they shall come again from the land of the enemy."* We worship a living God who does exactly as He says. We read in Is. 43:6:

"I will say to the north, Give up; and to the south, Keep not back: bring my sons from far, and my daughters from the ends of the earth;" Except for Russia in the north, there is also Ethiopia, exactly south of Israel, from where in recent years more than 57 000 Jews returned to Israel before 1996 alone. [77] Since then many more also returned to Israel.

There are numerous Jewish immigrants that return to the land of the covenant from numerous other countries, for example from America and Argentina. Is. 43:5 prophesied that they would also come from the *"west"*. According to the Jewish Agency, that monitors the immigration process in Israel (from all countries, not just from Russia), there was an average increase of 35% in 1999 in comparison to the figures of 1998. In 1999 a total of 78 000 Jews returned to their country (from all around the world) in comparison to the 58 000 in 1998. The 78 000 represent an average of 200 per day – for a whole year! Nearly a million Jews and their relatives returned to Israel in the decade of the nineties alone. [78]

It is an unusual phenomenon to see a nation returning to their old country in such numbers. It is without a doubt the Word of the only and true God that is going into miraculous fulfillment!

This is but one of the numerous occurrences at the end of time that is intensifying and becoming greater in frequency, shortly before the second coming of the Lord Jesus Christ. If it is still difficult to believe, pray for wisdom and study the Word of God, like never before.

To think that many believe that this remarkable and extraordinary phenomenon can in any way be compared to other people from other countries that are returning to their homeland. If you ask someone however, to name a few nations which returned in such numbers, they have no answer. The most interesting is that after all these centuries in other countries, the Jews still remain Jews. Currently

South Africans do emigrate more often than ever before, but they do not return to their old countries of origin like Germany, the Netherlands or France. No, they emigrate to countries like America, Canada, England or Australia. Furthermore, they do not emigrate in nearly such large numbers as the Jews. Furthermore, they are no longer Germans or Dutch people etc., but they are now South Africans. The Jews though, stay Jews.

Early in 2002 there were reports that even more Jews would return in the near future:

"Israeli Prime Minister Ariel Sharon reiterated his goal of bringing one million Jews to Israel over the next 10 to 15 years. He wants them to come principally from Argentina, France and South Africa." [79]

JEWISH IMMIGRANTS HIGHLY TRAINED

As mentioned already, the hundreds of thousands of Jewish immigrants from the former Soviet Union is a distinct fulfillment of the Word of God. In Jer. 16:15 the following is prophesied: *"that brought up the children of Israel out of the land of the north, and from all the lands whiter he had driven them: and I will bring them again into their land that I gave unto their fathers."* Yes, they are returning on a very large scale and specifically from the northern parts. In the period from 1989 to 1996 a survey was done among these immigrants and it revealed that they were the most trained and educated group of Jews that ever came to Israel, since the influx started nearly a hundred years ago. More than 40% of these immigrants from the north have 13 years of education or more behind them. It results in Russian officials accusing Israel of 'brain smuggling'. Among this group returning to Israel – in 1996 alone - there were amongst them the following professionals:

68 100 engineers
30 900 teachers
15 500 musicians and artists
10 950 scientists
14 590 medical doctors
14 231 nurses
1 831 paramedics
1 606 pharmacists
1 575 dentists [80]

Israel surely can be proud of this rich quota of professional people, which they will be able to put to great use in the difficult days ahead. In the time of great tribulation, this expertise will be of great necessity. God sends His judgments, but at the same time, He is also merciful. We have to remember that Israel is a very small country and that makes this inflow of people that much more important. If one does not want to see the hand of God in this, you just do not want to and probably never will. While disregarding these distinct signs that are happening in front of our eyes, there are still many who say that God rejected Israel forever. Nobody is of course as blind as he who will not see.

THE TEMPLE MOUNT

The struggle for the Temple Mount in Jerusalem is one of eternal proportions. This area is not known as the 'most sought after piece of territory on earth' for nothing. This struggle that exist between the Muslims and the Orthodox Jews is far from over yet. The Muslims have two mosques on the mountain, the Al-Aqsa and the Mosque of Omar (or 'Dome of the Rock). According to 'word of mouth' Mohammad ascended to heaven from the Al-Aqsa mosque. The Orthodox Jews are prohibited from worshipping on the Temple Mount, not to speak of their earnest attempts to rebuild their temple there.

A thousand orthodox Jews gathered in 1996 at the Temple Mount's 'Cotton Gate' with its tunnel like entrance to worship on the mountain. They were prohibited to enter by a strong police presence and then started praying where they stood at the gate. They prayed that God should take away Israel's disgrace and that the temple will be rebuild: "Just as we've seen it in ruins, let us merit seeing its rebuilding." A man blew an old silver trumpet – a replica of one from the ancient temple – the clear sound of the trumpet filled the tunnel and atmosphere. [81]

CORNER STONE FOR THE THIRD TEMPLE!

The *Temple Mount Faithful* group in Israel already has a cornerstone for their third temple in possession. The cornerstone of marble weighs 4.5 tons and was apparently obtained from the desert, not far from where the Israelites journeyed under Moses' guidance.

The stone is currently on display on a traffic circle, specially build by the municipality of Jerusalem for this purpose. The orthodox Jews awaits the return of their Messiah every day, but will unfortunately fall victim to the Antichrist (who will fill this role for them, but only for a short period of time). The groups in Israel, which are striving for the cause of rebuilding the temple, agree that we live in exiting times. They call it:

"A special exciting time of the redemption of the people of the land of Israel, the Temple Mount and Jerusalem. ... The members of the *Temple Mount and Land of Israel Faithful Movement* dedicated themselves to fulfill the wish of the God of Israel and the prophecies of the prophets of Israel for the end-times." [82]

The whole process of rebuilding the temple in Jerusalem

is actually a very tragic one. It proves that the Jews still reject the Lord Jesus Christ (the true corner stone) and want to return to a Old Testament type of temple service. It is well beyond the wishes of our Lord and Saviour, but is in truth a sign that the second coming is very near. Jews have to convert themselves to Jesus exactly like everybody else on earth and the time is running out very fast.

Gershon Solomon (his name says a lot), the chairman of the *Temple Mount and the Land of Israel Faithful Movement*, was one of the soldiers that fought in 1967 when Jerusalem was returned to Israel. On the fifth day of this infamous war of six days, Moshe Dayan, the previous minister of defense of Israel returned the Temple Mount to the Muslims though. Solomon is of the impression that this was a very big mistake. In an interview he explained the importance of the third temple: " ... the rebuilding of the third temple ... is a condition for the climax of everything which has happened in this country in the last 50 years, ... " Solomon also mentioned that he was looking forward to the soon "...coming of Mashiach ben David [The Messiah] ... "It will be wrong if I will not call this time, end times, days of Messiah, We are in the midst of the most exciting time in the history of Israel ..." [83]

A Jewish newspaper reported that 10 000 Jews went to pray at the Western Wall in the year 2000. They attempted, as before, to lay the corner stone of the third temple on the Temple Mount, but was restrained like before by the police from entering the temple area. [84]

The day will come however, that an international peace force will pave the way for the Jewish nation to rebuild their temple on the right place.

Although this will happen, no true Christian can really be in favor of the rebuilding of the temple in Jerusalem. Jesus Christ already paid the full price for our sins and now every Christian is a temple of God. For the Jewish people, much hardship and sorrow will also go hand in hand with the rebuilding of the temple. The Bible did however distinctly prophesy that a temple would be built at the end of time. This we can be sure of and nobody can deny this. In Dan. 9:27 we read about a man that will confirm a strong covenant with many for one week (a year week). And then, *"in the midst of the week he shall cause the sacrifice and the oblation to cease, and for the overspreading of abominations he shall make it desolate, even until the consummation"* These animal sacrifices will be discontinued in the temple. Mt. 24:15 refers to this verse: *"When ye therefore shall see the abomination of desolation, spoken of by Daniel the prophet, stand in the holy place, (whosoever readeth, let him understand)"*. Then we also read in 2 Thes. 2:4 *"who opposeth and exalted himself above all that is called God, or that is worshipped; so that he as God sitteth in the temple of God, showing himself that he is God."*

Finally (as mentioned already) we read of this temple in Rev. 11:1,2 where it is written: *"Rise and measure the temple of God, and the altar, and them that worship therein. But the court which is without temple leave out, and measure it not; for it is given unto the Gentiles:"* Could this area 'given unto the gentiles' refer to the area where the current Mosque of Ohmar or Dome of the Rock is found? The Bible is an amazing book. That this future building will be called the temple of God cannot be doubted. The third Jewish temple will sadly not be the temple of the true Messiah like so many Jews today hope it would be. No, it will be the temple of the false Christ – the Antichrist!

4

THE MIDDLE EAST – FLASHPOINT OF THE WORLD

For many centuries or even millennia, the center of the inhabited world has seen one war after another. The area better known as the Middle East is infamous as an area of confrontation – to a greater extent than any other place on earth. In all reality, it is the flashpoint of the world.

ISRAEL AND SYRIA

The tension between Israel and Syria is a long drawn-out one and at some point in time, it will eventually result in the fulfillment of an ancient biblical prophecy denoted by the prophet Isaiah many years ago. We read the following in Is. 17:1,3: *"The burden of Damascus. Behold, Damascus is taken away from being a city, and it shall be a ruinous heap ... The fortress also shall cease from Ephraim, and the king-*

dom from Damascus".

Damascus, the capitol of Syria, is today one of the oldest inhabited cities on earth. Never before in the whole history of Damascus, was it destroyed to a 'ruinous heap'. There never occurred anything quite like this prophecy from God's Word. The present situation in the north of Israel is of such a nature that the mentioned prophecy could go into fulfillment at any moment. Syria has already threatened many times to launch a surprise attack on the Golan Heights. If this were to be the case, Israel would have no other choice than to react immediately. The question remains, how will Israel react to such an attack from the north. It is a matter of common knowledge, from media reports, that Israel is currently in possession of more than 200 nuclear warheads. If they were to make use of it in retaliation to an invasion of the Golan Heights, it will affect the situation in the entire Middle East dramatically. It may result in the city of Damascus being left in complete ruin - and again God's infallible Word will be proven 100% accurate.

An Israeli minister uttered the following words in 1997, and they remind one unmistakably of this prophecy:

"If they [Syria] launch a snatch operation on the Golan Heights, we can carry out a military snatch operation <u>in Damascus. They should know that they will be obliterated from the face of the earth</u>.' ... [according to] Minister Eytan [from Israel]. ..." [85] (Emphasis added).

ISRAEL AND EGYPT

Old enemies for sure. Nothing has changed over the last few millennia. In 1996 Israeli leaders were shocked to learn that Egypt announced their plans of a major war exercise.

They view Israel as a nuclear power and as a result, as a huge threat to their neighbours. The ten-day maneuvers, 'Operation Badr', was the largest of its kind since the 1973 Yom Kippur war. The navy, air force, infantry, artillery and parachute units took part in the operation. Simulated exercises were held in the north of Egypt. The most interesting and most noteworthy was the sea landing at a port in the Red Sea. During this phase, the Suez Canal was also crossed. It was very close to Israel's border. [86]

This whole episode was only a prelude to what may become reality shortly in a real war situation. It makes one recollect the exodus of Israel thousands of years ago from Egypt. In their pursuit after the people of Israel, the Egyptians all met their fate in the waters of the Red Sea. This was after God parted the Red Sea and Israel advanced through on dry ground. God saved His people on that day and He will do it again if the situation necessitates it. In Scripture we find amazing prophecies regarding Egypt's future – it may be their near future. To tell the truth, it may in part already be true today. In Isaiah 19, we find God's prophecy regarding Egypt. We read in verse 17: "*And the land of Judah shall be a terror unto Egypt, every one that maketh mention thereof shall be afraid in himself, because of the counsel of the Lord of hosts, which he hath determined against it.*" If one take into account that the above-mentioned war exercises were held mainly because of Israel's nuclear arsenal, this passage comes into perspective. It is quite interesting to note the following two statements of Egyptian dignitaries:

"The war with Israel is a certainty and we are ready." (Former Egyptian minister of defense, Amin El Huwaidi in an Egyptian weekly gazette, *Rous el Yosef*). [87]

An interesting name for this gazette as one thinks back

to the days when *Joseph* supplied his father Jacob and his brothers with food – from Egypt!

The Lord Himself will eventually intervene between these two countries to restore the order and many will be amazed. At the moment though, the world holds its breath, for the critical situation in the Middle East could take a drastic turn any day. The following recent report proves that war between Israel and Egypt lurks in the near future:

"Twenty-one years after Israel and Egypt signed the first-ever Israeli-Arab accord ... a top Egyptian military commander has said that war with Israel is inevitable. Field Marshal Adb Al-Halim Abu Ghazaleh ... outlined what he sees as Israel's vulnerability to a concerted Arab attack." [88] (Emphasis added).

It appears now that in 2002, Egypt has further serious plans underway and this could destabilise the Middle East even more:

"Egypt is taking measures to obtain nuclear weapons, ... Egypt intends to mine natural uranium in the Sinai Peninsula and enrich it to weapons' grade material with the help of Chinese technology. The material would then be used on long-range missiles." [89]

THE WAR OF GOG AND MAGOG

"And the word of the Lord came unto me, saying, Son of man, set thy face against Gog, the land of Magog, the chief prince of Meshech and Tubal, and prophesy against him, and say, Thus saith the Lord God: Behold I am against thee , O Gog, the chief prince of Meshech and Tubal: and I will turn thee back, and put hooks into thy jaws, and I will bring thee forth, and all thine army, horses and horsemen, all of them clothed with all sorts of armor, even a great company

with bucklers and shields, all of them handling swords:
Persia, Ethiopia and Libya with them; all of them with
shield and helmet:Gomer, and all his bands; the house of
Togarmah of the north quarters, and all his bands: and
many people with thee. ... After many days thou shalt be vis-
ited: in the latter years thou shalt come into the land that is
brought back from the sword, and is gathered out of many
people, against the mountains of Israel ... And thou shalt
come from thy place out of the north parts, thou, and many
people with thee ... and thou shalt come up against my peo-
ple of Israel, as a cloud to cover the land; it shall be in the
latter days," (Ezek. 38:1-6,8,15,16).

This is one of the most interesting prophecies in the
Bible. This quotation stipulates that this war will occur at
the end of time. As a result we can be sure that it did not
occur as of yet. Many students of Bible prophecy also
reckon that this will not be the final war – the war of
Armageddon (Rev. 16:14, 16; 19:11-21). Others, on the
other hand, understand this to be the same exact war as
Armageddon. Regardless on how you view it, one cannot be
really dogmatic about it. Some of the possible differences
between the two mentioned wars (if they are two separate
wars) are the following: The latter, will occur in the valley
of Megidddo or the valley of Jehoshaphat. (Joel 3:1,2). The
war of Gog and Magog, however, it appears, will occur on
the mountains of Israel. During this war, only certain countries will come against Israel, while the final war will
involve all the nations of the earth (Zech. 14:2,3). This war
will also commence when the nation of Israel is convened
safely in their country. We know that the Antichrist will sign
a peace treaty with them for seven years and that there will
be a false peace for the first three and a half years of this
final seven year period in Israel (Dan. 9:27). There are
numerous points of view of when exactly during these seven

years, the Gog war will commence (if it is not the final war of course). In Ezek. 39:9 we read that the weapons, that will remain after the offensive nations are destroyed on the mountains of Israel, will be set alight and that it will burn for seven years (Ezek. 39:4). This verse may refer to the war occurring at the beginning of the seven years of tribulation. The other possibility is that it will occur shortly before the middle of the tribulation, because that is when Israel will live in 'peace'. Whatever the case may be, it is clear that the Antichrist will already be on earth during that time and that the true Christians (the bride) will already have been taken away to their home and their Father.

Previously, we referred to the destruction of Damascus. There we saw that this prophecy was written in Is. 17 and that it still has to be fulfilled. This war will also have to commence, most probably, only after the gathering of the true church of Christ to heaven. If it were to happen before that day, if will be a significant sign that the first phase of the second coming could occur in the time of the war. The Lord makes it very clear however, that we shall not know the day nor the hour of His coming. Our eyes should thus not be directed to these wars in the first place, but rather to Jesus Christ and to Him alone. It does not mean however that we should not be prepared for coming wars, but we will never precisely know when these final wars will commence. The way out interpretation that these wars lie in the far future, is totally ungrounded. The countries mentioned in Ezek. 38 are countries that are currently particularly active in arming themselves to the utmost - and not with spears, bows and arrows. It is true though, that Scripture refers to swords and shields as part of their armament. However, from the point of view of Ezekiel the prophet, a few thousand years ago, he probably described these events with the knowledge he had at that time. These countries currently arm themselves with nuclear weapons, chemical weapons and much more. If we read Is. 17, we note that the first three verses specifically refer to the destruction of Damascus in Syria. In verses 12-14 the Bible however speaks of "...*the multitude of many people, which make a noise like the noise of the seas; and to the rushing of nations, that make a rushing like the rushing of mighty waters: but God shall rebuke them, and they shall flee far off ...* " These verses might quite possibly refer to the invasion described in Ezek. 38 and 39. If Damascus is destroyed, it might well be that other countries that sympathize with Syria, will invade Israel to avenge the destruction. It is notable that the names of Syria and Egypt are not under the cited countries in Ezek. 38. It is possible that they could be part of the "*many people with you*", but it is however improbable, as the Lord always refer quite distinctly to these two countries as old enemies of Israel. In Is. 17 (as mentioned) and Is. 19 (the judgment of Egypt) there are the two well-known and distinct prophecies regarding Syria and Egypt.

We will now look specifically at the countries that are mentioned so distinctly in Ezek. 38 that will invade Israel at the end of time for the war of Gog and Magog. Gog and Magog itself refer to Russia and surrounding areas. From the earliest of times, the areas north of the Caucasian mountains were known under this name. The historian Josephus wrote in his *Antiquities and Wars of the Jews* distinctly that the ancient tribes of Magog settled themselves north of these mountains, thus in today's Russia and surrounding areas. In Ezek. 38:14,15 we read that Gog (derived from Magog) will come from the back parts of the north against Israel. The prophet Ezekiel lived in Israel when he wrote this prophecy and Russia and its surrounding countries are of course directly north of Israel. In truth, Russia is the nation that distinctly occupies the back parts of the north. No other nation lies further north than Russia. The Great Wall of China is also known in Arabic as the 'wall of Al Magog', as it was built to restrain the armies of Magog (Russia), from invading China. Gog and Magog undoubtedly also include the other states from the 'old Soviet Union.'

The Hebrew word for *"chief prince"* that Ezek. 38:2 refers to, is *rosh* - a reference to a king or monarch – in this case of Russia. There currently is a city in Russia with the name of Rostof, as well as state owned weapon export factories with the names Rosvooruzhenie and Rosoboronexport. It is a common name in that part of the world. Meshech refers to Moscow, the capitol of Russia and Tubal to the current city of Tobolsk. Much has been written on this subject and much more could be said on this topic. There is little doubt however, that the cited names refer to these cities. Then there are the Persians. It is commonly known that the ancient Persia is the current Iran. The ancient Persia was composed of a much larger area than today's Iran and that is why one could also include Iraq, Afghanistan and possibly Pakistan. We have to remember that these countries will be allies of Russia and that is why all the countries that have current alliances with Russia, could be candidates as partners during this war.

The reference to *"Ethiopia and Libya"* could include other African countries like Sudan and Somalia in the southeast and Algeria, Morocco and Tunisia in the north. These countries are mostly Muslim orientated and are sympathetic towards Russia – specifically when it comes to their hatred against the Jewish nation. The following name cited is that of *"Gomer and all his bands"*. It refers to Eastern Europe and specifically Germany. Remember, Yugoslavia is also situated in Eastern Europe and is regularly in the midst of wars. The name mentioned in conclusion is *Togarmah*. This refers to the current Turkey and surroundings. Here the passage also reads *"and many people with thee"*. This is a reference to all the countries that will convene with Russia during this war. From Ezek. 38 and 39 it is clear that Russia will be the leader in this invasion of Israel. It will however be God Himself that will *"cause thee to come up from the north parts, and will bring thee on the mountains of Israel."* The Lord will however also have them fail miserably and they will be thoroughly defeated on the mountains of Israel (Ezek. 39:2-4). They should actually expect this.

The Word is quite clear when it says: *"he that keepeth Israel shall neither slumber nor sleep."* (Ps. 121:4). Even if all these mighty nations convene, they will not be victorious in conquering the small nation of Israel. God Himself will intervene and will award the victory to Israel. He will however do this for a very specific reason. We read the following in this regard: *"it shall be in the latter days, and I will bring thee against my land, that the heathen may know me, when I shall be sanctified in thee."* (Ezek. 38:16); *"So will I make my holy name known in the midsts of my people Israel; and I will not let them pollute my holy name anymore; and the heathen shall know that I am the Lord, the Holy One of Israel."* (Ezek. 39:7).

This again proves that the Lord differentiates between Israel and the other nations. Those who still believe that the church is Israel, will find it difficult to explain how these countries will invade the church at the end of time (they will probably say that this is mere 'spiritual' warfare). Moreover, many will believe it as well. Others will say that the last days are already history – we are already living in heaven – it all depends on what you make of life, they say. The blind are presently leading the blind. The end result will be tragic though. If all is merely spiritual, I would like to know where the church is on the mountains of Israel. No, the concept is simple. God chose the nation of Israel and used them to make Himself known as the true God to everybody on earth. The Lord wants us to know whom He is – there is no other reason. It will still though, take terrible wars and great afflictions to convince but a minority on earth that He is the true God of heaven and earth. By His grace, He will do exactly that and it was all prophesied in His magnificent Word.

Let's return to the names of the countries which are described so distinctly in Ezek. 38:2-6. In Gen. 10:1-6 we find nearly all these recorded. They are the names of descendants of Noah. From the line of Noah's son Japhet we find the names Magog, Meshech, Tubal and Gomer. From the line of Gomer we find Togarmah. From the line of Noah's other son, Ham, we find Cush (Ethiopia) and Phut (Libya). These people moved far away to other parts of the world and various countries, regions, and tribes were named after them as a result. The two mentioned sons of Noah, namely Ham and Japhet and their descendants moved far away from the area of the future Israel. Also, they did not serve the Lord. Their brother Shem did know the Lord and from him Abraham descended – the one with whom God made the covenant through which all nations were eventually blessed (Gen. 12:3). From his bloodline the Messiah would eventually be born – the Saviour of the world. It is noteworthy that the descendants of two brothers, at a specific time in history, would convene against the nation of Israel, thousands of years later. In this country Israel, they will convene against the descendants of their own brother, Shem. Is it not amazing how the Lord keeps the entire history of the human race in His hands? Everything in God's Word fits together perfectly and no part of it can ever be ascribed to coincidence. The descendants of Magog and the others mentioned, did not convert themselves to the Lord yet – their leaders have definitely not and that is why God will let them convene against the country and nation of Israel to judge them there. By then, they would have had enough time to seek the Lord, but their pride and hardened hearts will lead them astray and they will go against the living God. The perfect and righteous God then uses this kind of people in His plan with man. All will fit together in the end. These mentioned nations want to exterminate Israel from the world map and do not want to acknowledge that Israel and the Jews are still God's chosen nation – for a very good reason – even for their own sake. As early as Gen. 12:3 God promised Abraham and by implication also his descendants, the nation of Israel: *"and I will bless them that bless thee, and curse him that curseth thee"*. For this reason the Lord says to Gog: *"Behold, I am against thee, O Gog"* (Ezek. 39:1). We can now acknowledge and comprehend why He gave this incredible prophecy.

CURRENT MOVEMENTS IN THE COUNTRIES OF EZEK. 38

If one look at the situation in the Middle East, it becomes quite apparent that the prophecy of the coming war of Gog and Magog on the mountains of Israel does not lie in the far and distant future. The world stage is now quickly being set for this big war that will become a reality at some point in the near future. Everything points to it. In fact, it seems as if this war is knocking at the door. We will now examine in short the current situation in the countries mentioned in this amazing Bible prophecy.

Russia

The new monarch or ruler of Russia, Pres. Vladimir Putin, seems to be in strict control of matters. Reportedly, he is busy restoring Russia to its 'former glory'.

The Russian economy seems to be in a horrendous state and this fact could mislead the world to a large extent. In spite of it, Russia is busy preparing themselves for a major war – and this on a large scale. They, for instance, posses a huge supply of the deadly smallpox virus, was reported in the media recently. Only they and the USA admitted officially that they were in possession of it. According to reports Russia is currently busy building an enormous underground base in the Ural Mountains. This base is reportedly as big as the metropolitan area of Washington DC. It is constructed at the Yamantau Mountain and is so deep that it will withstand a nuclear attack. In addition, in Moscow, there is currently huge activity as the Russians is busy preparing amongst others, tunnels and an underground city that may house up to 30 000 people. It will also be able to withstand nuclear attacks. This is made possible with the money that the West lends to Russia to consolidate their debt. If this is all true, it surely points to a coming war or wars. Somewhere somebody is busy manipulating matters - and a huge war, as the Bible predict, will surely commence with Russia at the forefront.

Meanwhile, Russia's new president, Putin, is leading the Kremlin to take control over the media:

> "the [Russian] government is attempting to acquire controlling stakes in ORT and NTV, the two dominant Russian TV channels. The Kremlin already owns ... the State TV and Radio Co., GTRK. If its new moves are successful, it will consolidate exclusive ownership of all three national TV channels, and will enjoy a virtual monopoly on televised news. That could have a serious impact on the prospects of freedom of speech and the media in Russia..." [90]

Why would he want to do this? This surely appears to be very much according to the pattern of the old Soviet Union when the communist state owned everything and controlled people's lives to the utmost. What is happening to the new democracy and what about so-called freedom of speech in the new Russia?

Putin is also busy reorganizing Russia's military:

> " ... Russian president, Vladimir Putin has methodically ticked off each item on a list of institutions ... Now he has turned his attention to the army. ... Russia has one and a quarter million men under arms, and a defense budget of about 3 billion pounds. More than 2 billion pounds goes into buying new equipment for the country's nuclear forces," [91]

The Biblical fact that Russia will fight with other Arabic nations against Israel becomes more clear as time goes by:

> "Russian President Vladimir Putin said ... that Moscow was 'ready to cooperate' with Arab countries in the search for a solution to the Middle East crises." [92]

(Emphasis added).

What will this solution be?

Iran

In May 1996 Iran held their largest military parade ever in the Middle East. Weapons of all kinds were exhibited in the parade in the Qom desert. Iran made a statement that it was to showcase to the world the readiness of their military forces. They noted that their military is under direct command of Ayatollah Ali Khamenei – their Islamic leader. A month later they proclaimed their plans of a great military exercise and that under the name: 'Road to Jerusalem.' [93]

Presently, calls for the total destruction of Israel is not uncommon. In an article with the heading: 'Iranian appeal: destroy Israel'_we read the following words from Iran's Speaker of parliament:

"Come out openly, like Iran, and <u>say you don't accept such a country as Israel on the world map</u>. Have courage. We can make good use of our <u>weapons, military equipment and all our forces,</u>...he urged <u>Arab countries</u> to believe in themselves." [94] (Emphasis added).

The root of the problem is right here. They believe in themselves and not in the infallible Word of God. Iran also has a nuclear reactor that they are working on and they are busy developing nuclear and chemical weapons.

A few years ago Iran also received their third Russian made submarine as it entered the Persian Gulf. Iran and Russia share a very strong relationship and it will become more evident in the days to come.

At the beginning of 1997 the *US Congressional Task Force on Terrorism and Unconventional Warfare* reported from the USA that the Mid-East is a flashpoint that is ready to explode.

According to the report, Iran, Iraq, Syria as well as the Palestinians are busy positioning themselves for a full-scale war against Israel.

According to the *Arutz 7* radio station in Israel, a UN report on arms budgets brought to light that the 13 Arabic nations surrounding Israel are spending twice as much on weapons than what the international average is. [95] They are definitely preparing for something and that is not peace!

Persia of old surely is preparing for war and they do not even hide it:

"Iran has launched its largest airborne exercise
near the Iraqi border as a state daily said Teheran

will not hesitate to develop nuclear weapons that can strike the United States. ... " [96]

- At the end of September 2000, Iran once again staged a war exercise that lasted 3 days
- Iran again called for the destruction of Israel in October of 2000. It came from their highest religious authority, Ayatollah Ali Khamenei. He said the following:

  "The only way to end the crisis in the Middle East is to dry up its roots. What is at the roots of the crisis? It is the Zionist regime that has been imposed on the region; ... 'clean Holy Qods (Jerusalem) of Zionists' ... Chants of '<u>Ready, Leader, we are ready</u>' and '<u>Death to Israel</u>' rippled through the crowd...." [97]

This country never stops preparing and exercising their military forces and the fact that they work closely with the Russians is no secret either. In March of 2001 they were at it again:

"Iran concluded a military exercise involving army, air force, marine units and more than 6,000 soldiers in the Gulf ... a week before Iranian President Mohammed Khatami is scheduled to arrive in Moscow. Diplomatic sources said Khatami's visit, ... is expected to pave the way for huge arms deals with Russia." [98]

This is exactly what the Word foretold!

Iraq

There are numerous reports on their efforts to restore

their army to its full potential after the Gulf War in 1991. Recently a special task team from the United Nations, designated to examine their weapon systems, declared that Iraq is probably hiding numerous Scud missile launchers. They apparently exchanged a number of self-made, useless missile launchers with operational ones and destroyed them for the sake of appearance. According to a treaty signed after the Gulf War, Iraq had to destroy these and other weapons. The UN's Security Council was approached by the investigative commission for a further amount of $30 million to monitor Iraq's movements more intensively. The UN's finances however, are trying and initially the money could not being granted. For many years the top positions in the Security Council of the UN were also filled by Russians and this further complicates the whole situation. Iraq possesses many Russian T72 tanks and hundreds of fighter planes. With Saddam Hussein at the head of affairs, anything is bound to happen. In August 2000, Iraq informed the UN that Kuwait was busy with 'deeds of aggression' on the border of Iraq. They cannot wait to invade this small country again. Kuwait is currently receiving support and protection from America, who warned Iraq to stop its wargames. In turn, America is quite concerned over its threatened oil interests in Kuwait.

The following report appeared regarding Iraq and their feelings towards Israel:

> "Iraqi leader Saddam Hussein has said that his country could <u>destroy Israel if it was given access to land next to the Jewish state</u> ... the president ... [said] <u>Iraq could put an end to Zionism in a very short time</u>" [99] (Emphasis added).

News about Iraq's supposed plans to 'liberate

Jerusalem', as they call it, has now also surfaced again and again:

> " ... A senior Iraqi diplomat said Saddam has <u>seven million combatants called the Quds [Jerusalem] Army</u>. The diplomat said Iraq would "<u>swallow Israel up</u>" if his country is attacked. "The Palestinian cause and <u>liberation of Jerusalem</u> as well as campaign against Israel is a <u>fundamental issue</u> for Iraq, just like <u>many other Islamic states.</u>" [100] (Emphasis added).

This is of course a futile exercise, but nevertheless a very interesting development to watch.

Is Iraq really working with Russia against Israel? Look at the facts:

> "Witnesses in Basra [Iraq] were quoted as saying that Iraq plans to import 1,300 tank transporters from Russia. Iraqi opposition sources said the tank transporters are key to the military's effort to regain control over the country <u>or join any Middle East war against Israel</u>." [101] (Emphasis added).

Ethiopia and Sudan

In January 1997 it was reported that Iran consigned Sudan with 60 Russian tanks, light artillery and chemical weapons via air. Sudan, together with Ethiopia, is of course part of the ancient land of Cush. Iran supports Sudan's Islamic government forces that are apparently in conflict with Ethiopia from time to time. It appears as if Sudan is taking the lead and that they can even invade communist Ethiopia (which seems in bad shape) at some stage in the future. There were reports in recent years of Sudanese forces shooting and killing hundreds of Ethiopian soldiers. The role of the Islamic religion should never be underestimated in the whole process. The Sudanese government is reportedly also busy negotiating with China for the acquisition of weapons. It seems as if some movement is coming forth in these Islamic controlled African countries. Their common target and enemy is and remains the land of Israel. Tens of thousands of Jews emigrated from Ethiopia to Israel in recent years. Their fellow countrymen of Islamic orientation, will however turn against them in the near future when Ethiopia and their neighbors will invade Israel with Russia. Presently Ethiopia is also engaged in conflicts with its other neigbor Eritrea.

Libya

The temperament of Muammar Ghaddafi is quite infamous. Under his guidance Libya is one of the world's most dangerous nations. According to a report from Spain (in reference to a confidential NATO document), Libya will have nuclear missiles that can travel up to 3 000 km ready by the year 2006. It will pose a great threat to NATO countries – especially Spain, France and Italy. If America attacks Libya for instance, they could then retaliate by attacking one of the above-mentioned countries. The missiles may also be fitted with chemical or bacteriological heads. According to the Pentagon, Libya is busy building one of the world's largest chemical plants inside a mountain. Russia's weapon export agency, Rosvooruzheniye, already provided Libya with Russian S-300 air defense systems. In 1999 the UN lifted sanctions against Libya and they are now able to acquire weapons on a large scale. [102]

Reports have also stated that Russia and Libya have been working together for some time now:

"At the time of the [international] sanctions [in Libya], Russia had thousands of workers and advisors in Libya." [103]

Interestingly enough a recent statement from Ghaddafi urged Libya and Egypt to unite. Just think how much closer they will be to Israel then.

Germany

Not much is mentioned in the media regarding their army and military readiness. In January 1997 however, there were some interesting political movements. A former aspirant Russian presidential candidate. Alexander Lebed, visited Germany as well as all the leaders of the big parliamentary parties. He also met with the former Counselor Helmut Kohl's lieutenant, Wolfgang Schaeuble, during this visit. Very notable were his words:

"Germany must look at me, I need to look at Germany, we have to decide whether we should work together or not. I hope that we come to the conclusion that we should work together." [104]

This sounded almost prophetic, but it could have been expected. The Lord said in His Word that they would work together in the last days. The report further stated that Germany is Russia's biggest creditor and supporter in the West. It fits perfectly with what the Word of God predicted.

More recently German forces, as part of a NATO offensive, were active in the war-torn Macedonia, part of Yugoslavia. Could these eastern European wars eventually lead to Jerusalem? Only time will tell.

Turkey

A few years ago Turkey and Israel signed an agreement to work together on certain matters of common concern. Turkey however, is an Islamic country (99% Muslims) and their former premier (in whose term the agreement was signed) made a very negative statement regarding Israel shortly thereafter.

The current crises in the Middle East though, forced Turkey to side with the other Islamic states against Israel again. Russia also very recently began to make the 'right moves' regarding Turkey:

> "Turkey and Russia said ... that they had agreed to increase cooperation in the military and defense industry fields ... "We have reached agreement to deepen and enhance our cooperation on military and security issues," visiting Russian Prime Minister Mikhail Kasyanov said at a joint press conference with his Turkish counterpart Bullent Ecevit." [105] (Emphasis added).

What incredible prophetically accurate moves are not being made in the world today? Is the Word of God not out of this world?

INVASION WITH HORSES?

Interestingly enough we read in Ezek. 38:4 and 15 that these countries will invade Israel with horses, amongst other weaponry. A possible explanation for this could be that Ezekiel, with his limited knowledge regarding the future, described it in this way. Another explanation could be that horses will really be used to a certain extent, as Russia will have to travel over mountainous areas (for example the

Caucasus Mountains) to invade Israel. An amazing piece of news concerning exactly this came forth at the end of the year 2001. According to the respected *BBC News*, Russia plans to conscript horses and other animals in case of a future war. The article even had the heading, '*Russia's four-legged conscripts*' and the caption of a photo of a horse in the snow, read: '*Horses will have to be registered.*' Look at the following:

> "In the event of war, the new conscripts called up by the Russian Defence Ministry could include pets ... Under the new proposals, donkeys, <u>horses</u>, camels, reindeers, sledge-dogs and four-wheel-drive vehicles <u>will have to be registered at local military commandants' offices across the country</u>. ... Deputy military commissar of Moscow Mikhail Prostodushev says ... <u>in the mountains in the south, travel is only possible on horseback</u>. So <u>could racehorses, for example, be the key to any future war effort in the south?</u>" [106] (Emphasis added).

What a question to ask.

A GREAT ARMY FROM THE EAST

IS CHINA IN THE BIBLE?

In Rev. 9:14 we read about the four angels that will be set loose in the great river Euphrates. Shortly after they are set loose, an enormous army of *"two hundred thousand thousand"* will appear on the world scene that will cause great destruction (verse 16). If one adds these numbers up, you come to two hundred million soldiers. In verse 17 we read that they are wearing breastplates *"of fire, and of jacinth, and brimstone"*. If you would look at colour photographs from the army of a certain Eastern country, you would see something astonishing. Their military uniforms have in them the colours of yellow (brimstone), a very fiery red (fire) as well as a light blue (jacinth) stripe on their caps. This army comes from Red China. We know that today China is by far the largest nation on earth with a population of more than 1.3 billion people. It is very interesting to also note that it was said that Mao Tsetung, their former leader, mentioned in his diary that his army, even in those days, could push 200 million into the battlefield.

More recently, the *Strategic Studies Institute* released a report by Col. L.M. Wortzel, with the title: 'China's Military Potential' wherein it is stated that:

> "China also has a potential manpower base of another 200 million males fit for military service available at any time." [107]

If we look at verse 18 of Rev. 9, we see that this army will kill a third of all people on earth. It strongly appears that this war will coincide or will culminate in the war of Armageddon. A third of the human race will die as a result during the seven years of tribulation that is to come. What a thought.

How do we know that a modern war is presupposed here, may be asked. In verse 17 we read that the heads of the horses are like *"heads of lions"* and that *"out of their mouths issued fire and smoke and brimstone"*. This could not be bows and arrows or anything of that sort. It is commonly known that in the days when John saw these visions, there existed no such weaponry. These type of modern weapons only made its appearance in the 20th century. In verse 19 we read: *"For their power is in their mouth, and in their tails:*

for their tails were like unto serpents, and had heads, and with them they do hurt." Today's fighter planes and fighter helicopters shoot from the front and some even from the back of the tail. Advanced missile launchers and different types of armored tanks can do the same. If we merely think of the various nuclear and atomic warheads that are in existence today, everything becomes that much more clear.

The whole issue regarding the river Euphrates and the fact that the mentioned army is connected with it in some way is also very interesting. The four angels that are bound at the river Euphrates in Rev. 9:14, refer quite possibly to the fallen angels that will initiate this war when they are loosened (Rev. 9:15). If we look at Rev. 16:12, it becomes very gripping. There we read: *"And the sixth angel poured out his vile upon the great river Euphrates; and the water thereof was dried up, that the way of the kings of the east might be prepared."* Shortly thereafter we read of Armageddon in Rev. 16:16. Presently China is the great rising force from the East. Can one still say that the book of Revelation is a vague and unclear book not written for modern times? Can one still say that all these events occurred many years ago or that this book of the Bible is only symbolic?

The river Euphrates is a very large river, as Scripture also seems to indicate. It presents no dilemma for the God of heaven and earth though. Interesting facts regarding this river came to the forefront in recent years that need our attention.

Late in 1989 the country of Turkey completed a huge dam, the Ataturk dam, and for the first time in history the flow of the mighty Euphrates could be stopped via human intervention. This prophecy can thus go into fulfillment any time the Lord will allow it to.

China seems to be the force from the East, but is this strange? The symbol of China is the dragon. The year 2000 in China was known as the year of the dragon! They also launched a so-called 'Dragon Project' and in the middle of February 2000 they hosted a 'dragon dance' on the Great Wall of China. Do they perhaps want to expand to territory on the other side of the wall?

In 1999, China held a big military parade for the first time in 15 years. It was to commemorate the 50th year of the communist rule there. During the festivities, half a million soldiers and civilians joined in the parade. [108]

At the end of 1998 China's large-scale military potential for the new millennium became known:

> "China's People's Liberation Army is building lasers to destroy satellites and already has beam weapons capable of damaging sensors on space-based reconnaissance and intelligence systems, ...
>
> China could blind U.S. intelligence and military space equipment, systems vital for deploying U.S. military forces in current and future warfare. ... The Pentagon report shows that China is preparing its forces to wage not only a 'Desert Storm-level' of regional conflict but a 21st century high-tech war," [109]

China, the land of the dragon is currently emerging as a military force that has to be reckoned with. The hour is much later than most would admit and the Word of God much more wonderful than could ever be imagined!

5

THE LAST FALL OF BABYLON

"We would have healed Babylon, but she is not healed." (Jer. 51:9)

"Babylon is fallen, is fallen" (Is. 21:9)

"Babylon is fallen, is fallen"(Rev. 14:8)

"Babylon the great is fallen, is fallen" (Rev. 18:2)

More than 2300 years ago a great world leader arose from Europe, fought and conquered wherever he went, but suddenly his vast empire came to an abrupt end – in Babylon! His name was Alexander the Great who died in the city of Babylon at the young age of 33. [110]

Of course Babylon is far more than an ancient city, it is a world system – it is a way of death. Eternity cannot be found within its parameters. Babylon always falls and they that go to Babylon, spiritually spoken, also fall – time and again.

Is it not compelling how the Word of God repeats itself? We read of the fall of Babylon in the Old Testament as well as in the New. The Bible reveals cycles of prophecies that build up to a point of climax. There are smaller fulfillments of biblical prophecies, further fulfillments, and eventually the final fulfillment at the end of the human dispensation on earth.

The above-mentioned cases refer to the fall of the ancient city and kingdom of Babylon. We know that we read of the tower of Babel as early as Gen. 11 and how God brought it to a fall. This was the first fall. In Is. 13:14 and Is. 21 as well as Jer. 50 and 51 we read of another fall of Babylon (this word comes from the root word Babel). Again it occurred in the same geographical area. In the book of Daniel we read how the Babylon of king Nebuchadnezzar came to a fall and how the Medes and Persians conquered them. The Bible prophesied these events and so it came to pass.

If we move to the New Testament, we read about the fall of Babylon in Rev. 14:8 and distinctly in Rev. 18. This time Babylon will fall a final time and the extent of its fall will be much greater.

A television program with this Babylonian theme is also very popular throughout the world these days. *Babylon 5*, is about a space station that has a majestic purpose, namely "to bring together representatives of a multitude diverse races – human and alien – to work out differences peacefully." This all developed at "the dawn of the third Age of Mankind, 13 years after" a big war that nearly obliterated humanity. Out of this state of chaos arose "the dream of the Babylon Project." Three so-called Babylons (space stations in the plot) already failed or were sabotaged. A fourth one disappeared in a mysterious way and now the fifth one looks like the final hope. As "Earth's government buckles under far-reaching corruption", this Babylon Project appears to be "the last, best hope for maintaining peace", according to the story line. [111]

This sounds almost apocalyptic. Even more than that, it appears to be almost exactly in line with what the Bible has to say regarding a last days Babylon. One big difference though, in the television version, Babylon is the place of great and final hope for mankind and in the Bible version, Babylon stands for the last and ultimate failure of a God forsaken humanistic world system.

ANOTHER TOWER OF BABEL?

Recently, news about a magnificent new space tower came forth. Scientists from *NASA* suggested such a tower and then talked about an incredible new space elevator that could take people high up in the atmosphere. From there we, they say, will be able to view earth from afar off. Look at a news report about this amazing concept that initially appeared in September 2000 (the same time the United Nations had their big Millennium Summit in New York):

> "ladies and gentlemen, welcome aboard NASA's *Millennium-Two Space Elevator.* Your first stop will be the Lunar-level platform before we continue on to the New Frontier Space Colony development. The entire ride will take about 5 hours … Current plans call for a base tower approximately 50 km tall … To keep the cable structure from tumbling to Earth, it would be attached to a large counterbalance mass beyond geostationary orbit" [112]

Quite a tall tower. Yes, quite a tall order. This of course makes one think of some well-known and even lesser known verses in Scripture. Do they really want to reach for the stars? In Gen. 11:4 we read that the people of that day started building a tower 'to reach heaven' and to 'make themselve a name.' This is also very typical of our Babylonian age. Everyone wants to make a name and reach for the stars. In Is. 14:13 we read about someone else who also wanted to *"ascend into heaven"*. This passage, inter-estingly enough, tell us earlier (in verse 4) about the king of Babylon and later (in verse 12) we see it actually points to Lucifer – the creator of Babylon. Man is very proud and want to ascend beyond all perceived limitations. Why would they want to ascend 50km into the sky? Who or what will they find there? The God of the Bible foresaw something like this, long ago: *"Though thou exalt thyself as the eagle, and though thou set thy nest among the stars, thence will I bring thee down, saith the LORD."* (Obadiah verse 4).

All Babylonian type activities, well-meant or not, will eventually come to a fall – a great fall. Why? Because the God of heaven and earth already came down to us – through His Son Jesus Christ. He wants us to rather humble our-selves and then He Himself will exalt us when the time is due. Meekness and patience though, are not attributes easily found in Babylon.

IRAQ IN PROPHECY

The areas that were associated with Babel in biblical times were known under different names at different peri-ods. It was known, amongst other names, as the land of *Shinar*, where the ancient tower of Babel was built; the land of the *Chaldeans*, from where Abram departed on his unknown journey; the name *Assyria* – the name of a former great kingdom that included that area; the well-known name

Babel which means 'confusion' – as God confused the tongues of the people there and because of their many gods. Bell was their main god – the sun god. Lastly also the familiar name *Babylon*, which is a mixture between Babylonian/Egyptian sun worship – On was an Egyptian god.

Today that infamous area is known as Iraq. Their president, Saddam Hussein views himself as the second Nebuchadnezzar and one of his military's infantry divisions is known as *Al-Nebuchadnezzar.* [113]

His eldest son, Uday, has a newspaper in Iraq with the name *Babel* – all this 2000 years after Christ. [114]

Hussein also rebuilt a part of the ancient city of Babylon. In 1978 the first work on it began and in 1987 the first arts festival was held there.

We read the following in a news report on the festival that was held there in 1998:

> "The magnificent Iraqi ancient city of Babylon, the crown jewel in the archaeological treasures of Mesopotamia, has been the locale for one of the best cultural festivals in the middle east. ... Babylon was known in Sumerian times as Kadinyirra and called by the Akkadians Bab-ilu, the 'gate of God.' Nebuchhadnezzar's and Hammurabi's artifacts, taken to Baghdad during the Gulf War, were only displayed during the festival which started September 22 – October 2 [1998] ... the 10th Festival that takes place in the reconstructed Greek Theatre of Nebuchadnezzar's fabled city on the River Euphrates." [115]

Following is also a short report on the Babylon Arts Festival of the year 2000:

"More than 47 countries will take part in the 10-day Babylon Cultural festival which opens on September 22 [2000] in the sanctions-hit Iraq, ... 'Several artistic groups ... will take part in the Babylon festival,' ... The annual festival <u>in the historic city of Babylon</u>, some 90 miles south of the Iraqi capital, was launched in 1987." [116] (Emphasis added).

These times though, could come to an abrupt end shortly. There is an amazing prophecy in Rev. 18:10,22 – *"Alas, Alas, that great city of Babylon, that mighty city! For in one hour is thy judgment come ... .And the voice of harpers, and musicians and of pipers, and trumpeters, shall be heard no more at all in thee; and no craftsman, of whatsoever craft he be, shall be found any more in thee;"*

Clearly, this prophecy did not go into final fulfillment yet. Is Hussein trying to prove the Scriptures wrong by hosting art festivals there? He however does not realize that this final fulfillment of the Word may come in his time!

Apparently, Iraq invaded Kuwait in 1990 to acquire their oil riches to further rebuild the city of Babylon. The palace and throne hall of Nebuchadnezzar has been rebuilt as well as the infamous Gate of Ishtar – named after the ancient Babylonian goddess. Hussein had his name put on many of the bricks that the walls were rebuilt with – as did Nebuchadnezzar of old. Recently reports stated that Iraqi soldiers was again observed at the border with Kuwait and that some of Hussein's military agents were also noticed in Jordan.

According to an Arabic news agency, Saddam Hussein has five people who resemble him closely (through surgery?) whom occasionally move out to his balcony for the TV cameras. He does this reportedly to try and save his own life in case of an assassination attempt. The question remains if all these precautions will be of any help at all.

The Lord has already destined the future of that country. Many today will be convinced that all the biblical prophecies regarding Babel were fulfilled in Old Testament times. It is not possible. Babel fell repeatedly only to rise again. Its final fall is still to follow. Some Old Testament verses disclose that the final fall of Babylon is still future. We read in Is. 13:20: *"It shall never be inhabited, neither shall it be dwelt in from generation to generation"*. This time that is referred to, surely cannot have been fulfilled finally and completely in Old Testament times. It must point to some future time – even future to our current time. Presently there are millions of people living in Iraq and the city of Babylon was rebuilt – a part of it anyway.

Earlier in the chapter of Isaiah, we read the distinct words that prove that it could not have been fulfilled previously. Here we read: *"The noise of a multitude in the mountains, like as of a great people; a tumultuous noise of the kingdoms of <u>nations gathered together</u>: The Lord of hosts mustereth the host of the battle. They come from a far country, from the end of heaven"* (Is. 13:4,5).

Nations gathered? It almost sounds like the United Nations. The UN was recently actively involved with weapons inspections in Iraq. Note that these nations come from 'a far country'. Can this possibly involve America? The USA is still busy patrolling the air above Iraq and a major attack is imminent. President Bush stated firmly that an attack on Iraq is next on the agenda after the US invasion of Afghanistan.

This will of course not be the first time that such an offensive will be launched against Iraq.

In 1999 a similar scenario was on the cards:

"The United States and Britain are gathering

171

steam for a large scale operation against Iraq, amidst almost daily air strikes against that country," [117]

In the following paragraph we read of a United Nations meeting held that September that had to decide on the fate of Iraq. The Security Council had to decide on this.

If we recollect 1990/1991 and how the West co-operated in invading Iraq, it could be like a prelude to what is still to come. In the book of Jeremiah, we read of this as well. In Jer. 50:9 – the prophecy concerning Babylon – we read: *"For, lo, I will raise and cause to come up against Babylon an assembly of great nations from the north country: and they shall set themselves in array against her; from thence she shall be taken".*

North America is certainly at the forefront of the attacks against Iraq – whatever their reason might be. The US and Britain come from the northwest. Is it not significant that no nations from the South want to take up arms against Iraq? Saddam Hussein has also many times declared that 'Iraq's victory would be certain' in a war against whoever. That especially includes Israel.

He added that the Western allied forces will in all certainty lose against Iraq, because Iraq is right and they are wrong. It is also interesting to note that America is usually very sympathetic towards Israel. Especially because there are many Jews in the United States. A while back however, Saddam made it clear what he thought about Israel:

"Palestine is Arab, The Zionists must depart from it. Jews who want to live with its people (with the Palestinians) have a right as citizens of one country ... if they do not, every person should go back to where he has come from." [118]

He cannot stand the Jews and want to wipe Israel from the world map. Clearly, he does not understand the Bible or know the God whom inspired the Holy Scriptures. On the other hand, maybe he does believe the Bible to a slight extent. Maybe he is panic-stricken that Israel will one day govern to the ends of the river Euphrates. This river is in today's Iraq!

But can Iraq really be the Babylon that the Bible speaks of - to this day?

Look at the recent and very candid statement and warning from Saddam Hussein's son:

> "All Iraqis are prepared to fight alongside Palestinians to chase Jews out of Israel, Saddam Hussein's elder son Uday boasted. ... 'The end of the Jews will be at the hands of the people of Babylon (Iraq) and they (Israelis) well know it', Uday said. ... sooner or later we, the inhabitants of Babylon, will break their necks'," (Emphasis added) [119]

Iraq wants to bring an end to Israel, but clearly do not understand the biblical prophecies that foretell that God will rather bring an end to them.

We can know for certain that God's Word in this regard will be fulfilled – in the future, the near future.

Yes, Babel will fall again and this time it will be the last fall! What we see happening now is merely a prelude to that which is to follow and it cannot be undone.

BABYLON THE GREAT

Babel or Babylon is also a term that refers to something

much larger. In the Bible a literal event always refer to a spiritual one and vice versa. The whole world is – in a certain sense – spiritually spoken – Babylon! Is it not significant that the Lord called Abram from Ur of the Chaldees (Babylon) with a covenant that he would lead him to the land of Canaan (the promised land)? To this day God calls His children from the world – from Babylon and Egypt so that they may please and serve Him. This is spiritually spoken. Will we be able to part with the spiritual Babylon in our lives today, remains the question. In a spiritual sense the current international society is very similar to the times of ancient Babylon. If we can merely think of the current confusion in the world as well as the many different idols that are worshiped by the multitude of nations, we know that it is clearly the case. Here we have the religious and endtime Babylonian system of Rev. 17. Then also we read of a commercial Babylonian system that will prevail at the end of the days in Rev. 18. In Rev. 16:19 we read about the judgment on political Babylon. Yes, the entire Babylonian system on earth, under the guidance of the devil and his human agents, will come to a certain and final fall. Exactly as Babel or Babylon (Iraq) will come to a final fall, this entire world system under human government will also come to a climactic end.

Note the following recent happenings from around the world and how it connects to the endtime scenario of the great Babylon that the Bible speaks of:

- From 9 – 20 March 1999 a session of the Provisional World Parliament was scheduled to have been held, guess where, no other location than Baghdad, Iraq - in Saddam Hussein's Peoples Palace! Can you believe that there was another effort for a one-world government in exactly the same geographical area where the ancient tower of Babel was built? This Provisional

World Parliament is part of the work of the World Constitution and Parliament Association. They strive towards one parliament for the whole world and in their own terms also the following: A 'Global Finance System', 'Planetary Banking System', 'World Executive', World Judiciary', 'The Enforcement System' with a 'World Police.' They also plan the disarmament of all nations and the protection of 'mother earth.' [120]

- In a special edition of the well-known international news magazine, *Newsweek*, a tower of Babel appeared on the front page. The heading read: EUROLAND. It reported on the Euro, the new single monetary unit of the European Union. At the top of the tower of Babel was a Euro sign – as if to say that the new Babel was now completed! [121]
This Babel will also come to a fall eventually.

- A few years ago there also appeared an image of the tower of Babel on the front page of the well-known *Time* magazine The heading read: 'BACK TO BABEL' In the report they also mentioned that half of the world's languages is disappearing. [122]

- There is also a web page on the Internet with the name *Babel*, to help you communicate in any language of the world through utilising of their translation services.

UNITY MOVEMENTS EVERYWHERE

The Council of Europe was founded in 1949 and was the first official step to unite Europe. The 'Council of Europe' coordinates legislation on the economic, social, cultural and scientific fronts. On 25 January 1996, Russia officially became the 39th member of the Council. They decided to openly mock God by making a poster for the council and depicting the new Europe as the Tower of Babel. Above the tower were various occultic pentagrams. The wording read: 'Europe, many tongues, one voice.'

The European Commission is now also seriously considering a *single capital* for the whole of Europe. This is an astonishing move, as it strongly reminds one of Babel again. They are thinking of Brussels, where the headquarters of the European Union is currently situated. [123]

- Not only Europe has Babylonian type plans, but now there is also strong talk about a new "African Union, modelled on the European Union, with its own parliament, central bank and court of justice." [124]

- In the same way, Arab nations in the Middle East now talk about "a single currency similar to the euro, in order to forge an Arab economic bloc." [125]

- Again, in exactly the same way Asia is now talking about a similar move as they want to promote "aggressive efforts to create a common currency in Asia, similar to the euro, to prevent financial turmoil." [126]

One can clearly see the pattern and it is nothing other than Babylonian in design.

FROM MUSIC TO RELIGION

Also the entertainment industry of this world is strongly *en route* to Babylon. This was long expected though. The following tell part of the story:

- At the end of 1997 the famous rock group, the *Rolling Stones*, began their new world tour with the theme *Bridges to Babylon*. [127] One of their previous recordings had the name: 'Sympathy for the Devil.' His fall is as certain as the fall of Babylon. Man does not want to understand that Babel or Babylon is not the place to built bridges to. Its judgment awaits and God will not prolong it. Some say America is Babylon. Concerning Hollywood and many other matters, it indeed seems true. The rest of the world however is not much better off. The whole world will be judged righteously – shortly! Iraq will come to a fall, but so also will the complete Babylonian world system come to a majestic fall. The one is merely a smaller prelude to the far greater one that will follow. Is it not perhaps why Jesus said in Jn. 17:9 that: *"I pray not for the world"*. We have to pray for all people, but not that this world system will be saved, as it will expire. The judgments of the Lord will come, but perhaps it will contain some grace as well. Is. 26:9 reads: *"for when thy judgments are in the earth, the inhabitants of the world will learn righteousness"*.

- A great Babylonian event was held in South Africa from December 1-8, 1999. It was the third *Parliament of World Religions* that was scheduled in the city of Cape Town (the first two events of this kind was held in Chicago, USA, in 1893 and 1993). An even greater smorgasbord of faiths gathered this time to envision a better future for the world. Some of the speakers included the Dalai Lama of Tibet as well as Stephen Rockefeller. About 6 000 delegates attended the many organized plenary sessions, seminars and lectures. Some of the catch-phrases of the week were: "'God is same', [according to] the Reverend Venerable G Ishibashi, a Bhuddist … The Aumists group carried a banner that proclaimed: 'God is one, whatever name we call Him'; and a Baha'i writing stated: 'The purpose of justice is the appearance of unity.'" [128]

One delegate from the United Nations that attended the above mentioned meeting also set the stage for the following organization, mentioned here below.

A STEP FURTHER – THE UNITED RELIGIONS

" *And they worshipped the dragon which gave power unto the beast ...* " Rev. 13:4

In **June of** 1999 the *United Religions* organization assembled **in San** Francisco. It was not their first assembly however. **This** organization was already initiated in 1997 and they **have** great plans for 'mother earth and her children.' The **religious** Babylon of Rev. 17 is now more clearly than ever coming to a distinct and final fulfillment. To follow are in short an extract from their own report on the 'coming together' of all the major religions of the world:

> "The fourth United Religions Initiative global summit commenced on a <u>sunny Sunday</u> afternoon in northern California on June 20, the day before the 1999 <u>Summer Solstice</u> ... From the Covenant of the Goddess to Catholicism, from Jainism to Judaism, we come from the grassroots, from faith sharing families the dream of an interfaith world at peace ... " [129] (Emphasis added).

Interesting time of year that they chose – like in days of old the sun is again very instrumental and very central in happenings of this kind. Yes, one could say without a doubt that this all is very Babylonian in nature. To the Babylonians of old the sun, moon and stars were very important indeed.

On the 26th of June 2000 the long awaited *United Religions* was officially constituted in Pittsburgh, Pennsylvania in the USA. As planned, the Charter of this Babylonian organization was signed. Coincidental, or maybe not, the signing took place on exactly the same date (day and month) that the United Nations was formed on, 55 years earlier. On this day 'greetings from the United Nations' were also received there.

The media reported on the occurrence as follows:

" ... Participants from six continents who formed a rainbow of nationalities, faiths and spiritual traditions ... [began] a six-day conference at Carnegie Mellon University. ... Drummers from Manipur, India, ... beat out a call to assemble. ... sacred sage was burned <u>to attract the spirits during a ritual earth blessing</u>. ... The mix of Hindu, Jewish, Wicca, Christian, Muslim and other faiths isn't in town only to affirm their differences. The United Religions Initiative prides itself on interfaith partnerships that work to cease religiously motivated violence and other international ills ... " [130] (Emphasis added).

A valid vision, but will it get done this way? Can there be real peace and harmony in this world without the real Christ of Scripture?

These people clearly believe this and a signing ceremony also took place in Pittsburgh:

"With the stroke of his pen, California's Episcopal bishop, the Rev. William Swing, signed off on a dream ... Delegates of the United Religions Initiative joined hands and danced to the music of African and Asian drums ... The initiative will be guided by a board of 24 trustees ... " [131]

(Surely this have nothing to do with the 24 elders of Rev. 4 and 5).

What an absolutely amazing world that we are living in. Never before has the world seen such specific and official moves toward a one world religion. The truth of God's Word has never been so clearly set before our eyes. Yet the majority will never comprehend what is actually happening around them. We are living in tragic times as never before, but also in very exciting times.

The road is now set for the end time Babylon and the Word of God will go into complete fulfillment, that we can be sure of.

THE UN's BIG RELIGIOUS SUMMIT

From August 28-31, 2000, summit talks were held with more than a 1000 religious leaders of all the major religions at the United Nations headquarters in New York.

It is interesting to note that this summit of world religions had a symbol or logo that was almost identical to the one used by the previously discussed United Religions Initiative. They must have the same ultimate goal in mind – a newly formed Babylonian system for the whole world.

Now it becomes quite clear that these different organizations were actually in cooperation all the time.

The following remarks came from delegates who attended the occasion:

> "This Summit of religious leaders, held before the Millennium Summit of world leaders ... is a defining moment for the humanity of the world." (Rabbi Arthur Schneier, *Appeal of Conscience Foundation*). [132]

> "In our different religious traditions <u>we have the answer</u> to conflicts. We are brothers and sisters in

God's human family." (Emphasis added).
(Theodore E. McCarrick, *Archbishop of Newark*). [133]

At the end of the 'religious summit', a document, "Commitment to Global Peace", was submitted and apparently all those present signed it. This document condemns all violence committed in the name of religion. It is sad that so many Christians though, are still being persecuted worldwide. The following closing ceremony was significant:

> "The summit concluded with a ceremony of 'sharing of the waters from around the world." [134]

In Rev. 13:1 we read that the Antichrist will arise from the sea and in Rev. 17:15 we read about the waters that the woman sits on and that it refers figuratively to nations and tongues. Is this mere coincidence?

A NEW WORLD SCRIPTURE

Not only are the religions of the world getting together on a formal basis now, but there are even more things happening in the last days Babylon. That there is a plan under way, cannot be denied anymore. A Babylonian 'bible' has already been put together and where will it go from here.

World Scripture first appeared in 1991 and consists of 928 pages and 4 000 passages. It was compiled from 268 'holy scriptures' and 55 oral traditions. This Babylonian compilation of scriptures had co-workers from all religions – people who were specialists in their field. Presently it is a book to please all tastes and viewpoints. Will it possibly be the ultimate book on which a new era world religion will be based? The compilers of the scripture agree that there are many roads to god. Read what they write in this regard under the heading, 'The Truth in many Paths':

" ... Hinduism, Jainism and Buddhism understand
the various deities to be expressions of a single
Absolute Reality, and the various paths lead to one
Supreme Goal. ... Furthermore, many religions
teach that a nonbeliever, if he does righteousness,
is acceptable before God and will receive a
reward." [135]

According to the Bible however, trusting in good works
can save nobody. Only through the name of Jesus Christ can
you be saved and only if you bow your heart before Him in
repentence of your sins.

SEPTEMBER 11, 2001

The incredible and almost unbelievably tragic events of
September 11, 2001 is still fresh in our memories.

What could this all mean? Many have sought for
answers and pondered this question over and over again. Are
there any specific messages for us in something as terrible
as that? We better believe there are.

God is a God of order and a God of love and therefore
He is a God that warns of coming judgments.

Many Bible researchers agree that the number 11 in the
Bible stands for 'judgment' and 'disorder.'

If one contemplates the events of September 11, 2001 in
New York City, you find some amazing statistics that can be
connected to that bleak day:

- The events took place on the 11th day of September
  2001
- The two towers next to each other had the architectural

appearance of a giant 11
- The first plane that crashed into the first tower, had the number 11
- The plane that crashed into the Pentagon had the number 77 (7x11)
- The state of New York was the 11th state in America that became independent
- Each tower had 110 strories (10x11)
- After September 11 there were still exactly 111 days left till the end of that year
- Furhermore it happened almost exactly 11 years after the start of the infamous Gulf war that incidently also involved Islamic nations, namely Iraq and Kuwait.

Is this a completely unique phenomenon? No, not at all.

The first world war (1914-1918) ended on the 11th hour of the 11th day of the 11th month.

Afterwards, almost everyone thought that real peace was in the air, but far from it. The far worse second world war came shortly thereafter and after that many wars raged even to this day.

In the same way, people who think that they will be saved on the 11th hour must also think again.

Why not come now to settle your case with God through His Son Jesus Christ. Time is certainly running out.

Is it biblical in any way to connect so much meaning to a number, like for example the number 11, as we just did?

In Gen. 9:25 we read about Canaan and how he was cursed of God and how he had exactly 11 sons (Gen. 10:15-18). Connected to this curse, was God's promise to Abraham that his offspring would eventually inherit that beautiful land. It happened exactly like that as well.

In Jer. 52:1,5 we see that Israel was judged by God after the godless king, Zedekiah, reigned only until his 11th year.

The king of Babylon then came to the forefront and Israel was taken into captivity.

In the book of Daniel, in chapter 7:7,8 we read of the ten horns that came from the fourth and last beast that the prophet Daniel saw in that vision. Then we also read about an 11th horn that came forth from amongst the other ten – that of the final Antichrist. Again it stands for God's judgment. Nothing in the Bible is coincidental .

HGH TOWERS HAVE A TENDENCY TO FALL

In the Bible there are quite a few passages that refer to falling towers. Some are prophetic warnings about towers that would fall in times gone by and others warn of future events.

Of course, by far the most well known case of a falling tower, is the tower of Babel. Must be a coincidence that we read about this tower in Gen. 11!

Then we also read about towers in Is. 30:25 and well in the following words: " ... *upon every high mountain, and upon every high hill, rivers and streams of waters in the day of the great slaughter, when the towers fall.*"

This is speaking of the great day of God's wrath that is coming.

In Ezek. 26 we read about the incredible prophecy against the city of Tyre (or Tyrus) - a city by the sea, just like the city of New York is by the sea. The prophecy about the great fall of the city of Tyre came in *"the eleventh year"* (Ezek. 26:1). In verse 4 we read that: " ... *they shall destroy the walls of Tyrus, and break down her towers ... "* and then in verse 9: *"And he shall set engines of war against thy walls, and with his axes he shall break down thy towers."*

Also remember that New York is the city with the great statue in her harbour – the Statue of Liberty – but can this statue really provide liberty in this world?

In Zeph. 1:14-16 we read about the great and awesome day of the wrath of God that is near and about: *"the trumpet and alarm against the fenced cities, and against <u>the high towers</u>"* – (verse 16).

Even in the New Testament do we read of a tower that fell, where people were killed as a result. Jesus Christ Himself spoke of this event and at the same time it served as a warning to bystanders that day, and of course to us that live in the third millennium: *" ... except ye repent, ye shall all likewise perish. Or those eighteen, upon whom the tower in Siloam fell, and slew them, think ye that they were sinners above all men that dwelt in Jerusalem? I tell you, nay: but, except ye repent, ye shall all likewise perish* (Luk. 13:3-5).

What happened in New York is a type of what God always does. This is a set pattern throughout the Bible. The high and exalted works of man – on which man readily trusts – will always come to a fall. The proud human race must be humbled to learn God's ways and then eventually those that trusted only in Him will be exalted at the appointed time.

We must understand clearly that God is always and in all circumstances in complete control despite all that happens on earth. He does, though, give Satan certain freedom to do certain things because of man's rebellion against Him. The devil is of course a very intelligent, though darkened being and he plans certain events to fit his ultimate scenario – his own exaltation. If God let him go for a while and man goes against the will of the Almighty, tragic events take place on earth. Satan though is the murderer of men (Joh. 8:44), and definitely not God.

The New York events also did remind one of the words in Rev. 18:10,11 namely: *"Alas, alas, that great city Babylon, that mighty city! for in one hour is thy judgment come. And the merchants of the earth shall weep and mourn over her; for no man buyeth their merchandise any more"*.

Clearly was this event not the final fulfilment of this prophecy, but still it was a strong type of what can be expected in the near future. It were like two towers of Babel that fell — they always fall. Remember it was the *World Trade Center* that fell — this world is nothing but Babylon!

Most people in Babylon hope only on Mammon, but this idol fails them every time.

Does man ever learn?

The world economy was severely shaken by the events in New York. The *Dow Jones,* situated on Wall Street in New York, has tremendous influence across the whole globe and whenever the Dow falls, other stockmarkets follow suit. Exactly this happened after September 11, 2001.

Several airlines experienced a huge setback. The once mighty *Swissair* was down on the ground and *Sabena* from Belgium suffered badly. Others had to cut back on spendings in a serious way.

After September 11, close to 1.2 trillion US dollars were wiped out in market value. [136]

The Word of God does prophesy about a large scale ecomomic crises in the last days and surely we are moving in that direction now more than ever (Ezek. 7:19; Jas. 5:1-3). Despite these clear and straightforward warnings, most people are getting into debt more and more evey day, and never has there been a time when it was so easy to acquire credit from financial institutions.

Can we see that the almighty God is warning us that this

worldly and thus Babylonian system is on the brink of a great fall? Shall we take heed?

Another great warning came recently and again it is connected to the tragic New York events.

While working away in the rubble of the fallen towers, a man came across something that should make us sit up and take notice, to put it mildly:

> "Buried under tons of World Trade Center steel and rubble, rescue workers found <u>a page from the Bible that spoke of a tower that reached to the heavens</u>. It was a shocking revelation ... said photographer Gary Gere, who found the passage from Genesis, about the Tower of Babel, amid the ruins. 'After more than 93 days of fires, a skinny little frail page from the Bible survived. I find it quite unbelievable,' ... " [137] (Emphasis added).

After the incredible events of September 11, 2001, a cry for more control has gone up. People are afraid for their lives more than before and certain measures are already being taken.

In Florida in the USA, a family decided to get silicon chip implants – the first official implantation of this kind that was also made public through major television news networks and news magazines. Some elderly people also made use of this opportunity as these current chips were mainly developed for people with health risks. This was done in the month of May, 2002, and most definitely one cannot help but to think of the infamous mark that the book of Revelation speaks of in chapter 13. Of course this is not that mark, but could it point to a near future period where similar technology would be implemented to curb terrorism and armed robberies etc.? In news articles about these silicon chips, that are implanted under the skin (by the way), they have supposed over and over again that it could be used very succesfully for exactly the above-mentioned reasons. One article also did mention that within the next few years a micochip that functions with the help of global positioning satellites will be ready for the marketplace. [138]

It could then be used to track people literally anywhere, but of course for the purest of reasons – their 'safety and security'!

One monetary system and currency for the whole world (Babylon?) was also recently proposed by former Nobel peace prize laureate Robert Mundell. This was done at the highest possible level - at an International Monetary Fund (IMF) meeting late in the year 2000. [139]

At the end of 2001, in a United Nations meeting, a singular electronic database for all of humanity was also proposed. [140]

Will all of this help in any way? For a very short period of time maybe – by the initial appearance thereof, but not even this will save Babylon from its final majestic fall and therefore our hope surely can never be in this world.

The last fall of Babylon will be great indeed and time is running out at an alarming rate!

6

ALL ROADS LEAD
TO ROME

During the last two thousand years, the city of Rome continually played a particular and prominent role in the history of the world. It may well be said that this city earned its prominent place on the world map. The question remains however, will the world as we know it (and that of course includes the city of Rome), exist for all eternity? Yes, many do like to call Rome the *eternal city* – a title that the living God actually designated for the one and only Jerusalem. In addition to this, almost everybody knows the two familiar expressions connected to the city of Rome, namely that *'all roads lead to Rome'* and that *'Rome was not built in a day'*. Why did such universal expressions – and those distinctly referring to Rome – remain fixed in the conscience of man? It is something to contemplate. Is the world's eye still directed, perhaps unconsciously, towards Rome and will this city perhaps play a big and important role in the near future?

In Dan. 2 we read of the image that Nebuchadnezzar saw in his dream. Ultimately only Daniel could interpret the dream, as history had proved:

Head of gold – Babylonian empire (end of verse 38)
Breast and arms of silver – Medes and Persians
Belly and thighs of brass – Greek empire
Legs of iron – Roman empire (legs divided approximately 330 AD)
Feet part of iron and part of clay – the revived Roman empire

How do we know that the feet and toes refer to a revived Roman Empire? In Dan. 2:44 we read that *"And in the days of these kings"*, referring to the last kingdom (the Roman Empire – the fourth empire), *"shall the God of heaven set up a kingdom, which shall never be destroyed"*. This is the thousand year empire of Christ that will lead to eternity. Never again will a human government or kingdom reign over the earth. For 6 000 years human efforts failed miserably, but gracefully the Lord will take control and He will at long last ensure true peace and righteousness for ever. The important point to remember is that the Roman Empire reigned after the Greek empire and approximately to 300 AD. After this, the so-called 'Holy Roman Empire' with the Roman Church at the forefront came to power.

Incidentally, did you ever wonder why everybody that are describing the period around 500-1500 AD use the term 'dark middle ages'? If this was the middle ages, then Jesus' birth and crucifixion roundabout the year 0, was the beginning – and we that are living today, 2 000 years later, are living right at the end!! It is true. Christ's first coming to earth was the beginning of the church dispensation and His second coming will end this period.

After the fall of the Roman empire there will never be a

world empire of like sort again. In Dan. 2:45 we read how a stone (The Rock – Jesus) came loose and destroyed the final empire. The words *"in the days of these kings"* are of utmost importance. It will happen in the days of the kings of the Roman empire. This Roman Empire however came to an end hundreds of years ago, how then could Christ take over this empire? There is merely one answer. The Roman Empire will revive shortly before the return of Jesus Christ!

It is exactly what is happening today, at the end of the 20th and the start of the 21st century.

The following groups and organizations played a big part towards the creating of a unified new Europe:

THE EUROPEAN COMMUNITY MARKET

After signing the 'Treaty of Rome' in 1957, the EC and the ECC integrated under the same name, the European Community Market in 1967. It is interesting that it was the year when Israel won the six-day war. The time was right for reviving the old Roman Empire.

THE EUROPEAN PARLIAMENT

This parliament was elected in 1979 for the first time and had its first session in 1980. In 1984, with the second election of the European Parliament, they released a post stamp with a remarkable illustration on it. The stamp illustrated a women riding on a beast. Under the animal, there were seven waves that might also refer to mountains. Read Rev. 17:1-3,9,15. In 1994, 567 members were elected to the parliament, among which many Social democrats and Socialists. In 1999, a new parliament was elected.

THE EUROPEAN UNION

Just over a decade ago, the major news magazine, *Time*, had a long article on the new Europe that was to come. Even the cover told the story. Inside there were many surprises. Clear colour depictions of Europe as a woman on a beast met the reader of this edition. One depiction even had red spots on the beast that supposedly pointed to 'sins' such as *nationalism* and *patriotism*. [141] It appeared that the European Parliament stamp of earlier was not a give away.

The European Union was officially established in November 1993 with the implementation of the Maastrict Agreement. The name stipulates distinctly what they envisaged, namely One Europe. Included in this union are all the European organizations that work for unification. Counted among them are currently 15 countries that are members of the union. The European Union plans expanding rapidly and many other European nations are awaiting membership.

They surely are serious about their future role in the international community:

"The European Union would create a fully fledged foreign service, with its own embassies around the world and an elite training academy, under plans approved by the European Parliament." [142]

The European Union with its initial twelve member states started using the single monetary unit, the Euro, in January 1999. In 2002 other countries in Europe joined them in this monetary union. Most interesting is the symbol of the European Union, as well as the Euro itself. The EU's symbol is twelve stars and the Euro has two sunrays shining into a quarter-moon. In the Roman symbolization of their gods, Jupiter is the sun god, and one of Jupiter's moons is known as his daughter Europa. In Rev. 12:1 we read about a woman dressed with the sun and under her feet is the moon, while she is wearing a crown of twelve stars. This also reminds us of Joseph's dream in Gen. 37:9 when the sun, moon and eleven stars bowed before Joseph. Joseph himself was the twelfth star and it also refers to the twelve sons of Jacob (Israel). The EU wants to govern the city of Jerusalem and Israel exactly like the Roman Empire governed Israel at Jesus' first coming to earth. In Acts 7:42,43 we read that God once gave Israel up to *"took up the tabernacle of Moloch"* (sun and moon worship) and to worship the *"star of your god Remphan"*. What strange star is this?

Today, Europe is mainly Roman Catholic and with its religious wing, it is aiming towards the land of Israel. It is the center of the inhabited world and an ideal venue to govern from.

The EU is moving on thin ice however, their officials making certain very challenging statements. According to EU External Affairs Commissioner, Chris Patten:

> "The European Union needs to be seen 'to do more for itself' on the world stage ... "In the past, people asked God to deliver them from evil." ... "Today they look to international institutions – and in Europe, that means the European Union." [143] (Emphasis added).

What brave, but prophetical words of Patten about what the new European Union actually stands for.

Note the following statement from Henri Spaak, former secretary general of NATO, from a *BBC* documentary on the European Union:

> "we felt like Romans on that day ... We were con-

sciously recreating the Roman Empire once more." [144]

More distinct it cannot be. The *European Union* is without a doubt the Roman Empire revived. Spaak referred with those words to another occurrence in Rome in 1957 – the *Treaty of Rome* that began the whole movement towards the revived Roman Empire officially. Why was this treaty signed in Rome of all places? To bring all into perspective, we now look at what had happened in Rome over the last 40 years:

1957 – Signing of the *Treaty of Rome*
1962 – 2nd *Vatican Council* started in Rome
1968 – *Club of Rome* instituted
1998 – *Statute of Rome* proclaimed

The *Treaty of Rome* was the official start of the political unification of Europe. The 2nd *Vatican Council* was the Roman Catholic Church's attempt to become more acceptable to the Protestant Churches of the world as well as to attract the other religions. The *Club of Rome* was initiated to bring about one world government. The *Statute of Rome* entails the newly founded *International Criminal Court* which was initiated in July 1998 – also in Rome! This court started to function on July 1, 2002. That is not all that Rome has to offer. To think that after all these years Roman Law is still with us in the Western World and even further. If one does not realize the implications of this today, prayer for guidance and wisdom is the only answer.

In Dan. 2:42-43 we read that the final empire before Jesus' return will be the feet and toes. We know in this regard that a person has ten toes – the lowest part on the human body. Most important about this prophecy in the Bible is the following fact. According to the prophet Daniel, this dream of Nebuchadnezzar referred to *"what shall be in the latter days"* (Dan. 2:28). It was clearly not all fulfilled in the days of Daniel or Nebuchadnezzar.

This last human empire on earth will resemble iron and clay that cannot mix. May it possibly refer to Christians (clay) and anti-Christian groups with hardened hearts of iron that will never be one? The Lord said that His children should be like clay in His hands. They with callous hearts, resembling iron, do not want to bow before the living and only God. I believe that it is specifically referring to the intermingling of religions. In Old Testament times the Lord did not want his nation of Israel to marry into the surrounding nations, specifically as a precaution against their heathen religious practices. In a further sense the iron can refer to the Roman Empire and the clay to the nations that do not want to become any part of it. In this sense the Roman Empire of iron will submit the other nations of clay – but just because God will allow it for a short while to fulfill His Word.

In a more concrete and literal way, to put it in these words, the formation of the European Coal and Steel Community in 1951 was the real starting point of the European (new Roman) unity that would follow. Of course the old Roman Empire was known to reign with an iron fist, but would it be any different in the revived Roman Empire?

More specifically, we read about the ten toes of the image of Nebuchadnezzar. In Dan. 7:24 and Rev. 17:12 we get a very distinct impression that ten kings will rise in the time of the end and that they will govern for a period of time with the Antichrist (the beast). For this reason the following piece of information is so astonishing and prove how infallible the biblical prophecies are. On 17 September 1973 the *Club of Rome* released a report with the title, *Regionalized and Adaptive Model of the Global World System."* In this document, this Roman organization divided the current world into ten political/economic zones or 'kingdoms' (as they described it). [145]

If this is not the fulfillment of a Godly prophecy, what is it?

Very recently, shortly before the Millennium Summit of the United Nations that was held in New York (September 2000), even more amazing news came to the front. Note the following:

> "The United Nations will face more peacekeeping failures in the 21st century without major overhaul, <u>according to an international panel</u>. ... The <u>10-member panel</u> did not endorse a United Nations army, but did encourage the 188 UN member states to form several brigade-size forces of 5 000 troops each that could deploy in 30 to 90 days," [146] (Emphasis added).

It is also not the only progression in the direction of the ten possible kings or kingdoms. The UN also began to contemplate expanding their permanent Security Council to ten members!

The following report relates:

> " ... The [UN] Security Council is made up of the <u>five</u> veto-wielding permanent members ... The United States, Britain and France favor <u>adding five new permanent</u> seats – Japan, Germany and one member from Asia, Africa and Latin America, to be selected by their regional groups." [147] (Emphasis added).

Then there will be ten permanent members and it does not seem to differ much from the ten zones the *Club of Rome* had in mind! Currently it is <u>merely a possibility</u> and we cannot ascertain if these ten members are the ten kings of Scripture. It is however very interesting to follow.

THE FOUR BEASTS OF DANIEL 7

In the book of Daniel, chapter 7, we read of four strange looking beasts. They have a strong prophetic significance. These four beasts clearly refer to the Babylonian, Medo-Persian, Grecian and Roman empires of old. It seems though that these beasts could also refer to countries and their rulers (verse 17 says they point to four kings from the earth) that were prominent on the world stage during the 19th and 20th centuries.

- Regarding these beasts we read: *"The first was like a lion"* (verse 4) It may refer to the Babylonian Empire, because their symbol was a lion. I believe it could also refer to Great Britain – yes to imperialistic Britain. The wellknown phrase 'Britannia rules the world' (or the way) certainly meant something. In 1917 England liberated Jerusalem from Turkish rule. Many biblical prophecies have multiple fulfillments and it makes it that more significant. To this day, a lion standing upright, is the emblem of the British Empire. Is it perhaps why verse 4 refers to the lion as: *"lifted up from the earth, and made stand upon the feet as a man"* (the British Lions rugby team, representative of all the British Islands, is well-known to many). In Rev. 13:2 the final beast has a mouth like a lion – does he perhaps speak English? Today it is the international language!

The words in Dan 7:4 is very insightful in other ways as well. The lion had wings like that of an eagle, but it was plucked. America's emblem is the eagle – also on the dollar notes. America did stand under Britain's rule at one stage!

- The second beast is *"like to a bear"* (verse 5) and can refer to Russia. This land has been known under the symbol of the great red bear for quite some time. Communist Russia captured many countries with their Marxist ideologies. Under the cruel Stalin they expanded widely. In 1917 the Bolshevist revolution changed Russia forever.

- The third beast is *"like a leopard"* (verse 6) and could refer to Germany. To this day, the leopard or 'panther' is to be seen on products in Germany. Some of their war armory also carries this emblem, like for example, the famous German *Panther* tank that was used in the second world war. Since the 1960's a German company, Krauss-Maffei, also manufactured the *Leopard I* tank and they are still manufacturing the *Leopard II* tank. In March of 2001 Germany used some of them in the war in Macedonia as "two Leopard tanks were ordered to move to Macedonia from the Prizren barracks in Kosovo. The Bild newspaper reports ... that tank units in Germany have been placed on 24-hour alert." [148]

Further, we may ask: Who will ever forget Hitler? It was 1939 – 1945! The leopard in the prophecy incidentally has four heads. Was Hitler's Germany not the infamous 'Third Reich'. Some are already speaking of a 'Fourth Reich'. Rev. 13:1,2 continues with this vision.

- The fourth beast is *"dreadful and terrible, and strong*

exceedingly ... it was diverse from all the beasts that were before it; and it had ten horns." (verse 7). Could this beast at least partially refer to something like the United Nations, that was founded as a 'peace organization' in 1945? Many would say never. This organization though, was initiated after World War II, in which the previous one, Germany, was instrumental. In verse 23 we see that the fourth beast "*shall devour the whole earth, and shall tread it down, and break it in pieces.*" Although the UN is presently working for peace in the world, the situation could change drastically at anytime. The UN is not a Christian institution at all. The Prince of peace, Jesus Christ, is not the One they are looking up to. The UN is currently busy assembling a world military force that could use their power to subdue all that would not comply with the so-called New World Order. The fourth kingdom is indeed diverse from the previous three. Interestingly enough the fourth kingdom also includes the previous three. Britian (or the United Kingdom), Russia and Germany form part of the UN. Germany is also the main player in the European Union (especially in the process towards a full European Monetary Union – the European Central Bank is situated in Frankfurt) and Russia and the United Kingdom are almost part of it. The UN, EU and NATO could have much to do with this amazing prophecy. Also remember that the revived Roman Empire will probably reign the whole known world of our day. The UN (or its successor) and the new Roman Empire could thus eventually be the same kingdom at the end.

The three beasts (the kingdoms with their leaders) do not govern the world today, but these countries remain active to this day. It is precisely what Dan. 7:12 says: "*As concerning* *the rest of the beasts, they had their dominion taken away: <u>yet their lives were prolonged for a season and time</u>.*" Only the Lord will know when that time will come to an end.

The fourth beast has ten horns (as Daniel saw it – Dan. 7:7). The 'Club of Rome' has already divided the world, as we know it, into ten zones or regions. In Dan. 7:24 we see that the ten horns refer to ten kings. From the fourth beast (that is referred to as a kingdom in this verse) will these ten kings eventually arise.

If we return to Dan. 7:8 we read the following amazing words: "*I considered the horns, and, behold, there came up among them another little horn, before whom there were three of the first horns plucked up by the roots: and, behold, in this horn were eyes like the eyes of man, and a mouth speaking great things*." Here Daniel clearly speaks of the coming Antichrist!

A GREAT LEADER FOR THE NEW EUROPE?

Plans are now also underway to elect a new president for Europe by 2005 - 2006. He is supposed to be the EU's 'face in international affairs':

> "France and Britain joined forces ... to demand the creation of a powerful new president of the European Council ... The goal is to give Europe a high-profile political leader, who would also serve as the European Union's face in international affairs and take a key role in developing defence and foreign policies." [149]

THE SPIRITUAL WING

A major movement like the European Union surely cannot function solely as a political entity. They need a religious arm to further their dream and they have one that grasps the vision.

The Roman Church's role in this whole process is under-estimated. The Pope has suggested many times that he want to contrive unity between the Catholics and the Protestants and at the same time the Vatican is part of the unification process in Europe.

The revived Roman Empire will thus most probably be Christian in appearance.

In 1997 a special television program about the new Europe and its spiritual partner was aired worldwide. Note the following:

> "The television program 'Europe and John Paul II' ... will be transmitted throughout the world in a unified satellite coverage ... from Rome's City Hall and from Brussels, ... The occasion for the transmission is the 40th anniversary of the Treaty of Rome. ... Participants also included representatives of the European Commission, the European parliament, the Italian government and Rome's City Council." [150] (Emphasis added).

Here one can again clearly see the importance of the 1957 Treaty of Rome in the unification process of Europe.

In the year 2000, the Vatican had a whole project running regarding the city of Rome – which according to them will relive – in our age!

One reads the following about Rome on one of their main Internet web pages under the heading, *Vatican Exhibit*:

> " ... The City Reborn – How the City Came Back to Life – Rome now is one of the grandest cities in

<u>the world</u>. Millions of pilgrims and tourists come every year to admire, and be awed by, its treasures of architecture, art and history." [151] (Empasis added).

The Word of God is true – indeed! The new or revived Roman Empire's religious wing though, is aiming way further than merely Europe. The Vatican has Jerusalem in mind – they have long held the belief that they are the new Israel of God.

The Pope views matters as follows:

"Pope John Paul II ... urged creation of a special international status for holy sites of Jerusalem, ... [and] urged the power brokers "<u>not to overlook the importance of the spiritual dimension of the city of Jerusalem</u>." ... only a special statute, internationally guaranteed, can effectively preserve the most sacred areas of the Holy City," [152]

The Roman Pope has many friends in and around Jerusalem and his dream of an international Jerusalem is not far fetched at all. Chances are great that his church could play an important part in setting up a climate of peace in Jerusalem as well as on the much sought after temple mount area. The question is though, will there be real and lasting peace without the intervention of our Lord Jesus Christ?

Will this peace come through man-made relations? In May 1999 the Pope conversed with three Muslim leaders in the Vatican. At one stage, he kissed the Koran (their holy book). This was apparently broadcasted more than once on Iraqi television. [153]

It is not that strange, as the new *Catholic Catechism* of the Catholic Church, 1994, point 841, declares that this

Church and Islam worship the same deity. The deception in the world is far greater than many can conceive. That is why Christ warned us so drastically agaits deception in Mt. 24:4 and 11.

The Church of Rome and her Pope is also busy uniting with the other religions of the world and in a serious manner. In 1986 and again in 1999 leaders of all the major religions (even snake worshipers) were invited to Rome for joint times of prayer.

On January 24, 2002 the Pope again took the stage as the great leader of the world's faiths, to unite 200 religious leaders from vodoo priests to 'protestant clergy' for the sake of bringing forth the ever illusive 'era of peace.' The incredible inspired words of the Holy Bible that we find in 1 Thessalonians 5:3 was (as expected) not read at this gathering. The truth thereof would just be to revealing: *"For when they shall say, Peace and safety; then sudden destruction cometh upon them,"* As one could have expected, the terrible events of September 11th, 2001, was a great motivator for this 'urgent (Babylonian) gathering.' The magnificent prophetic Word of God though new all about this, since events of this kind was already prophesied thousands of years ago. The Bible clearly states that this type of event would be the order of the day in the endtime – shortly before the blessed return of our Lord Jesus Christ. [154]

During the recent Religious Summit at the United Nations, at the end of August 2000, the Church of Rome also played an essential role.

The Vatican's main representative there was the Cardinal Francis Arinze, president of their 'Pontifical Council for Inter-religious Dialogue.' He said the following regarding the occasion:

"Collaboration between people of all the religions

of the world is needed for the proper motivation of hearts and consciences. <u>Pope John Paul II gives a personal example as a promoter of reconciliation and harmony between peoples of different religions</u>, cultures and languages." [155] (Emphasis added).

The Pope himself was not present, but he sent a letter to the meeting:

"In a written statement, Pope John Paul II said that 'It is a sign of hope when religious and spiritual leaders can say to the world <u>with one voice</u> that peace is possible, ... <u>I assure all the participants that I am spiritually close to them</u> as they seek to promote the good of the whole human family." [156] (Emphasis added).

One has to realize that the Pope sees himself and his Church as much greater than any global interreligious body of whichever sort. The religions of the world will have to bow before him if they want to co-operate with them on a high level. This is precisely what is going to happen. The role of Rome in international religious affairs was never more prominent than it is today.

The new single Europe with their spiritual capital Rome is then actually working towards a new inclusive type of religion that can be called nothing other than Babylonian. This is exactly what the Bible foretold would happen towards the end. Few, incidently, see the coming fall of this system, because few really believe the whole Bible.

THE WORLD NOW DEVOTED TO 'MARY'

On October 7 and 8 of the year 2000 the Roman Church held a big Marian jubilee in Rome. They started by praying the so-called 'Rosary' in honour of the deceased Mary.

This prayer prayed with a string of beads, dates back from the old Babylonian religions. Prayers to the deceased and to statues were very common then – as it is today. According to Deut. 18:10 this is an abomination to the living God.

The Vatican reported on the big occasion as follows:

"Pope John Paul and 1, 500 bishops from around the world who are celebrating their Jubilee were joined in St. Peter's Square ... by tens of thousands of priests, religious and lay faithful to pray the rosary. ... Before the Holy Father entered the square to begin the Marian prayer [a prayer to the statue], he processed through St. Peter's Basilica with the statue of Our Lady of Fatima ... The statue of Our Lady was placed on a pedestal in the square. ... " [157] (Emphasis added).

These events are amazing but also saddening as one knows that God forbids this practice in the strongest way.

On the 8th of October the Pope complied with the long awaited wish of many Catholics when he devoted the whole world to 'Mary'. The prayer to Mary was shocking - if we recall that Jesus Christ already died for us on the cross and through His death and resurrection, ensured salvation for each one who believes on Him.

The following are from that prayer:

" ... you are the Immaculate One, through you there shines the fullness of grace. Here, then, are your children, gathered before you at the dawn of the new millennium. The Church today, through the voice of the Successor of Peter, in union with

so many Pastors assembled here from every corner of the world, <u>seeks refuge in your motherly
protection</u> ... <u>O Mother, intercede for us,</u> ... <u>We
entrust to you all people,</u> ... <u>To you, Dawn of
Salvation, we commit our journey through the
new Millennium</u>." [158] (Emphasis added).

How sad that these praises that should only be bestowed
on our Saviour and Lord, Jesus Christ, are given to his
earthly mother who died a normal death and was buried two
millennia ago.

In the days of Babylon of old, a woman that was called
the queen of heaven, was also adored and prayed to in this
same manner (Jer. 7:18; 44:19). The current Mary is also
called the queen of heaven by many and this Babylonian
title is even given to her in official Marian prayers!

In the last days Babylon, all roads indeed lead to Rome.

7

A WEEK HAS SEVEN DAYS

"for in six days the LORD made heaven and earth, the sea, an all that in them is and rested the seventh day" (Ex. 20:11)

The verse above confirms that Gen. 1 distinctly points to the fact that God had completed His creation in six literal days (of 24 hours each) and that He put aside the seventh day to rest (later more on the literal nature of the 24 hour day). As a result a week was born.

Seven days was a period fixed by God, during which He composed a whole creation - and completed it with a day of rest. *Seven days* is a term of completion and fulfillment in God's eyes. It includes work and rest, but in the fixed borders of time. We would be able to say that eternity is not part of this fixed time of seven days or in other words, a completed week. God created time and is therefore in no way in submission to it. He fixed the end and beginning of time before time even commenced (Is. 46:9,10).

There are various other places in Scripture were the number seven is found. It appears that God attaches a very special meaning to this number. In Ps. 12:6 we read: *"The words of the LORD are pure words: as silver tried in a furnace in the earth, purified <u>seven times</u>."*

The living God could have chosen any other number to prove the perfection of His Word, but He did not. In His supreme wisdom though, He chose the number seven. One day we will fully understand and we will stand in awe before His almighty and majestic plan.

This number appears all over the Old Testament and refers to completion and conclusion. The people of Israel had to walk around Jericho once each day for six days, and *seven* times on the *seventh* day before they conquered the city. *Seven* priests with *seven* rams' horns had to walk in front, blowing their trumpets as they went around (Josh. 6:15,16).

In the book of Revelation we find more than a few references to the number seven. Is it because this book is the completion and conclusion of the whole Word of God? In this book we read that Jesus Christ is the *Alpha* and the *Omega*. The One that began all and will end all on earth – before the commencement of the new heaven and new earth.

He is not the incarnated Word by pure chance (Jn. 1:14). In Rev. 1:4 we read that the book was written to the *seven* churches of Asia, and the *seven* Spirits before God's throne are also mentioned. We read that Jesus Christ is standing in the midst of *seven* candlesticks (Rev. 1:12,13). *Seven* seals are opened, *seven* trumpets are blown, and *seven* angels cast *seven* vials of God's wrath on the earth's inhabitants. Seven is therefore also the perfect number when it comes to the judgments of the Lord. The sins of the human race need to and shall be punished righteously– precisely what they deserve, they will receive. If one rejects Jesus Christ, it is an absolute rejection. That is why these punishments for sin (even on earth) will in a certain sense be complete. God is a God of a distinctly, fine and measured order and nothing happens outside His designated plan.

Nature reveals His Godly order and how He keeps it every day. Even here the number seven is very prominent.

The time period in which the eggs of different birds hatch, is also in multiples of seven: chickens – 21 days (three 7's); canaries – 14 days (two 7's) etc. The same principle applies to animals: house cats – 56 days (eight 7's); lions – 98 days (fourteen 7's). The spectrum of light also consists of seven colours (recall the colours of the rainbow). There are also seven notes in an octave (A-G). The first and eighth notes are in essence the same. A new life thus begins at the end of a cycle of seven. In spite of this, there are very few who want to accept God's Word and bow themselves before Him. He however planned everything – also man's free will, and all is intertwined in His perfect eternal agenda.

SEVEN DAYS – SEVEN THOUSAND YEARS

"But, beloved, be not ignorant of his one thing, that one day is with the Lord as a thousand years, and a thousand years as one day." (2 Pet. 3:8)

Unfortunately, this one matter evades many of the beloved and many are ignorant of this truth. If people are told that the second coming is near, this verse is quickly cited as proof that one cannot know anything about the approximate timing of the Lord's coming, 'because this biblical time frame has little or no value to the Lord at all' and because many think that a day in the eyes of the Lord can just as well point to a million years or even to eternity.

They forget that He is the Creator of time. In Dan. 11:35

we read that the end will come at: " … *a time appointed.*"
God's time frame is a set one and it will not be altered.

The entire 2 Pet. 3 portrays the second coming. In verse
1 and 2 Peter urges the beloved that he is writing this "*second epistle*" to them to urge them to have "*pure minds*" and
to be "*mindful of the words which were spoken before by the
holy prophets.*" Presently, few heed the words of the holy
prophets of old. Many maintain: 'the old testament is not
applicable today.' We will however, in near future, realize
how applicable the Old Testament remains for our modern
society.

The Old Testament prophets, in many places, wrote and
prophesied about the return of Christ and the time thereafter.
Peter reminded his beloved of these passages. In verse 3 and
4, he warns about the scoffers that " … *shall come in the last
days*" and who shall ask, "*Where is the promise of his coming?*" There are many today who hold to the belief that
everything is the same as "*from the beginning of creation*".
People use this argument to explain that we will not know
when the second coming is near, as everything always
remains the same. This while the Word indicates this viewpoint to be false and misleading. In verse 8 we read that one
day is like a thousand years and shortly thereafter in verse 9:
"*The Lord is not slack concerning His promise, as some men
count slackness.*" We have to read this entire part in context
and the meaning will become very clear. The fact that a day
and a thousand years are compared, is a sign that the second
coming will not take place in the far future (without someone expecting it). It is a specific instruction to the beloved
not to remain in the dark regarding this day. It corresponds
completely with 1 Thes. 5:6. That is why Peter says in all
earnestness: "*be not ignorant of this one thing*" He warns
them to not expect the second coming only in a million
years' time. Satan desires this though, because then many
will not convert themselves to the Lord. Man likes to post-

pone matters. In addition, those reborn has to prepare themselves to meet the Lord. They need to live with pure hearts and walk in holiness before God, as verse 14 of the same chapter alludes to.

This verse then is rather a prophetic revelation through which many other parts of Scripture could be interpreted. The Lord wants to teach us that a day is like a thousand years for Him. He created the earth in seven days (which includes the day of rest) and that is why it may be like seven thousand years to Him. Why should this be the case? What does He want to teach us through this? In six days + one day God completed all of creation. In the same way the entire history of man will come to an end in six days + one day. God worked for six days, in the same way man will work for six thousand years – because of the fall of man. God rested one day and man will rest for one thousand years.

Prophetically speaking, seven days are thus equivalent to seven thousand years – in the eyes of the Lord.

Are there other places in Scripture that can confirm this? Yes, Heb. 4:4 reads *"For he spake in a certain place of the seventh day on this wise, And God did rest on the seventh day from all his works"*

A few verses further, in verse 9 and 10 we read: *"There therefore remaineth a rest to the people of God. For he that is entered into his rest, he also hath ceased from his own works, as God did from his."*

The book of Hebrews was directed specifically and in the first place to the Jews (the Hebrews). They are the literal nation of God, which of course does not mean that they are all perfect or are all going to heaven just because of this truth. It is rather about the fact that Christ, the Light of the world, was given to the world through them. They have to be converted to Christ the same as everybody else has to. God did not however reject them finally and completely and the church surely did not replace them. The above quoted words refer on one level to the literal people of Israel, but clearly it also refers to the church of Christ (the spiritual people of God). We know further that the above mentioned verses does not speak of one literal day of 24 hours (as verses 9 and 10 clearly indicate). Here, prophetically speaking the seventh day, the Sabbath, can point to the thousand years of peace or the millennium that we read about in Rev. 20 and in many other places in the Word.

The reborn Jews (Zech. 13:1,8,9) will enter the thousand years (the seventh day) and will govern from Israel with Christ (Zech. 8:22,23). In a similar way, the church (though in glorified bodies) will also govern as kings with Christ during this time.

Thereafter the eighth day – the 'day' of eternity will arrive.

There is more confirmation from Scripture that a day is like a thousand years before the Lord. In Ps. 90:4 we read: *"For a thousand years in thy sight are but as yesterday when it is past, and as a watch in the night"*

The fact that a night watch is mentioned here in connection with a time of a thousand years, is very insightful and certainly not accidental at all. A night watch alludes to a time of being on guard and on watch in the night. The watchman does not sleep but is seriously watching and guarding for himself and for others. In Mt. 24:43,44 we read: *"But know this, that if the goodman of the house had known in what watch the thief would come, he would have watched, and would not have suffered his house to be broken up. Therefore be ye also ready: for in such an hour as ye think not the Son of man cometh."*

Is it not the Lord Jesus who will come like a thief in the night?

We also read in Lk. 21:36 *"Watch ye therefore, and pray always, that ye may be accounted worthy to escape all these things that shall come to pass, and to stand before the Son of man.*" It means to acknowledge the signs of His coming and to persist in prayer so that you will be ready and others will be ready as well.

Psalm 90 is a key Psalm in coming to describe the end of time. In verse 12 we read the words that definitely correlates with what was already mentioned: "*So teach us to number our days, that we may apply our hearts in wisdom.*" Will we take it seriously and comprehend that seven days refer to seven thousand years? Will we apply our hearts in wisdom?

In the following verse (13) we read that the Psalm writer asks: "*Return, O Lord, how long?*" – could this be about the second coming of the Lord and on how long we have to wait till that blessed day! That the Psalms reveal much about the last days is not a strange phenomenon! We have to remember that Jesus Christ Himself said "*that all these things must be fulfilled, which were written in the law of Moses, and in the prophets, and in the psalms, concerning me.*" (Lk. 24:44). That includes His return!

Shall we calculate then where we stand today in context with this biblical schedule? Shall we number our days?

THE DAY OF ADAM

We know that Adam lived to the ripe age of 930 years (Gen. 5:5). Is it then not significant that God warned Adam in all earnestness not to eat of the tree in the middle of the garden, "*for in the day that thou eatest thereof thou shalt surely die.*" (Gen. 2:17). Adam did eat of the fruit, but did not die literally on the same day. He did die spiritually however. We already know that one day is like a thousand years before God and that is why we can understand the prophetic significance that Adam died before the end of that day (thousand years) at the age of 930 years. God's Word came to be true again. It is interesting that Adam missed the thousand-year mark by only seventy years. Is it not perhaps why we read in Ps. 90:10 that *"The days of our years are three-score years and ten"* (70 years). It is a good average today. The years Adam lived, we now complete in a certain sense to one day – a thousand years.

SIX DAYS – SIX THOUSAND YEARS

According to biblical chronology, six thousand years have passed since Adam. It may be calculated as follows:

Adam to Abraham – 2 000 years; Abraham to Christ – 2 000 years; Christ to today – about 2 000 years. Thus approximately 6 000 years of human history have passed till now.

How do we know this? The exact ages of all the earliest forefathers (from Adam onwards) and their generations are stipulated in the Bible and numerous individuals have calculated it to be roundabout 4 000 years untill the birth of Christ. Since then a further 2 000 years have been completed, bringing the total to 6 000 years of human history thus far. One person who did research on this was an Anglican Bishop, James Ussher. He made his calculations during the 17th century, in which he lived. It cannot be calculated up to the precise day or date, but God also said in His Word that we would not know the precise day and hour of His return.

It is also very interesting to note that many of the old church fathers held to a similar belief in the first few centuries after Christ.

The *Schaff-Herzog Encyclopedia* (Part III, pp. 1514, 1515) confirms that Justin Martyr, Irenaeus, Eusebius, Papias, Ignatius, Lactantius, Victorinus and others firmly believed that there would be six thousand years of human governance, followed by a thousand years of peace under the guidance of Christ the King. The encyclopedia explains: "The general belief among the fathers was that the Lord would appear at the end of the sixth millennium. The ancient belief was, that this final kingdom, that correlates with the Sabbath of the creation, would be a thousand years." This then refers to the thousand years of peace of Rev. 20. The *New Schaff-Herzog Encyclopedia of Religious Knowledge* also mentions that: "The early fathers most commonly looked for the second advent at the end of 6000 years of the world's history." [159]

We also read what Irenaeus specifically said regarding this viewpoint:

> "For in so many days as the world was made, in so many thousand years shall it be concluded ... and God brought to a conclusion upon the sixth day the works He made ... This is an account of the things formerly created, as also it is a prophecy of what is to come ... in six days created things were completed: It is evident, therefore, that they will come to an end after six thousand years." [160]

Barnabas also wrote the following in his epistle:

> " ... in six thousand years the Lord God will bring all things to an end ... in six days, that is, in six thousand years, shall all things be accomplished." [161]

Today we are living at the end of that 6 000 years!

The Word of God, in numerous places, make prophetic statements that point to the time of the end. Some can be observed and noticed more openly and some are more concealed – at the first look! In this way the whole issue of six days being like six thousand years in the eyes of God is also referred to more than once in the Bible. It is not conspicuous that most of the time one reads certain passages and words in the Bible, you will at first not attach any deeper or prophetic meaning to it. It is also the case with the issue that we have been dealing with so far. We read in Mk. 9:1-13 of Jesus' transfiguration on the mountain. The passage starts with the words: "*And after six days Jesus taketh with him Peter, and James, and John, and leadeth them up into a high mountain apart by themselves: and he was transfigured before them. And his raiment became shining, exceeding white as snow; so as no fuller on earth can white them.*" (verses 1-3).

These words "*after six days*" have no other distinct meaning than its reference to the end of human government on earth. Very notable is that Jesus took three of His disciples with Him to a high mountain. It surely refers to His second coming at the end of the six thousand years. Jesus was transfigured there and in like manner Moses and Elijah also appeared to them (verse 4). They had glorified bodies which points to a special time in future. In 1 Cor. 15:53 we read that the children of the Lord will also undergo a transfiguration at the last trumpet when Christ will again appear with us. We will be clothed with immortality and then ascend to meet the Lord in the air (also see Phil. 3:21).

On the mountain of the transfiguration Peter surprisingly enough wanted to built them each a tabernacle (verse 5). If one comprehends that the Feast of Tabernacles of the Old Testament is a shadow of the thousand years of peace or coming millennium, everything becomes even more apparent (Col. 2:16,17 – please read these verses!)

Here Jesus and His disciples went up the mountain at the end of six days and Peter wanted Jesus' earthly Kingdom to commence immediately. Peter however did not realize that the time for it had not arrived yet. He did not understand that there had to be a church dispensation of two thousand years before this glorious time would come.

In Zech. 14:16 we read regarding the thousand years of peace, that the people remaining on earth after the big war of Armageddon, will proceed year after year to attend the Feast of Tabernacles in Jerusalem. This seventh 'day' follows 'six days'. Are the Scriptures not absolutely amazing? Or is it all too much to believe?

HOW OLD IS THE EARTH?

If one keeps all this in mind, the question regarding the age of the earth definitely comes to the front. If the historical time of human government on earth is a mere six thousand years, how can the earth be millions or billions of years old? The earth then should only be six thousand years old as well, or is that impossible? It is not at all what is being reported in the media each day, but the evidence is overwhelming. Let us look at this very important issue now.

We regularly hear about excavations of 'prehistoric animals' and even 'prehistoric men' that should have 'lived' hundreds of thousands of years ago. Archaeologists and other scientists use different methods to calculate the age of these fossils. One of the most familiar methods used, is the C-14 (carbon 14) test. This and other radiometric dating methods have been proven – on numerous occasions - to be so unreliable that it cannot be taken seriously. The media, however, will never report on these fiascos. The problem remains that man does not want to believe in God in general. That is why he is continually busy searching for methods to prove the Bible as fallible and that the living God is not the Creator of all and everything. This, sinful humanity does, to try and avoid the very awkward situation that will face each human being at the end of their life – that of standing before a holy and righteous God to give account of the life that he lived here on earth.

If man can disprove the existence of an almighty God, it

automatically will excuse him from all responsibilities before such a Lord and God. If however, there truly is a God who created man personally, then this God have the right to direct man in the way which he is to live on this earth that was also created by Him. Then man can also expect to be judged for not adhering to God's laws and rules. It is the last thing the fallen and unregenerate human being wants to know about. For this reason he has been busy right throughout the ages to put to doubt what had been written in the holy Scriptures and to explain God's non-existence through 'scientific knowledge'. It is however, a fatal game that man will have to pay dearly for. Most people are familiar with the theory of evolution as perpetuated by Charles Darwin. Many Christians will immediately confirm that they do not agree with the theory. They do believe that God created man, but they do not really believe everything that has been written in the Bible. 'Everything cannot be understood so literally' they usually will say. A new theory has thus been developed, one with which almost everybody will have no real problems. You just take a little bit of biblical truth and mix it with a good dose of 'scientific knowledge' and there you have it: 'Theistic evolution'.

They take the Satanically inspired evolution theory and include God in it. They take a theory from the world and add God and there they have a 'Christian' theory. In the same manner people take 'rock music' from the world, writes Christian words for it and then have 'Christian rock music'. You take something Satan offers and Christianize it – give it a Christian colour or adorn it in Christian attire. Then you please both God and the world, man thinks. Unfortunately, this is totally outside God's will. The Word says: "*whosoever therefore will be a friend of the world is the enemy of God.*" (Jas. 4:4) and Rom. 12:2 also warns: "*be not conformed to the world*".

Man has to make choices at all times, but to compromise with the world is never a wise decision. It remains foreign words though for someone who does not know the Lord. The problem with 'theistic evolution' is that it is a lie from the heart of the father of lies. This theory declares that there was a big bang, but guess what, God started it. The almighty God created everything in this manner – they say. God started the evolutionary process and now that we have passed the year 2000, the next step is just around the corner. The next stage for the human is apparently divinity. It correlates 100% with the new age theory.

Everybody who believes in theistic evolution also believes that God made the earth in billions of years. The biblical description of creation in six literal days is thus rejected. These people loose sight of the fact that God created the entire creation through His Word. If one starts to engage in these things, it gets dangerous. Jesus Christ is the Word and in Jn. 1:3 we read: "*All things were made by him, and without him was not anything made that was made.*" God thus created everything through Jesus Christ (the Word). He uttered a word and something was there. If you now suggest that the days of creation, mentioned in the book of Genesis, do not refer to ordinary days, but to different ages of a few million years each, the divinity of Jesus Christ is questioned. If His divinity is questioned, then His shed blood on Calvary was not sufficient to save us from our sins.

This whole issue is of far more importance than it initially appears. Any evolution theory (theistic evolution included) is a direct attack on Jesus Christ and the gospel of salvation. God's Word create and recreate immediately and not over long indefinite periods.

Man does not improve over time until he becomes worthy to enter heaven. One is rather born-again in one moment through the work of God's Holy Spirit and your name – at that moment – is written in the Book of Life. This is, of course, if you believe unequivocally that Jesus Christ died for you on the cross and that He was resurrected from the dead – because it really happened that way.

The other problem with the misguided viewpoint that each day of creation could account for millions of years, is so logical and clear that it is almost mystifying how those highly educated could overlook this fact.

If each creation day was pointing to a time of a million years or more, how could the insects have pollinated the flowers that were already created on day three? The winged creatures (surely insects included) were only created on day five. How could the plants and flowers that were only created on day three use the process of photosynthesis and thus exist for 'millions of years' when the sun was only created on day four? In addition, Adam was created on day six, he thus lived through day six and seven, and long thereafter, but he only came to be 930 years old. God's Word remains wonderful and humans with their worldly 'wisdom' will always be rendered foolish in comparison to the wisdom of the eternal Word.

What does it have to do with the age of the earth? Excavations of human and animal fossils apparently 'prove' that the earth is millions or billions of years old. If the earth was created in six literal days of 24 hours each (as the Bible teaches – we regularly read the words: "*And the evening and the morning were the first [second,third ...] day*" etc.), then the basis of the theory of evolution is already crumbling. The rest that proponents of evolution believe, is utterly dubious, to say the least. Still, the masses believe almost everything that is presented to them in the name of 'science'.

Then of course there is the 'gap theory', about a possible gap between Gen. 1:1 and Gen. 1:2. Supposedly, this gap then accounts for the millions or billions of years before the 'final creation' or the one mentioned in Scripture. Today however, there are just too much scientific evidence that the earth is in fact very young and the evidence increases almost day by day. The whole issue of dinosaurs that supposedly lived 'millions' of years ago is to this day merely a theory. They did live of course, but in the pre-flood era.

The case of the coelacanth (fish) of which quite a few discoveries have been recorded during the 20th century, is a very interesting one to look at. This while they were supposed to have become extinct around 60 millions years ago.

Following below are just some of the logical and scientific reasons why the earth cannot be older than 10 000 years, but quite possibly not even older than 6 000 years.

1. Comets disintegrate too rapidly.

Every time a comet nears the sun, it loses enormous amounts of matter. If comets are as old as the solar system (as evolutionists suppose), then everything is much younger than is generally accepted. Many comets do not have a lifespan even touching on 10 000 years. [162]

2. Too little mud on the ocean floor.

To assert that the earth is a few billion years old is a wild guess. Every year a certain amount of mud is deposited onto the ocean floor and it does not fit in with the evolutionists' theory. [163]

3. Too little sodium in the sea.

Rivers and other sources continuously supply the sea with sodium and the amounts measured per annum, prove that the sea is not that old. [164]

4. Earth's magnetic field loses energy too rapidly.

Because of this the magnetic field cannot be older than 10 000 years, possibly younger. [165]

5. Too few human skeletons from the Stone Age are being excavated.

Evolutionists are of the impression that the Stone Age continued for at least 100 000 years. It means that about 4 billion people from that time should have been buried. Excavations however prove that a lot less people have been buried during that time and it prove that that time period was much shorter. [166]

6. Recorded history is much too recent.

History was first recorded from 4 000 – 5 000 years ago. Why would people from the Stone Age, that made numerous rock-engravings, not also leave behind their own history (on rock) for the following generations? Why would these people have lived for nearly 100 000 years (according to the evolutionists) and then only started to engrave their own history 4 000 years ago? [167]

This is not all. There is more evidence that the time of human history is merely 6 000 years old. Recently archaeologists of the University of Chicago discovered a wall in a city in the northeast of Syria. They are of the impression that the city can be no older than 6 000 years and this is the oldest city wall ever discovered! [168] Why have there no other cities been discovered from earlier periods? Why was this one discovered in Syria of all places (the Middle East – confirming the Biblical timeline)? Why were these cities discovered between the Tigris and Euphrates – where the first people lived according to the Bible? Until this discovery the oldest cities discovered were in average about 4000 years old – surely not in the region of 100000 years.

7. Too little cosmic dust on the earth.

Every year a few million tons of cosmic dust descend from the atmosphere to the earth. If the earth is 4.5 billion years old as the evolutionists maintain, the dust should have been many feet deep on the earth. Where is all the dust?

8. Coal does not take long to form.

Some wooden bridges built in 1870, was found to be very close to real coal in the mid 1950's when it was removed. Coal does not take millions of years to form. [169]

9. The rapid erosion of Niagara waterfall.

The slopes on the top of this waterfall erode at a tempo of more or less 7 ft per year. The ravine formed by the fall is currently about 7 miles or 36 000 feet long. A simple calculation shows that this waterfall cannot be older than 5 000 years. It fits in 100% with the time of Noah's flood as described in the Bible. This waterfall is as a result surely not millions of years old.

10. Sediment in the Grand Canyon points to a young age.

If the Colorado river is 10 million years old (as evolutionists believel), the river would have moved enough sediment through the Grand Canyon to cover the whole California under miles of sand and slime. Quite clearly, this has not been the case.

11. Earth's population increases too rapidily.

If one takes the current population of the earth and calculates it back by halving it every 170 years (a fair average), it fits in very well with the time since Noah's flood. About 4 300 years ago 8 people survived the flood and the current world population could easily have come from those 8 people. On the other hand, if you believe that humans and their 'predecessors' have been on the earth for hundreds of thousands of years, then we would have had a few million people per square meter on the earth's surface. Where are all the people?

12. Radio metric dating methods are extremely suspicious.

There are some interesting cases that prove distinctly that the radio-metric methods of dating cannot be taken seriously. This type of dating information can never ever be promoted above the Scripture. In 1980 the Mount St. Helens volcano erupted spectacularly in the USA. This mountain was volcanically active until 1986. Numerous samples of the molten lava were analyzed in 1996 (10 years later) by the Geochron laboratory in Cambridge, Massachusets. They wanted to ascertain the solidification period of the particular rock. The ages were affirmed to be between 350 000 and 2.8 million years. This for rock that was still molten merely ten years before. [170]

Many people from our day and age are addicted to numbers and figures. They enjoy speaking in terms of millions or billions. It sounds impressive and great. Scientific knowledge is used for the good in the world, but if the human being does not want to believe in God's Word, he devises for himself his own inventions and calls it science in order to sidestep the Lord. Unfortunately, this is futile. In 1 Cor. 1:20 we read clearly: "*hath not God made foolish the wisdom of this world*". Paul writes to Timothy in 1 Tim. 6:20,21: "*O Timothy, keep that which is committed to thy trust, avoiding profane and vain babblings, and oppositions of <u>science falsely so called</u>:*

Which some professing have erred concerning the faith."

Science is merely knowledge arrived at through empirical research methods and is not at all above the Word of God. Humans are humans and they do make mistakes – all of them. There are of course good science and bad science, but if a preconceived theory directs your science, it becomes dangerous.

The above mentioned examples are but a few points of evidence that the earth is younger than generally proclaimed. There is a great amount of additional evidence that could also have been mentioned in this regard.

It proves that the biblical scenario of six thousand years of human history on earth is absolutely correct, as the Bible is 100% accurate in every area.

TWO DAYS - TWO THOUSAND YEARS

If we look at what the Word teaches concerning the whole issue of 'the days', everything becomes increasingly more interesting. We find the words, 'the last days', in many places in Scripture. What exactly does this mean? In Heb. 1:1 we read: *"God ... who spake in time past unto the fathers by the prophets, hath in these last days spoken unto us by his Son."* We know the Son is Jesus Christ - the incarnated Word (Jn. 1:1,14). God speaks to us through His Word. To what would the term *'last days'* then refer? This term is repeated in many places in the New Testament. Could it be that the terms 'last days' or 'latter days' refer to the last two days before His return? In other words to the dispensation of the Church – the last two thousand years? It becomes clear from Scripture that the last days commenced with the crucifixion and resurrection of Christ. Today we are living almost 2000 years after His ascension and therefore we are living in the latter days – more than ever before. Is there more evidence in the Bible to prove this? In Lk. 13:32 we read the infor- mative words - but with a much deeper meaning than on first appearance: *"I cast out devils, and I do cures today and tomorrow, and the third day I shall be perfected."* We know for certain that Christ did not only heal the ill and cast out devils for two literal days of 24 hours each. His earthly min- istry was for approximately three and a half years. If two days then, prophetically spoken, points to two thousand years of human history, it spans the church dispensation pre- cisely. For the past two thousand years many sick people were cured when they prayed to God and devils were cast out by people who received salvation through the blood of Jesus Christ. It means that we are standing on the verge of entering the third day or that we just entered it. In Lk. 24:1,2 we read of the resurrection of the Lord Jesus Christ: *"Now upon the first day of the week, very early in the morning, they came to the sepulchre ... they found the stone rolled away..."* Jesus Christ thus rose very early on the third day. It was also the first day of the week, the day of the resurrection - the Sunday.

As Christ rose from the dead early on the third day, those who followed Him in life will also rise from the dead on the third day, prophetically spoken. We read in 1 Thes. 4:16-18 that *"...the dead in Christ shall rise first: then we which are alive and remain shall be caught up together with them in the clouds, to meet the Lord in the air: and so shall we ever be with the Lord. Wherefore comfort one another with these words."*

This will happen when He comes to collect those who belong to Him. We (His disciples) will follow Him into heaven. It will happen early on the third day – early in the third millennium. That is why our generation has to be on guard, as the third day (the third millennium since He ascended to heaven) is here. Is it not notable that the signs of the times – especially in our time – are going into fulfillment in such a rapid way?

Nobody can say for sure when the day will be. It is also not our intention with this study.

The precise date of birth of Jesus Christ is also not attainable and therefore we do not know the exact date and year when two thousand years since His birth will have passed. It may already be that we have gone passed that mark and that we may have entered the early hours of the 'third day'. Many historians are under the impression that Christ was born in 4 BC. If this is the case, then 1996 was already the end of the 'second day' or second millennium since Christ. There are however different viewpoints on when Christ was born, but whatever the case may be, we are living close to the second coming of the Lord and that is why we have to be ready at all times. Every person who answers to His call, have to ensure themselves that they are truly born again and that they live a holy life so as not to be ashamed before Him at His return

(1 Jn. 2:28). We are however not saved through any good works, but solely through our faith in Christ Jesus. If this faith does not produce any works on the other hand, it is a dead faith and the Word warns against that in Jas. 2.

The Word of God contains many scriptures that have more than one meaning – thus on more than one level. This does not mean conflicting interpretations either. No, both are correct and the one may be complementary to the other. One may be spiritual and the other literal and then there are also many prophetical truths and explanations throughout the Bible. Sometimes there are words that can not be approached in any other manner than in a prophetical context. Otherwise, it has no specific meaning. We read for example in Jn. 2 about the wedding in Cana where Jesus turned water into wine. Verse one begins: *"And the third day there was a marriage in Cana in Galilee, and the mother of Jesus was there: and both Jesus was called, and His disciples, to the marriage"* (verses 1 &2).

Why would the Word refer to this event as happening on the third day? In Jn. 1:29 we read of John the Baptist meeting Christ for the first time. In Jn. 1:35 we read of the *'next day'* – in other words the day after Jesus' baptism (the second day) and in chapter 2:1 of *'the third day'*. It is the historical events of the first three days of Jesus' administration that are being described here. It is interesting that the wedding was held on the third day and that Jesus' disciples were also invited – with Him. We know that the marriage of the Lamb (Christ) will take place in heaven shortly after His descending in the clouds to collect His children (His disciples). We read about it in Rev. 19:7,9. If this wedding is to take place on the third day (early in the third millennium after Christ), these verses are of particular importance. I believe that every verse in Scripture that refer to a wedding or marriage have to teach us something about the great heavenly marriage of the Lamb that is still to come.

In the same way, all references to brides in the Bible are in one way or another a typology of the true church of Christ – the bride. These typologies regarding the end times can be found not only in the New Testament but also early in the Old Testament. In the book of Exodus there is an extra-ordinary reference to the second coming of the Lord that convincingly parallels the aforementioned explanations. In Ex. 19 we read where God called Moses to the mount Sinai. There He gave Moses certain instructions that he had to give to the nation of Israel in return. Moses told them - amongst other things - the following: *"And the Lord said unto Moses, Go unto the people, and sanctify them today and tomorrow, and let them wash their clothes, and be ready against the third day: for the third day the Lord will come down in the sight of all the people upon the mount Sinaï"* (verses 10,11). A reference to the church of Christ that also have to cleanse her clothes for two days (two thousand years) to be the pure and unspotted bride of Christ – with her eyes fixed upon the soon coming marriage with her heavenly bridegroom (2 Cor. 11:2). In verse 15, 16 and 17 we also read: *"And he said unto the people, be ready against the third day: come not at your wives. And it came to pass on the third day in the morning, that there were thunders and lightnings, and a thick cloud upon the mount, and the voice of the trumpet exceeding loud: so that all the people that was in the camp trembled. And Moses brought forth the people out of the camp to meet with God.*" Are you ready for the third day? An idolatrous woman in the Bible is a clear type of idol worship – anything that comes between God and man. Are there any idols in your life? Are your clothes washed in the blood of the Lamb (Rev. 1:5). The *"voice of the trumpet exceeding loud"* is a beautiful reference to the return of Christ to receive to Himself those whom He had bought with His own blood.

Continuing in Ex. 20, God gave the law to the people of Israel and we know that Jesus Christ Himself is the fulfillment of the law as well as the end of the law. It is a reference to Him – exactly as everything in the entire Scripture refers to Christ, who Himself is the Word.

In the book of Hosea we also read of the interesting fact, that one day is like a thousand years for the Lord and vice versa. In Hos. 5:14,15 we read: *"For I will be unto Ephraim as a lion, and as a young lion to the house of Judah: I, even I, will tear and go away; I will take away, and none shall rescue him. I will go and return to my place, till they acknowledge their offence, and seek my face: in their affliction they will seek me early."* Then in Hos. 6:1,2 we find the following literal promise to the people of Israel, but in a prophetical way it also points to the church: *"Come, and let us return unto the Lord...After two days he will revive us: in the third day he will raise us up and we shall live in his sight."* What important words these are not. The Jewish people (to whom these words were directed literally and in the first place) were scattered all across the world in 70 AD, after Jerusalem and the temple had been destroyed. After nearly two thousand years (two days) they regained their land in 1948 and they have been returning to Israel in vast numbers since then. They were 'dead' for two days and are now in a sense politically 'healed'. The spiritual healing of the nation of Israel will however only follow later – at the end of the great tribulation, when the remainder of the

Jewish people will call out to God in their affliction and the Lord will forgive them their trespasses. (Zech. 12,13). This part in the book of Hosea, however also refers to the true church that will rise after two days or two thousand years (many are currently resting in their graves) and they will live before Christ on the third day – in the thousand years of peace, the coming millennial kingdom.

Even the well-known South African theologian, Prof. Murray Janson (Dutch Reformed), once suggested the following on this subject: "Jesus Christ was absent for two thousand years, but still it is like merely two days for the Lord. He may return on the third day – like His resurrection!" (translated).

A PROPHETIC REFERENCE TO THE TIME SURROUNDING 2000 AD?

The Word of God is full of surprises for everyone that wants to study this remarkable and unique Book under the guidance of the Holy Spirit. In Jn. 2:20 we read that all those reborn and spirit filled children of the Lord "… *have an unction from the Holy One, and ye <u>know all things</u>.*"

This is everything we need to know about how to receive salvation and how to understand the Word. That which we do not understand fully now (1 Cor. 13:9,12) is the finer detail of our day-to-day existence – why certain things cross our path etc.

Life is like an enormous tapestry, viewed from behind and therefore we also have a very limited notion of God and heaven where He lives, as well as a very limited insight in the time hereafter. The Lord, however, nowhere stated that we could not understand His Word – His letter to us. On the contrary, He mentioned in quite a few places that we have to and need to comprehend its meaning. Jesus, for example, said that "*man shall not live by bread alone, but by every word of God."* (Lk. 4:4). This was, very informative, the words He used when Satan tempted Him in the wilderness. We may comprehend the Word, but only through the Holy Spirit that Christ send us as Comforter and enlightener after He left the Earth. In Jn. 14:26 we find Jesus' clear explanation regarding this: *"But the Comforter, which is the Holy Ghost, whom my Father will send in my name, he shall teach you all things, and bring all things to your remembrance, whatsoever I have said."*

We return to 1 Jn. 2, verse 21 and 27 regarding a true Bible Christian's anointing by the Holy Spirit: *"I have not written unto you because ye know not the truth, but because ye know it, and that no lie is of the truth...But the anointing which ye have received of him abideth in you, and ye need not that any man teach you: but as the same anointing teacheth you of all things, and is truth, and is no lie, and even as it hath taught you, ye shall abide in him."* It is interesting that the rest of this passage refers to the Antichrist, as well as to deception and the second coming. In many churches, there is still some unwritten rule that only the church or the preacher or bishop or priest may teach the Word of God. Supposedly the 'ordinary church member' could not 'comprehend' the Word without these people. They take over the role of the Holy Spirit (God) in many cases. It stands in direct contrast with the Word itself. The Roman Church prohibited their members to read the Bible for many centuries and today, although not official, the same applies to a certain extent in many 'protestant' churches.

Members 'prohibit' themselves from reading and studying the Bible, because they can apparently not 'comprehend' it.

The same people will however, study complicated scientific and other books in all earnestness. The plan of Satan behind it all is very clear and he is quite focused in his endeavour to mislead the human race.

Jesus Christ is the Light of the world and Satan is the father of darkness. In 1 Jn. 1:5 we read: *"This then is the message which we have heard of him, and declare unto you, that God is light, and in him is no darkness at all."* Everyone that knows Him and seeks the truth in His Word, will find it. The question remains - does one want to accept the truth if one finds it.

Very few want to accept God's Word as it stands, not to mention a true belief in the Word of God. Faith only stems from adhering to the Word of the Lord. (Rom. 10:17). Many are deceived today and this merely because they do not know Scripture. Jesus had to proclaim this Himself to the Sadducees in Mt. 22:29. He also said in the same verse that they wandered astray because they did not know the power of the Lord. Would He have said it if we were not able to understand something of His power?

In 1 Pet. 1:9-12 we read about salvation as the destiny of our souls in these beautiful words: *"receiving the end of your faith, even the salvation of your souls. Of which salvation the prophets have inquired and searched diligently, who prophesied of the grace that should come unto you: searching what, or what manner of time the Spirit of Christ which was in them did signify, when it testified beforehand the suffering of Christ, and the glory that should follow.*

Unto whom it was revealed, that not unto themselves, but unto us they did minister the things, which are now reported unto you by them that have preached the gospel unto you with the Holy Ghost sent down from heaven; which things the angels desire to look into."

These ancient prophets were people just like us – flesh and blood and with an intellect. They inquired and searched regarding Christ's first coming to earth. Today we can also be diligent in our search and inquiry regarding the second coming of Christ. The Word of God is complete (the Alpha and Omega) and no new extra-biblical revelations can be added to the Scriptures, but new discoveries and insights from the existing Scriptures clarifies everything that much more in our times. In the book of Daniel, we read that certain words and prophecies will remain sealed until the end of time and that knowledge regarding this will increase (Dan. 12:4). Presently, this is happening at an unprecedented tempo.

A while back someone fixed my attention to an amazing passage in the Old Testament that have a distinct prophetic implication and that could refer to the current generation. To be quite honest, the prophetic importance that surrounds the current period (the time surrounding 2000 AD), is increasingly becoming more clear every day.

We read about this in the book of Joshua. This man (Joshua) that ultimately led the people of Israel into the Promised Land, is a very good type of Jesus Christ. Exactly like Joshua led the Israelites into Canaan, Jesus leads people who were in Egypt (the world) or in the desert (an unfulfilled life), into the spirit filled life and eventually into the eternal glory of heaven. The name Joshua, in Hebrew, is very similar to the name Jesus, and pointed to Him that was to come. Here the resemblance merely begins, but it is a study all on its own.

In Josh. 3 we read the passage that describes Israel's journey through the Jordan. It is of course a beautiful type of the death of the self life - of the previously carnal Christian. The Jordan flows down into the Dead Sea. On the other side of this river, there is a new life of abundance, unbeknown to those who never experienced it.

In Josh. 3:3, Joshua instructed the people on how to cross the river. They had to follow these instructions to the letter. We read: *"When ye see the ark of the covenant of the Lord your God, and the priests the Levites bearing it, then ye shall remove from your place, and go after it.*" In Deut. 10:1-5 we read more regarding the Ark of the Covenant and how Moses placed the two tables of stone (with the law) in the ark. The Ark of the Covenant with the law therein points to Jesus Christ. We find prove of this in the New Testament, in Rom. 10:4 where we read: *"For Christ is the end of the law for righteousness to every one that believeth"*. As previously mentioned, the entire New Testament is foreshadowed in the Old Testament and it becomes very clear in this case too. The passage in Josh. 3 continues and in verse 4 and 5 we read Joshua's clear words to the nation: *"Yet there shall be a space between you and it, about two thousand cubits by measure: come not near unto it, that ye may know the way by which ye must go: for ye have not passed this way heretofore. And Joshua said unto the people, Sanctify yourselves: for tomorrow the Lord will do wonders among you."*

As mentioned earlier, Scripture often speaks of two days in which a certain task is to be completed and then it is follwed by a new time or event commencing on the third day. It may refer to the period of two thousand years between Christ's first coming and His return. Often, the Bible refers to two days in a certain way, with the third day thereafter being completely different in appearance.

This bears a very strong resemblance to the current generation. It is even more applicable if we recollect the enormous changes and upheavels the world is experiencing around the time of 2000 AD. The part in Joshua 3 is merely another passage referring to this amazing pattern in Scripture, but offers a further and more distinct image of what is to follow. As mentioned, the Ark of the Covenant refers to Jesus Christ. Two thousand years ago, He already ascended to Heaven. The people of Israel had to remain two thousand cubits behind the ark while they followed it. May it refer to the past two thousand years, the dispensation of the church? Will the true church (those reborn) follow the Lord shortly into the glory of heaven? Very important is the word "*about*". It speaks volumes. The Word teaches us that we shall not know the day and hour of His coming, but only the season. We may thus ascertain, more or less, the time of His second coming. The time surrounding two thousand years after Christ, is therefore of cardinal importance to the church. It is not at all to be compared with the time of 1000 years AD. Then, many Christians also awaited His return, but there is no prophetic reference in the Scriptures that it would be a specific time of importance.

The reference to the fact that the nation of Israel did not pass the same way "*heretofore*" further intensifies the typology. The people would pass through the Jordan and enter a completely new dispensation. For two thousand years, the children of God (the true Christians) passed around the earth, but now everything is changing. The words "*Sanctify yourselves: for tomorrow the Lord will do wonders among you*" may be descriptive of the third day dawning for the bride of Christ – on the way to entering heaven. It will surely be the greatest event, unbeknown to anything we ever experienced on earth before. Many will now ask, may we draw such conclusions from the Word, and is all this really pointing to our generation that is presently living on earth.

In 1 Cor. 10:11 we read the remarkable words: "*Now all these things happened unto them for ensamples: and they are written for our admonition, upon whom the ends of the world are come*". The end of the days clearly fell upon our generation. We may accept with a sound heart that there is no coincidences or unimportant passages in the Bible. Everything written in this wonderful Book was inspired by God Himself and is useful to us for study.

THE 'NEW AGE' AND TWO THOUSAND YEARS

It is interesting to note that the followers of the new age movement also attach great value to periods of two thousand years. According to them, this phenomenon is found institutionalized in the star signs of the zodiac.

They believe that, aside from the annual movement of the sun through the twelve constellations, there is also a further path the sun follows in periods of two thousand years each, through the constellations. Therefore the period between 2000 and 4000 BC was the age of the Bull (Taurus). The time thereafter, from 2000 BC until Christ, was the era of the Ram (Aries). In this time the sheep ram (as an offering) as well as the scapegoat was on the forefront in the lives of the Israelites. In this dispensation, Israel was solemnly reprimanded when they worshipped a golden calf - from the previously expired era. The following era was that of the Fish (Pisces). It commenced with the coming of Christ and has continued until the current time. During this time, the Christian Church had been associated to a certain extent with the fish. In the New Testament, there are many references to fish and some of the disciples were fishermen as well, who later became fishers of men. In the same way, every child of God in the dispensation of the Church needs to be a fisher of men.

According to the 'New Agers', the world transcended, roundabout the year 2000, into the era of Aquarius – the next one in line. They then also await a Messiah or Christ figure in this 'new age'. This new era movement fixes much importance on the symbol of the rainbow. The connection lies in the fact that the era of the waterbearer (Aquarius) is to have commenced around 2000 AD. That is why, in the last decade and even more so now, one finds many symbols of rainbows whereever one travels. It is the announcement of the new age of Aquarius that supposedly has just dawned upon the earth. The Lord knew all these things beforehand and made an indication to it long ago in His Word. In Lk. 22 we read of the last Passover or the institution of the Holy Communion. If one keeps the 'new era of the waterbearer' in mind, then the following is very informative. Jesus sent Peter and John to prepare the Passover. When they asked Him where to go and prepare it, Jesus answered: " ... *when ye are entered into the city, there shall a man meet you, bearing a pitcher of water; follow him into the house where he entereth in ... and he shall show you a large upper room furnished: there make ready"* (Lk. 22:10,12).

If one keeps in mind all that were discussed already, it is clear that the second coming of Christ and the entering into the next millennium (the Kingdom of Peace under Christ) and the 'new era of Aquarius' according to the 'New Agers' have some things in common. That is only an appearance of similarity though, because the one is a Biblical truth and the other a lie from Satan.

If we look further, the last Passover before Christ's crucifixion is surely a type of the coming marriage supper of the Lamb (Rev. 19:9) that will be in heaven.

Differently said, the marriage supper of the Lamb is a reference back to the last Passover and the crucifixion. That is why it is distinctly called the marriage supper of the *Lamb*. It follows on the second coming of Christ. In the cited quotation in Luke, the reference to a man that bears a pitcher of water is not incidental. It appears that the Lord wants to give us another sign of when we may expect the second coming – close to the time when some will expect the coming 'new era' - according to the constellations. We are not speaking of astrology here. Remember that God Himself created the stars and gave them names (Ps. 147:4).

The reference to a waterbearer is in fact a reference to Jesus Himself. He is the One who said: *"If any man thirst, let him come unto me, and drink."* (Jn. 7:37) and also *"but whosoever drinketh of the water that I shall give him shall never thirst*" (Jn. 4:14). Yes, it is Him whose voice sounds like "*many waters*" (Rev. 1:15). It is Him of whom it is said in Rev. 22:17: "*let him take the water of life freely*". My friend, have you drunk of this water? Are you born-again through the Holy Spirit? Do you realize what is happening around you – that He whom we spoke of is on His way back to them that await Him?

Satan of course is an imitator of everything that God has created and that is why that which the world offers – namely the new era of Aquarius, is not from God. A false water-bearer (the Antichrist) is on the way and everyone that drinks from his water, their thirst will never be quenched. On the contrary, an eternal thirst will be their destiny (Lk. 16:24).

We have to follow Christ to the house where He entered into. It is He that prepares the large upper room for us, His children (in heaven – Jn. 14:1-3). It is there where we will enjoy the marriage supper of the Lamb with Him. All this information does not implicate that the second coming of the Lord will occur in any specific year. It is merely point-ing toward the season of His coming. That we are in that season is quite clear. The day of His return may become a reality at any time. Nobody will be able to say. The question remains however, are we ready to meet with God?

8

THE TIME OF JACOB'S TROUBLE

"Alas! For that day is great, so that none is like it: it is even the time of Jacob's [Israel's] trouble; but he shall be saved out of it." (Jer. 30:7)

"for then shall be great tribulation, such as was not since the beginning of the world to this time, no, nor ever shall be." (Mt. 24:21)

We have already shown and documented that this world is not paradise at all. Everyone that wants to be honest, has to admit that this world is in dire need of a great redemption. Even the creation cries out for a time of real God-worked quickening and refreshing (Rom. 8:18-23). Before those glorious days arrive though, and they surely will, God first has to settle some matters on this earth – especially with those whom rejected His Son Jesus Christ. The Word of God speaks of troublesome times that will come on this earth before the redemption of this planet will become a reality. When contemplating this topic, one first has to remove some old misconceptions though. The biblical prophesied period of *great tribulation* or also called the *time of Jacob's trouble*, is not a reference to the daily tribulations and afflictions one has to endure on earth. The fact that every person – in general – has to endure suffering and hardship in this world, are directly related to the fall of mankind, in the Garden of Eden. Through Adam, every person shares in the fall of man because sin found its way into this world through that historic event. The reborn child of God will particularly endure suffering in this world, because the Lord says very clearly: *"therefore the world knoweth us not, because it knew him not."* (1 John 3:1). As Christ suffered here, so shall we. Everyone who knows the Lord, will be a stranger in this world and will therefore have a difficult time, to various degrees, in this world. The great tribulation have nothing to do with the day to day tribulation we read about in Jn. 16:33. There John writes: *"In the world ye shall have tribulation: but be of good cheer; I have overcome the world"*

If the Bible speaks of the great tribulation, it refers to a very specific time in the history of mankind on earth. It refers to a time that never was and that never again will be. The term 'great tribulation' is a prophetical term and refers to an extraordinary period in God's prophetical program for man. In the first place, it is a judgment over His people of the covenant, namely Israel. We read very distinctly in Mt. 24:9 about a time when *"they shall deliver you up to be afflicted, and shall kill you: and ye shall be hated of all nations for my name's sake."* This is part of Jesus' answer to His disciples after they questioned Him about His return and about the end of the world. Jesus Christ spoke as a Jew to His Jewish disciples and told them what was to be expected at the end of time. All the nations of the world would hate Israel and the Jewish people because Christ was born from them. Right through the centuries, Jews were hated and persecuted very cruelly, without any logical reason, except that salvation is of the Jews (Jn. 4:22). In the time of the great tribulation, it will reach an unprecedented climax. The entire Mt. 24, the Olivet discourse or prophecy of the Lord Jesus Christ, was distinctly written from a Jewish perspective and in the first place it points to the literal destiny of the nation of Israel during this time. The main reason for this is the fact that the Jews deny the Messiah to this day and because they crucified Him 2 000 years ago. During that event, they shouted: *"His blood be on us, and on our children"* (Mt. 27:25).

God, infallible and righteous, cannot and will not leave sins unpunished and did not forget those words. That is why the nation of Israel will suffer greatly during that time. It is, unfortunately, not only them that will suffer greatly during the great tribulation, but also everyone who denies Jesus' atoning blood.

In Lk. 21 we find another rendering of the Olivet prophecy of the Lord, but now directed more specifically to the gentile nations – verse 24 and 25. The gentile nations include all nations, except the nation of Israel. Hereby the Word draws a distinction between Israel and other nations. It does not mean that Israel is more important to the Lord than the other nations, but only that Jesus was born from the people of Israel and that God still have a definite plan with them. The covenants with Abraham, Isaac and Jacob were not completely fulfilled yet and we know that the Lord will never go back on His Word. The church did not replace the literal Israel, but learn from God's dealings with the literal Israel. In this way the disciples of Christ (His true followers from all nations) can learn much from the Olivet discourse for example. The true Christians also suffer persecution in this world and to a far greater extent than others. In this, Jews and Christians have much in common except that the

Jews suffer greatly because they rejected Christ and the Christians because they excepted Him. During the time of great tribulation the history of the world will be rewritten and nothing will ever be the same again. According to all indications from Scripture, this time is at hand and may commence at any moment. There are literally hundreds of reasons why this statement could be made – especially because of what is now happening on the world stage, and specifically because it was all prophesied in God's Word – to the minutest detail.

HOW LONG?

The question arises, how long will this tribulation period be. The Bible is very clear on this issue and no person need to be in the dark regarding this matter. If we look at the book of Daniel (that always have to be studied in conjunction with the book of Revelation), we begin to see the light on this issue. In chapter 8 of this book, Daniel saw a vision that distressed him greatly (Dan. 8:27). The angel Gabriel (in verse 26) said to him that he had to keep the vision secret as, "*it shall be for many days*". In chapter 9 of this book we read of Daniel's prayer to God for his people who were in exile. While he was praying the angel Gabriel appeared to him again to give him insight into the future. In Dan. 9:24-27 we read: "*Seventy weeks are determined upon thy people and upon thy holy city, to finish the transgression, and to make an end of sins, and to make reconciliation for iniquity, and to bring everlasting righteousness, and to seal up the vision and prophecy, and to anoint the Most Holy. Know therefore and understand, that from the going forth of the commandment to restore and to build Jerusalem, unto the Messiah the Prince, shall be seven weeks, and threescore and two weeks: the street shall be built again, and the wall, even in troublous times. And after threescore and two weeks shall*

Messiah be cut off, but not for himself: and the people of the prince that shall come shall destroy the city and the sanctuary; and the end thereof shall be with a flood, and unto the end of the war desolations are determined. And he shall confirm the covenant with many for one week; and in the midst of the week he shall cause the sacrifice and the oblation to cease, and for the overspreading of abominations he shall make it desolate, even until the consummation, and that determined shall be poured upon the desolate."

This prophecy is distinctly referring to the nation of Israel. The language used is very clear, when it says *"thy (Daniel's) people"* and *"thy holy city (Jerusalem)"*. The seventy sevens refer to seventy year weeks, in other words, 70 times 7 years – a period of 490 years.

There are numerous passages in the Scriptures that shows that a week, as mentioned above, may also refer to a year week. In Lev. 25:8 we read about this when the Lord gave the orders to Moses regarding the sabbath years and years of Jubilee: *"And thou shalt number seven sabbaths of years unto thee, seven times seven years; and the space of the seven sabbaths of years shall be unto thee forty and nine years."* We also find in Gen. 29:27,28 a passage of Scripture concerning the same truth. Laban related to Jacob that he had to serve him for seven more years before he could take Rachel as his wife. He told him: *"Fulfill her week [Leah's]; and we will give thee this also for the service which thou shalt serve with me yet another seven years. And Jacob did so, and fulfilled her week"*. From these verses, the principle of the year week comes to the front quite clearly.

If we look at Dan. 9:25, we can calculate precisely when this seventy sevens commenced. There we find that it correlates with the time of the decree to rebuild Jerusalem. We read about this in the book of Nehemiah. In chapter 2:1 we read that Nehemiah served king Artaxerxes with wine in the month of Nisan (March or April according to our calendar). The king noted that Nehemiah was sad and upon acquiring about it, the whole issue of the desolated Jerusalem came to the front. In verse 6 the king granted him permission to return to Jerusalem and to start rebuilding it. This was the beginning of the seventy sevens (yearweeks) determined upon the nation of Israel. The *Encyclopedia Britannica* denotes that the reign of king Artaxerxes commenced in 465 BC and admits that the rebuilding of the walls in Jerusalem started in the 20th year of his reign, thus in 445 BC. According to Dan. 9:25,26 the first of the seven sevens commenced on this date. During this time, the walls of Jerusalem were literally rebuilt. After that the other sixty two sevens also went into fulfillment. It continued until the Messiah was crucified, but without His Kingdom in place yet . These first two periods together, in other words the 69 weeks of years (the 7 plus the 62), give us a total of 483 years (69 times 7), and resulted in a very special event.

Before we continue, it would be fitting to first find out how long each of these years are. Biblical or prophetical years are not 365 and a quarter day as is presently the case. We can also see this from Scripture. The events surrounding Noah and the ark and the specific time he and his family spent in the ark, shows how long a month was for the Lord. In Gen. 7:11 we read that the fountains of the deep broke open and the windows of heaven were also opened on the 17th day of the 2nd month. In chapter 8:3,4 we read that exactly *"hundred and fifty days"* later, on the 17th day of the seventh month – thus five months later, the ark came to rest on the mountains of Ararat and the water began to abate. We can thus see that five months is equal to 150 days. That is why one month is equal to 30 days. A prophetical or biblical year therefore is 12 times 30 days = 360 days. It was of course also as a result of the lunar or moon calendar that was used during that time. Today we use the sun calendar that is slightly longer.

AN AMAZING CALCULATION

The brilliant British criminologist and Bible student, Sir Robert Anderson, calculated the first two periods, namely the 69 sevens, to their precise number of days. This can be found in his book, *The Coming Prince*. The 483 years then came to exactly 173 880 days. He went and counted the days onward from 14 March 445 BC into the future. His results were astonishing. The date he came to was 6 April 32 AD. What was so special about this date, you may ask. It was the day when Jesus Christ, on the back of a donkey, entered the city of Jerusalem. It can easily be determined today. On this day – only on this day - Jesus Christ was acknowledged as King (or Messiah as He was referred to in Daniel). It was the only time in all His earthly ministry that He was worshipped in this way. We read about this event in Lk. 19:29-38. In verse 38 we read the following words that was shouted by the people: *"Blessed be the King that cometh in the name of the Lord"*. It was the day when the Jews thought that He would become their political redeemer, to free them from the ruling Roman government of that time. They did not however realize or understood that which was to follow shortly afterwards. In Lk. 19:41,42 we find the following profound and meaningful words of the Lord Jesus Christ Himself – that He uttered that amazing day: *"And when he was come near, he beheld the city, and wept over it, saying, If thou hadst known, even thou, at least <u>in this thy day</u>, the things which belong unto thy peace! but now they are hid from thine eyes."* The Jewish nation sadly did not know what day it was, simply because they forgot about the prophecy in the book of Daniel. What an incredible thought. We can thank God today that our eyes need not be closed anymore. What a great privilege! Sadly though, most still do not know about this day or understand this prophecy. The prophetic Word of God is 100% accurate. It is absolute unique to the Bible. No other 'holy' book of any other religion prophesies any specific and detailed prophecies for the future. They would not even dare doing that. The first 69 sevens thus came to a magnificent fulfillment on this day. The question now remains, when did the last yearweek, the 70th or last seven go into fulfillment? Did this time transpire already or does it still remain for sometime in the future. In Dan. 9:26 we read that the Messiah (Jesus Christ) would be cut off, but not for Himself (the crucifixion in 32 AD). After this He ascended to heaven with the promise to return again. Now we will look at the coming of a 'prince' connected to a nation that would destroy the holy city Jerusalem. This part of the prophecy also went into fulfillment literally, in the year 70 AD. The Roman army under General Titus destroyed the city of Jerusalem and the temple during that year. The nation of Israel was scattered across the entire world as a result and the seventieth week of Daniel could not go into fulfillment. In 1948 though, the people of Israel became a nation again in their land of old. If the final year week (the 70th) had commenced during that year, the end could have been expected to be around the year 1955. We know however, that this was not the case. There are quite a number of prophecies that still have to go into fulfillment before the end will come. The 'prince' to come, according to Dan. 9:26, refers to the Antichrist that will rise from the revived Roman Empire. He will be a world leader that will try to unite the entire world under his leadership. The passage in Daniel continues and prophesies that the prince's end will come with a flood. It has never happened and refers to the last great earthquake and the battle of Armageddon. Further we see that there will be wars until the end of time. We know that the end has not come as of yet, and that is why it has to lie in the future – maybe the near future. The seventieth week of Daniel or the last seven year period prophesied by him, still lies in the future and did not go into fulfillment directly after the previous 69 weeks of years. In Dan. 9:27 we read that the 'prince' or Antichrist will make a strong covenant with many (nations) and that his governance will eventually result in the end of the current dispensation.

This last seven years is the biblical prophesied time of the great tribulation that we read of in Mt. 24. We can see that there is a span of nearly 2 000 years between the 69th and 70th year weeks prophesied by Daniel. This truth in the Bible is not as strange as it appears. We have to remember that these prophesied periods are specifically applicable to the nation of Israel. In Hosea 3:4,5 we read another remarkable prophecy regarding Israel, that brings to the front the span between the 69th and 70th year week distinctly. We read there: "*For the children of Israel shall abide many days without a king, and without a prince, and without a sacrifice, and without an image, and without an ephod, and without teraphim: afterward shall the children of Israel return, and seek the Lord their God, and David their king; and shall fear the Lord and his goodness in the latter days.*" This only partially refers to the Babylonian exile. It was not the last days then. This prophecy points to current times. Israel did not have a king for literally 1900 years. They also did not have a temple (teraphim or house gods) where they could bring their offerings. To tell the truth, they still do not have a temple to this day. Currently, they are working in all earnestness to bring about a third temple. There are already a couple of schools in Israel that are training Levitical priests for temple service and numerous other projects are also underway to rebuild the temple in our generation, as was mentioned before.

It is one of the most important signs that the time of great tribulation is at hand. The temple has to be rebuild, because Daniel 9:27 refers to the Antichrist as stopping the sacrifices in the middle of the year week. It is a distinct reference to the temple in Jerusalem (compare 2 Thes. 2:4; Mt. 24:15 and Rev. 11:1,2). The quotation from Hosea 3:5 concerning Israel's conversion, refers to the third part of the Jewish nation that will convert to Jesus Christ at the end of the great tribulation, with His return (Zech. 12:10 and 13:1,8,9). The reference to David their king, could be to Jesus Christ (the Son of David) that will establish His Messianic reign on earth after His second coming on the Mount of Olives (Lk. 1:32,33; Zech. 14:4 and Acts 15:16,17).

TWO SHORT PERIODS

Now that we have established that the tribulation period will introduce the final seven years of human governance on earth, we can look at other complimentary passages of Scripture regarding the length of this time. It is clear from the Bible that the period of seven years can be divided into two equal parts of three and a half years each. The first half will introduce a time of false peace, while the second will be the prophesied time of great tribulation. In Rev. 11:2 we read that the gentile nations will trample the streets of the holy city (Jerusalem) for 42 months. It is exactly three and a half years. In verse 3 we see that the Lord will send two witnesses (possibly Enoch and Elijah or Moses and Elijah) to prophesy for 1260 days (again three and a half years). In verse 7 we see that these two witnesses will be conquered by the beast from the earth and they will eventually be killed. These periods refer to the first three and a half years. If we go to Rev. 13:5, we find that the beast from the sea (the Antichrist) is given power for 42 months. With him the beast from the earth (the false prophet – Rev. 13:11) will reign for that time. They will thus play a very important role during the second three and a half years (the real time of great tribulation) – after the two witnesses will have ascended to heaven (Rev. 11:12). In Rev. 12:6 we read that the women (Israel) will flee to a place in the desert prepared for her by God. There Israel will be kept for 1260 days. It seems that this could refer to the city of rock – Petra, in Jordan. This city with carved rooms and temples from pink rock, can house more than a million people. Chances are great that the remnant of Israel will flee to this hiding place during the time of great tribulation. 'Petra' means rock and the literal nation of Israel could be concealed in this literal rock until they convert themselves to the true spiritual Rock, Jesus Christ – 1 Cor. 10:4. In Mt. 24:15,16 we also read of Israel's fleeing into the mountains during this troublesome times. In verse 14 of Rev. 12 we read of the same event, but here "*a time, and times, and half a time*" is mentioned in the Bible. It is a Jewish way to again describe a period of three and a half years. It seems as if the Lord wanted to assure us that 1260 days are equal to the above mentioned time period. If we interpret the book of Daniel using this key, it comes in very handy. There we read twice of 'time, times and half a time' (Dan. 7:25; Dan. 12:7).

The first one mentioned (Dan. 7:25), correlates beautifully with Rev. 13:5-7. Through this we can see that the seventieth seven (or yearweek) will definitely be seven literal years. All this may sound very technical, but proves that nothing in the Bible were left to mere chance. Everything was recorded for us and no one will have an excuse that they did not know. The Lord gave us His Word and what a privilege it is to study it with the help and guidance of the Holy Spirit. There is a viewpoint however, that we were not supposed to know it all. No human in this life will ever know everything about God, but that which He wanted us to know, He recorded for us in His Word. That which is not in His Word, is that which we were not meant to know in this dispensation.

OLD TESTAMENT DESCRIPTIONS OF THIS TIME PERIOD

In Dan. 12:1 we find the following description of how it will be on earth during that time: "*And at that time shall Michael stand up, the great prince which standeth for the children of thy people; and there shall be a time of trouble, such as never was since there was a nation, even to that same time: and at that time thy people shall be delivered, every one that shall be found written in the book.*" Here we can see that the nation of Israel will be on the foreground during this time. We also read in Jer. 30:7 the following description of this period: "*Alas! For that day is great, so that none is like it: it is even the time of Jacob's trouble; but he [Jacob or Israel] shall be saved out of it.*" It surely will be an unprecedented time in human history. The best and most commonly used term for this period in the Old Testament is the term 'The day of the Lord.' It appears in many places and includes the second coming of Christ. It also refers specifically to the judgments of God that will be brought about by Him on earth during the great tribulation. In Joel 1:15 we read the following in this regard: "*Alas for the day! For the day of the Lord is at hand, and as a destruction from the Almighty it shall come.*" Today we can just echo these words. This day is near indeed. In Zeph. 1:14-18 we find the terrifying and most distinct description of this day of the Lord: "*The great day of the Lord is near, it is near, and hasteth greatly, even the voice of the day of the Lord: the mighty man shall cry there bitterly. That day is a day of wrath, a day of trouble and distress, a day of wasteness and desolation, a day of darkness and gloominess, a day of clouds and thick darkness, a day of the trumpet and alarm against the fenced cities, and against the high towers. And I will bring distress upon men, that they shall walk like blind men, because they have sinned against the Lord: and their*

*blood shall be poured out as dust, and their flesh as the
dung. Neither their silver not their gold shall be able to
deliver them in the day of the Lord's wrath; but the whole
land shall be devoured by the fire of his jealousy: for he
shall make even a speedy riddance of all them that dwell in
the land."*

These words sound harsh and terrifying, but we can
expect this to happen to the letter – exactly as prophesied.
The living God never states something without fulfilling it.
This God always does what He says, to the finest detail. We
have to remember that God saw this happening beforehand,
that is why it is as good as if it already happened.

WHAT DOES THIS PERIOD ENTAIL?

The Word is quite clear in what the human race is to
expect during this time of great tribulation. This time is
described in detail in the book of Revelation. From Rev. 6-
19 we read about the circumstances on earth during this
time. In Rev. 6:2 we read of a man on a white horse. In Rev.
19:11 we again read of a Man on a white horse. Between
these two events, the time of great tribulation or Jacob's
trouble occurs. Except for the apparent similarities between
these two persons on the white horses, there are also major
differences between them:

- The first appears to start a war, the second to end a
  war.
- The first brings a false peace, the second brings true
  peace
- The first comes from the underworld, the second
  comes from heaven.
- The first comes in his own name, the second comes in
  the name of His Father
- The first receives power through the god of this world

(Satan), the second from the God of heaven and earth
- The first will represent himself as god; the second is God Himself.
- The first person is the Antichrist; the second Person is the true Christ.

The Antichrist will introduce terrible times on earth. Jesus Christ will come to end those terrible times. During this time, the world will be characterized by terrible wars. (Rev. 6:4, Rev. 9:15-19, Rev. 16:14,16; Rev. 19:11-21).

There will also be widespread starvation (Rev. 6:5,6,8) and diseases and pests (Rev. 6:8; Rev. 16:2).

In addition, it will be a time of enormous earthquakes (Rev. 6:12; Rev. 8:5; Rev. 11:19; Rev. 16:18) and other great natural disasters (Rev. 8:7-12; Rev. 11:6; Rev. 16:4-10,21). In Revelation 16:21 we read of a tremendous hail storm (it reminds you of one of the plagues of Egypt), where the hail stones will weigh around 60 kg and it will rain on earth's unconverted inhabitants that hated God. Many are of the impression that this is simply impossible. Recently however, an enormous hail stone of 10 kg fell from the air in Spain and one of 1,4 kg hit a women. [171]

These passages correlate greatly with the prophetic words of Jesus in Mt. 24, Mk. 13 and Lk. 21. It proves that God wants to ensure us over and over that no part of Scripture is to be ignored or is of less importance. The above-mentioned is however not all that the human race can expect during this time. Also, at a certain point in time, every person on earth will be expected to take the mark of the beast (Rev. 13:16-18). The worst though, will be the demonic activities on earth (Rev. 9:2-11; Rev. 12:9) and open Satan worship and sorcery (Rev. 9:20; Rev. 13:4).

Those who will live on earth during this time and think that they will be able to sidestep these terrible events, have to keep the following in mind also: Early in the time of tribulation, wars, famines and diseases will be the order of the day through which a fourth of all people will eventually be killed (Rev. 6:8). It will be followed by further wars where another third of the earth's population will lose their lives (Rev. 9:15,18). First a quarter and then another third - thus half of the world's population will die during this unequaled period of time. From all people, the unbelieving Jews will suffer the worst and that is why this time is also known as the time of Jacob's or Israel's trouble. It is all very upsetting to contemplate, but we can be sure that this will be the scenario of events during the great tribulation. There is also a very specific reason why God will allow all of this. Mankind's measure of sin will come to a climactic fulness. Yes, the measure of man's sin will overflow and will ask to be judged rightly.

The question remains if we can really believe all of this from the Bible. Will all of this really happen in such a literal way? Does the Bible ask of us to take it all literally or may we spiritualize it? Will a God of love really bring these terrible judgments over this earth? To those who are in doubt, contemplate the following:

- Did the God of love send literal plagues over Egypt, or were it merely spiritual plagues?
- Were the people of Noah's time annihilated by a literal flood or was it a spiritual flood?
- Were Sodom and Gomorra destroyed by a literal fire from heaven or a spiritual fire?
- Did this God of love not let his own creations nail His own Son literally to a cross and did He not shed literal blood for our literal sins – or was it all merely a spiritual event?

One does not even want to contemplate the consequences if the latter did not take place literally. Would it be unfair or shortsighted of this God to make human beings pay for their ungodly deeds? In fact, this whole tribulation period is still another short time of pure grace, because everyone that – at this stage – did not yet accept the Lord Jesus as his or her Saviour, may then have an opportunity to do so. A big emphasis has to be placed on the word 'may' though. According to the Word a great multitude will be saved during the great tribulation (Rev. 7:9,14), but to count on this would be foolish. The circumstances of this time will be such that most will call to some or other supreme being. May it be to the living God!

Those who denied the offer of salvation through Jesus Christ before hand, cannot rely at all on seeking Him during this time. We read in 2 Thes. 2:10-11 the following distinct statement regarding this: "*and with all deceivableness of unrighteousness in them that perish; because they received not the love of the truth, that they might be saved. And for this cause God shall send them strong delusion, that they should believe a lie*"

It is wise to rather get ready today, to meet the Lord.

THE PURPOSE OF THIS TIME

It is clear that the time of great tribulation will be a tremendous judgment from God. It will be the righteous judgment of a loving God over a sin filled world. The sins of the current generation were a disgrace for a long time now and call for righteous judgment. The Lord can and will not let sin go unpunished and that is why there will be such a time on earth. In Rev. 19:2 we read that these judgments will be literal and necessary: "*for true and righteous are his judgments*". In Jer. 30:14,15 we also find the following words to Israel, but also as a lesson to every other nation on earth: "*I have wounded thee with a wound of an enemy, with the chastisement of a cruel one, for the multitude of thine iniquity; because thy sins were increased, ... I have done these things unto thee.*" This passage relates to the prophesied time of the tribulation. In Is. 13:11 and 13 we also read of this time and why the Lord punishes the earth and its inhabitants: "*And I will punish the world for their evil, and the wicked for their iniquity; and I will cause the arrogancy of the proud to cease, and will lay low the haughtiness of the terrible ... Therefore I will shake the heavens, and the earth shall remove out of her place, in the wrath of the Lord of hosts and in the day of his fierce anger.*"

The Bible is clear that there will be such a time and that nobody could ever charge God with unrighteousness. The fact that these prophesies are found written in the Bible is another sign of His mercy. The question remains, do we heed these warnings? We also read in Ps. 96:13 that "*before the Lord: for he cometh, for he cometh to judge the earth: he shall judge the world with righteousness, and the people with his truth.*" In Revelation we see that those who died because they did not want to take the mark of the beast, will sing songs in heaven with the following words: "*Great and marvelous are thy works, Lord God Almighty; just and true are thy ways, thou King of saints.*" (Rev. 15:3).

In the next chapter, we read the following words of an angel, right after another plague just hit the earth: "*Thou art righteous, O Lord, which art, and wast, and shalt be, because thou hast judged thus.*" (Rev. 16:5). We may well realize that every judgment and plague that will hit this earth, will be absolutely necessary and righteous.

WHEN WILL IT BE?

"*For when they shall say, Peace and safety; then sudden destruction cometh upon them, as travail upon a women with child; and they shall not escape.*" (1 Thes 5:3).

255

Is this not the cry all over the world today? Everywhere these words are heard, but still there is no peace. The 'they' mentioned here are referring to the world – those not reborn. Peace and safety is what everybody desires, but when 'they' cry for it, we know it will not be realized. Without God and His Christ, this world will never know true peace. The other aspect of the tribulation period is that it will arrive quite suddenly. We read in Lk. 21:35 the following: *"For as a snare shall it come on all them that dwell on the face of the whole earth."* Even though we have all the signs of the times before us, we need to remember that this time will still take most by surprise. The reason being - the Scriptures are being ignored and especially because this subject is seldom if ever preached in most churches. These passages in the Word are not taken literally and that is why the sudden commencement of this time will be a great shock to many. Most people will not know what hit them. The fact of the matter remains that the great tribulation period is at hand. All the Biblical prophesies that should proceed this time, except one, already went into fulfillment in a literal way. In spite of this, people continue in their normal day-to-day existence, without thinking about the Lord or the coming judgments that will shortly come upon this earth. This in itself is also a fulfillment of the Bible, as was mentioned already. No human can separate himself from the Word of God. In one way or another, all our activities are prophesied in Scripture and no one on this earth can escape that fact.

9

WHEN IS CHRIST COMING?

What a question? Many have tried to answer this question in many different ways, but dare we even ask this question. Much uncertainty exist among Christians on when Christ will come to collect His bride unto Himself. Here we do not mean the *precise day and hour* - nobody knows that - but we speak of the biblical sequence of events at the end. Many Christians are of the opinion that the sequence of the final moments on earth is of no importance. They are of the impression that we merely have to be 'ready' and that alone can mean different things to different people.

Others believe that it is impossible to know anything about the final moments on earth. They maintain that we should not delve too deep into the Word (Satan also believes this of course), because, as they say, we may get confused. In fact, the exact opposite is true. If you do not know the Word of God, chances are you will get confused that much easier – and you will be without a true and real biblical faith.

Satan is the one sowing the seeds of confusion and the Word of the Lord clears up that confusion. Yes, it ends confusion. It *"giveth light"* and *"giveth understanding unto the simple"* (Ps. 119:130). God is not a God of confusion, but rather of a finely created harmony.

What about the various points of view different people have on various subjects in the Bible? What is true, is that everybody does not share the same zeal to search the Word of God. Many do not want to spend time with the Bible and even less time is spent in prayer before the Lord.

Concerning the return of Christ for His bride, great controversy is the order of the day. Many Christians do not believe in the rapture or the gathering of the saints. A great number of arguments exist against this day of Christ. We will take a closer look at this matter in this chapter. Some say that it (the rapture) is a sectarian interpretation, or that a woman (active in the occult), introduced this theory in the 1800's or even that a Jesuit priest from the Roman Catholic Church, who lived in the 18th century, was responsible for the spread of this 'lie'. Yes, some interpret this as being an immense lie from Satan himself. Others reckon that people who do believe in the pretribulation 'rapture theory', as they put it, are frightened over that which is to come upon the earth and that they look for an escape from reality. This may be either true - or the matter has a very different side to it that is completely neglected and ignored.

Can those who expect a rapture (the gathering of all true Christians – from out amongst all Christian churches and house churches – to meet Christ in the air – 1 Thes. 4:16,17), perhaps be the most realistic of all people living on earth? World happenings are viewed from a biblical perspective rather than from a humanistic one. They merely believe that the Word of God has to be understood in a straightforward manner.

It seems however, that there is someone who is trying

with all his power to make this truth appear to be a lie. He uses everything in his might to keep the children of God from having hope (seated in Christ) and that is why the result is an incredible onslaught against this biblical doctrine. The devil wants us to regard him as our hope in this world. See, he is the 'god of this world' (2 Cor. 4:4) and wants our faith to rather reside in him – even though only in an indirect manner. The rapture of the true church (all real believers in Christ) is a controversial subject. Few doctrines in the Word has to withstand such fierce attacks as this one. Yes, one of the most beautiful messages in the entire Bible (in particular relevant to our time), is interpreted by most theologians as wishful thinking and absurd. Often one hears about someone stating in a sarcastic way that there cannot and will not be a 'secret rapture.' They accentuate that this event will not occur in 'secret'.

It is true that man dislike situations that could catch him off guard. Man wants to remain in control at all times – of his own circumstances and even further if possible. The unforeseen and unexpected many times bring fear and that has to be avoided at all cost – even though God said that there would be an unexpected time when He would come to swiftly gather His bride. Yes, man never wants to admit that there is Someone greater than himself who controls everything on this earth to the finest detail. The average world citizen or even worldly Christian does not want to admit that he is totally subject to an almighty God that plans and decrees all major events beforehand. Man with his free will is always busy with future prospects and the dreaming of dreams about *this passing world* and the 'things I still want to do.' Plans wherein Jesus Christ is central, is something quite different. The problem is that many view God as the One whom wants to interfere and 'spoil the fun.' They however forget that it is this same God that created us and it is He who keeps us, in spite of our rebellion against Him.

Furthermore, He still provides us with a chance, to this moment, to set things straight with Him. Yes, every person on earth has an issue to settle with God. In Is. 1:18 He invites everyone to come and settle this issue with Him – forever.

Concerning Christ's sudden coming for His church, we have to be prepared and ready, for according to the Word, there will be a gathering of the true believers and it will remain a secret event even for those who will remain behind. In 1 Thes. 5 we find the following:

"But of the times and seasons, brethren, ye have no need that I write unto you. For yourselves know perfectly that the day of the Lord cometh <u>as a thief in the night</u>. For when they shall say, Peace and safety; then sudden destruction cometh upon them, as travail upon a woman with child; and they shall not escape." (verses 1-3).

When a thief comes in the night, will he not come in secret? Will he appear openly and declare that he is there? Would such a thief succeed in stealing anything? Remember, Jesus comes *like* a thief and not *as* one!

This event will occur suddenly and unexpectedly, especially for those who did not know Christ. In the next verse (1 Thes. 5:4) the Word continues:

"But ye, brethren, are not in darkness, that that day should overtake you as a thief." Two clearly distinguishable groups are present here. They who will be caught totally unaware and the children of God who will be prepared and not be overtaken as by a thief. To which one of these two groups do you belong? Are you awaiting the second coming of the Lord Jesus Christ? Paul already awaited this event in his days!

PRE, MIDDLE OR POST?

The question remains, at what stage on the prophetic calendar of God will the rapture take place? Will it be before, in the middle or after the great tribulation. (Mt. 24:21). Unfortunately, there are also those who want to reason away the coming great tribulation, but that is another tragedy. In Dan. 9:27 we read of the Antichrist who will confirm a strong covenant with many nations for a week (a year week – seven years). As was mentioned before, this is clearly the time in which the events of Rev. 6-19 will occur on earth. Without a doubt, it will be a terrible time one earth – a time like never before (Dan. 12:1). Everything points to the fact that the beginning of this time could be at hand.

The world is in a chaotic state and it is worsening daily. The collective sins of the human race have been calling for righteous judgement for quite a long time now. The Lord will intervene at a certain stage – we can be sure of that. The prophetic Word of God states this frankly.

To answer the question of when the rapture will be, we have to look at the well-known passage in Lk. 17. In verse 24 we read more about the sudden coming of the Lord Jesus Christ: *"For as the lightning, that lighteneth out of the one part under heaven, shineth unto the other part under heaven, so shall also the Son of man be in his day."* In the following verse, the Lord Jesus Himself relates how the days before His coming will be like. It does appear to be 'normal' times, almost like today: *"And as it was in the days of Noah, so shall it be also in the days of the Son of man. They did eat, they drank, they married wives, they were given in marriage, until the day that Noah entered the ark, and the flood came, and destroyed them all."* (verses 26 and 27). It was quite ordinary times. Noah, the prophet, warned everybody, but everyone 'knew' better.

Think how remorseful they must be now. They continued with their lives as if everything would just carry on for ever, but it was not the case. They were so busy with themselves and their own things, that they did not hear the voice of the Lord in their lives. The voice, which kept on pleading: 'Prepare to meet your Lord', was ignored. The crux of the matter is that the flood came when nobody expected it. It took the entire ancient world by utter surprise and only eight people's lives were spared. Alternatively, do we have to spiritualize the flood away, as many do these days? Is this not done mainly to take the accent away from God's coming judgments in the days shortly before the second coming? God said that the latter days will be like the days of Noah. That there was a flood and that it was a worldwide flood cannot be denied anymore. The evidence in the thousands of seashell fossils found high on the Himalayas, is but one example. Much evidence exists in this regard and numerous Christian and non-Christian scientists confirmed this. What we read in the newspapers - that this all is but myths - is an onslaught from another side. There are more than 250 legends of a flood that previously occurred right across the world. The fact that all the details do not always correlate exactly, actually strengthens the case. If different witnesses in a court case testify about a specific event, but everybody tells it from his of her own perspective, a good case exists and the judge will act accordingly.

On the other hand, if all the witnesses tell the same story, and that word for word, the judge will suspect that something serious is wrong.

This placed aside, the Word of God speaks in many places, in the New Testament, about the flood and Jesus Christ Himself refers to it, amongst others, in the mentioned Lk. 17.

The most important point to remember though, is that this tragedy (the flood) occurred under very 'ordinary' circumstances. People were eating, drinking, marrying etc. It will be the same when Jesus comes to gather His bride (Lk. 17:30). Will this be the situation at the end of the great tribulation? Will the end not come after an enormous war? Will this be normal, ordinary circumstances? Will people eat, drink and marry in a normal way? It is not what the book of Revelation explains regarding the final part of the seven years of tribulation!

Look at the following: Rev. 6:6,8 (as well as Mt. 24:7) speaks of the famines of those days; water (the sea water and fresh water) will change into blood - as in the days of Egypt (Rev. 16:3-6). Incredible wars will be the order of the day (Rev. 6:4,8; Rev. 9:15-19; Rev. 16:14-16 etc.) Will these people eat and drink and marry in a normal way? Most young men will probably be away on the war zone! Is this how the days of Noah were before the flood came? We need to be honest. Remember the Lord is honest and true to us (Num. 23:19).

If we return to Lk. 17 we read: *"Likewise also as it was in the days of Lot; they did eat, they drank, they bought, they sold, they planted, they builded ... Even thus shall it be in the day when the Son of man is revealed."* (verse 28 and 30). Again, the Bible speaks of buying, selling, planting and building. It sounds like a normal day, like we still enjoy, by the grace of God, to this day. The Lord will return when this type of life is still the order of the day.

Will this be the case at the end of the great tribulation? Or even in the middle of that time? In the middle of the seven years, the Antichrist will force his mark on all people and nobody will be able to buy or sell if he does not have this mark (Rev. 13:16-18). Many will however be converted to the Lord Jesus Christ and they will not take the mark. We can see this clearly from the passage in Rev. 20:4. Many will not be able to buy and sell normally. They will lose their lives because they will not accept the mark. Today, the world is planting and building, but will it be possible during the great tribulation? In Rev. 8:7 we see that a third of all the trees and green grass on earth will be burnt. The two witnesses will also have the power to close the heavens for three and a half years so that no rain will fall on earth during this time (Rev. 11:3-6).

There will be no likelihood of any planting and building in a normal way during this time. In addition, there will be terrible judgments - the sun scorching people (Rev. 16:8) and hail (each a talent in weight = 60 kg) that will fall on earth's inhabitants (Rev. 16:21). The Lord will not come to collect His children under such circumstances. Jesus Christ, the Bridegroom and coming King, will not hit His bride to be (the re-born Christians) to pieces before the glorious marriage in heaven. No, the day of Christ will be like the days of Noah and Lot, SHORTLY BEFORE THE JUDGEMENTS OF THE LORD CAME DOWN ON THE GODLESS PEOPLE OF THE EARTH. The Scriptures teach that the gathering will occur in ordinary circumstances – LIKE FOR EXAMPLE: TODAY!

The question remains, how long will everything remain 'normal.' We can see that events in the world are moving into a specific direction and fast too – as God predicted.

Another important point, usually missed by most people, is the fact that the Lord explicitly said: *"Therefore be ye also ready: for in such an hour as ye think not the Son of man cometh."* (Mt. 24:44). It will be sudden, unexpected and like a thief in the night. In the book of Revelation, we read in numerous places (amongst others Rev. 12:6 and 13:5) that there will be a final period of three and a half years before Jesus comes back with His saints (Rev. 19:14). It is also called a period of 42 months or specifically 1 260 days. It could then be that Christians who would live in those days (if there was no rapture before that time) that they will be able to count the days precisely (the 1260 days) to know exactly when the Lord will come.

The Lord says however, that no one will know the day

and hour of His coming. These events of the great tribulation culminate in the second phase of Christ's coming and not in the rapture or gathering. It will climax in the time when Jesus will stand with His feet on the Mount of Olives as prophesied in Zech. 14:4,5. The bride of Christ will then be in heaven for seven years for the marriage week and will return triumphantly with Christ to set up the thousand year Kingdom that will climax in the eternal Kingdom. We also read distinctly in Mt. 25:13: *"Watch therefore: for ye know neither the day nor the hour wherein the Son of man cometh"*. This verse, as well as Mt. 24:44 and similar passages refer specifically to the gathering or taking away of the bride of Christ. It will occur suddenly and unexpectedly (1 Cor. 15:51,52).

That is why we have to be ready to meet our Heavenly Bridegroom at any time. The saints (the bride of Christ) will be in heaven for the entire period of seven years, where first the judgement seat of Christ (2 Cor. 5:10) and then the marriage supper of the Lamb will take place (Rev. 19:7,9). On earth, the terrible judgements of the Lord will be ongoing, as mentioned already. This time is also known as the time of God's wrath (Rev. 6:17). In 1 Thes. 5:9 (referring specifically to the events at the end), Paul says distinctly: *"For God hath not appointed us to wrath, but to obtain salvation by our Lord Jesus Christ"*. He speaks of the true church - the reborn Bible believing Christians. The true children of God will escape the entire period of tribulation and will be in heaven around the throne of God (Lk. 21:36 says we will stand before the Son of man). In Rev. 19:8 the bride of Christ is clothed with *"fine linen, clean and white"* for the marriage supper and in Rev. 19:14 we read that *"the armies which were in heaven followed him [Jesus] upon white horses, clothed in fine linen, white and clean"*. This will happen right at the end of the seven years of great tribulation. Then the King comes with His bride, the war of

Armageddon is ended (Rev. 19:15-21; Zech. 14:1-5) and the thousand year Kingdom (the reign of peace) will commence (Rev. 20:1-6).

The Word of God is quite clear on when the gathering of the saints will be and that there will be such an event. The rapture or gathering is the next great event on God's prophetic calendar – according to the Bible. It will happen quite suddenly though. Nowhere in the Bible did God say that this world would be ready for this day. The world is in direct opposition to God (Jas. 4:4). This day will catch the world unawares – when they will still be crying *"peace and safety"* (1 Thes. 5:3). A further truth is that even the nominal church (as an institution) will not be ready for this day. The Word teaches that the apostate, lukewarm church of Laodicea (which means 'human rights' or 'rights of the people') will be present on earth before the Lord comes (Rev. 3:14-22).

In 2 Thes. 2:3 we also see that there first have to be an *"apostasy"* (*apostasia* in Greek) – a falling away from the truth, before the final events will come to pass. Some are of the impression that this even relates to a 'departure' of the saints – the gathering! Whatever the case may be, no great sign or signs have to precede the rapture of the true church. It could be any day my friend, are you ready? Yes it is very important that we as the children of God understand these things and share it with others – the time is really short. Speaking of 'in the secret', the prophet Isaiah prophesied about such a time more than two and a half thousand years ago: *"The righteous perisheth, and no man layeth it to heart: and merciful men are taken away, none considering that the righteous is taken away from the evil to come. He shall enter into peace: they shall rest in their beds, each one walking in his uprightness"* (Is. 57:1,2).

Are you walking in this way?

We will now look in more detail at the biblical promise of the day of Christ – that unique and blessed day when God's trumpet will sound and everything on earth will change forever.

THE BLESSED HOPE

"looking for that blessed hope, and the glorious appearing of the great God and our Saviour Jesus Christ" (Tit. 2:13)

What can this blessed hope be? From the Word we have clearly pointed out that the time of great tribulation will be the time of God's righteous judgement over this sin filled world. Would it be fair or righteous of God to also bring those who had served Him in truth and sincerity into this period of His wrath? It does not make sense and seems quite illogical in the context of the Scriptures. To tell the truth, we were not left in the dark regarding this 'difficult' question. In the Word of God we find numerous distinct references that all those that are reborn, those that were washed by the blood of Jesus Christ (Rev. 1:5), will not endure this time. The Lord says in no uncertain terms that they that belong to Him, are not destined for His wrath that will come upon this earth: *"For God hath not appointed us to wrath, but to obtain salvation by our Lord Jesus Christ, who died for us, that whether we wake or sleep, we should live together with him."* (1 Thes. 5:9,10) and also *"to wait for his Son from heaven, whom he raised from the dead, even Jesus, which delivered us from the wrath to come."* (1 Thes. 1:10).

The *wrath to come* is clearly a reference to the time of the great tribulation that is to come. We see that Rev. 6:15-17 refers specifically to this period of judgement as the time of God's wrath: *"And the kings of the earth, and the great men, and the rich men, and the chief captains, and the mighty men, and every bondman, and every free man, hid themselves in the dens and in the rocks of the mountains; and said to the mountains and rocks, Fall on us, and hide us from the face of him that sitteth on the throne, and from the wrath of the Lamb: for the great day of his wrath is come; and who shall be able to stand?"*

Here, it is clear that the wrath that is to come refers to the great tribulation. Chapters 6-19 of the book of Revelation, as was mentioned earlier, relates specifically to this terrible time of God's wrath on earth and its inhabitants. This time is also called *the day of the Lord* – a reference to the same day of His great wrath (also see Rom. 1:18). The mentioned passages in 1 Thessalonians, that we will escape the wrath of God, are in connection with the second coming of Christ as well as the time of great tribulation. From the Word it is very clear that this time will introduce the end of the human dispensation on earth. The children of God will be taken away before this time commences - to their home in heaven. These type of events and way of dealing from the Lord is not strange in comparison to other parts of Scripture. In the time of Noah, he and his family were first brought into the safety of the ark before the Lord brought His judgements onto the earth. The ark is also a type of the Lord Jesus Christ. Everyone that resides in Him, will first be brought to safety before the Lord will pour out His wrath on this earth. In the time of Lot, he and his family was also brought to safety first before the Lord destroyed Sodom and Gomorra with fire and brimstone. Then it is not strange to again read the words in Lk, 17:26,28,30: *"And as it was in the days of Noah, so shall it be also in the days of the Son of man ... Likewise also as it was in the days of Lot ... Even thus shall it be in the day when the Son of man is revealed."* As it happened in those days, it will be again in the day of Christ. No person belonging to Him will be in the cross fire when God's judgements hit the earth. We have to remember that it is God Himself who judges the world. Even in a war situation, the offensive nation will first remove all of their own citizens from the country they want to invade. To this day, it is still the modus operandi. Never in all history did God treat those who belong to Him and those who hate him, in the same manner. Even Rahab and her family were spared when the city of Jericho was destroyed, because she believed in God (Josh. 6:23,24). We (the saved) are in this world, but not of this world (Jn. 17:16). We are citizens of heaven on a journey through a foreign land. We belong to the One whose place of residence is not in this world. Those that are in Christ, will therefore not enter the time of great tribulation.

We read in 1 Jn. 2:28 the following in this regard: "*And now, little children, abide in him; that when he shall appear, we may have confidence, and not be ashamed before him at his coming*". If we notice all the signs of the endtimes so clearly, we know that the time of great tribulation is near. There is however an event that will precede this event and that is the blessed hope for every born-again child of God. We read in Lk. 21:28: "*And when these things begin to come to pass, then look up, and lift up your heads; for your redemption draweth nigh*". The mentioned "*these things*", are the signs of the end of time that are pointed out in the previous verses in Lk. 21 – particularly concerning the tribulation period and the events that will introduce that time. All these things are about to happen and that is why we have to look up "*unto Jesus the author and finisher of our faith; who for the joy that was set before him endured the cross, despising the shame, and is set down at the right hand of the throne of God.*" (Heb. 12:2).

A further strong consolation can be found in Lk. 21 in verse 36: "*Watch ye therefore, and pray always, that ye may be accounted worthy to escape all these things that shall come to pass, and to stand before the Son of man.*" It is clear

– once again – that everyone that is accounted worthy will not endure these things (the judgements). It is however, only with Christ in you, through the working of the Holy Sprit, that one may be accounted worthy to escape these judgements.

Nobody can eradicate this truth. God's Word can never change – it stands firm until all eternity. Rev. 3:10 states also that they that know the Lord, will not go into the hour of temptation – the tribulation period: *"Because thou hast kept the word of my patience, I will keep thee from the hour of temptation, which shall come upon all the world, to try them that dwell upon the earth."*

This is the blessed hope for every child of God that lives today and with it comes the incentive to live a holy life and to never stop praying. It is not done from our own strength, but *"in the power of his might"* (Eph. 6:10).

One of the objections against the doctrine of the rapture of the church - before the start of the tribulation period - is the view that it will cause the children of God to become lukewarm, because they now know that they will be taken to heaven anyway. This is poor reasoning though. One does not live holy in fear of the coming hard days, but rather because you truly met with the Lord Jesus Christ and because you trust Him to fill you with His Holy Spirit. If you learn to know Him and you become familiar with His will – from the Word – you will always serve Him, in good or bad times. The fact that the gathering of the saints could occur any day and does not have to be preceded by any sign, is a further inspiration for a biblical Christian to live in all holiness. As a result, you do not have to be on the lookout for the Antichrist or a certain war, because Jesus can come today! That is why we have to be ready at all times. The expectation of the rapture thus results in the fact that our eyes are fixed on Jesus Christ and not on this world.

WHO IS THE WITHHOLDER?

From Scripture it is clear that the Antichrist will be revealed early in the tribulation period. He will make a strong covenant with many nations (Dan. 9:27) and will introduce a time of false peace. With regard to his revelation, we read in 2 Thes. 2:6-8: "*And now ye know what withholdeth that he might be revealed in his time. For the mystery of iniquity doth already work: only he who now letteth will let, until he be taken out of the way. And then shall that Wicked be revealed,*". The question remains, who is this withholder that has to be removed before the Antichrist will be revealed. Some are of the opinion that it is the government systems of the world. Could that be? Today there remains no governments with constitutions that are based on the Word of God anymore. Such a government could never withhold any sin, not even to mention the "*man of sin*" (2 Thes. 2:3). The Antichrist will rather rise from such an antichristian foundation. The current scenario on earth is of such a nature that this person may rise at any time. There is however somebody else Whom is the true Withholder. God alone can prevent this man from making his appearance. God works in this world through His Holy Spirit and through His children (the church) in which the Spirit dwell. The true church or body of Christ (filled with the Holy Spirit) is the withholder that prevents this person from being revealed to the world. The Holy Spirit will not be taken away completely from the earth – that would be impossible. God is omnipresent. After the rapture however, the Holy Spirit will not be present on the earth in His Pentecostal fullness. The rapture will be the end of the church dispensation which began on Pentecost Sunday, and in the great tribulation that will follow, the world will shortly return to a Old Testament type of dispensation with Israel as the main focus. In Dan. 9:24–27 we see that the seventieth week (a period of seven years) is determined upon Israel as a nation. It will go into fulfillment then.

In addition, we have to remember that the prayers of the reborn Christians keep the current world from rotting completely on a moral level as well as on all others. God listens to the prayers of His children, because He promised this in His Word. We read in Jas. 5:16 that the fervent prayer of the righteous achieves much. There is however nothing for the Christian to boast about, all the glory and honour belongs to God. It is mere grace that He did not come to judge this earth yet. It is also not strange to view the true church as the withholder. In Mt. 5:13 we read: *"Ye are the salt of the earth; but if the salt have lost his savor, wherewith shall it be salted?"* Salt keep and prevent food from going off or even rotting, and give taste at the same time. It is also much more effective if sprinkled – more so than when all is on one heap. That is why Paul says in Col. 4:6 *"let your speech be always with grace, seasoned with salt"*. It is also interesting to note that Lot's wife, after she left Sodom, changed into a pillar of salt (Gen. 19:26). She was disobedient to God, but through this, we can clearly see that the Lord first removed the 'salt', before He send His judgements. Whichever way you want to view this, Lot's wife escaped the judgements and was not consumed by fire and brimstone. One of the angels told Lot that he could do nothing before they reach the city of Zoar. Only then the cities were destroyed. It is a type of the body of Christ that will be taken away before the great tribulation. The Antichrist will be revealed shortly thereafter and the final seven years will then commence - ending in Christ's glorious appearing to the world.

THE SECOND COMING IN PHASES

There are certain parts of Scripture that are more difficult to understand than others. Only the enlightenment of the Holy Spirit of God can reveal these things to the born-again Christian. When you study the passages concerning the return of the Lord in the Bible, one realizes that it is not that simple a matter. The general perception that the Lord will only come after thousands or even millions of years, and that He will instantly separate the goats from the sheep - sending some to heaven and some to hell, is a misrepresentation of the Word. This point of view usually presides with those who never study this matter in real depth. Some others again may even be afraid of the subject of the second coming. This is often the case if you are not really ready for the day of Christ and most of the time this is merely because of a lack of Scriptural knowledge. Sustained prayer and a systematic study of the Word bring the full picture into perspective though.

The second coming occur in two clearly distinguishable phases. This does not mean that there will be two second comings. Presently there is a strange point of view held by some of the opposers of this interpretation. They believe we teach a 'first' second coming before the thousand years of peace and also a 'second' second coming after the thousand years of peace. This interpretation however, does not exist at all. Both phases of the second coming occurs before the millennium of peace. (They however also do not believe in a literal millennium, but rather that we are currently living in that time and that Satan is bound now!)

The first phase, the rapture of the church, introduces the great tribulation and the second phase will come at the end of that period. The second coming of Christ includes both phases as well as the millennium of peace (Rev. 20:1-6) that will follow. The main reason being that He will return to set up His Kingdom on earth. In 1 Cor. 15:25 we read: *"For he must reign, till he hath put all enemies under his feet."* It is not how we experience the world today. The apostle Peter alluded to this matter centuries ago and warned that few would understand these truths. Every child of God who shares a healthy and living expectation of the second coming, will ensure that he or she walks with God. Such a Christian need not be in the dark regarding these amazing and sometimes difficult passages in Scripture. Concerning this Peter wrote: *"Wherefore, beloved, seeing that ye look for such things, be diligent that ye may be found of him in peace, without spot, and blameless. And account that the long-suffering of our Lord is salvation; even as our beloved brother Paul also according to the wisdom given unto him hath written unto you; as also in all his epistles, <u>speaking in them of these things; in which are some things hard to be understood</u>, which they that are unlearned and unstable wrest, as they do also the other Scriptures, unto their own destruction. Ye therefore, beloved, seeing ye know these things before, beware lest ye also, being led away with the error of the wicked, fall from your own steadfastness."* (2 Pet. 3:14-17). This passage has to be interpreted in the context of the whole of 2 Pet. 3, which specifically speaks of the second coming of Christ. We will also see that it was the apostle Paul that initially expounded on the first phase of the second coming. It is to these matters that Peter alluded as *"some things hard to be understood"*. It does not have to remain this way however, for we have the Holy Spirit and the whole Word to teach us.

The fact that the second coming will occur in phases, is not a strange phenomenon in the Bible. If we look at Jesus' first coming to this earth, we find that there were also different phases. He did not appear on one day and disappeared again immediately. There were the phase of preparation when the angel appeared to Mary; the birth, His childhood; His life as a carpenter; His earthly ministry of about three and a half years; the crucifixion, death, resurrection and eventual ascension. Combined, this is interpreted as the first coming of Christ to this earth. Only at the age of thirty, did Jesus' earthly ministry really begin. Generally, His last three and a half years are known as His first coming – when He came and revealed Himself as the Son of God, but that was merely the most important phase of His first coming. When He returns shortly, it will initially only be for those who belong to Him. This phase will only start the time of the second coming (when He will eventually also return to earth to set up His Kingdom), as we will see later. This will be the final fulfillment of the prophecy and promise concerning His second coming.

Now, let us look at the distinguishable aspects of the two phases of Christ's second coming:

- In the first phase, Christ returns in the air (1 Thes. 4:16,17)
  In the second phase, He will stand with His feet on the Mount of Olives (Zech. 14:4,5)
- In the first phase He comes as a thief in the night (Mt. 24:42,43)
  In the second phase every eye shall see Him (Rev. 1:7)
- In the first phase He will come *for* His saints (1 Cor. 15:51,52)
  In the second phase He will come *with* His saints (Jude 14; Rev. 19:14)
- The first phase is known as the *day of Christ* (Phil.1:10)
  The second phase is associated with the *day of the Lord* (Zeph. 1:14-18)
- In the first phase, the body of Christ - His church - is central (1 Thes. 4:16,17).
  In the second phase, the nation of Israel is central (Zech. 12:10-13:9)

THE DAY OF CHRIST

It is this day that every Bible believing Christian awaits in anticipation. Paul writes the following in this regard: *"And this I pray, that your love may abound yet more and more in knowledge and in all judgment; that ye may be sincere and without offence till the day of Christ"* (Phil 1:9,10). Also read 1 Cor. 1:7,8 regarding the day of Christ. It is that special day when Christ will return to collect His bride to be with Him for all eternity. The bride of Christ has to be prepared for this great moment. We read in 1 Thes. 4:16-18 of this wondrous event: *"For the Lord himself shall descend from heaven with a shout, with a voice of the archangel, and with the trump of God; and the dead in Christ shall rise first: then we which are alive and remain shall be caught up together with them in the clouds, to meet the Lord in the air; and so shall we ever be with the Lord. Wherefore comfort one another with these words."* How many times have you been comforted with these wonderful words? Today, I want to comfort every true child of God with these blessed words. It is however a very rare message in the age that we live in. For every true Christian this day is a great expectation though. The tribulation period is approaching, but if you are born-again and you truly know the Lord – then you will not enter this terrible time. However, it must be said again, this only applies to them who have settled their case personally with the Lord – through the blood of Jesus Christ. In the above-mentioned verses, we can see that the Lord Jesus Christ will only come in the air and not, in the true sense of the matter, to the earth. This is the first phase of the second coming. Only those who died in Christ and those who truly know Him in life, will ascend to heaven on that day. What does it mean to be in Christ? Surely it does not mean to merely be a member of a denominational church. There is a big difference between *being in church* and *being in Christ*.

In 2 Cor. 5:17 we read: *"Therefore if any man be in Christ, he is a new creature; the old things are passed away; behold, all things are become new."* These are not mere cheap words. Paul wrote it in all honesty and under the inspiration of the Holy Spirit. If you did not become a new creature, can you then say that you are in Christ? It would be very dangerous to assume that. The true Christ of the Scriptures will never leave your life unchanged after you have really met Him. He is the God of the universe! That is why all church members need to heed the warning that they will not be taken away with Christ merely because they belong to a church. Everyone that is truly in Christ though – thus surrendered to Him, have the assurance from the Word that this will be an indescribable day for them.

The truth of the rapture is very clearly stated in Scripture in 1 Thes. 4:16 and 17. The Lord Jesus Christ – on that occasion – will come only for His holy ones – those that He had sanctified through His blood. Now in Zech. 14:4,5 in comparison, we read that Jesus will stand with His feet on the Mount of Olives near Jerusalem and all the *"saints"* will be there with Him. We find the same truth in Jude 14,15 when we read of the coming of the Lord *"with ten thousands of his saints"*. This is no reference to angels, as some believe. Angels are never called saints in the Bible. This group will be compiled out of every reborn human, washed in the blood of the Lamb. This is the second phase of His coming.

If Jesus thus comes with His saints, He had to come for them first. This is the glorious day of Christ, when His body – the true church, will be united with Him as the Head. This event, the rapture, will take place in the air as Scripture describes.

The word rapture is derived from the word *rapere* - the Latin translation of the Greek word *harpazo*. The *King James Version* of the Bible translates this with *'caught up'*.

It is precisely what it is.

Sadly though, many associate this word and belief with some or other sect and miss the wonderful biblical truth surrounding this very special event. Oftentimes when you mention this to someone, you are stared at and even regarded as strange. It is tragic and mainly because of ignorance regarding this biblical teaching. The message of the gathering or rapture is very relevant today – more so than ever before. There is literally no other prophecy in the Bible that needs to go into fulfillment before this great event will become a reality. For most (even for many Christians), this truth is too magnificent to believe. They just cannot envision that God will perform such an act of grace. Those who do not believe in the coming rapture do focus on the fact that God is a God of love (which He is of course). The problem is that they also believe that He will not come to judge this world in righteousness – in any way not in such literal terms as the Bible explains. If this is your way of thought, then the normal outflow thereof is that the tribulation period will not be nearly as severe as is portrayed in the Word. In other words if you believe that the church will not be raptured, then the other prophecies in Scripture regarding the end time could also be spiritualized away. Is this the way to handle God's infallible Word though? The irrefutable truth from the Scriptures is that the nation of Israel will have to endure the great tribulation. The problem arises when the bride or church of Christ (Eph. 5:25-32) is positioned in the place of the literal Israel. That is why many believe that the true church will also have to endure this time.

Remember that Satan hates the message of the rapture, because it brings hope to the child of God in this godless world. Do not allow that your blessed hope is stolen from you in this way. Some people do not want to believe in the rapture, because they fear that it could lead to the devil deceiving them, or that it will lead to a lukewarm relationship with the Lord. The opposite is true. If the Lord Jesus can come at any time (which He can of course), you have to be ready all the time anyway. This is the message.

PROBLEMS WITH THE 'THEORY' OF THE RAPTURE

Today, many Christians doubt if there will be anything like a rapture or gathering of the saints, and that for various reasons. Some do believe that the church will have to endure half of the tribulation period before they will be taken away and others believe that the saints will have to endure the entire tribulation before being taken away at the end thereof. It is understandable that there are different points of view regarding this matter, but in the end, it merely matters what God says in His Word. Some of the objections people have against the idea that the bride of Christ will be taken away before the entire period of the great tribulation, are the following:

* They say that if Christians in the time of Nero and other Roman emperors, and during the time of the Roman inquisition, as well as under leaders like Hitler and Stalin had to endure so much suffering, why would God save our generation from the tribulation. They ask why if eleven of the twelve apostles and Paul had to die cruell deaths - as martyrs, how can we expect not to also meet our end this way. It is a very good point, but merely a little further biblical and extra-biblical research brings everything into perspective. In the past 2 000 years there were millions of Christians that had to die for their faith. To tell the truth, missionaries have stated that in the 20th century alone, more Christians died for their faith than in all of the previous 19 centuries of the church dispensation combined. Now as I am writing, Christians are suffering severely for their faith in

Christ and many die in countries like Sudan, Morocco, Saudi-Arabia, Pakistan, Afghanistan, Indonesia and Red China, to mention but a few. The reason why few Christians in the Western world die for their faith in Christ, is because most people's Christianity cost them very little. If you actively begin to minister to the spiritual needs of people of other religions, with the motive of seeing them become converted to Christ, you may also lose your life, sooner or later. In Muslim countries, the Christian faith is simply not tolerated, but in the 'Christian' countries of the West all religions are tolerated and accommodated. Why is that?

The persecution of the children of God through the centuries – even to this day – is not to be compared with the coming time of great tribulation that the Bible speaks of. It will be a time like never before (Mt. 24:21). It would be unfair of God to select our generation and the members of the true church of Christ that is living presently, to live through this unique time. What about all the Christians that died already but lived a tranquil life without having experienced severe persecution at all? God is righteous and that is why we have the promise of a rapture before this time commences. No Christian have a guarantee that he will survive the great tribulation. According to the book of Revelation, everyone who will not take the mark of the beast will be killed. In Mt. 16:18 we read: "*...and upon this Rock I will build my church; and the gates of hell shall not prevail against it*". The entire body of Christ will not be exterminated on earth.

Further we have to remember that the time of great tribulation is not the time of Satan's wrath or the Antichrist's wrath. The past 2 000 years the church suffered greatly under Satanic attacks, but that is not even comparable to the terrible days awaiting the world in the near future. No, the great tribulation is the time of *God's wrath*.

In Rev. 6:17 (right at the beginning of this incomparable

time) we read these words: *"for the great day of his wrath is come; and who shall be able to stand?"* Then God self, through His angels, will judge this world and all them that are in the world whom have rejected the atoning blood of His Son Jesus Christ.

* Another objection against the pretribulation rapture, is the interpretation that this doctrine had its origin somewhere in the 19ᵗʰ century. This is not true. Note the following church father as well as other preachers who believed and preached this message a long time ago:

- Ephraem of Syria – 425 AD
- Peter Jurieu – 1687
- Philip Doddridge – 1738
- Morgan Edwards – 1743
- Dr. John Gill – 1748
- James Macknight – 1763
- Thomas Scott – 1792 [172]

THE NATURE OF THE RAPTURE

From the Scriptures we can clearly see that this event will occur suddenly and abruptly. We read in 1 Cor. 15:51,52 the wonderful words: *"Behold, I show you a mystery; We shall not all sleep, but we shall all be changed, in a moment, in the twinkling of an eye, at the last trump: for the trumpet shall sound, and the dead shall be raised incorruptible, and we shall be changed."* This truth remained a mystery until this moment, but then Paul revealed it to the church of the Corinthians under the guidance of God the Holy Spirit. How terribly sad that for so many it still remains a mystery to this day. Paul here speaks to us or ('we') – the children of God, some of whom have already died and others that will still be alive on that glorious day. Here is no reference to those living in the world, those without God and without hope. They will be left behind. There is no question about it. The Word teaches very distinctly in Lk. 17:35-36: *"Two women shall be grinding together; the one shall be taken, and the other left. Two men shall be in the field; the one shall be taken and the other left."* (Tragically enough there are those in our day and age that suggest that the sinners will be taken away and the righteous ones will be left behind. Many 'new age' writers and supporters also believe this).

We find these words following the passage that refers to the coming of Christ as being like the days of Noah and Lot, in other words in context with the blessed day of Christ – the rapture or gathering of His saints!

Where will you be when this trumpet sounds? As we conclude from Scripture, this event will occur very unexpectedly. In this regard we read in Lk. 17:24: *"For as the lightning, that lighteneth out of the one part under heaven, shineth unto the other part under heaven; so shall also the Son of man be in his day."* (His day – the day of Christ). This will be when the Lord comes like a thief in the night (Mt. 24:42-44). The comparison with the thief in the night is very striking and exactly what will happen that day. Jesus Christ will come to collect those who are precious to Him, those who knew Him personally – those whom He has bought with His own blood. We have mentioned this before, but a thief always surprises the people of the house. The rapture will occur instantly and without prior notice.

The Word also speaks of a trumpet – the last trumpet – that will sound at that moment. Many wonder how this fits in if the Lord Jesus is coming like a thief in the night. In Rev. 4:1 we also read of a voice like a trumpetsound. The apostle John wrote that he heard a voice crying unto him with the words *'come up hither'*. It is a prophetic reference to the true church that will be taken away and it corresponds with 1 Thes. 4:16 – the sound of a trumpet and a shouting. The Lord will call His children on that day and only they will recognize His voice. One recognizes only the voices of those you know. Jesus Christ explained this in Jn. 10:3,4 as well as in verse 27: *"My sheep hear my voice, and I know them, and they follow me"*. Further on in Jn. 12:28-30, we read of where God spoke from heaven to His Son on earth. Some of the people present recognized God's voice and others again thought it to be a clap of thunder. We read the following: *"Father, glorify thy name. Then came there a voice from heaven, saying, I have both glorified it, and will glorify it again. The people therefore that stood by, and heard it, said that it thundered: others said, An angel spake to him. Jesus answered and said, This voice came not because of me, but for your sakes."* On the day of the rapture, only the true children of God will recognize His voice and others will not know what had happened. Will you recognize His voice when the trumpet sounds?

TYPES OF THE RAPTURE

In the Bible we find quite a few types or examples of raptures that have occurred in the past. It is a strong reminder that there is such an event waiting in future. In Eccl. 1:9 we read: *"The thing that hath been, it is that which shall be; and that which is done is that which shall be done: and there is no new thing under the sun"* Early in the Old Testament we find the well-known case of Enoch. He was a man close to the heart of God – he walked with God. The Scriptures relate: *"and all the day of Enoch were three hundred sixty and five years: and Enoch walked with God: and he was not; for God took him"* (Gen. 5:23,24). Interesting how Enoch (Gen. 5) was taken away before the flood in the days of Noah (Gen. 6-8). In the New Testament, we also read of this special event. In Heb. 11;5 we read: *"By faith Enoch was translated that he should not see death; and was not found, because God had translated him: for before his translation he had this testimony, that he pleased God."* At the time of the rapture, it will only be them that pleased God – those that believed in Him, that will go away with Christ.

There also was the time when Elijah was taken up by the Lord. We read in 2 Kgs. 2:1,11: *"And it came to pass. When the Lord would take up Elijah into heaven by a whirlwind, that Elijah went with Elisha from Gilgal ... and Elijah went up by a whirlwind into heaven"*. It will be the same when the Lord Jesus comes to gather those who belong to Him. It will only be on a much larger scale and with more far reaching results.

Not only in the Old, but also in the New Testament do we find types of the rapture. In 2 Cor. 12:2 we read: *"I knew a man in Christ above fourteen years ago, (whether in body, I cannot tell; or whether out of the body, I cannot tell: God knoweth;) such an one caught up to the third heaven."* Paul here refers to himself and that he was raptured unto God's residing place – the third heaven. He himself is not sure if it was in or out of the body. When the church of Christ will be taken away, we will all get new glorified bodies. We read in Phil. 3:20,21 that: *"our conversation is in heaven; from whence also we look for the Saviour, the Lord Jesus Christ: who shall change our vile body, that it may be fashioned like unto his glorious body, according to the working whereby he is able even to subdue all things unto himself."* It is noteworthy that everyone that had such a rapture-like experience, knew the Lord firsthand. Paul says distinctly *"a man in Christ"*. Can you say the same today?

There are even more raptures found in Scripture, for example when Jesus ascended to heaven. Rev. 12:5 reads that He was *"caught up"*. Some others are still to come. In

Rev. 11:12 the two witnesses are also taken up into heaven. Then there are the 144 000 sealed Jews. In Rev. 14:1 they stand on the heavenly Mount Zion. Verse 4 of the same chapter reads: *"These are they which follow the Lamb whithersoever he goeth."* At least two thousand years later, they follow Him into heaven. The rapture of the bride will occur before this time, because these last mentioned raptures will occur during the time of the great tribulation.

The Old Testament – in quite a few places – have interesting (possible) references to the rapture. In the time when this was written, those people could not understand it in this sense, but today with the New Testament as our major reference, it is very insightful to study these passages of Scripture.

- In Ps. 27:5 we read that God will come to our rescue and that *"in the time of trouble he shall hide me in his pavilion: in the secret of his tabernacle shall he hide me"*.

- In Eccl. 12:5 we read of terrible times: *"because man go to his long home, and the mourners go about the streets"*. Clearly two very distinct groups.

- In the book of Isaiah we find two such passages. The first is in Is. 26:17-21 regarding the resurrection. Verse 17 relates about a women in labour and it fits in with other similar passages that refers to the second coming in Mt. 24:8 and 1 Thes. 5:3. Verse 20 says that the people of God must be *"hid"* until God's wrath has passed. Verse 21 relates that this refers to the great tribulation.

In Is. 57:1,2 we read that the rapture will occur in secret: *"The righteous perisheth [disappear], and no man layeth it to heart: and merciful men are taken away, none considering that the righteous is taken away from the evil to come. He shall enter into peace: they shall rest in their beds, each one walking in his uprightness."*

- In the Book of Daniel, we find an amazing illustration

of the rapture before the seven years of tribulation. Except therefore that every part of Scripture has a literal meaning, there always is a spiritual meaning as well. In many cases, you can also find guidelines of a prophetical illustration that is found just under the surface. These illustrations explain the bigger picture of the Scriptures and are at times difficult to understand at first. In Dan. 2 and 3 we find such an illustration, that has to remind us of the depth of the Scriptures. It is there for us to find under the guidance of the Holy Spirit. If we look at Dan. 2:48 we see the following: *"Then the king made Daniel a great man, and gave him many great gifts, and made him ruler ... "* In the following verse, we see that three of his friends Shadrach, Meshach and Abednego was appointed under him. The following verse (the final one of Dan. 2) however ends like this: *"but Daniel sat in the gate of the king."* In chapter 3 we read of the events surrounding the image that had to be worshipped and that every one who did not comply had to be cast into a fiery furnace. It is noticeable that Daniel was absent and that his three friends, after they refused to worship the image, was thrown into the furnace. In verse 19 king Nebuchadnezzar ordered that the furnace be made seven times warmer. Daniel's friends were however visited by a fourth Person (the *"Son of God"*) and they were kept safe and escaped totally unhurt. The guards who threw them into the furnace, were consumed by the fire themselves (verse 22).

Note the possible prophetical interpretation: In the passage at the end of chapter 2, Nebuchadnezzar as king is a type of God. Daniel is exalted by him and he finds himself in the king's quarters. This could refer to the bride of Christ being raptured and exalted unto heaven. The great gifts that Daniel received (chapter 2:48), could refer to the judgment seat of Christ (2 Cor. 5:10; Rev. 4:10) that will commence shortly after the rapture. Daniel in the palace of the king, could refer to the saints before the throne of God in heaven. The image could refer to the antichrist and his image (Rev. 13:14,15). The furnace to the great tribulation. The fact that it is made to be seven times worse, may refer to the intensity and the length of the tribulation – 7 years. While Daniel is absent – in heaven, his three friends refused to worship the image or take the mark of the beast. Here they could be a type of Israel (they were Jewish of course) that has to endure the great tribulation. The fourth Person is Jesus Christ Himself. He was present literally and represent the everlasting promise of God to His children: *"I will never leave thee, nor forsake thee"* (Heb. 13:5). The guards could refer to those who will deny God's gift of salvation and who will eventually burn in the lake of fire for all eternity. This is a very clear and interesting illustration of what the world is to expect shortly. Nobody can say with certainty when this will be, but it is quite near – that is not to be doubted.

- Micah 7:1,2 is also very revealing. We read that the summer fruits have already been gathered (the harvest of those born-again) and the we read these words: *"The good man is perished out of the earth; and there is non upright among men"* That what follows is a description of the great tribulation.

- In Zeph. 2:1-3 the reference is also astonishing: *"Before the decree bring forth, before the day pass as the chaff, before the fierce anger of the Lord come upon you, before the day of the Lord's anger come upon you. Seek ye the Lord, all ye meek of the earth ... it may be ye shall be hid in the day of the Lord's anger."* The term *'day of the Lord'* and *'anger of the Lord'* are used throughout the Bible as referring to the events at the end of time - in the great tribulation. Note the repeated use of the word *'before'*.

- Malachi 3:17 reads: *"And they shall be mine, saith the Lord of hosts, in that day when I make up my jewels; and I will spare them, as a man spareth his own son that serveth him.*" Do you serve the Lord with all your heart? Malachi 4 that follows, is one of the clearest descriptions of the tribulation period in the entire Bible. Here again we can see that the tribulation will only become a reality after the rapture or gathering of the saints. There we read: *"For, behold, the day cometh, that shall burn as an oven; and all the proud, yea, and all that do wickedly, shall be stubble: and the day that cometh shall burn them up, saith the Lord of hosts, that it shall leave them neither root nor branch. <u>But unto you that fear my name shall the Sun of righteousness arise with healing in his wings</u>"* (Mal. 4:1,2).

THE BOOK OF REVELATION

Another great piece of evidence that the bride of Christ will be taken away before the great tribulation, can be found in the book of Revelation. The entire book of Revelation (which is in fact a revelation – an unveiling and not a concealment) is telling proof of this. In Rev. 3:20 we read that Jesus stands at the door and knock. It is the closed door of the church of Laodicea. This church also represents the final church dispensation and all indications are that it points to our generation. It represents the luke-warm apostate time in the church's history, the time of human rights (Laodicea). This is the time when the church exalts man rather than God. Is this perhaps why we read in Rev. 3:14, regarding the church of Laodicea, that this letter is addressed to: *"the church <u>of</u> the <u>Laodiceans</u>"*? It is a mere church of people and people's opinions. Human 'wisdom' took over. In the letters to the other churches, we read that they were addressed differently - to the churches *in* Smyrna or *in* Pergamos for example. Few would admit though that this is the sad case that we experience in many churches today. Many reckon that we have revival today, but much of the hype points to apostasy rather.

If we move to Rev. 4:1, we read of the following event after the end of the Loadicean church age: *"After this I looked, and, behold, a door was opened in heaven: and the first voice which I heard was as it were of a trumpet talking with me; which said, Come up hither, and I will show thee things which must be hereafter."* After the closed door of Rev. 3:20, there now is an open door, not on earth – but in heaven. The final church age has been completed and the bride of Christ now is gathered before the throne of God in heaven. John, who hears this Voice calling him, immediately follows the saints into heaven. In Rev. 4 and 5 the scene thus moves from the earth to heaven. John then describes the events that are to occur in heaven. In Rev. 5:8 we read of the 24 elders and in verse 9 they sing a new song with the words: *"Thou art worthy to take the book, and to open the seals thereof: for thou wast slain, and hast redeemed us to God by thy blood out of every kindred, and tongue, and people, and nation"*. These 24 elders are representative of the entire body of Christ, which will reside in heaven at that time. This group of elders cannot just refer to 24 people if we look at this new song in heaven. They sing about the fact that they come out of every kindred, tongue, people and nation on earth. There are far more people groups and nations on earth than just twenty four. This also cannot refer to angels, for they were not bought with the blood of the Lamb. In verse 10 we see that they will also be kings and priests unto God. If we compare this with 1 Chr. 24 in the Old Testament, we see that David divided the nation of Israel into 24 priestly orders. It represented the entire nation of Israel then, just like the 24 elders represent the entire body of Christ in heaven here. In verse 11 we see that their number (the four beasts and the angels included) is given as *"ten thousand times ten thousand, and thousands of thousands"* Those born again will indeed be in heaven at this stage while earth's inhabitants will await the judgments of

God. If we examine the book of Revelation closely, it is clear that the New Testament church of Christ is absent from chapters 6 to 19. These chapters give a detailed exposition of the tribulation time and the church is in no way part of it. Where we do find a reference to saints, it refers to those people that will be saved during the tribulation time – Rev. 7:9,14. This truth is also made clear in the letters to the seven churches that we find in Rev. 2 and 3. At the end of every letter we read the following words: "*He that hath an ear, let him hear what the Spirit saith unto the churches*". This is a message to the churches on earth – before the tribulation period commences. In Rev. 13:9, in the middle of the tribulation, we however only read: "*If any man have an ear, let him hear*". The church of Christ then is no longer present on earth and it is a message to those still living in the world – an urgent appeal to them to turn to God.

We also read in only one verse, Rev. 11:18, of the church of Christ in heaven and at the same time of those who were left behind on earth: "*And the nations were angry, and thy wrath is come, and the time of the dead, that they should be judged, and that thou shouldest give reward [judgment seat of Christ?] unto thy servants the prophets, and to the saints, and them that fear thy name, small and great; and shouldest destroy them which destroy the earth.*" Remember, right at the beginning we proved from Scripture that those who know the Lord, is not designated for His wrath. Here two scenes are described, one on earth and one in heaven. God will surely not reward His children on earth during the great tribulation. This will however occur before His throne in heaven at the judgment seat of Christ.

TWO RESURRECTIONS

The general point of view that with the second coming of Christ, there will be merely one resurrection of the dead, cannot be defended from the Bible. The Scriptures teach distinctly that there will be two different resurrections. The one group will be those who died in Christ and the others those who died without Him. We read of this in 1 Cor. 15:22-24. There we learn that: *"For as in Adam all die, even so in Christ shall all be made alive. However, every man in his own order: Christ the firstfruits; afterward they that are Christ's at his coming. Then cometh the end, when he shall have delivered up the kingdom to God"*. The first resurrection will occur at the rapture of the saints, as we can see from in 1 Thes. 4:16. There we read: *"and the dead in Christ shall rise first"*. The second resurrection will only occur at the end of the thousand years of peace – the millennial reign of Christ. Then the King, Jesus Christ, will hand over His Kingdom to God. We read of this in Rev. 20:5 – *"But the rest of the dead lived not again until the thousand years were finished."* Then those whom have rejected Jesus Christ will rise from the dead. They will appear before the great white throne of God to be judged (Rev. 20:11-15). It contrasts strongly with the first resurrection. The first resurrection is specifically and only for those who accepted the offer of salvation through the blood of Jesus Christ. Paul spoke of this special resurrection when he said the following: *"Yea doubtless, and I count all things but loss for the excellency of the knowledge of Christ Jesus my Lord: for whom I have suffered the loss of all things, and do count them but dung, that I may win Christ, and be found in him, not having mine own righteousness, which is of the law, but which is through the faith of Christ, the righteousness which is of God by faith: that I may know him, and the power of his resurrection, and the fellowship of his sufferings, being made conformable unto his death; if by any means I might attain unto the resurrection of the dead."* (Phil. 3:8-11).

This is a reference to the first resurrection. Paul would not have longed to die to himself merely to have part in one general resurrection of lost and saved people. This refer distinctly to the day of Christ, the rapture. There are various other statements in Scripture that distinguish the first resurrection from the second one. The following passages refer to that wonderful first resurrection:

- " ... *for thou shalt be recompensed at the <u>resurrection of the just</u>.*" (Lk. 14:14)
- "*neither can they die anymore: for they are equal unto the angles; and are the children of God, being the <u>children of the resurrection</u>.*" (Lk. 20:36)
- " ... *for the hour is coming, in which all that are in the graves shall hear his voice, and shall come forth; they that have done good, unto <u>the resurrection of life</u>; and they that have done evil, unto the resurrection of damnation.*" (Jn. 5:28,29)
- " ... *and preached through Jesus <u>the resurrection from the dead</u>.*" (Acts 4:2)
- "*and the <u>dead in Christ</u> shall rise first*" (1 Thes. 4:16)
- " ... *that they might obtain a <u>better resurrection</u>*" (Heb. 11:35)
- "*Blessed and holy is he that hath part in <u>the first resurrection</u>: on such the second death hath no power ...*" (Rev. 20:6)

THE SEVEN JEWISH FEASTS

In Lev. 23 we read where the Lord instructed Moses regarding the feasts that the nation of Israel had to keep. Seven different feasts are mentioned that were appointed unto Israel as an annual institution. All seven these feasts refer to prophetic events and some have already been fulfilled through Jesus Christ and others will still be fulfilled by Him in future. Everey single one of these feasts are a reference to Jesus Christ – as the entire Scripture is also a reference to Him. The Word is clear that these feasts refer to future events and we can see this in Col. 2:16,17 where we read: *"Let no man therefore judge you in meat, or in drink, or in respect of an holyday, or of the new moon, or of the sabbath days: which are a shadow of things to come"*.

Now we will shortly look at the seven Jewish feasts and how the rapture is also foreshadowed in them:

THE FEAST OF PASSOVER

In Lev. 23:5 we read of the feast of Passover. It refers to Jesus Christ, our Passover Lamb, who died for our sins on the cross of Calvary. The New Testament describes it as such: *" ... For even Christ our Passover is sacrificed for us: therefore let us keep the feast"* (1 Cor. 5:7,8). This feast was fulfilled at the crucifixion.

THE FEAST OF UNLEAVENED BREAD

We read of this feast in Lev. 23:6. It refers to Jesus Christ, the 'corn of wheat' that fell into the ground and died, but germinated and brought forth much fruit (Jn. 12:24). Through this He became the unleavened – thus the sinless bread of life. This feast was also already fulfilled.

THE FEAST OF THE FIRSTFRUITS

In Lev. 23:10,11 we read of this feast. It refers to Christ who rose as the firstfruits from the dead (1 Cor. 15:20). This feast was thus also already fulfilled.

PENTECOST

In Lev. 23:16 we read of this feast. On the day of Pentecost the Holy Spirit was poured out and the feast was also fulfilled in Christ (Acts 2:4). The promise of Jn. 16:7 (the Comforter who came in place of Jesus Christ) went into fulfillment that day.

THE FEAST OF TRUMPETS

In Lev. 23:24 we read of this feast. We find the following words there: " ... *In the seventh month, in the first day of the month, shall ye have a sabbath, a memorial of blowing of trumpets, an holy convocation.*" We also read in Num. 29:1 about this: " ... *it is a day of blowing the trumpets unto you.*"

This feast has not been fulfilled as of yet. It refers to the rapture of the church of Christ. On the day when the trumpet will sound, this feast will also be fulfilled in Christ. It refers to the trumpet of 1 Thes. 4:16; 1 Cor. 15:52 and Rev. 4:1. The body of Christ will then enter the wonderful rest. Even though this feast is annually held in September or October by the Jews, it does not mean that the rapture have to necessarily occur in one of those months. No, the day of Christ could come at any time and we have to be ready at all times.

THE DAY OF ATONEMENT

In Lev. 23:17 we read of this feast. The fulfillment of this day or feast still remains in the future. It refers to the glorious appearance of Christ at His second coming (Zech. 14:4,5). On that day the remaining third of the Jews will recognize Him and they will eventually turn to Him and He will forgive their sins (Zech. 12:10; 13:1,8,9).

THE FEAST OF TABERNACLES

We read of this feast in Lev. 23:34. It remains to be fulfilled in the future and refers to the millennium of peace, when the Lord Jesus Himself will govern from the throne of David in Jerusalem (Zech. 14:16; Mic. 4:1-3 and Acts 15:16,17).

We can see how four of the seven feasts already went into fulfillment literally. It is logical that the last three feasts will also become a literal reality and that they will also be fulfilled in Christ. The majesty and absolute order of God's prophetic plan with man becomes a reality in an amazing way through these seven feasts.

As a result it is very important to remember the next event on the feast calendar - the rapture of the body of Christ!

A JEWISH PERSPECTIVE

We always have to keep in mind that Jesus Christ was born a Jew and therefore He had a Jewish upbringing. His disciples were also Jews and that is why he often, as it came quite naturally, shared with them parables from a Jewish perspective. After He told them that He had to leave them, they did not understand Him at first and became quite distressed. He consoled them with the words: *"Let not your heart be troubled: ye believe in God, believe also in me. In my Father's house are many mansions: if it were not so, I would have told you. I go to prepare a place for you. And if I go and prepare a place for you, I will come again, and receive you unto myself: that where I am, there ye may be also"* (Jn. 14:1-3). Here, the Lord Jesus referred to the rapture of His church (of which eleven of the twelve would also become a part of). He shared it from a Jewish perspective however. The Jews followed a specific routine before a marriage finally took place.

After the engagement, the intended bridegroom would go away for a time to prepare a home for his intended bride and that at his father's home. To this day it is the custom among some Jewish families. The house is prepared and then the father of the intended bridegroom has to inspect it first. If he finds everything in order, the man may collect the intended bride from her home. This he usually does in secret. He will 'steal' her away 'secretly' although sometimes he or someone else would blow a trumpet at around midnight. Then she is taken to the intended bridegroom's family house, where they are eventually married.

Amazingly enough the Jewish marriage feast is made to last seven days in some cases. The prophetic significance of this is underestimated by most. It is a prophetic reference to the seven years of tribulation that will prevail on earth. In that time the bride will already be in heaven for the marriage of the Lamb and the marriage supper thereafter. Compare Samson's wedding feast of seven days in Judg. 14:12 as well as the seven years that Jacob (Israel) had to work extra to take Rachel as his wife (Gen. 29:27). The Jewish nation will as a result remain on earth for an extra period of seven years before their remnant will accept Christ as their Messiah at the end of the seven years of tribulation. In this manner, God will also take Israel as His wife, for whose conversion He will wait seven years longer than that of the New Testament church. Initially God wanted Israel as His 'wife', but they rejected Him. He then turned to the gentile nations and got Himself a bride from among their midst. Eventually He will go back and save the remnant from Israel also. This is the amazing story (the truth) of what is to happen with the bride of Christ. At this moment we are in the engagement period and when our place in the house of the Father has been brought to readiness, the Lord Jesus Christ will come to collect us. The church of Christ on earth, as a virgin, is being prepared for that day. That is why Paul writes in 2 Cor. 11:2: *"for I have espoused you to one husband, that I may present you as a chaste virgin to Christ"*. It will become a reality the day when the trumpet sounds.

ARE YOU READY?

The question remains if we are ready for this day. Were all your sins washed away by the blood of Christ? Are you born-again through the Holy Spirit of God? Are you part of the body of Christ who longs for His return and " … *our gathering unto him*" (2 Thes. 2:1). Does the idea of this make you anxious or does it fill you with unprecedented joy and peace in your heart? The time is little, the day of Christ is at hand, "*Therefore be ye also ready: for in such an hour as ye think not the Son of man cometh*" (Mt. 24:44).

We have to remember the following regarding Christ and that day: " … *unto them that look for him shall he appear the second time without sin unto salvation.*" (Heb.9:28).

Do you look for Him?

This is our blessed hope and it remains so for everyone that wants to take God upon His Word. Where does your hope lie for this life and the one hereafter?

- "*Surely I come quickly: Amen. Even so, come, Lord Jesus.*" - Rev. 22:20

10

THE SEVENTH DAY – THE COMING KINGDOM

"Blessed and holy is he that hath part in the first resurrection: on such the second death hath no power, but they shall be priests of God and of Christ, and shall reign with him a thousand years" (Rev. 20:6).

"For he spake in a certain place of the seventh day on this wise, And God did rest the seventh day from all his works ... would he not afterward have spoken of another day. There remaineth therefore a rest to the people of God ... For he that is entered into his rest, he also hath ceased from his own works, as God did from his ... Let us labor therefore to enter into that rest" (Heb. 4:4,8,9,11).

In Revelation 20:1-7 we read of this thousand years – no less than six times. Some believe that this number (thousand) is merely symbolic. Who though said that this passage in the Bible needs to, or could be spiritualized? Who gave anybody the right to make the Word imply anything different than that which is written? In Ps. 90:4 and 2 Pet. 3:8 we see that a day could be likened to a thousand years in God's sight, or that a thousand years could mean a day. Nowhere do we read that a thousand years may represent two thousand years or longer. God is a God of order and does not use misleading methods in His Word to reveal His thoughts to us. Particularly not in the book of the Bible that is called the Revelation. This definitely is not the character of the merciful God.

In a previous chapter, we looked at the passages in Scripture that refer to the fact that the current human dispensation on earth could come to an end after six thousand years. The true age of the earth, approximately six thousand years, also fits in beautifully with this interpretation. It leaves us with another day, the seventh, to bring the week or seven thousand years on earth to a perfect end.

The first two verses of Rev. 20 describe how an angel from heaven binds Satan for a thousand years that *"he should not deceive the nations no more, till the thousand years should be fulfilled ... "* (verse 3). Those who believe that we are currently living in the millennium of peace will have great difficulty to explain to God who the force is who is currently misleading the nations of the world. Could it perhaps be God Himself who has mislead the nations through all the centuries - by spurring on war - also the two tragic world wars? Is that which the world is currently experiencing, God's time of peace? Is this His promised Kingdom? Is this how the peace of the almighty God look? Can we then as Christians still marvel at the small number of people in this world, that converted to God. Jesus Christ – with His first coming to this earth – said: *"Think not that I am come to send peace on earth: I came not to send peace, but a sword."* (Mt. 10:34).

The chance of someone ridiculing the living God and

His infallible Word is great if one does not heed the fine detail of the Bible - and that through the guidance of the Holy Spirit. It is the Holy Spirit who inspired the entire Holy Scripture.

The matter is very important and those who call themselves children of God need to be very careful. We must take heed not to diminish the glory of God and Christ, and to bestow even some of that glory upon Satan. Even though God created heaven and earth and it belongs to Him, a temporary transfer of power was introduced on earth after the fall of man into sin. In Mt. 4:1-11 we read of Satan's tempting of the Lord Jesus. In verse 8 and 9 we read that the devil took Jesus to an *"exceeding high mountain"*, showed Him all the kingdoms and boasted: *"all these things will I give thee"* if He would bow before him and worship him. Jesus of course did not do this, but also did not mention that these kingdoms are not in temporary possession of the devil. In Jn. 12:31 Jesus Himself referred to Satan as: *"prince of this world"*. In 2 Cor. 4:4 Paul calls him: *"the god of this world"* and in 1 Jn. 5:19 we read that *"... the whole world lieth in wickedness."* The devil is not bound in this dispensation - no the Word explains: *"...because your adversary the devil, as a roaring lion, walketh about, seeking whom he may devour"* (1 Pet. 5:7). These passages entail that there can be no peace on earth, or in this world, in the present situation. This is the current reality.

It is true though that every truly born-again Christian will surely experience peace in his or her heart. This does not mean that we have complete peace on earth however. The passage in Lk. 2:14, where the angels sung at the birth of Jesus: *"Glory to God in the Highest, and on earth peace, good will toward men"* clearly did not refer to an immediate peace. This same Jesus was crucified in a cruel manner and died on the same earth - and as mentioned already, He Himself declared that He did not come to bring peace. After

His ascension, there was still no peace on earth. This was a prophetic reference to a time that is still to come, a time - now much closer than ever before. When He returns, He will come to establish this promised peace and it will differ greatly from the peace offered by the 'god of this world'. The Word has been warning us for a long time now against the false 'peace' that the devil and his associates has to offer, particularly in reference to the second coming of Jesus Christ: *"For when they shall say, Peace and safety; then sudden destruction cometh upon them, as travail upon a woman with child; and they shall not escape."* (1 Thes. 5:3).

The whole question of a new age of peace and the establishment of a new world order, as promised by many of today's world leaders, is nothing but an imitation of the true reign of peace that will become a reality on earth shortly. It is the thousand years of true peace Scripture speaks of in Rev. 20 and it will commence only after the second coming. The short-lived new age/new world order, under leadership of the Antichrist (Satan's imitation of Christ), will be brought to a sudden end by the true Jesus Christ – with His second coming and specifically at the war of Armageddon (Rev. 16:14,16;19:11-21).

The danger is that even Christians could glorify Satan by declaring that we are now living in the period which – according to Scripture – is destined to be to the glorification of Christ. The current increase in Satanic activities is prove enough. Many Christians continually pray for peace on earth, the right thing to do, but stand disappointed because their prayers are not being answered immediately. Every effort seems to fail, as the 'peace process' in the Middle East, for example, proves every time. The Lord hears our prayers, but that time lies in the future – in the near future now. In Is. 62:7 we read that we should not stop to remind the Lord of His promises, *"till he establish, and till he make Jerusalem a praise in the earth."* Another danger is that many do not want the second coming to occur too soon, because they are not ready to meet their God and that is why they want the current dispensation to continue. We are however living in the time of 'strong delusion.' Often this is not well understood and therefore it leads to misconceptions, even among Christians. To believe that we are currently in a symbolic period of peace results in dishonor to God's name. God's promises of real peace on earth are thus reasoned away and many Christians want to rather establish their own concepts of peace. For this reason we find so many groups today that believe that man has to establish peace on earth first, and then the second coming will occur. They believe that the church will introduce the Kingdom of peace on earth. Jesus Christ however said with His first coming to this earth: "...*My kingdom is not of this world: if my kingdom were of this world, <u>then would my servants fight</u>*" (Jn. 18:36). Christians have nothing physical to fight for in this world. We wrestle not against flesh and blood, but against principalities and powers and the forces of darkness (Eph. 6:12). This passage proves how unbiblical was, for example, the crusades of the Roman Church a millennium ago. They wanted the land of Israel and much more for themselves, because they believe they are Israel and that the kingdom of God is an earthly kingdom.

There are numerous examples of other Christian groups today that support this type of unbiblical interpretation, for example the Kingdom Now Theology, Dominion Theology, Reconstructionism, Restorationism, Latter Rain Movement and of course Replacement Theology, that believes the church currently replaces Israel. They also forget all the distinct warnings in Scripture that refer to the last days as being very difficult and as a time of a great falling away from biblical truths. Further the Bible states clearly that the Lord will only come back to earth after the time of great tribulation

(2 Thes. 2:3; 1 Tim. 4:1). Shortly before the second coming of Christ, many will become apostate and there will definitely not be a wonderful Christian kingdom on earth.

The mentioned groups – unknowingly – play a great role to mislead many Christians and non-Christians to welcome the so-called new age with open arms. They are part of the spiritual apostasy that is overflowing the world currently. Only with the second coming of Christ, will He, the Prince of Peace, set up His Kingdom on earth for a thousand years. This will eventually usher in eternity, and the new Jerusalem.

In Rev. 20:4 we read that the children of God who was decapitated because they did not worship the beast and did not take his mark on their hands or foreheads will also govern with Christ on earth for a thousand years. They are those who will become converted during the great tribulation. People who want to believe that we are currently living in the thousand years (and that it commenced with Christ's first coming), find it difficult to explain when the Antichrist governed (usually this is Nero for them), when the mark of the beast was enforced and when these Christians died. They are thus currently governing with Christ from their graves or they were resurrected and nobody knows about it. Interestingly enough, God does not call this group of believers 'blessed' as He does the others whom will take part in the first resurrection. They will though share eternal life with the other Christians, but they were not ready for the first resurrection (the rapture) – they were not yet born-again by that time. They had to endure God's wrath and lost their lives - not to deny Him. This group will be resurrected at Christ's appearance at the end of the great tribulation.

In verse 6 we read: *"Blessed and holy is he that hath part in the first resurrection"*. It is the occasion many children of the Lord long for – the *'blessed hope'* of Titus 2:13 – the rapture or gathering of God's own. In 1 Thes. 4:16-18 and 1

Cor. 15:51-53 we read about this as well. What *'blessed hope'* can a child of God have today if he knew beforehand that he is going to loose his head soon? God does not play around with His bride (the true church) on these matters – no, His Word is distinct and very clear regarding this.

JESUS, THE COMING KING

The coming thousand years of peace on earth will be a time when Christ will be exalted and honored. He will be glorified as King of the entire earth and if we want to reason away this period, we are robbing Him of this glory. It is also not supposed at all that He will be limited to earth during this period of Godly governance. He is God and will surely move between heaven and earth as King, while the final dispensation on earth (the last 1 000 years) is being completed.

In the book of Daniel, we read of Nebuchadnezzar's dream of the image. Eventually a stone came and destroyed the image. In Dan 2:35 we read: "…*and the stone that smote the image became a great mountain, and filled the whole earth.*" This stone is of course a reference to Jesus Christ – the eternal Rock (1 Cor. 10:4). We read in verse 44 that a kingdom will be established, which shall never again be destroyed – after the final kingdom on earth comes to an end. The New Testament confirms this truth. 1 Cor. 15 addresses the matter of the resurrection of the believers and in verse 23-25 we read: "*But every man in his own order: Christ the firstfruits; afterward they that are Christ's at his coming. Then cometh the end, when he shall have delivered up the kingdom to God, even the Father; when he shall have put down all rule, and all authority and power. For he must reign, till he hath put all enemies under his feet.*" Christ will surrender His Kingdom to the Father after the final war of Gog and Magog (Rev. 20:7-9) and after the thousand years will be ended with fire from heaven and Satan will finally be cast into the lake of fire (Rev. 20:10).

With the announcement of Jesus' birth nearly 2000 years ago, the angel shared with Mary that she would fall pregnant and bear a Son and that she had to call Him Jesus. The angel also said: *"He shall be great, and shall be called the Son of the Highest; and the Lord God shall give unto him the throne of his father David: and he shall reign over the house of Jacob for ever; and of his kingdom there shall be no end."* (Lk. 1:32,33). The book of Zechariah also referred to this time: *"and speak unto him, saying, Thus speaketh the Lord of hosts, saying, Behold the man whose name is the BRANCH; and he shall grow up out of his place, and he shall build the temple of the LORD: even he shall build the temple of the LORD; and he shall bear the glory, and shall sit and rule upon his throne; and he shall be a priest upon his throne; and the counsel of peace shall be between them both."* (Zech. 6:12,13). For the first time in history there will prevail real peace between church and state.

In Is. 9:7 we find a prophecy of Jesus' first coming and that He will be a Prince of Peace and that *"Of the increase of his government and peace there shall be no end, upon the throne of David, and upon his kingdom, to order it, and to establish it with judgment and with justice from henceforth even for ever."* This cannot be a reference to the heavenly kingdom, because David's kingdom was never established in the heavens. King David governed from Jerusalem and in the same manner Jesus Christ will, after His second coming to earth, also govern in the thousand years of peace. In the book Jeremiah 23:5,6 we read: *"Behold, the days come, saith the LORD, that I will raise unto David a righteous Branch, and a King shall reign and prosper, and shall execute judgment and justice in the earth. In his days Judah shall be saved, and Israel shall dwell safely: and this is his name whereby he shall be called, THE LORD OUR RIGHTEOUSNESS."*

Since the first coming of Christ, Israel has never lived in complete safety under the rule of Christ – this time is still to come! If we move to Zechariah, chapter 14, we read of the great war and the coming of Christ. In verse 4 we see that He will stand with His feet on the Mount of Olives. In verse 5 we read: *"and the Lord my God shall come, and all the saints with thee"* and then distinctly *"And the Lord shall be King over all the earth: in that day shall there be one Lord, and his name one."* (verse 9) – in this seventh day or seventh and final millennium. We also find interesting information regarding that time in verse 17, *"And it shall be, that whoso will not come up of all the families of the earth unto Jerusalem to worship the King, the LORD of hosts, even upon them shall be no rain."* In Zech. 9 we read more regarding this millennial period, right after the prophecy about Jesus' entering into Jerusalem on a donkey. This, of course, has already occurred – it was the one and only event when Jesus was honored as King by the masses at His first coming. We also read, in this passage, that the Lord will end a war in Jerusalem and then *"he shall speak peace unto the heathen: and his dominion shall be from sea even to sea, and from the river even to the ends of the earth."*

It is also interesting to note the words that was put on the cross via Pontius Pilate's instruction: *"THIS IS THE KING OF THE JEWS"* (Lk. 23:38). There were some like the high priest that wanted Pilate to change it to read that Christ Himself said that He was the King of the Jews. Pilate however prevailed and declared: *"What I have written I have written."* (Jn. 19:21,22). It was an act of immense prophetic significance. In the book of Acts, we read more about this time – a time still to come. As early as the first chapter, in verse 6, the apostles asked Jesus: *"Lord, wilt thou at this time restore again the kingdom to Israel?"* He did not say that there will be no such a time, but "*... It is not for you to know the time or the seasons, which the Father hath put in* *his own power. But ye shall receive power, after that the Holy Ghost is come upon you...*" (verse 7 and 8). At that time, they could not understand these words, but after the Holy Spirit came upon them at Pentecost, everything changed. The same Jesus Christ promised in Jn. 16:13: "*Howbeit when he, the Sprit of truth, is come, he will guide you into all truth: for he shall not speak of himself; but whatsoever he shall hear, that shall he speak: and he will show you things to come.*" The future millennium of peace is one of these "*things to come*". Since Old Testament times God is busy communicating this truth to humankind through His Word and He still is doing this today. In Acts, in chapter 15, we find more regarding the events right after Christ's return. In verse 16-17 we read: "*After this I will return, and will build again the tabernacle of David, which is fallen down; and I will build again the ruins thereof, and I will set it up: that the residue of men might seek after the Lord, and all the Gentiles, upon whom my name is called, saith the Lord, who doeth all these things.*" Heaven has never fallen down or become destitute and this refers – without a doubt – to the earthly city of Jerusalem and the millennium temple (Ezek. 40). It is also clear that people will still seek the Lord after the second coming – a strange concept to many. If we return shortly to the book of Zechariah, we see a correspondence between the above-mentioned verses and Zech. 14:16. There we read: "*And it shall come to pass, that every one that is left of all the nations which came against Jerusalem, shall even go up from year to year to worship the King, the Lord of hosts, and to keep the feast of tabernacles.*" It is the remainder of the people that will still be living on earth after the war of Armageddon and Christ's second coming – another piece of evidence that everything on earth will not end with the coming of Christ.

The prophet Jeremiah prophesied: "*At that time they*

shall call Jerusalem the throne of the Lord, and all the nations shall be gathered unto it, to the name of the Lord, to Jerusalem: neither shall they walk anymore after the imagination of their evil hearts." (Jer. 3:17). In Zech. 2:10,11 we also read: "*Sing and rejoice, O daughter of Zion: for, lo, I come, and I will <u>dwell in the midst of thee</u>, saith the Lord. And many nations shall be joined to the Lord in the day, and shall be my people: and I will dwell in the midst of thee, and thou shalt know that the Lord of hosts hath sent me unto thee.*" From the following passage in Micah, chapter 4:1-3, that also refers to this future period, we again see that the Lord will govern from the earthly Jerusalem: "*But in the last days it shall come to pass, that the mountain of the house of the Lord shall be established in the top of the mountains, and it shall be exalted above the hills; and people shall flow unto it. And many nations shall come, and say, Come, and let us go up to the mountain of the Lord, and to the house of the God of Jacob; and he will teach us of his ways, and we will walk in his paths: for the law shall go forth of Zion, and the word of the LORD from Jerusalem. And he shall judge among many people, and rebuke strong nations afar off; and they shall beat their swords into plowshares, and their spears into pruning hooks: nation shall not lift up a sword against nation, <u>neither shall they learn war any more</u>*" (We find the same words in Is. 2:2-4).

Clearly these passages refer to a future earthly governance. In heaven it will not be necessary to judge among people.

In Rev. 12:5 the Word teaches that Christ will govern the nations with a rod of iron. The devil will not be present anymore to mislead the nations, as is the case presently, but he will be bound and kept in a safe place. No military service, no wars – what a wonderful prospect. Will you be there? Did you already receive eternal life through Christ Jesus? In that very important prayer to His Father, Jesus noted how one could receive this gift of eternal life: "*And this is life eternal, that they might know thee the only true God, and Jesus Christ, whom thou hast sent.*" (Jn. 17:3). God makes Himself known through His Word and through prayer.

In Mt. 25:31-46 we read of the second coming of Christ and how He will judge the nations and set up His kingdom. Verse 31,32 and 34 reads: "*When the Son of man shall come in his glory, and all the holy angels with him, then shall he sit upon the throne of his glory: and before him shall be gathered all nations: and he shall separate them one from another, as a shepherd divideth his sheep from the goats ... Then shall the King say unto them on his right hand, Come, ye blessed of my Father, inherit the kingdom prepared for you from the foundation of the world*".

In Rev. 5:10 we find a distinct reference to this time, which will commence when the true blood-washed children of God will sing a new song before the throne of God in heaven (verse 9) and then we also read: "*and hast made us unto our God kings and priests: and we shall reign on the earth.*" The born-again children of the Lord will already be in heaven during that time – before the great tribulation commences – and from there we will sing this new song. In Rev. 19:6, when the great tribulation on earth speeds to its end, a wonderful event will occur in heaven: "*And I heard as it were the voice of a great multitude, and as the voice of many waters, and as the voice of mighty thunderings, saying, Alleluia: for the Lord God omnipotent reigneth.*" Only then will Christ accept His Kingship – shortly before His visible coming. The voices of the bride of Christ will be heard in heaven and this will occur shortly before Jesus Christ leaves heaven with His saints, to end the war of Armageddon on earth (Rev. 19:11-21). Then He will establish His Kingdom on earth and govern as Prince of Peace for a thousand years.

THE NATURE OF THE COMING KINGDOM
OF PEACE

What will it be like during this particular time on earth? In Acts 3:19 we read of *"times of refreshment"* for everyone who will come to Christ. The following two verses in this chapter describe that heaven has to receive Christ until *"the time of restitution of all things, which God hath spoken by the mouth of all his holy prophets since the world began."* (verse 12). Yes, surely did God prophesy by means of all the Old Testament prophets regarding this coming millennial reign of peace. These verses cannot refer to the restoration of heaven. Heaven has never deteriorated and does not need to be restored. The earth and the human race however, did enter into a state of deterioration with the fall in Eden and it will be restored in the thousand years of peace.

The book of Romans, chapter 8, continues in verse 18,19,21: *"For I reckon that the suffering of this present time are not worthy to be compared with the glory which shall be revealed in us. For the earnest expectations of the creature [or creation] waiteth for the manifestation of the sons of God ... because the creature itself also shall be delivered from the bondage of corruption into the glorious liberty of the children of God."*

The earth even awaits them who will govern as kings with the King of kings and the Lord of lords. The millennium of peace will be a return - in a way - to the time between the fall of man into sin and the flood in the days of Noah. In Gen. 3:17 we read that the earth was cursed as a result of the sin of Adam and Eve. God also said: *"thorns also and thistles shall it bring forth to thee."* (verse 18). The earth that we live in today, was seriously affected as a result of the sin of the human race. God made provision for this in His perfect plan though, and He is going to end the final dispensation on earth on a climactic note – even better than it was initially. This will be the start of eternity and then time will be no more.

If we move to the Old Testament and particularly to the book of Isaiah, you stand amazed when you read of the glory that God plans for those who love Him. In Is. 11:6-10 we read more about this refreshing time – for which every true child of God can long for: *"The wolf also shall dwell with the lamb, and the leopard shall lie down with the kid; and the calf and the young lion and the fatling together; and a little child shall lead them. And the cow and the bear shall feed; their young ones shall lie down together: and the lion shall eat straw like the ox. And the suckling child shall play on the hole of the asp, and the weaned child shall put his hand on the cockatrice' den. They shall not hurt nor destroy in all my holy mountain: for the earth shall be full of the knowledge of the Lord, as the waters cover the sea. And in that day there shall be a root of Jesse, which shall stand for an ensign of the people; to it shall the Gentiles seek: and his rest shall be glorious."* This is how the seventh day shall be. In Is. 35:6-10 we read more regarding this wonderful time: *"Then shall the lame man leap as a hart, and the tongue of the dumb sing: for in the wilderness shall waters break out, and streams in the desert. And the parched ground shall become a pool, and the thirsty land springs of water: in the habitation of dragons, where each lay, shall be grass with reeds and rushes. And a highway shall be there, and a way, and it shall be called The way of holiness; the unclean shall not pass over it; but it shall be for those: the wayfaring men, though fool, shall not err therein. No lion shall be there, nor any ravenous beast shall go up thereon, it shall not be found there; but the redeemed shall walk there: and the ransomed of the LORD shall return, and come to Zion with songs and everlasting joy upon their heads: they shall obtain joy and gladness, and sorrow and sighing shall flee away."*

Is. 41:18-20 continues: "*I will open rivers in high places, and fountains in the midst of the valleys: I will make the wilderness a pool of water, and the dry land springs of water. I will plant in the wilderness the cedar, the shittah tree, and the myrtle, and the oil tree; I will set in the desert the fir tree, and the pine, and the box tree together: that they may see, and know, and consider, and understand together, that the hand of the LORD hath done this, and the Holy One of Israel hath created it.*"

Regarding the position of Jerusalem and Israel during this time, the prophet Isaiah, through the inspiration of the Holy Spirit, wrote the following: "*Therefore thy gates shall be open continually; they shall not be shut day nor night; that men may bring unto thee the forces of the Gentiles, and that their kings may be brought. For the nation and kingdom that will not serve thee shall perish; yea, those nations shall be utterly wasted ... I will also make thy officers peace, and thine exactors righteousness. Violence shall no more be heard in thy land, wasting nor destruction within thy borders; but thou shalt call thy walls Salvation, and thy gates Praise. The sun shall be no more thy light by day; neither for brightness shall the moon give light unto thee: but the LORD shall be unto thee an everlasting light, and thy God thy glory. Thy sun shall no more go down; neither shall thy moon withdraw itself: for the LORD shall be thine everlasting light, and the days of thy mourning shall be ended. Thy people also shall be righteous: they shall inherit the land for ever, the branch of my planting, the work of my hands, that I may be glorified. A little one shall become a thousand, and a small one a strong nation: I the LORD will hasten it in his time.*" (Is. 60:11,12,17-22). It almost seems to be a reference to heaven, but we will see that there is a very clear distinction between heaven and the thousand years of peace. No nation will be able to grow, deteriorate or be destroyed in heaven, but it is still possible in this time – through God Himself (verse12). For Jerusalem and Israel, the sun and moon will not be a necessity anymore, for Jesus will reside in Jerusalem – the Light of the world.

In Is. 65:19,20,25 we find further promises regarding this blessed time: *"And I will rejoice in Jerusalem, and joy in my people: and the voice of weeping shall be no more heard in her, nor the voice of crying. There shall be no more thence an infant of days, nor an old man that hath not filled his days: for <u>the child shall die a hundred years old; but the sinner being a hundred years old shall be accursed</u> ... The wolf and the lamb shall feed together, and <u>the lion shall eat straw like the bullock</u>: and dust shall be the serpent's meat. They shall not hurt nor destroy in all my holy mountain, saith the LORD."* (Also see Ezek. 34:25-27).

True peace will reign in Jerusalem: *"Rejoice ye with Jerusalem, and be glad with her, all ye that love her: rejoice for joy with her, all ye that mourn for her ... For thus saith the LORD, Behold, I will extend peace to her like a river, and the glory of the Gentiles like a flowing stream: then shall ye suck, ye shall be borne upon her sides, and be dandled upon her knees. As one whom his mother comforteth, so will I comfort you; and ye shall be comforted in Jerusalem"* (Is. 66:10,12,13).

Almost everybody will come to worship in Jerusalem and those who rebel against Christ will be punished: *"And they shall bring all your brethren for an offering unto the Lord out of all nations upon horses, and in chariots, and in litters, and upon mules, and upon swift beasts, to my holy mountain Jerusalem, saith the Lord, as the children of Israel bring an offering in a clean vessel into the house of the LORD ... .And it shall come to pass, that from one new moon to another, and from one Sabbath to another, shall all flesh come to worship before me, saith the LORD. And they shall go forth, and look upon the carcasses of the men that have transgressed against me: for their worm shall not die, neither shall their fire be quenched...*" (Is. 66:20,23,24).

In the book of Amos we read: "*In that day will I raise up the tabernacle of David that is fallen, and close up the breaches thereof; and I will raise up his ruins, and I will build it as in the days of old ... Behold the days come, saith the LORD, that the plowman shall overtake the reaper, and the treader of grapes him that soweth seed: and the mountains shall drop sweet wine, and all the hills shall melt. And I will bring again the captivity of my people of Israel, and they shall build the waste cities, and inhabit them; and they shall plant vineyards, and drink the wine thereof; they shall also make gardens, and eat the fruit of them. And I will plant them upon their land,and they shall no more be pulled up out of their land which I have given them, saith the LORD thy God.*" (Amos 9:11,13,14,15).

Although some deep spiritual lessons can be found in these verses, this cannot be a symbolic reference to the church of Christ, for her fate cannot be changed. It is another reference to the fallen tabernacle or temple of David in Jerusalem and the literal people of Israel. The remnant of the nation of Israel will be redeemed and they will finally fulfill their part of the covenant. They will live in the land of Israel with boundaries similar to those in the days of king David.

The prophet Zechariah wrote about this period and said the following: "*Thus saith the LORD; I am returned unto Zion, and will dwell in the midst of Jerusalem: and Jerusalem shall be called A city of truth; and the mountain of the LORD of hosts, The holy mountain. Thus saith the Lord of hosts; There shall yet old men and old women dwell in the streets of Jerusalem, and every man with his staff in his hand for very age. And the streets of the city shall be full of boys and girls playing in the streets thereof. Thus saith the*

LORD of hosts; If it be marvelous in the eyes of the remnant of this people in these days, should it also be marvelous in mine eyes? saith the LORD of hosts. Thus saith the Lord of hosts; Behold, I will save my people from the east country, and from the west country; and I will bring them, and they shall dwell in the midst of Jerusalem: and they shall be my people, and I will be their God, in truth and in righteousness." (Zech. 8:3-8). For many Christians these precious promises from God's infallible Word just seem to good to be true. Many do not even realize that these passages are to be found in Scripture. Some gives it a completely different meaning.

Finally, another passage to describe the character of the magnificent millennium of peace: *"and the inhabitants of one city shall go to another, saying, Let us go speedily to pray before the LORD, and to seek the LORD of hosts: I will go also. Yea, many people and strong nations shall come to seek the LORD of hosts in Jerusalem, and to pray before the LORD. Thus saith the LORD of hosts; In those days it shall come to pass, that ten men shall take hold out of all languages of the nations, even shall take hold of the skirt of him that is a Jew, saying, We will go with you: for we have heard that God is with you."* (Zech. 8:21-23).

In this manner, God will restore His nation of Israel in honour. All of this though, is too much for many (including Christians) to believe and to anticipate. Many believe that God rejected Israel in all finality. Rom. 11:1,2 and 25-28 however defines clearly how this nation fits into God's plan. In Rom. 11:12 we read regarding the fall and the eventual restoration of the Jewish nation: *"Now if the fall of them be the riches of the world, and the diminishing of them the riches of the Gentiles; how much more their fullness?"* It will lead to the wonderful seventh day – a thousand years of peace for all the nations that remain after the final great war. Many of these people will still not be born again, but because

Satan will be bound, there will be peace. The children of God (the bride of Christ) from all the different nations will govern as kings with Christ in this time. Then eternity with God will dawn for the saved. Even if the nation of Israel is presently still blind and apostate, Christ was born from them (Jn. 4:22) – the greatest gift ever to the human race!

From all these quoted passages about the millennial reign of peace, it is clear that there never has been such a time on earth before. We can safely assume that we did not experience such a time on earth yet. Every true child of God possesses the peace of God in his or her hearts, but it does not mean that real peace has come to planet earth as a whole.

Those who believe that these passages refer to heaven, leave something out of the picture. Let us look at eight differences between the thousand years of peace on earth and the new Jerusalem that will follow thereafter:

1. Christ will govern in the thousand years (Rev. 20:4)
   God Himself will govern in Heaven (Rev. 21:3)
2. There will be a temple in the thousand years (Ezek. 40-47; Zech. 6:12,15)
   There will be no temple in heaven (Rev. 21;22)
3. The sea will still exist in the thousand years (Ezek. 47:8; Zech. 9:10)
   There will be no sea in the heavens (Rev. 21:1)
4. There will still be sin in the world in the thousand years (Is. 65:20; Zech. 14:16) There will be no sin in heaven (Rev. 21:8; Rev. 22:15)
5. In the thousand years, man will still be bound by time (Is. 65:20; Is. 66:23)
   In heaven there will be no more time (Dan. 12:3)
6. In the thousand years the gospel will still be spread (Is. 66:19; Mt. 24:14; Acts 15:16,17)
   In heaven this will no longer be necessary (Rev. 21:27)

7. It will still rain during the thousand years (Is. 30:23; Zech. 14:17)
   It will no longer be necessary in heaven (Rev. 22:1,2)
8. During the thousand years people will still have children (Is. 60:22)
   In heaven, this will no longer be the case (Mt. 22:30)

This thousand years of peace, with Christ as King, is a period that every child of God may and should look forward to. There will be rest and joy after the six thousand years of work and sorrow and also it will be a time of great blessings after the terrible time of great tribulation. It will be a period of refreshment after the six thousand years of human efforts to achieve true peace.

Many Christians often ask: Why are we living on earth? Of course, we are living for Christ, in the first place, but we are also living for that which He had promised and prepared for us. Sadly though, the message of the coming millennium of peace is for the most part an unknown (and therefore unloved) message. It is suppressed from the pulpits, probably because there are so many different interpretations of the subject. This way of treating the Word of God is actually disrespectful of God's infinite ability to communicate important truths to those He created. It is true that man has many differing interpretations of certain passages in the Bible, but we have to remember that the Lord has merely one literal interpretation. He is not ambiguous in character. To speculate that God leaves us in the dark regarding some biblical truths, does not make sense and is unfitting of whom God says that He is. Christians who for example do not believe in the rapture (the blessed hope) before the great tribulation, and also not in the literal thousand years of peace, rob themselves of immense blessings and hope. In such a case, it is easier to take your eyes of God and focus on the world with all its desires. (In most cases it is merely because the subject have not been studied properly).

On the other hand, there are unfortunately also children of God that do believe in these truths, but their lives tell another story. One cannot though reason away a biblical truth merely because some Christians lead a worldly life. God will reward them on the appropriate time. The Word stands firm and cannot be changed. That is why the foundation of all our beliefs have to be grounded in the Scriptures and not in people and in what they do. Man often change, but never the Lord and His Word! (Mt. 24:35). To recall this time of refreshment (the millennium) and await it in anticipation, is no different than thinking about Jesus and awaiting His return. He will then stand central in everything and our eyes will be fixed on Him at all times (Heb. 12:2). The thousand years of peace is, firstly, a time of the glorification of Christ. It is a proclamation of His already settled victory on the cross of Calvary. This will be a time filled with glory - to God all the honor for the wonderful promises in His eternal Word. May this seventh day commence very soon!

11

THE GLORY OF HEAVEN

*"But as it is written, Eye hath not seen, nor ear
heard, neither have entered into the heart of man,
the things which God hath prepared for them that
love him."* (1 Cor. 2:9)

The idea of heaven is almost too much to contemplate.
The mere thought of it is overwhelming. There are too
many who are of the opinion that such an utopia only exists
in dreams. Others are of the opinion that we have to do
everything possible to create heaven on earth ourselves. It is
true that we cannot even begin to comprehend the concept of
the eternal heaven and its glory in this temporary existence
on earth, but the question remains: What does the Word of
God say about heaven and the time here after?

Early in the Bible, even right in the first verse of
Scripture we read that heaven was created: *"In the beginning
God created the heaven and the earth."* (Gen. 1:1) Heaven
did not always exist. No, God is eternal – He was never created, but heaven was created by Him. Heaven was created at

the same time as earth. The Word says so. Heaven was created in the beginning – from the beginning of time. The earth was also created at the beginning of time. Before heaven and earth were created, there was no time. Eternity was before and will be after. The current heaven will also cease to exist on a certain day. In Mt. 24:35 we read that heaven and earth shall pass away. Only the Words of God shall never pass away. Unfortunately, it is not what most Christians believe or understand. In 2 Pet. 3:10,12 we read clearly that "*the heavens shall pass away with a great noise, and the elements shall melt with fervent heat*" and specifically that "*heavens being on fire shall be dissolved*". It sounds strange, but it will happen. We also read in Is. 34:4 that "*the heavens shall be rolled together as a scroll*" and in Rev. 6:14 that "*heaven departed as a scroll when it is rolled together*". The words of Ps. 102:25-27 tells the entire story: "*Of old hast thou laid the foundation of the earth: and the heavens are the work of thy hands. They shall perish, but thou shalt endure: yea, all of them shall wax old like a garment; as a vesture shalt thou change them, and they shall be changed: but thou art the same, and thy years shall have no end.*" From Scripture we understand that there are three heavens that are referred to in the Word. Firstly, we find the atmospheric heaven, as the Word for example refers to the birds from heaven. Secondly the starry heavens and thirdly the heaven as current residing place of God – the place from whence Jesus descended to earth, when He lowered Himself for our sake. The apostle Paul was swept up to the "*third heaven*" (2 Cor. 12:2).

In the book of Ezekiel, we read of an astonishing vision that this prophet of the Lord had about heaven and about God Himself. In Ezek. 1:4 we read: "*And I looked, and, behold, a whirlwind came out of the north, a great cloud, and a fire infolding itself, and a brightness was about it, and out of the midst thereof as the color of amber, out of the midst of the fire.*" He continues and relates about the four creatures that he saw – a description of God in all His facets.

Interesting that this whirlwind came from the north. In Is. 14:13 we read of God's place of residing "*upon the mount of the congregation, in the sides of the north*" Also read Job 26:7,11. Ezekiel continues: "*And there was a voice from the firmament that was over their heads, when they stood, and had let down their wings. And above the firmament that was over their heads was the likeness of a throne, as the appearance of a sapphire stone: and upon the likeness of the throne was the likeness as the appearance of a man above upon it. And I saw as the color of amber, as the appearance of fire round about with it, from the appearance of his loins even upward, and from the appearance of his loins even downward, I saw as it were the appearance of fire, and it had brightness round about. As the appearance of the bow that is in the cloud in the day of rain, so was the appearance of the brightness round about. This was the appearance of the likeness of the glory of the Lord. And when I saw it, I fell upon my face, and I heard a voice of one that spake.*" (Ezek. 1:25-28).

What an image of the living God and His high and exalted throne. This passage correlates beautifully with the vision the apostle John had and that we read about in the book of Revelation.

In the book of Isaiah, we read the touching account of the calling of the prophet Isaiah and how he had to warn the people of Israel. He also saw heaven and described it as follows: "*...I saw also the Lord sitting upon a throne, high and lifted up, and his train filled the temple. Above it stood the seraphim: each one had six wings; with twain he covered his face, and with twain he covered his feet, and with twain he did fly. And one cried unto another, and said, Holy, holy, holy, is the LORD of hosts: the whole earth is full of his* *glory. And the posts of the door moved at the voice of him that cried, and the house was filled with smoke. Then said I, Woe is me: for I am undone; because I am a man of unclean lips, and I dwell in the midst of a people of unclean lips: for mine eyes have seen the King, the LORD of hosts."* (Is. 6:1-5). The absolute glory and holiness of God in heaven overpowered the prophet Isaiah, and that is why he could not but utter these words.

It is interesting that both Ezekiel and Isaiah (and later also John in Revelation) described how God sits on a throne covered with angels. In Ps. 18:10 we read how David described God: *"and he rode upon a cherub, and did fly: yea, he did fly upon the wings of the wind."*

In the book of Daniel we also find a wonderful and special description of God on His throne: *"I beheld till the thrones were cast down, and the Ancient of days did sit, whose garments was white as snow, and the hair of his head like the pure wool: his throne was like the fiery flame, and his wheels as burning fire. A fiery stream issued and came forth from before him: thousand thousands ministered unto him, and ten thousand times ten thousand stood before him: the judgment was set, and the books were opened."* (Dan. 7:9,10). The words in Heb. 12:29, that our God is a *"consuming fire"* now has new meaning. In His holy presence only absolute righteousness can enter – that righteousness that Christ became for us, His children, on the cross of Calvary. All imitated, human made righteousness and holiness will be consumed by the fire. This vision of Daniel gives us an idea of whom God is and what it will be like in heaven – in the presence of the living God.

Paul wrote about our home in heaven - that we await in great anticipation: *"For we know that, if our earthly house of this tabernacle were dissolved, we have a building of God, a house not made with hands, eternal in the heavens. For in this we groan, earnestly desiring to be clothed upon with our house which is from heaven*" (2 Cor. 5:1,2). The well known servant of God, Abraham, is infamous for his great faith in God. His faith was such that he then, a thousand years ago already "... *looked for a city which hath foundations, whose builder and maker is God*" (Heb. 11:10). Abraham then already awaited the new Jerusalem and that is why he moved from Ur of the Chaldees, to a country that God directed him to. Today, shortly before the second coming of Christ, there are few left who still anticipate this house - not made with hands. The world with all its grandeur is just too charming and wonderful to most to even think of something like a heavenly home. Paul desired to go, because it would be – according to him – by far the best, but today even many Christians do not want to be reminded of heaven. Some think naively that heaven will be a place of only singing and that in fact, with respect, it will be quite boring in heaven. Such ideas are far from the truth. If God created this earth so breathtakingly and amazingly, we cannot even begin to comprehend how awesome heaven will be.

Paul said that when he was caught up to paradise, he heard "*unspeakable*" words that were "*not lawful for a man to utter*" (2 Cor. 12:4). Did this vision in heaven perhaps had something to do with his tremendous diligence for the work of God right to the end of his life? In Heb. 12:22,23 we read about "*the heavenly Jerusalem ... the general assembly and church of the firstborn, which are written in heaven*". What a prospect for every born again Christian! The apostle John had a vision of Jesus Christ in heaven that correlates with that of Ezekiel and Daniel. He saw seven golden candlesticks and much more: "*And I turned to see the voice that spake with me. And being turned, I saw seven golden candlesticks; and in the midst of the seven candlesticks one like unto the Son of man, clothed with a garment down to the foot, and girt about the paps with a golden girdle. His head and his hairs were white like wool as white as snow: and his eyes were as a flame of fire ... and his voice as the sound of many waters."* (Rev. 1:12-15). In Rev. 4:2-6 John reveal even more of heaven: *"...a throne was set in heaven, and one sat on the throne. And he that sat was to look upon like a jasper and a sardine stone: and there was a rainbow round about the throne, in sight like unto an emerald ... And out of the throne proceeded lightnings and thunderings and voices: and there were seven lamps of fire burning before the throne, which are the seven Spirits of God. And before the throne there was a sea of glass like unto crystal. And in the midst of the throne, and round about the throne, were four beasts full of eyes before and behind."*

We could enter this throne room any day. Are we ready to meet this almighty holy God? Every one proclaiming that he or she is a Christian has to contemplate this at one stage or another. In heaven, some things will be no more. If we look at what the Word teaches us, we find that the following will no longer be present in eternity:

1. There will be no sea
2. There will be no tears
3. There will be no death
4. There will be no sorrow
5. There will be no pain
6. There will be no temple
7. There will be no sun
8. There will be no moon
9. There will be no night
10. There will be no sin
11. There will be no closed doors
12. There will be no curse

(Rev. 21:1,4,22-25,27 and Rev. 22:3).

We will also not think about the things that were before

and it will not even enter our hearts anymore – never again any negative or bad thoughts. God says: *"For, behold, I create new heavens and a new earth: and the former shall not be remembered, nor come into mind."* (Is. 65:17).

The following wonderful things will be present however:

1. A new heaven
2. A new earth
3. A new Jerusalem with twelve gates of pearls and twelve foundations
4. A street of solid gold like transparent glass
5. A clear river with water like crystal
6. The tree of life that bears fruit twelve times a year
7. The Lamb (Christ) as the lamp to light the city

(Rev. 21 and 22)

The question remains, will you be there? Were you cleansed through the blood of the Lamb?

- Is it worth it to sacrifice eternity for a little, short-lived 'pleasure'?
- Why serve the world now if you are going to serve God one day in heaven anyway?
- Why cling to senseless, worthless things if you will not be able to cling to it in eternity?
- Why serve the devil 70 or 80 years and then hope to enter heaven and serve God there forever? This life is not the end of everything; it is the beginning of everything!

This life is merely a period of trials and testing before eternity that is awaiting. The second coming of Christ will end this period and then the rest of your life begins.

Everyone that knows the Lord, will enter the glory of heaven! (Jn. 17:3). To think that we will meet Noah, Enoch,

Moses, Abraham, Isaac and Jacob in heaven. Also Joseph, Elijah, David and Daniel. Yes, also Peter, John and James and of course Paul. Above all, we will also meet Jesus and we will see the marks on his hands and feet and we will realize that we have – finally – come home.

ENLIGTHENED EYES OF THE MIND

Is everything about the so-called time of the end really true, or is it merely a flight of the imagination? Why does everybody in the world not believe that the second coming of Christ is near? To answer these and other questions we have to direct ourselves to the inspired Word of God. The Word gives a definite answer to all our questions. Paul said to the congregation of Ephesus that he did not stop praying for them: *"that the God of our Lord Jesus Christ, the Father of glory, may give unto you the spirit of wisdom and revelation in the knowledge of him: the eyes of your understanding being enlightened; that ye may know what is the hope of his calling, and what the riches of the glory of his inheritance in the saints"* (Eph. 1:17,18). The Holy Spirit of God is in possession of all the knowledge and wisdom in existence. If we are born again and if we remind God in our prayers of His inspired promises, He will answer us and His light will shine on us. We will never have to run around in darkness. Everyone who seeks shall find, and for everyone who knocks the door shall be opened. In spite of all the negative things of this world, we will know the *'hope of His calling.'* We will also realize that this world, as it is today, is not our eternal home, but that we can look forward to the *"glory of his inheritance in the saints"*. The Holy Spirit enlightens the eyes of our mind, that we may understand what is written in God's wonderful Word.

Nearly one third of the Bible consists of prophecies and up to now each one was fulfilled to the letter. The Lord says in Rev. 3:18 to *"anoint thine eyes with eyesalve, that thou mayest see"*. This salve is the Holy Spirit – why would the Father not give the Holy Spirit to those that pray to Him (Lk. 11:13). Everyone who still maintain that everything in the world is still exactly the same as before, needs the salve of God – the Holy Spirit, to receive the enlightened eyes of the mind. Everyone that can see on the other hand, should also be aware not to gradually close his or her eyes. The simple biblical instruction of 1 Thes. 5:17 to *"Pray without ceasing"* was never more applicable than it is today.

The almighty, only wise God, in His infallible Word, gives us the following wonderful and consoling words:

"Call unto me, and I will answer thee, and show thee great and mighty things, which thou knowest not" (Jer. 33:3).

Be true in heart and test God and He will never disappoint you.

AN INVITATION TO THE WEDDING

There is only ONE way of accepting this invitation. It is completely free of charge, but not easy to attain at all. It can only be obtained through grace, but is definitely not cheap. It all depends on where you enter, for the Bible says: *"Enter ye in at the strait gate: for wide is the gate, and broad is the way, that leadeth to destruction, and many there be which go in thereat: because strait is the gate, and narrow the way, which leadeth unto life, and few there be that find it."* (Mt. 7:13,14)

For this reason *"Strive to enter in at the strait gate: for many, I say unto you, will seek to enter in, and shall not be able."* (Lk. 13:24)

Jesus made it clear how to enter at this strait and narrow entrance when He said: "*I am the door: by me if any man enter in, he shall be saved*" (Jn. 10:9)

He (Jesus) however only came to seek and save those that are lost (Mt. 18:11), in other words those that admit and know that they cannot exist without God. Are there some people who are not lost in sin? The Word is clear: "*For all have sinned, and come short of the glory of God*" (Rom. 3:23). Yes, "*There is none righteous, no, not one*" (Rom. 3:10). What about all the *good* people on earth? Surely there are many *good* people on earth? Scripture is clear and decisive: "*...there is none that doeth good, no, not one*" (Rom. 3:12). People are good in the eyes of each other, but not in the eyes of a perfect and holy God!

The solution?

The Word states simply: "*that if thou shalt confess with thy <u>mouth</u> the Lord Jesus, and shalt <u>believe</u> in thine heart that God hath raised him from the dead, thou shalt be saved*" (Rom. 10:9). It however does not merely entail a faith in a historical Jesus that lived on earth a long time ago. No, it entails a faith in the entire Word of God, because Jesus Christ Himself is the incarnated Word (Jn. 1:14). This same Jesus said: "*If a man love me, he will keep my <u>words</u>*" (Jn. 14:23).

What is eternal life? Jesus prayed to His Father in heaven and said:

"*And this is life eternal, that they might know thee the only true God, and Jesus Christ, whom thou hast sent.*" (Jn. 17:3).

Do you know this God? We may know Him through His Word. This is eternal life. This life is more rare than diamonds. More valuable than fine gold. It costs us nothing to attain, but in fact, it costs everything. It is a new life. A new beginning. Eternity with God and His Christ is the reward.

Nothing on this earth can be compared with this life, but you can only receive it while still on this earth.

Today is the day to start searching for this life!

The invitation remains after two thousand years :

"And the spirit and the bride say, Come. And let him that heareth say, Come. And let him that is athirst come. And whosoever will, let him take the water of life freely." (Rev. 22:17)

But for how long?

ENDNOTES

[1] *Weekly Telegraph*, January 5-11, 2000

[2] *Die Volksblad*, September 15, 1999

[3] *The Media Wise Family*, Dr. T. Baehr

[4] *US News and World Report*, April 15, 1996

[5] *Fort Worth Star-Telegram*, September 21, 2000

[6] *Rapport*, November 5, 1995

[7] *The Citizen*, December 27, 1995

[8] *BBC News*, December 24, 1999

[9] *Agence France Presse*, October 1, 1999

[10] *Religion Today* News, July 14, 2000

[11] *Die Volksblad*, October 31, 1998

[12] *Military Balance, International Institute of Strategic Studies*, 2000

[13] *Millennium Alert*, March 2000

[14] *Vatican Information Service*, October 7, 2000

[15] *Die Volksblad*, December 18, 1998

[16] *Die Volksblad*, October 2, 1997

[17] *The Citizen*, January 28, 1998

[18] *CNN*, August 31, 1999

[19] *The Citizen*, August, 17 2000

[20] *Millennium Alert*, March 2000

[21] *Die Volksblad*, May 27, 2000

[22] *The Citizen*, September 21, 2000

[23] *BBC*, June 6, 2002

[24] *Insig*, July 1996

[25] Ibid.

[26] *Insig*, January 1999

[27] *The Citizen*, August 25, 1997

[28] *The Citizen*, February 3, 1998

[29] *Die Volksblad*, May 5, 1999

[30] *The Citizen*, June 23, 1999

[31] *Netnews*, July 5, 2000

[32] *The Citizen*, June 20, 2000

[33] *CNN*, June 26, 2002

[34] *The Times*, Augustus 12, 2001

[35] *The Weekend Australian*, 8-9 July 2000

[36] *Beeld*, 25 April 2000

[37] *The Weekend Australian*, 8-9 July 2000

[38] *United States Geological Survey* and the *National Earthquake Information Center*, 1998, 2000, 2002

[39] *Associated Press*, February 1, 2001

[40] *CNN*, February 22, 2001

[41] *Bloemnuus*, July 21, 2000

[42] *Die Volksblad*, May 27, 2000

[43] *Associated Press*, October 24, 2000

[44] *Die Volksblad*, October 1, 1998.

[45] *Die Volksblad*, May 27, 2000 and *The Citizen*, September 21, 2000

[46] *The Star*, August 6, 1998 – main article on front page

[47] *The Citizen*, January 19, 1999 – main article on front page

[48] *Die Volksblad*, September 17, 1998

[49] *Light*, May/June 1998

[50] *Die Volksblad*, November 14, 1998

[51] *The Citizen*, June 30, 2000

[52] *CNS News*, August 25, 2000

[53] *Die Burger*, May 20, 2002

[54] *Ma'ariv*, August 14, 1996

[55] *The Citizen*, December 4, 1996

[56] *Atlas of Israel*, 1985, p. 17

[57] *Israel Wire*, April 7, 2000

[58] *BBC*, January 21, 2000

[59] *The Jerusalem Post*, August 24, 1996

[60] *Israel National News*, June 27, 2002

[61] *Ha'aretz*, August 30, 2000

[62] *London Times*, August 8, 2000

[63] *Temple Mount and Land of Israel Faithful Movement*, May 25, 1999

[64] *Jerusalem Post*, July 2, 2002

[65] Heading of an article in the *Beeld*, December 4, 1998

[66] *The Citizen*, August 31, 2000

[67] *London Guardian*, September 6, 2000

[68] *Associated Press*, December 31, 1999

[69] *South China Morning Post*, January 5, 2000

[70] Migrating birds know no boundaries, *International Center for the Study of Bird Migration – Israel Ornithological Center, www.birds.org.il* (English site)

[71] *Sandgrouse*, Volume 18(1) May 1996, 'Spring raptor movements at Gebel el Zeit, Egypt - major new raptor bottelneck described'

[72] *Raptors 2000, www.ortra.com/raptors2000/*

[73] *Bird-watching Festival*, Aloft 2000, as reported on in *Gems in Israel*, December 1999

[74] *Ma'ariv*, June 24, 1996

[75] *The Citizen*, July 15, 1999

[76] *CNN*, January 10, 2000

[77] *Middle East Digest*, Sept./Oct. 1996

[78] *Dateline Israel*, April 12, 2000

[79] *Jordan Times*, February 22, 2002

[80] *Middle East Digest*, Sept./Oct. 1996

[81] *Jerusalem Report*, October 3, 1996

[82] *The Temple Mount Faithful*

[83] *Jerusalem Courier*, May-July 1998

[84] *Ha'aretz*, October 16, 2000

[85] *Yediot Aharonot*, June 23, 1997

[86] *Israel News Digest,*October 1996

[87] *Rous el Yosef*, January 29, 1995

[88] *CNS News*, July 21, 2000

[89] *Ha'aretz News*, June 22, 2002

[90] *UPI*, August 7, 2000

[91] *London Telegraph*, August 13, 2000

[92] *Agence France Presse*, October 22, 2000

[93] *Intelligence Digest*, June 21, 1996

[94] *The Citizen*, January 16, 1999

[95] *Arutz 7*, January 5, 2000

[96] *World Tribune*, February 11, 2000

[97] *Reuters*, October 20, 2000

[98] *World Tribune*, March 6, 2001

[99] *BBC*, October 5, 2000

[100] *World Tribune*, December 4, 2001

[101] *Middle East Newsline*, June 17, 2001

[102] *The Citizen*, April 24, 1999

[103] *The Citizen*, August 2, 2000

[104] *The Citizen*, January 16, 1997

[105] *Agence FrancePresse*, October 23, 2000

[106] *BBC News*, December 27, 2001

[107] *Strategic Studies Institute*, September 2, 1998

[108] *The Citizen*, April 13, 1999

[109] *Washington Times*, November 3, 1998

[110] Alexander the Great, *Encarta Encyclopedia, 2000*

[111] *e-TV advertisement*, Issue number 11, July 2002

[112] *NASA Science News*, September 7, 2000

[113] Iraq's Republican Guard, *http://www.cnn.com/SPECIALS/1998/iraq/guard/*

[114] *Die Volksblad*, November 20, 1998

[115] *The Living Channel*, October 6, 1998

[116] *Agence France Press*, September 21, 2000

[117] *The Citizen,* August 27, 1999

[118] *CNN*, July 19, 1999

[119] *The Citizen*, April 11, 2002

[120] *www.wcpagren.org*

[121] *Newsweek*, Special Edition, November 1998 – February 1999

[122] *Time*, July 7, 1997

[123] *San Francisco Chronicle*, March 24, 2002

[124] *Agence France Presse*, July 8, 2001

[125] *Jordan Times*, January 3, 2002

[126] *UPI*, July 11, 2002

[127] *The Citizen*, August 27, 1997

[128] *Pretoria News*, December 2, 1999

[129] *United Religions Initiative*, July 1999, *www.united-religions.org* -

[130] *Pittsburgh Post-Gazette* June 26, 2000

[131] *Pittsburgh Post-Gazette*, June 27, 2000

[132] *Worldwide Faith News*, September 2, 2000

[133] Ibid.

[134] Ibid.

[135] *World Scripture*, http://service-net.org/ws.cfm

[136] *New York Post*, September 21, 2001

[137] *New York Post*, February 12, 2002

[138] *The Star*, May 10, 2002

[139] *Die Volksblad*, November 10, 2000

[140] *Sydney Morning Herald*, *www.smh..com.au*, December 17, 2001

[141] *Time*, December 9, 1991

[142] *London Telegraph*, September 6, 2000

[143] *Agence France Presse*, June 9, 2000

[144] Grant. R. Jeffrey, *The Signature of God*, (Frontier Research Publications, 1996), pp. 190-191

[145] Gary H. Kah, *En Route to Global Occupation*, (Huntington House Publishers, 1992), p. 40

[146] *Associated Press*, August 23, 2000

[147] *Associated Press*, September 7, 2000

[148] *London Telegraph*, March 17, 2001

[149] *EU Observer*, May 16,2002

[150] *Vatican Information Service*, March 18, 1997

[151] *www.ibiblio.org/expo/vatican.exhibit/Vatican.exhibit.html*

[152] *Associated Press*, July 23, 2000

[153] *The Christian News*, October 18, 1999, p.16

[154] *The Telegraph*, January 25, 2002

[155] *World Wide Faith News*, September 2, 2000

[156] Ibid.

[157] *Vatican Information Service*, October 7, 2000

[158] *Vatican Information Service*, October 8, 2000

[159] *New Schaff-Herzog Encyclopedia of Religious Knowledge*, Vol.VII, p.376

[160] *The Writings of Irenaeus*, Vol 1, p. 577

[161] *Epistle of Barnabas*, chapter 15, *The Apostolic Fathers,* pp.151-152

[162] D. Russel Humphreys. Ph.D., *Evidence for a young world, Answers in Genesis*

[163] Ibid.

[164] Ibid.

[165] Ibid.

[166] Ibid.

[167] Ibid.

[168] *The Citizen*, May 24, 2000

[169] Dr. Kent Hovind, *Creation Seminar part 1*, *Creation Science Evangelism*

[170] Austin, S.A., 1996, Excess Argon Within Mineral Concentrates from the New Dacite Lava Dome at Mount St. Helens Volcano,. *Creation Ex Nihilo Technical Journal*, 10(3):335-343

[171] *Die Volksblad*, January 22, 2000

[172] Thomas Ice and Timothy Demi (editors), *When the Trumpet Sounds*, (Harvest House Publishers, 1995)